A Mo

Alex Kane is a writer from Glasgow, specialising in gang-land crime and psychological thrillers. When not writing, Alex can be found relaxing at home reading, or drinking tea and/or gin (sometimes all of the above).

# Also by Alex Kane

# A MOTHER'S
# REVENGE
## ALEX KANE

**hera**

First published in the United Kingdom in 2024 by

Hera Books
Unit 9 (Canelo), 5th Floor
Cargo Works, 1–2 Hatfields
London SE1 9PG
United Kingdom

A CIP catalogue record for this book is available from the British Library.

Print ISBN 978 1 80436 792 6
Ebook ISBN 978 1 80436 791 9

Look for more great books at www.herabooks.com

Printed and bound in Great Britain by Clays Ltd, Elcograf S.p.A.

1

*For Lindsey Mooney*

# Prologue

The whistling sound was odd to her. She couldn't quite put her finger on what it was or where it was coming from. No, not whistling; it was more like a gush of air. Fast. Rushed. It gained speed, getting closer and closer.

When the body hit the ground, she screamed, louder and harder than she thought her voice was capable of.

She stared down at the face she recognised even after it had been pulverised into the ground. The face of the person who'd caused her so much heartbreak; so much terror. Their body now a mass of blood and guts mashed into the gravel path. The bridge above leered over them like a concrete giant.

*Jesus*, she thought. But even *he* couldn't help now.

She didn't know how she felt in that moment. Relieved? Terrified? Perhaps both. Either way, she couldn't breathe. She tried hard to suck air into her lungs, to try to calm herself. The almost instantaneous stench of iron filled her nostrils and she gagged a little.

Pulling her gaze away, she looked into the eyes of the woman standing in front of her. 'Breathe,' the woman said, cupping her face. 'In and out. Slowly.'

She did what the woman said and imagined life from that moment. She couldn't see a thing. Only a blank space where life should be better.

# Chapter 1

Sitting in the passenger seat of her boyfriend Leo's car, Cheryl remembered the first moment she'd laid eyes on him. She'd been at a sleepover with a few friends from school. The evening had been an extra special one with her friends, as they were celebrating the fact that it was Cheryl's fifteenth birthday. A Saturday night down at the golf course. She and the other girls had chipped in for a few bottles of cider and one of them had a portable speaker for music. Cheryl had always loved those nights. Her parents would have had a stroke if they'd known what she'd been up to. That night, the girls had been walking through the golf course towards the car park; they had a curfew of ten p.m., which was always adhered to, but after her friend's mum had gone to bed, they'd all snuck back out again through the bedroom window and stayed out until five in the morning. They'd never been caught. And that was when she'd seen him for the first time. His car was parked by the entrance, the window down and his music playing quiet enough not to disturb the peace of the night.

Her stomach had swirled when she looked at his face. He'd been the most handsome person she'd ever seen in her life. He'd smiled at her, and she'd smiled back.

'Hope you girls are heading straight home. It's past your bedtime,' he'd said. A few of the girls ignored him; some of them giggled.

'We'd get home quicker if you gave us a lift,' Cheryl had replied with a smile, and she'd felt her cheeks flush. She'd never flirted with anyone before; especially not a man. He had to be at least eighteen. Possibly older?

One of her friends had elbowed her in the ribs. 'Shut up. If we pull up to my house in that thing, my mum will fucking kill me.'

'Can't, I'm still on shift,' he'd replied, ignoring the comment. 'But why don't you give me your number and I'll phone you later?'

Again, her stomach had fluttered. She hadn't known if he was joking, but she'd walked up to the window, leaned in and told him her mobile number; thankfully she'd just been given one by her parents.

She'd walked back to her friend's house and, later, Leo had phoned her. They'd chatted for an hour or so and then Cheryl had decided to climb out the window and go for a drive with him. It was the most exciting thing to ever happen to her. Some of the girls were nervous, telling her she shouldn't go. The others were as excited as she was. That was the night she'd understood the term: love at first sight. Now, she couldn't live without him.

'I still think you should wait a little while longer, you know, before you tell them,' Leo said, with his hand on her knee, giving it a gentle squeeze. Cheryl thought about how she was going to tell her parents about him. She'd avoided it over the course of the last ten months, but soon she'd be turning sixteen and there would be nothing they could do or say to change her mind about him. He was incredible. So gentle, caring, loving. And

3

she felt so safe around him. Cheryl had never known love like this existed. But she knew how awfully her parents would react to it. They'd tell her she couldn't go through with it. They'd attempt to ground her; as if they still had that authority. She wasn't looking forward to the strain it would put on her relationship with them. But she'd be married to the love of her life. She'd be able to get through it. And maybe they'd come to accept it. Maybe.

'Why? I'm almost sixteen,' Cheryl replied, pushing all of the doubt out of her head and forcing herself to be stronger about her decision. 'I'm sick of keeping you a secret. I love you, there's nothing they can do about that. If they want me to be happy then they'll just have to accept it.'

Leo's expression soured. 'I don't know. Maybe we could tell a little white lie then?'

Cheryl eyed him curiously. 'Like what?'

'Maybe...' His voice trailed off like he was thinking. 'Maybe shed a couple years off my age?'

Cheryl looked through the windscreen at the woodlands in front of her as the sky fell dark. Another reason she wanted to be open about her boyfriend: they wouldn't have to sit in his car in a deserted car park every time they wanted to be together. 'Like... eighteen?' It could work, she thought. It might soften the blow when they thought about the fact that she had only been fifteen when she met Leo.

Leo nodded. 'Hmm. Means I'm still old enough to have a licence, and it's a little less severe than my *real* age. I'd still be over the legal age to be with you. Which sounds so wrong, I know. I feel like a bit of a dick, to be honest. I should have waited until you were actually sixteen before we got together.'

4

Cheryl felt her eyes widen. 'Oh my God, no way. That would have been awful. It *would* be awful. I can't live without you.'

'Me either,' Leo replied softly. 'I just don't want your parents to worry about you. I don't want them thinking I'm some kind of weirdo, which they would. Of course they would. You're their daughter. But you can't help who you fall in love with, can you? We didn't *choose* for this to happen. I just clapped eyes on you and, bang, nothing else mattered.'

Cheryl couldn't stop the smile that crept onto her face. 'I love you too. They're my parents, of course they're going to worry. But I really think that once they meet you and see how happy I am, they'll accept it.'

'Hmm,' Leo said. 'I wish I shared your faith. If my daughter told me she was going out with a guy six years older than her when she was only fifteen, I'd probably want to break the guy's legs.'

Cheryl rolled her eyes and laughed.

He took her left hand in his and ran his thumb over the massive diamond on her fourth finger. 'Might want to hide that. It'll be hard enough for them to accept that your boyfriend is older than you let alone that you're engaged to be married to him.'

Cheryl stared down happily at her engagement ring and smiled. 'I don't want to take it off. I haven't since you put it on.'

Smiling at the memory of when he'd asked her to marry him just a week earlier, Cheryl felt an excited giggle rise up from her stomach. They'd been parked in the Gleniffer Braes – known as the car park in the sky – overlooking the city. Cheryl had been sat on the bonnet of the car, admiring the stunning view when he'd simply handed her the ring and asked her to marry him. She'd squealed with excitement and, of course, said yes. She didn't have to think about it. Cheryl loved Leo more than she ever thought possible; there was never going to be another answer to that question.

Leo frowned. 'How have you managed to hide it from them?'

Cheryl shrugged. 'Like you suggested: I wear it on a chain round my neck when I'm at home, and school for that matter. My parents don't pay much attention in the mornings. Getting up and out for work and shipping me off to school is all they're concerned about.'

Leo sighed. 'I'm glad you thought the chain was a good idea. Trust me, Cheryl, it's better that way, and better you lie about my age. In fact, better to wait until you're actually sixteen before telling them about us altogether.'

Cheryl nodded disappointedly. 'Okay. I'll wait. But on one condition.'

A smirk raised the corners of Leo's mouth. 'What?'

'As soon as I'm sixteen, we get married.'

Leo's eyes widened. 'Seriously?'

'Yeah. I won't need their permission by law. If we're married, there's nothing they can do about us being together,' Cheryl said. 'Look, I know it's quick, but we love each other and that's all that matters. I mean, it's not like they're strangers to marrying young.'

'Oh yeah?'

'Mum and Dad met when they were sixteen and got married at twenty.'

'Yeah, that's a tad older than what you would be, Cheryl,' Leo said.

'Yeah, but only by four years. So they can't tell me I'm too young to know what I'm doing or what I really

6

want because they were young too. Plus they had me pretty much a year after they got married. It's not like I'm pregnant or about to be. We can still plan our lives together, work to get what we want before all that stuff, can't we?'

Leo squeezed her hand, leaned in and kissed her. He was hesitant and Cheryl began to panic a little. Maybe he was going to say no. He pulled away, parted his lips and smiled widely. 'I think it's a fucking *belter* of an idea.'

'Really? You do?' Cheryl said, feeling the worry leave her.

'Aye, of course I do. But do you really want to get married alone? No family there at all? Don't you want your dad to walk you down the aisle?'

Cheryl thought about it. Of course she did. But she knew that he'd refuse, given the circumstance.

'Obviously I'd want them there, but I know what they'll say. They'll try to stop me, threaten me with their absence. I don't want the hassle or the heartbreak of actually being faced with having to choose. If I make the choice, then it's within my control from the beginning. If I tell them we're married and that I'm happy then there's no going back. They'll either have to accept it, or not.'

Leo looked thoughtful. 'I just don't want them thinking badly of me. I *am* older than you, Cheryl, regardless of whether you're sixteen or not. And they'll think I've pushed you into this.'

Cheryl grabbed at his hands and their fingers entwined. 'But you've not. I want this. It's not like you're some bad man who's kidnapped me off the street and holding me captive somewhere while you arrange our wedding without my consent. It's not like that at all. I won't lie, if

7

you hadn't proposed, I probably would have. I *want* this. I want us.'

Leo pulled his lips into a thin smile. 'I know you do. Me too. I just hope they see it that way.'

—

The registrar blinked and stared into Cheryl's eyes. The same way she imagined her mother would when she finally told them about the wedding and about Leo: judging, worrying. Why couldn't people just smile and be happy for others?

Leo had taken care of everything. Booking the ceremony, witnesses. Well, that was it, really. There was no big, fancy wedding dress or kilt, there were no bridesmaids or groomsmen. It was just Cheryl, Leo and two people she didn't know who would sign the marriage licence to make it legal. She hadn't even known that was a thing. Cheryl just thought that when you said your vows and kissed, it was done. You were married. They'd have to send away for the certificate before it was legal. Cheryl had decided she would have the certificate in her hands before she told her mum and dad.

'You ready?' Leo asked, gripping her hand as they stood by the double doors of the registry office.

Cheryl took a deep breath. She might only be sixteen, a young girl, but she understood the commitment she was making, the sacrifices she was making to be with the man she loved. She knew what it would all mean. She'd lose her family. They'd never go for this; never accept it. But she knew what she wanted and how she felt. Cheryl loved Leo more than she ever thought you could possibly love a person and there was nothing else in the world that mattered to her. She and Leo had a deep connection and they'd talked about their future. He'd said that he'd be able to give her everything that she'd ever wanted. Being an only child, she'd always wanted a sibling, so dreams of a bigger family felt closer than ever because Leo had said that when they got married, they could have as many children as she wanted. She didn't need immature friends when she was going to be a wife and a mother. She wouldn't have time for any of that silly girly stuff once she was looking after her babies and her husband.

'Absolutely,' she replied chirpily, pushing thoughts of a future absence of family out of her head.

Leo nodded at the couple standing by the registrar and the man pressed play on a CD player in the corner. Cheryl and Leo's song played and she felt tears pool in her eyes.

'I can't believe you picked this,' she said as 'You're Not Alone' by Olive played. Every time she heard it, she was transported back to the night she met him. It was the song playing in his car when she'd left the golf course with her friends.

'It's our song, why wouldn't I?' Leo smiled.

Cheryl knew she'd never be alone so long as she had Leo by her side. And as they took their vows and promised just that, Cheryl knew she'd made the right decision to marry Leo Davidson.

# Chapter 2

Leo Davidson stood tall, his shoulders pushed back and his expression stern. But no matter what he did, he'd never be able to intimidate Marek Kaminski. To look at, the man oozed class and sophistication with his designer clothes, flash jewellery and calm manner that did him well in his legit business dealings in Poland and the UK. He needed said businesses to keep up appearances. The only person who truly knew the extent of Marek's other business interests was Leo; in the UK, of course. Marek's sinister tone was what made him his cash. That and his ruthlessness. He wasn't the type to feel fear and neither was Leo. Yet, as he stood there, ready to face the wrath of his boss, Leo felt a fear inside he'd never felt before. But that wasn't something he could show. He needed to appear strong and unaffected by Marek's anger.

'You were my second in command here in Glasgow, Leo. The fact that I had to find out that your boy fucked up by one of my other employees who is lower down the chain than you fills me with anger, Leo. Dean fucked up *big* time and neither of you had the decency to tell me about it; you especially. And what would have happened if I didn't find out? Would it have happened again? One fuck-up leads to another, always. Do you understand the basic need for discretion in our business?' Marek said, jabbing his finger into Leo's chest.

Leo raised an eyebrow at the assumption that Dean would make another mistake like that. Leo had already warned him not to do it again because of the possible repercussions. He understood the severity of the situation. Leo had dealt with it perfectly fine. Like Marek had said, discretion was key and that's what Leo had done.

'Did you hear what I said, Leo?' Marek said, his voice growing louder and more agitated.

'Yes, Marek. Of course I understand the need for discretion in this business; we all do. It's just, well, Dean couldn't have predicted that this was going to happen, could he?'

'He may not have been able to predict it, Leo. But he could have prevented it. He could have told that little bitch of his to keep her mouth shut about their relationship. But did he?'

'I believe he did, yes,' Leo replied, unsure if that was truly the case or not. Dean assured him he had advised Molly Rose Hunter not to tell anyone about them because he was older, but that was after her mother had turned up at the house and threatened to go to the police.

'Well, it didn't fucking work, did it?' Marek said, continuing to jab Leo's chest. 'Which means, Dean wasn't thorough enough with his selection. He should have picked a girl from the gutter. Instead, he picked up a little rich bitch with a mouth for a mother and I lost out on thousands of revenue because we had to go to the ground for a while. That was all Dean's doing, Leo.'

Leo looked down at Marek's hand and took a deep, steadying breath. The man was being a total cunt and if he wasn't careful, boss or no boss, he'd knock him out.

Marek seemingly noticed the look on Leo's face and dropped his hand, but he kept his eyes fixed on Leo's and shook his head. 'I am disappointed, Leo. *You* disappoint me. Dean goes *way* beyond that. Not only did he fuck up on what we were looking at being one of our finest servants over in Poland, but he messed up on passports, both quality and time. If passport control got hold of them, do you know what would have happened? My entire empire would be ripped to shreds by the authorities. I cannot have that. He's a liability, Leo. And I cannot, no, *will* not have someone like him mess up my business. I make a lot of revenue from this, and I will not have it taken away from me because some little Glasgow fucker got too big for his boots.'

Leo frowned. 'What do you mean?'

'Come on, Leo, you're a smart man. You can figure it out,' Marek said.

His frown deepened. 'You're firing him?'

If anything, he was relieved that was the only punishment that his son would receive.

Marek tutted. 'No, Leo. I've already put the order in. It's done. Like I said, Dean is a liability. I can't have someone like him putting me at risk and I can't have the police sniffing around me, or my interests. He's out, Leo.'

Something inside Leo froze in that moment. Out?

'You've put out an order to *kill* him?' Leo exclaimed.

'It's business, Leo. Nothing personal.'

Leo's eyes widened and he threw his arms up in the air. 'How the fuck can you say it's nothing personal? You've just told me my son's about to be fucking killed by your men. Jesus fuck, Marek. No. I won't let you do this.'

Marek glared at Leo through narrowed eyes. 'You won't *let* me? I'm sorry, Leo, but there is no one or the other here. It's not a choice and certainly not yours. My business, my men, my rules.'

Leo couldn't believe what he was hearing. After everything that Leo and Dean had done for Marek's operations in Glasgow. They'd worked hard, sought out young girls who no one gave a shit about; the ones who were easy to mould. Leo had been promoted to Marek's second in command, with Dean being trusted with passport production alongside his recruitment responsibilities. Leo and Dean were the reason the Glasgow operation was raking Marek in a shit ton of money. The reason it had been so successful was because Dean was good at what he did. He'd made one mistake: he'd picked the wrong girl. He should have gone for one without a wealthy family who cared. *Fuck sake, Dean*, Leo thought. Now he'd ended up with a fucking target on his back.

Feeling the rage build inside him that Marek was making this choice, Leo said, 'He's *my* son, Marek. You think I'm going to just stand by while you order his death? Fuck that. And fuck you!' He glanced down at the desk Marek was standing next to and eyed the almost empty bottle of whisky.

In one swift move, Leo shot out his hand, broke the end of the bottle on the table and held it at arm's length, right into Marek's face.

Marek, who eyed the bottle with contempt, barely flinched at the idea that Leo might kill him. And if Leo was being honest with himself, he wasn't sure he had the guts to do it if it really came to it. Yet he held the broken bottle steady at Marek's face.

'Cancel the hit. *Now*,' Leo said, his heart thrumming so hard in his chest it felt like it was in his throat.

'I can't do that,' Marek said. 'I've had men killed for a lot less, Leo. You know as well as I do that if Dean continues to work for my firm, he'll get us all put away.'

He mustered up as much of the anger from the pit of his stomach as he could, raised his voice and gritted his teeth. 'I'd rather do life in prison than allow you to do this.'

'And if you go to prison, it wouldn't take long for my operation to be taken down by the authorities. I won't have that.'

Leo knew his place. He had no power against a man like Marek.

'I don't care. I said cancel the *fucking* hit!' He waved the bottle a little in front of Marek's face, hoping that he'd find it in himself to think about what was about to happen to Dean and have a change of heart.

Marek narrowed his eyes and sighed. 'Fine. If I must.'

Leo, as surprised as he was, relaxed a little as he watched Marek lift the phone from the desk and put it to his ear.

'It's me,' Marek said, his tone low. 'Cancel my order.'

Silence filled the tiny space Marek called an office. Not that he needed a big office in Glasgow. He was barely ever in the country. Leo took care of things on this side of the continent. Marek was only there to oversee things every so often, like the girls his staff were getting ready for shipment.

'Good. Okay. I'll speak to you later,' Marek finally said before ending the call. He glanced at Leo and shook his head. 'Too late, Leo. My order was carried out less than half an hour ago.'

Leo felt his stomach drop as he stared into the darkness of Marek's eyes. 'What?'

'Dean's already dead, Leo. No longer a threat to my business, or to your freedom.'

Leo Davidson watched as the broken bottle shook in his trembling hand before Marek carefully removed it from his grasp.

'You killed him? You killed my son, you fucking *bastard*. I'll kill you!'

Just as Leo was about to launch at Marek, the office door flew open and three of Marek's men from Poland wrestled him to the floor. He kicked, punched and screamed in anger and fury as much as in grief.

'You bastard, Marek. I'll fucking kill you. I'll fucking kill you.' The words came in broken sobs.

'You will do nothing, Leo. Because without me, you *are* nothing. Now, if you don't calm yourself, I'll pay a visit to that wife of yours. Not only will I tell her about those little parties you like to attend for yourself after a long, hard slog at the office – you know, the ones where you like to dominate young women, young enough to be your daughter. But I'll also make sure that she understands that it was you who killed Dean and once I've done that, I'll kill her myself. Trust me, it wouldn't be hard. Unless that's what you want, I'd suggest you take a few deep breaths and consider your freedom, with your wife in one piece and her perception of you and your son intact.'

Everything had happened so fast in a few short minutes. Dean was dead. Marek had threatened to expose Leo's secrets to Cheryl. How the hell was he supposed to deal with that?

Leo succumbed to the strength of the three men holding him down and tried not to let the sobs of grief escape him.

'Now, are you going to relax?' Marek teased. 'If you do, my men will let you up. But a word of warning, Leo; a little reminder, if you will? One wrong move and not only will you die, but after I've made your little wife aware of your affairs, I'll make sure she's killed just for the privilege of knowing about it all. Is that what you want?'

Leo was silent, the blood thrumming in his ears as he tried to process what was happening.

'I said is that what you want?' Marek pressed, his tone firmer this time.

'No,' Leo said, gritting his teeth so hard that they might shatter in his mouth.

'Let him up,' Marek said. The men pulled Leo to his feet and he stared at Marek. 'I know it's tough, I get it. But we need to come to an understanding here, Leo. Not only does the threat still stand, but remember, I'm your source of income. Your employer. What I say goes.'

Leo breathed heavily as the men held him in their grip.

'Remember, without me, you have nothing. It was necessary to get rid of Dean. I'm sorry it hurts; I get it. Losing a child can't be easy. But trust me, Leo, if you think you're going to leave here today with a revenge plan, you're wrong. You'll *never* outsmart me or my men. And if you think for one moment that you're going to get out of this game just because Dean was taken out to protect my business, then you're highly mistaken. You're our lifeline to this city. And you work for me now and always. No matter what.'

Leo slumped under the grip of Marek's men. As hard as it was to hear, Marek was right. There was no way he was going to be able to take Marek down unless he went to the police. Even though Marek had killed Leo's son, he couldn't go up against that rule. In their world, grassing was never an option. Not even a last resort.

'Do I make myself clear, Leo?' Marek asked, bending down so he was face to face with Leo.

Leo nodded, trying to control his emotions. Each time a new sob threatened, he swallowed hard. What would happen to Dean's body? Would it ever be recovered? Would he and Cheryl be able to have a funeral for him?

'I didn't quite hear you.'

'Yes.'

Marek raised an eyebrow and said with a growl, 'Yes, *Marek.*'

Leo gritted his teeth and said, 'Yes, *Marek.*'

'Good,' Marek said. 'And let me make this very clear to you. You will need to earn my trust back after this incident. You will have to earn your right to be by my side in this operation. Do you understand what I'm saying?'

Leo glared at Marek, quite sure of where he was going.

'You're on a probationary period until I can be sure your work ethic, eye for detail and ability to prevent this kind of mistake from happening again is at the top of your priorities. This is non-negotiable. Again, do you understand?'

Leo nodded, biting at the inside of his cheek.

'Say it,' Marek growled.

'Yes, Marek. I understand.'

# Chapter 3

## NOW

### TWO PEOPLE IN HOSPITAL IN GLASGOW AFTER CAR SMASH ON RURAL ROAD

Police and ambulance crews were called out to a stretch of the A81, just past Strathblane, yesterday when it was reported that a car had been run off the road. Two people have been taken to hospital. It's reported that the injured are Northern Irish businesswoman Janey Hallahan and her husband Ciaran Hallahan.

Janey Hallahan has very recently opened a luxurious beauty salon in the West End of Glasgow, reportedly creating several jobs for the area.

A source linked to the Hallahans, who asked to remain anonymous, said, 'It's awful what has happened. Why would anyone leave the scene of an accident like that? I hope they both pull through.'

Detective Inspector James Pearson of Police Scotland said, 'We are investigating the incident and anyone who was in the area at the time who may have information, we are asking that you come forward as soon as possible. It's of high importance that the people who caused this collision are brought to justice.'

# Chapter 4

## NOW

'Happy twenty-first birthday, baby boy,' Cheryl sobbed as she crouched down in front of Dean's grave, feeling like she couldn't get enough air into her lungs to let out another wail. She felt Leo's hand on her back and she didn't have the energy to shrug him off. She inhaled deeply to steady herself and blew the air out slowly, wiping the tears away from her eyes so she could read her son's name clearly.

Cheryl ran her fingertips over the letters on the headstone. That was all her son was now, an engraving on a fucking headstone.

Closing her eyes, she felt the enormity of the situation she was faced with and would forever feel the pain of it. She had never imagined outliving her child. She had never imagined when he was growing in her belly that he would be murdered, his body left in such a cold, callous way. The newspapers had reported on his death in a way that made him sound like a monster, which Cheryl knew he wasn't. He was just her son, caught up in a situation he never should have been in. *Man with Links to European Gang Found Dead* had been the headline. Strange how the police had never uncovered said gang and found out who had killed him. It seemed no one was able to do that. Well, all that was about to change.

She opened her eyes, stared at Dean's name and felt the lump in her throat grow again. 'I promise to get you justice, my lovely, beautiful boy. I'll fucking *hang* the bastard who did this to you.' The words hissed through gritted teeth and she released her jaw so as not to shatter them.

Leaning forward, Cheryl put her lips to the cold granite headstone, kissed it and swallowed down the lump in her throat. She had to get a grip of herself; had to be strong for her son.

'Come on, Cheryl,' Leo said, his hand still on her back. 'He wouldn't want you sobbing over his grave.'

Getting to her feet, Cheryl turned to her husband and raised an eyebrow. 'And you think he'd want to be six feet underground in a wooden fucking box after *your* boss left his body in that fucking scrapyard with a bullet in the back of the head? It was a fucking execution, Leo. He was a fucking child compared to your boss. He was no threat at all.'

Cheryl thought back to the day the police showed up at the front door. It felt like yesterday instead of two months ago. In fact, it felt like just yesterday that the midwife placed Dean in Cheryl's arms after she'd given birth to him. Twenty-one years was nothing and so much all at once.

Leo blinked but kept his eye on her. With his voice low and meek like a child himself, he replied, 'It wasn't actually Marek who killed him.'

Cheryl's mouth fell open. 'Really, is that all you've got to say?'

Leo puffed out his cheeks. 'You know what I mean. And I said I'd sort it.'

The sound of the police officers' words hadn't been audible. When she'd opened the door with Leo by her side and seen them standing there, hats in their hands, she'd known what they were going to say before they'd said it. Her heart felt like it was going to burst out of her chest; the physical pain was the only reason she knew she wasn't trying to wake up from a nightmare. How was she going to live with the knowledge that she hadn't been able to protect her son? That Leo hadn't been able to stop his boss from doing what he did?

Cheryl sneered. 'Aye, if you say so, Leo. I'll tell you something, if you'd had the balls to stand up to Marek and tell him that you weren't getting involved in his disgusting scheme in the first place then Dean would still be alive. You should've just stuck to the drug and gun deals like you'd always done and this would never have happened.'

She pushed past him and moved across the grass, walking between headstones as she kept the car in sight.

'Cheryl,' Leo called, following close behind her. 'Marek isn't a man to be negotiated with. Once he had the operation in his sights, there was no way I wasn't going to be involved. You know I had no choice in the matter. If I had refused, he'd have killed both me and Dean. You'd be standing over both our graves today if I'd done that.'

*Maybe that wouldn't be such a bad thing*, she thought. She'd much rather her son was still alive than her fuck-up of a husband. 'You know what? I can't believe how blind I was to it all,' she said, turning to face him.

Leo stopped, stared at her. 'What do you mean?'

She felt her jaw tense and she was aware they were outside in a public space; quieter than any other because it

22

was a cemetery. Thankfully, there was no one else around, not within earshot anyway. 'Leo, *you* got our son into human *trafficking*. *You* dragged him into a world where he became the worst kind of human. And the mother of the girl Marek had him working on, Molly Rose' – she cleared her throat, unable to comprehend that she had just said it out loud – 'came to our door and threatened him. You brought this shit to our front door, Leo. And you kept it all from me. I could have talked some sense into Dean; could've stopped all this if you'd just let me. But you didn't tell me because you knew how fucking disgusted I'd be with you.'

She watched as Leo chewed the inside of his cheek. He was angry with how she was speaking to him; that was obvious.

'I said I'd sort it,' Leo said, his words low and angry.

The face of Molly Rose Hunter swirled around inside her head. As did the face of her mother, Orla. The more she thought about them and what had happened, the angrier she became.

Cheryl turned her back on her husband as he rounded the front of the car and stood at the driver's door. In the early days of their marriage, Leo had spoiled her with designer clothes and handbags, lavish meals out and a lifestyle that she could only have dreamed of. But as the years had gone on, and Marek had come into their lives, things changed and by then it was far too late for her. She was years deep with a son to raise and, thanks to Leo, she was on her own with no family to support her other than him. Cheryl had always been happy to be blissfully ignorant to the actual job of running drugs and guns around the city. But if she'd had any inkling that her son would end up dead because of it, she'd have done something to stop it.

And now that Cheryl was aware of the Hallahan family and their power over the city, it was a mystery to her how he'd got away with it for so long. She couldn't believe that Leo had the audacity to even go down that road, knowing that he was working off someone else's territory. Leo knew about Janey Hallahan. He knew she was one of, if not Glasgow's biggest crime boss even before Dean had got involved with Janey's granddaughter, Molly Rose Hunter; before he realised they were related. It demonstrated to her just how ruthless Leo had been to make his money. There had been a time when she'd questioned whether Dean bringing Molly Rose in had been intentional, a way to weaken Janey's hold on the city. But that wasn't the case, he'd assured her. How could she ever trust that he was telling her the truth?

'I get it, all right. You blame me; nothing's changed there.'

A tear dropped down her cheek and she wiped it away furiously.

Leo held his hands up and sighed. 'I'll get them. I'll get them all. The Hallahans, Marek.'

She drew her eyes away from her husband and got into the car. He climbed in beside her and started the engine. She knew there was no way he'd be able to take revenge on Marek Kaminski. That was an impossible task. But she wanted him to try. And if he died in the process, then that was the price he'd have to pay for Dean.

'And how am I supposed to trust you? For all I know, you could still be working for that disgusting bastard.'

'I'm not. I wouldn't,' Leo replied, his voice softer than she expected.

The silence was deafening between them for a few moments. Cheryl imagined how she was going to get justice for Dean and, as if Leo could read her thoughts, he said, 'How would you like me to deal with the rest of the Hallahans?'

'You mean since you fucked the original plan of killing Janey?' Cheryl sneered and looked up at the sky. Sitting back and playing the good, innocent little wife to a gangster didn't do it for her any more; not that it ever had. She needed to take control, be part of getting justice for her son. Leo had fucked up, time and time again. Janey Hallahan was supposed to be dead by now. Instead, she was as close to Molly Rose as she could get, making this whole quest a lot harder. 'Let me do it,' she said solemnly. 'I'll be able to get a lot closer to them a lot quicker than you could. I can gain their trust. Then...'

And then what? What would she do with her life when she'd taken care of it all? Go on as if nothing had happened? Carry on in a marriage she loathed, with the aching knowledge that she'd live the rest of her life with a gaping hole in her chest?

Leo looked on, waiting for her to finish.

She cleared her throat. 'And then we can move on.'

Leo pulled out of the cemetery and Cheryl kept her eyes on the road.

# Chapter 5

Zofia felt her boyfriend give her hand a tight squeeze and her heart surged in her chest.

'I'm so excited about this,' she said, referring to their holiday to London. 'I've never been there before.'

Szymon smiled and gazed out of the front windscreen as he drove along the road. 'You're going to love it. It's the most amazing city and it'll be a good way for you to keep practising the English language. You already have so much vocabulary; this will only help.'

Szymon had been unexpected. Someone who had come into Zofia's life when things had become hectic. Her mother was in a care home for early-onset dementia. She was mute, with no idea who she or Alina, Zofia's sister, were. Zofia loved the fact that Szymon had taken her out of that hard time. If it wasn't for him, she'd probably be on the streets.

'And you said Alina and Krzysztof are meeting us at the airport?' Zofia asked, checking that she had her passport in her bag for the millionth time.

Szymon shook his head. 'Actually, there has been a change of plan. We're picking them up at Krzysztof's apartment and all travelling together.'

Zofia raised an eyebrow. 'Okay,' she said slowly. 'Why the change of plans?'

Szymon shrugged. 'That's my brother for you. Likes to keep us on our toes.'

'I'm surprised Alina didn't say anything when I was messaging her this morning.' Zofia narrowed her eyes and glanced out of the window. Then she decided to text her sister. Pulling her phone out of her bag, she began typing out a text when Szymon placed a hand on her wrist.

'No need, all the details are sorted,' he said.

'I know,' Zofia replied. 'But I just want to check in with her before we actually get there.'

Szymon's hand fell from her wrist as he replaced it back on the steering wheel. Zofia tapped out a WhatsApp and hit send. She watched as one grey tick appeared. She waited. And waited. The second tick didn't show up on the screen, which meant the message hadn't gone through.

'That's strange,' she said, tapping on the number and calling it. It went straight to voicemail. Zofia stared at the screen, as though there might be something wrong on her end. Bad signal, perhaps?

'What's the problem?' Szymon asked, keeping his eye on the road.

'Alina's phone is off. She never switches it off,' Zofia said, now full of worry.

'Don't worry about it, Zofia. She will be fine. She's with Krzysztof, waiting for us at his apartment.'

His voice was flat, his expression off. Something didn't feel right. Maybe he was annoyed because she was going on about Alina?

'Fine,' she said, sitting back in her seat and staring down at the single grey tick.

Half an hour later, the car pulled into what she could only describe as an industrial estate; a disused one at that. She glanced at the units, their shutters down and the buildings grey and depressed-looking. A few lorries were parked outside the unit that Szymon parked the car in front of and then Zofia noticed Krzysztof's car on the other side of the shutter.

'Why are we here?' Zofia asked.

'I've got a surprise for you. Something I ordered especially for you. You're going to love it,' Szymon said, switching off the engine.

Zofia stared at Szymon. 'What is it?' she asked, a feeling of uncertainty swirling around inside her.

'Remember that dress you wanted, the one you said would be perfect for dinner in that London restaurant that we booked? I bought it for you.'

Zofia glanced back at the closed shutters and said, 'This doesn't look like the kind of place you'd be able to pick up a designer dress from, Szymon.'

He got out the car, closed the door and walked around to the passenger side; all the while, Zofia's eyes darted between the shutter and Krzysztof's car. Where was he? And where was Alina?

Szymon pulled open the passenger door and smiled down at Zofia. 'Come on,' he said.

'Why is your brother's car here? And where are they?'

Szymon's smile, the one she'd fallen for, changed to a frown. His eyes darkened. 'Please, don't make this any harder than it needs to be.'

Zofia frowned. 'What is that supposed to mean?'

Before she knew what was going on, Szymon was pulling her from the car, his fingers digging into the flesh on her upper arm.

'What are you doing, Szymon? Let go, you're hurting me,' she shouted.

Ignoring her pleas, he dragged her from where the car was parked towards one of the industrial units. A door set to the side of the shutter opened and a man appeared. Krzysztof stared into her eyes as Szymon pushed Zofia towards him.

'What the fuck are you doing?' Zofia cried. She stumbled forward, unable to keep her balance, and fell to the ground. Spinning quickly, she looked up at her boyfriend and his brother.

'Where is her passport?' Krzysztof asked, without looking at Szymon.

'In her bag in the car. Her phone is there too,' Szymon replied.

Zofia tried to get to her feet but, before she could, Szymon pulled a gun out from behind his back and pointed it at her. 'Don't move. Just stay where you are.'

Panic rose to her chest, constricting, and she felt like she couldn't breathe. And then a voice from behind her said, 'She'll do what you want. You don't have to point the gun at her.'

Turning, Zofia stared at her sister, sat on the floor at the other side of the unit. She wasn't alone. There were a few other young girls, all crying or looking like they had been.

'Alina?' Zofia sobbed.

'Just do what he says, Zofia,' Alina replied, her tone sombre.

'Stand up,' Szymon said. 'Go and sit with the others. The boss will be here soon to take a look at you all before you're put into transit.'

Transit? Boss? What the hell was going on?

Zofia got to her feet, limbs trembling, and began to walk towards her sister, trying to breathe through the rising panic. Alina appeared calm. How long had she been here? It occurred to Zofia that she hadn't properly spoken to her sister in over twenty-four hours, only via messages; Zofia had been too busy and excited while she prepared for her first trip away with Szymon.

Zofia sat down next to her sister and, up close, Alina's eyes were bloodshot; tired. She glanced around at the other girls. Their faces resembling zombies. All staring down at the ground. All unblinking.

'Alina,' Zofia whispered as quietly as she could. 'What is going on?'

Alina shook her head. 'Don't speak. Just do what they say. It's not worth getting them angry. Trust me.'

Narrowing her eyes, Zofia could truly see how terrified her big sister, Alina, was. The fact that she wasn't saying anything, wasn't telling Zofia what had happened before she arrived, had alarm bells ringing loudly in her ears.

She glanced back at Szymon and Krzysztof, who were stood together at the door she'd just come through. The sound of a car pulling up outside made Zofia's skin prickle.

'Boss,' Krzysztof said, and Szymon nodded before they moved to the side, allowing a taller, broader man to enter the unit.

He rubbed his hands together as he took in the sight in front of him with a smile on his face. The act made Zofia shiver, and she felt Alina's hand slip into her own.

The man walked towards Zofia and the other girls. The rest of them almost resumed the foetal position, but Zofia remained as she was. She wanted to see this man's face up-close; even though she herself felt a terror she'd never experienced before.

'Stand up,' the man said as he positioned himself in front of them. The shape of his broad, muscular shoulders could be seen through his leather jacket and Zofia knew this wasn't going to end well. She had a fair idea of what was about to happen, but without confirmation, she couldn't be sure. 'Let me get a good look at you all.'

Zofia watched as the girls stood to attention and she felt Alina's hand fall from her grip as she got to her feet too. Reluctantly, Zofia did the same, not wishing to be the odd one out or be seen to be causing trouble.

'Yes,' he said, rubbing at his short stubble, his dark eyes glistening under the very faint light above them. 'Yes, very, very good work, you two.' He turned to Szymon and Krzysztof. 'Excellent, in fact. A lot better than the shit that I've had to deal with back in the UK.'

The UK, Zofia thought. That was it. She knew now.

'Thank you, boss,' both Szymon and Krzysztof said in unison. They too seemed scared of this man.

Suddenly, the man's phone began to ring in his pocket. He slid it out to answer it and placed the phone to his ear. 'Yes?'

Zofia kept her eyes on him, tried to listen to the voice on the other end. Not that she knew what she was listening for. But he left the unit, gesturing back in the direction of Zofia and the others before he went outside.

Szymon and Krzysztof were stood in front of them now, and Szymon's face was suddenly different. No longer the sunny, smiley boyfriend she thought she knew. His smile was gone, as was the light in his eyes.

'Turn around, face the wall,' he said.

The girls all did what he said. Zofia took a deep breath and shook her head. 'Not until you tell me what is going on.'

The corners of Szymon's mouth raised a little before he lifted his hand so quickly, she didn't have time to react. The force of the back of his hand against her cheek made her think her face was going to explode.

'I said turn the fuck around!'

Reluctantly, she did as she was instructed and turned to face the wall. Her hands were bound behind her back with what felt like sharp plastic which dug uncomfortably into her skin. She felt hands on her shoulders and was spun back around to face Szymon. Some of the girls were crying now, their fear ignored by Szymon and Krzysztof as they gagged all of the girls. Zofia wanted to fight back, to refuse, but fear rooted her to the spot.

She watched as the others were guided out of the unit; she was the last one, with Szymon at her back. Outside, Krzysztof forced each of them into the back of one of the lorries she'd noticed when she'd arrived. Not one of the girls refused; they did exactly what was being instructed. Alina was in front of Zofia and climbed in. Zofia stopped walking, her face in agony from the backhanded slap Szymon had delivered. She didn't want another one of those, so decided to climb into the lorry behind Alina.

'Get comfortable,' Szymon said, eyeing each of them. 'It's going to be a long journey.'

Zofia glared at him and studied every inch of his face. She had never believed that hate was a real emotion, but as she looked into Szymon's eyes, she felt it deep in the pit of her stomach. It was a hopeless feeling, because there was nothing she could do with it other than hope something happened to him that would make him feel as desperate as she did in that very moment.

Then, he shut the back doors, plunging them all into darkness, and that's when the tears finally came.

Her body ached, as did her face when she opened her eyes. The jutting and jerking of the lorry for however long she'd been in there had taken its toll on her. But they weren't moving any more. The lorry had stopped.

She turned her head towards Alina, whose eyes were wide with terror and staring at the back doors. The look on her sister's face made Zofia's stomach lurch.

A voice speaking English but in an accent she didn't recognise bellowed from somewhere outside the lorry. Shit, where were they?

The back doors swung open and bright, artificial light shone into the space, blinding her from what was behind it.

'This is all of them?' came a man's voice from behind the light.

'For now, yes,' another voice came. One she did recognise, only having heard it briefly before she'd been placed in the lorry. Szymon and Krzysztof's boss.

'Nice one, Marek,' the other man said with enthusiasm. 'They're all much better than Molly Rose Hunter.'

The light died and Zofia blinked rapidly to get rid of the spots in her vision.

'Molly Rose Hunter is lost revenue, Leo. Lost revenue isn't good for business. These girls are only replacing that loss, which in itself isn't a profit,' the man named Marek said.

*Marek and Leo*, Zofia thought. She'd store those names in her memory. Alongside Szymon and Krzysztof.

'And while we're on the subject of lost revenue?' Marek said.

'I'm working on it,' Leo said, his voice lowering.

'Work *faster*,' Marek snapped. It was clear he was angry with Leo about something. 'It's a good thing you don't have another son to offer up to the slaughter, Leo.'

The words echoed in Zofia's ears and they terrified her.

'I won't fuck up again,' Leo said.

'No, you fucking won't,' Marek replied. 'Because you know what will happen if you do. Thankfully, I have a team back in Poland who were able to do a much better job than Dean ever could. I really do hope you can finish the job he started?'

'I'm on track,' Leo replied. 'It's being taken care of. Molly Rose will be in Poland before the end of the month.'

'I hope you're right. I had some of my very prestigious clients go through my catalogue and that girl was on reserve. I've assured them that their deposits are still valid. You better not lose me thousands, Leo.' Marek took a breath, smiled and rubbed his hands together. 'Now, get these girls to their required destinations. Get them trained up and on the job quickly. I want what they're worth too. So, your best client list for them. Understood?'

'Loud and clear, boss,' Leo said, climbing into the space.

The conversation she'd just witnessed made her feel sick to her stomach. A catalogue of girls for prestigious clients? Deposits? Whoever this Molly Rose was, she was going to be put through hell. As was Zofia by the sounds of it all. A terrible sense of dread took over at the thought of what awaited her. She couldn't even begin to imagine what kind of people she would encounter. There were certain types of people out there in the world, with very specific tastes, and it was becoming clearer with every passing second that Zofia was going to come face to face with them very soon.

Pulling a sheet of paper out of his pocket, Leo read over what was on there and then glanced down at them all. He read out their names, made them stand one by one and led them out of the lorry. Zofia, again, was the last aside from Alina, who was led out in front of her.

Leo led Zofia out of the lorry, her hands still bound behind her back, her entire body aching and shivering from the pain and exhaustion of the journey. She noticed two white Transit vans parked with their back doors open and facing her. Alina was in the one to the left, with three other girls. Zofia glanced to the van on the right. Three girls sat inside and she was led by the arm towards it.

*No, no, no*, she thought. Why couldn't she go with her sister? Why were they being split up? Angry tears pooled in her eyes as the English-speaking man named Leo pushed her into the van. She turned, tried to speak through the gag covering her mouth. She wanted to plead to be able to go with Alina. But before she could say anything, the van doors slammed shut, and once again she was plunged into darkness.

# Chapter 6

## ONE MONTH LATER

Leo Davidson stood at the door of the cramped room inside the flat with his arms folded across his chest and stared at each and every one of them. Some were of age, but no older than twenty. Others were as young as fourteen. Whatever the punters wanted, they got because it paid Leo well.

'Right,' Marek said. 'Get them prepped and on the job tonight.'

Leo turned and looked at Marek. 'Tonight?'

The sound of quiet cries and sniffles coming from the back of the room made Marek's back stiffen.

'Oi, shut your mouth or I will shut it for you.' The cries turned to silence, and Marek turned back to Leo. '*Yes*, Leo. Tonight.'

Leo frowned. 'But I haven't had a chance to set up a venue.'

Marek raised an eyebrow and scoffed. 'Then I suggest you get to work, Leo. You know what happens if things don't go as I plan, don't you? I can't kill Dean again, but if I could I'd make you watch so that you wouldn't question me so much. Remember that you are on probation until I see improvements, and part of that probation period is you doing as you're expected otherwise that lovely wife of yours is next on my list.'

It felt like a stab to Leo's gut. *Fucking probation.* If he knew he could get away with it, Leo would strangle Marek there and then just for being a disrespectful prick in front of these girls. It could make him look weak, perhaps give them an in to try to get out of their work. He refrained, of course, because he would never get away with something like strangling Marek Kaminski.

Marek suddenly gave Leo a playful, yet stern, slap on the back and said, 'Oh, come on, Leo. With your client list, you'll be able to put these servants to work quicker than you think. All you have to do is find a venue and the rest is ready and waiting. I have faith in you.'

It wasn't a compliment; it was a warning and Leo Davidson knew it.

'Yes, boss,' Leo said through gritted teeth.

'Don't look so down about it, Leo. Why not change it from probationary period, to improvement plan?' Marek suggested patronisingly, and Leo gritted his teeth so hard he heard them crunch together. 'Here's what I suggest, if you can get a payment for each and every one of these new servants, then I'll let you have a go for *free* on that one you like,' Marek said, clicking his fingers. 'What's her name again? Ah, yes, Maja. She's a feisty little thing. That what you're into? Blonde hair, long legs, small breasts? Or if that's not your thing, we can get you, let's say, the fuller kind?'

Leo wanted to punch the face off Marek. He felt eyes on him from all around. He turned his back to them as Marek was about to walk out the door.

'Marek?' Leo said.

'Yes, Leo?'

37

He lowered his voice. 'If I make it double per servant, I want her for an *entire* night.'

Marek raised an eyebrow, laughed loudly and slapped him on the shoulder again, harder this time.

'I tell you what, you make it triple, you can have her for twenty-four *fucking* hours. Do whatever the fuck you want with her, just make sure she's still alive at the end of it. She's our most sought after in the east side and I don't want to lose her.'

At that, Marek slammed the door shut, leaving Leo inside the flat with six new servants from Poland.

They all looked at Leo in horror. Maybe they understood English well enough to comprehend the exchange between Leo and Marek.

'What the fuck you all staring at?' he barked, and they all lowered their gaze.

Something stirred deep inside him. He was going to get what he wanted. If working for Marek, the man who had ordered the kill on Dean, was going to work, then he wanted certain benefits.

He pulled out his phone and sent a group message to all of the clients he knew would be interested in this evening's activities. One replied with the offer of using one of his properties for the occasion.

'Right.' Leo smiled, his phone still in his hand. The faces on the screen saver stared up at him, smiling, like they didn't know what lay ahead of them. And they hadn't known. Not even Leo could have guessed what would happen between Marek and Dean. 'Looks like we're all going to a party tonight. So, let's go over the rules, shall we?' He turned to his right and smiled. 'Explain it all, won't you, Zofia? After all, your English is superb; almost as good as your mother tongue. One of the main reasons you were chosen.'

She stood by his side, her eyes low and her stance weak. Then he noticed that her eyes weren't on the floor. They were on his phone; she was looking at the screen-saver image of his family. Of himself, Dean and Cheryl. He quickly clicked the power button once and the screen went dark.

'Oi, don't be such a nosy bitch,' he said, shoving her in the shoulder. 'Get on with it.'

She snapped into action then, stood tall with her shoulders back. He watched as Zofia moved across the floor from the corner, stood in front of everyone and started to talk about Leo's expectations in Polish. He smiled as he listened, even though she could be saying anything to them. Although he had trained her not to be so stupid. She'd been the most obedient girl he'd ever found. She did everything he said and often was rewarded for her loyalty. Sometimes, he left her out of the sex parties. Not because he felt sorry for her, but to keep her in line. If he did that, then his job was easier. He also had another plan for Zofia, one that would help him with his final objective when it came to the Hallahan family. She was perfect for the role and it was the best idea he'd ever had. For that he was proud of himself.

# Chapter 7

'Mrs Hallahan,' the surgeon said. He let her name hang there longer than necessary. It was like he was trying to make her think the worst.

'Is he dead?' Janey asked bluntly.

The surgeon shook his head and Janey didn't think she'd heard him right.

'So I can see him?' she asked, unsteadily getting to her feet. Kristo rose with her and stood by her side, like he always did during the hard times.

'No, not right now,' the surgeon replied.

Janey stared at him, wondering about the state her husband was in if she couldn't see him after the surgery.

'Why not?' Kristo asked, his tone calm, as though he knew that Janey's anger might result in their ejection from the hospital.

'Your husband's injuries are very serious, Mrs Hallahan. He's had a significant brain bleed. The surgery *did* go as planned, but we need to keep him in intensive care to monitor his condition.'

The words were like a vice around her neck. Who had done this to them and why?

Kristo supported Janey under her arm as she leaned on him. Her own injuries were insignificant in comparison. A sprained wrist, twisted ankle and a bump to the head. She'd been lucky in that respect.

'So, when *can* I see him?' Janey sighed, trying to keep her patience intact.

The surgeon looked at her, and she could tell he understood the tone. She wasn't asking when, she was demanding now.

'Today,' the surgeon replied. 'He's in an induced coma so that he can recover better. Let me just make sure he's comfortable first and I'll get back to you.'

Kristo smiled at the man and stood firm. 'You understand the importance of the man in your care to my boss, don't you? You must do whatever you can for a good outcome.'

Janey felt an aching lump in her throat. Her daughter, Orla, was dead, and now her husband was in a coma; could possibly die too. How had life become this?

'Of course,' the surgeon said, his voice barely audible. He left the family room and Janey's legs almost buckled.

'Kristo,' Janey said, her voice almost cracking with a mixture of emotions. 'You get out there and find the bastard who ran us off the road.'

'The team are already on it,' Kristo replied.

Janey nodded and then gave in to the shock of Ciaran's prognosis and sat down. How was all this going to affect the running of her business? She still needed to give the go-ahead for the cocaine shipments and distributions, she still had to check in to make sure the money was coming in, being cleaned, and she still needed to make sure that the legit businesses were running as they should be. It was all so much to think about when she was grieving the loss of Orla and worried that she would lose Ciaran too.

As though he'd read her thoughts, Kristo said, 'You don't have to worry about the business. I can take care of things until you're feeling up to it again. And I mean all of it; but only if you want me to.'

Janey sighed heavily. 'Maybe it would be better if I just carried on as normal, you know, keep my mind busy.'

'Possibly. But you know I'll do whatever I can to help. And Ciaran *will* be fine, Janey. Although, I can't say the same for the person responsible for putting him here,' Kristo replied.

Janey Hallahan wasn't going to take this lightly. Someone had run her and her husband off the road. Given that she was the head of a criminal firm, it was likely it had been intentional, especially since those responsible had left the scene as soon as it happened.

Her whole family could be in danger. Given what they'd all been through recently, she wasn't willing to take any risks.

'When you find out who did this, tell me immediately. Whether Ciaran dies or not, I want to make sure I end them myself.'

Kristo nodded but remained silent.

'And another thing. I want Molly Rose under constant security. Please, collect her from the salon. Bring her to the house in Rhu. She's not living on her own in that huge house with all this going on.'

'Anything else?' Kristo asked.

Janey sighed. 'Yes, don't take no for an answer. I know what my granddaughter is like. She'll fight you on this, Kristo. But make sure she gets in that car with you today.'

'Mrs Hallahan?' a familiar voice said. Both Janey and Kristo turned to see Detective James Pearson standing just a few feet from them with a gentle smile on his face.

'James,' Janey said, her voice a little shakier than she'd like. It was a relief to see him, this man that she and Ciaran could rely on to get their information for them if they needed it; to keep their names out of any dodgy business around the city.

'How is he?' the detective asked, stepping forward and placing a hand on Janey's upper arm.

'He's in an induced coma,' Janey replied with a sliver of anger in her tone.

'We're on it,' James said. 'We're going over every piece of information we can to find who did this. I won't let you down.'

Janey glanced at Kristo. Was it a good idea to let the police take the lead with this? If they did, and they found the person responsible, what would they get? A few years behind bars? Nah, Janey didn't want that. She wanted the person responsible to suffer in the worst way. There was no easy way out of this for them.

'What is it?' James asked.

'Nothing,' Janey replied.

'No, come on. I've worked with you and Ciaran a long time now. I know that look. What are you thinking? In fact, I know what you're thinking. You don't want us to find them, do you? Or at least, you don't want us to do anything about it once we've found out who ran you off the road?'

Janey looked down at the floor and closed her eyes. He was bang on the money with that one. But could she tell him? Could she really be *that* honest?

'This is personal against the Hallahans, you know that, right?' Janey said.

'You're sure about that?' James asked.

'Never been surer of anything. It was deliberate. Another car didn't just bump into us, James. We were

43

literally rammed off the road. I want the person or people dead. I don't give a fuck who they are.'

James took a long, deep breath. 'This person or persons left the scene of an accident, Janey. I can't just ignore it.'

'It wasn't an accident. It was a target hit,' Janey replied sternly.

'And for that, I have to do my job. Who would you want investigating it? Me, or some other DI who could dig a little deeper into your life and, well, you know what?'

Kristo cleared his throat loudly and then whispered, 'Janey has enough on her plate without that. We all do.'

James nodded. 'Exactly. Look,' he said, lowering his own voice now. 'I know it's hard and given what you all went through with Orla's death, I just think it might be better to let me lead on this. Let me do my job. I'll find them, and then I'll tell you who it is. Once I've done that, I'll arrange for you to do what you want. It won't come back to you. But you can't kill them. They need to come to justice. It needs to look legit otherwise my job is on the line.'

Janey rolled her eyes before raising her head and looking at James. *Your job was on the line the second you took your first pay cheque from us*, she thought.

'Fine. But I'll be doing my own digging, James. And if I get there first, it's my game, my rules. Got it?'

The DI nodded. 'Okay. But just... be careful, Janey. This person, these people; they could be more dangerous than any of us realise.'

Janey smirked. 'No one's more dangerous than me right now. You can trust me on that one.'

# Chapter 8

Cheryl Davidson watched Molly Rose Hunter as she busied herself around the salon.

She was a young and beautiful girl, but that didn't penetrate Cheryl's feelings towards her. Her baby boy was dead. That was a situation no parent should ever have to deal with.

'Are you okay?' Molly Rose asked.

Cheryl blinked at the sound of Molly Rose's voice. 'Yes, why?'

'You've been staring at me for the best part of five minutes. I'm beginning to think I've got something growing out my head; or my arse.'

Despite her bitter hatred for the girl, Cheryl laughed. 'Sorry. I was just thinking about...' She raced through her brain to think of an answer. 'Janey. Are you doing okay? You know, after what happened to your grandparents, you must be upset.'

Molly Rose sighed. 'I'm fine. Ciaran's not my grandfather. But yeah, it's still shocking. But my gran, Janey, will be fine. It feels weird to call her gran. I've only known her a short time. Anyway, she's made of tough stuff.'

Cheryl raised an eyebrow. 'Really? Because from where I'm standing, your face doesn't share the same sentiment. And it can't be easy going through all this after just losing your mum too.'

45

Molly Rose frowned. 'How do you know about that?'

'Janey told me about it when I started working here,' Cheryl replied quickly. 'She said it was quite sudden?'

Molly Rose raised an eyebrow. 'Yeah, it was. I'm beginning to think my family are cursed. Dead mum, Dad's fucked off to America because he can't cope, auntie in rehab. Now Janey's in the hospital and her husband's in a coma.'

Cheryl nodded. Good, she thought, the girl was opening up to her. Gaining her trust was the single most important thing in Cheryl's plan to bring her and the rest of the family down to the ground. 'It's all just so horrible, Molly Rose. I'm so sorry. You've been left on your own, pretty much. It must be so tough.'

'I've been through a lot in the last year. I'm tougher than I look. I don't want to talk about it, if I'm honest. It's a waste of my fucking breath.'

'It's not though, is it? A waste of your breath, I mean. Maybe talking about it all would help ease some of the stress?' Cheryl pressed again. She saw the look on Molly Rose's face; she was scowling, like she was disgusted that the suggestion had been made. 'All I'm saying is I'm happy to lend an ear.'

'I'm not the type to blabber on about my shitty trauma. Believe it or not, knowing I'm on my own for a bit has forced me to think about how to approach life. I need to fend for myself for a while. I can do it. I've lived on the streets, I've been kidnapped by a psycho and almost murdered...' The words trailed off like she suddenly realised she'd said too much.

'Jesus,' Cheryl said, narrowing her eyes. 'You were kidnapped?'

'Long story, but as you can see,' Molly Rose opened up her arms like she was presenting herself to the world, 'I'm fine. Well, *surviving*.'

Cheryl watched as Molly Rose gave a smile before she carried on sweeping the salon floor.

'No boyfriend to help you through it all?' Cheryl asked, realising that it was quite the subject change and hoping it wouldn't rouse suspicion.

Molly Rose let out a laugh and said, 'Nope. Last one turned out not to be very nice. In fact, that's an understatement. He was an utter dickhead. I just didn't find out until well after he was gone.'

Anger burned in Cheryl's chest. 'Oh? What happened?'

Molly Rose sighed loudly but continued sweeping. 'Turned out he was trying to have me trafficked.'

Cheryl dug her nails into her knee. She had to pull her best acting skills out of the bag here. She gasped and said, 'Are you *serious*?'

'Yep,' Molly Rose said, her tone turning sour. 'Prick. Thankfully my mum warned him off me otherwise who knows what would have happened to me. Hope the wee prick rots in hell.'

'Whatever happened to him?'

'The best thing that could have happened. He's dead,' Molly Rose replied, her face expressionless. 'Means he can never hurt anyone like me ever again if he's six feet under.'

A huge wave of pain surged through Cheryl's whole body. To hear Molly Rose state that she was glad Dean was dead was like finding out he'd been killed all over again. She'd only learned the truth about what Dean had been dragged into by his own father just days after his

47

death. She remembered the conversation; or more Cheryl sitting with her head in her hands as Leo was forced to tell her the truth because he was dead. It had all been so much to take in. The trafficking, the fact that Dean had inadvertently picked the granddaughter of a fucking gangster, even if at the time none of them knew this to be the case. Massive fucked-up coincidence, she'd thought at the time. Leo had explained to Cheryl how Molly Rose's mother had come to their door and demanded Dean stop seeing their daughter or she'd go to the police because she was underage. If Orla hadn't done that, if Molly Rose had kept her mouth shut about the relationship, Marek would never have been told by one of his other employees about it and he'd never have killed Dean.

The need for justice for Dean had driven her from the moment she'd discovered he was dead. Getting Marek was going to be an impossible task even if Leo said he'd try. Marek had made the order, but it all stemmed back to Molly Rose. Dean was dead because of her.

She closed her eyes, wished she could turn back the clock. But how far back would she go? Her life had been a mess the moment she married Leo. Then again, if she'd never married him, Dean would never have been born.

'Did you love him?' Cheryl asked, trying not to sound too invested in the life story of a young girl she'd only known for a few weeks.

Molly Rose sighed and stopped sweeping. 'I thought I did. Like, I was excited to see him, I thought about him all the time. He made me laugh, made me feel safe and wanted. I suppose that was his plan. Suck me in, gain my trust then, bang, jet me off to sex-slave land.'

Cheryl's eyebrows crept up her forehead and Molly Rose noticed.

'Sorry, I don't mean to be so blunt but that's basically what he had planned for me.'

Cheryl smiled thinly and held a hand up. 'It's fine,' she said, not sure if she could listen to any more of what Molly Rose had to say about her son.

'Anyway, if eternal damnation is a thing, I hope Dean is in the thick of it. What he had planned for me was fucked up. In fact, he was lucky Janey wasn't around at the time.'

Cheryl felt the burning rage inside her chest intensify but, somehow, she managed to keep it down.

'Janey? Why would you say that?' Cheryl asked. 'Your gran doesn't seem like someone a young lad would be scared of.'

'Haha.' Molly Rose's laugh was loud and sarcastic.

Cheryl bit her tongue. She couldn't break character now. 'What's so funny about that?'

Molly Rose smiled and raised an eyebrow. 'You know who she is, right?'

Cheryl nodded and continued to play dumb. 'She's my boss and a businesswoman, from what I can gather.'

'Yeah, she's a business woman all right.'

'What I meant was, she doesn't seem the type of person to hurt anyone, for any reason.'

'Okay,' Molly Rose said. 'Maybe you don't know her well enough then. Anyway, all that matters is the fucker's dead and he can't hurt me again. Or anyone else.'

Cheryl rose to her feet and stared at Molly Rose as she filled the mop bucket; she felt the anger flush her cheeks.

'Sorry,' Molly Rose said, seemingly shocked by Cheryl's sudden change in position. 'I swear a lot more now than I used to. I think I picked it up from Kassy, my best friend.'

Molly Rose turned her back to Cheryl and poured some bleach into the bucket. Cheryl balled her fists on the desk and tried to breathe through the rage. She was surprised she was holding it together. Her thoughts were interrupted when the salon door opened and a man walked in.

'Kristo, what are you doing here?' Molly Rose said, turning from the sink at the back of the salon. Cheryl relaxed her shoulders and released her fists as she glanced between this man and Molly Rose.

'I've been asked to keep an eye on you.'

'Eh?'

The man, Kristo, looked worried. Cheryl wondered what was going on. Was Janey in a bad way, more so than this man was letting on? Cheryl prayed that would be the case. That woman wasn't supposed to survive. None of them were.

'Janey, she thinks what happened to them was deliberate,' Kristo replied.

Cheryl kept her expression neutral, but inside she was screaming. Yes, it was fucking deliberate and it hadn't worked.

Molly Rose leaned her back against the sink and sighed. 'Of course it was deliberate. This family is cursed. Everyone who comes into contact with us is cursed.'

'What do you mean, deliberate?' Cheryl interjected. She needed to be seen to be concerned. And she was, just not in the way they would think.

'They were run off the road on purpose.' Kristo frowned, looked at her with suspicion. 'What else would I mean when I say deliberate?'

'Sorry, it's just, I don't believe it. How could someone do that? Is she okay?'

Kristo's frown deepened and, for a moment, Cheryl thought her face said it all. But then his expression softened a little and he said, 'Janey is fine. Ciaran...' He cleared his throat.

Cheryl looked across at Molly Rose, who was staring at Kristo, her eyes wide and unblinking.

'He's not so good,' Kristo finished. 'Molly Rose, you've to come with me.'

'Why? I'm fine here, at work.'

'Yeah,' Cheryl interrupted. 'I need her here. We have an appointment sheet as long as the desk today.'

Kristo looked around the shop slowly. 'There's no one here. You can deal with whoever is coming in today, Cheryl. Janey's instructions were clear.'

Cheryl took a deep and steadying breath. She couldn't let Molly Rose out of her sight. Now that this had happened, that the Davidson vendetta against the Halla-hans had started, Janey wouldn't trust anyone around her, especially no one new and that meant Cheryl.

'I can't run this place on my own. I need Molly Rose here.'

'No, you don't,' Kristo replied forcefully. 'Like I said, Janey's instructions were clear. Molly Rose is not to be left alone until we find out who ran them off the road.'

Molly Rose sighed loudly, clearly annoyed herself. Cheryl wanted to scream, but there was really nothing she could do.

'So I'm actually expected to run this place by...' She stopped, reminded herself that protesting would only bring on more suspicion from this man. 'In fact, you're right. Molly Rose, you shouldn't be away from your family right now with what's happened.'

Molly Rose rolled her eyes. 'Am I actually expected to stand here and take instructions from you two, who have absolutely nothing to do with me? I like you, Cheryl, but you're my boss, not my mum. And you.' She looked at Kristo. 'You're Janey's heavy. I'm not listening to either of you. I'll make my own decisions.'

Molly Rose turned her back on both of them and Cheryl noted how she gripped the edge of the sink.

'She's your gran,' Kristo interjected and Molly Rose rolled her eyes. 'Get your things together. You're coming with me, now.'

'No,' Molly Rose replied, without turning.

'Excuse me?'

'I'm not going to stop living my life because of this. Charlie has already taken enough from me. I'm not about to let some stranger put me back to square one.'

Cheryl narrowed her eyes at the mention of the name and wondered who he or she might be to Molly Rose.

'It's not a request, Molly Rose. It's an order; from your gran and my boss. Get your things.'

Molly Rose spun around, her face contorted. 'Can you stop referring to her as my gran? Yes, she is by blood, but to me she's still just Janey. And also, what are you going to do about it if I don't do what you say?'

Cheryl raised an eyebrow, surprised at how feisty this girl was. And then it occurred to her, maybe Molly Rose would rebel against Janey and the rest of her family – what was left of them anyway. That in itself could work in Cheryl's favour.

Kristo closed his eyes for a brief moment. 'Molly Rose, think about why you're being asked to come with me. I mean, *really* think about it. The last few months, what has happened to your family? Nothing but bad things. And it seems that isn't stopping anytime soon. Janey only wants to keep you safe.'

Silence fell heavy over the room, and Cheryl watched in anticipation, hoping that Molly Rose wouldn't back down.

'Urgh,' she grunted loudly. 'Fine. You win. Where am I going?'

Cheryl sighed inwardly. She could feel the revenge plan slipping from her fingers already.

Kristo nodded and relief washed over his face. 'You'll be staying with Janey until things settle down.'

'And when the hell will that be?'

Kristo shrugged. 'I'll take care of that. Just you do what your gran tells you and you'll be fine.'

'So, how long will Molly Rose be away from the shop for? I'll need to get someone in to cover her while she's away,' Cheryl said.

'You'll need to take that up with Janey yourself, I'm not a PA.'

Cheryl stifled a laugh. That was exactly what he was, with muscle.

She sat back down in her seat behind the desk as Molly Rose went into the back to get her things. She'd have to think this through. She was going to have to get close to Janey, gain her trust. Make her think that she could help.

Revenge was going to be a slow process.

# Chapter 9

Climbing out of the car at the house, she looked up at the grandeur of the place. It made her family home look like something from a slum. It was the biggest house she'd ever seen in her life. No, it wasn't just a house. It was a mansion; the kind you only saw in an episode in one of those reality real estate shows. How the hell had she managed to make so much money to be able to build something like this from scratch? What the hell was she selling? Gold?

'Jesus *Christ*,' she said as she took it all in. 'I can't believe my mum kept me away from a family member who is *this* minted.'

Kristo could be heard laughing gently from the car but she ignored it, remembering why. Orla hadn't wanted a relationship with Janey after being given up as a baby. She and Sinead had gone down completely different paths because of what happened in their childhoods. Although now that she thought about it, if Janey hadn't given them up as babies, where would that have led them? Where would they be now? Her mum would probably still be alive, perhaps Sinead wouldn't be an addict. It was Janey's fault, wasn't it? That one decision led to her mum's death and Sinead's spiral into a dark hole. It was Janey's fault that Molly Rose was essentially an orphan. A sixteen- almost seventeen-year-old orphan, whose mum wouldn't be around for big life events. The eighteenth birthday, the twenty-first. If she got married, Orla wouldn't be there. Molly Rose's children wouldn't have a gran on her side. Molly Rose was going to feel Orla's absence for the rest of her life.

Swallowing down the lump in her throat and blinking back tears, she focused her attention on the house again. How long had Janey been living here? And how much had it cost to build this place? Orla would have rolled her eyes and said it was nothing but a bragging house. Anything to keep her hardened exterior intact, when really it was all a defence mechanism for how she'd really felt about everything she'd been through in childhood.

A sadness weighed down on Molly Rose's chest. Every time she closed her eyes, she saw her mother's face, moments before she died. It didn't matter how hard she tried to think of something else, Orla would always be staring back at her.

'Has anyone been in contact with my Auntie Sinead about this?' she said, trying again to refocus her attention on something other than the shitshow her life had become. She didn't know Janey well but they were connected by blood. And now, she had to rely on her new grandmother to get her through the latest target on her back. Something she should be used to now, she supposed.

'I told Janey I'd let Sinead know what happened, but she insisted on doing it herself,' Kristo replied, opening the boot and pulling out Molly Rose's bags.

'Am I staying here by *myself*? When is Janey getting out of the hospital?'

'Today; I'm going back to pick her up later. She just wanted to stay with Ciaran for a while.'

'They've discharged her already? It's only been a day,' Molly Rose replied.

'No, she's discharging herself. I advised her not to, but you know what she's like.'

In that moment, Molly Rose realised that, actually, she didn't know what Janey was like. Not really.

Kristo pulled out a set of keys and unlocked the front door, allowing Molly Rose to go inside first. As she walked into the house, she sighed. She'd been living at home alone since Orla had died two months earlier; her dad having left for America to live with his brother because he couldn't cope with the grief. Even though she was grieving at the same time as trying to get on with things, she'd enjoyed the independence. Now, it would feel like she was under surveillance.

The sound of bags being dumped on the marble floor in the entrance hall made Molly Rose turn round.

'I'll be back with Janey in a couple of hours. Make yourself comfortable. Do not, and I repeat, do not answer the door to anyone, do not leave this house unless it's to go on the balcony and do not answer any calls that aren't either myself or Janey. Do you understand?'

Molly Rose glared at Kristo in disbelief. 'I can't *leave*?'

Kristo shook his head. 'No. But there will be plenty here to occupy yourself with. I'll be back soon.'

She watched him go and felt utterly imprisoned. She could leave if she really wanted to. She could just walk out the door and do what she wanted to do. But what good would that bring? If Janey was serious that this was some personal attack on the family, then Molly Rose could once again be in real danger. And once again, it was all down to Janey.

'Fuck sake,' Molly Rose muttered as she heard Kristo lock the front door. Walking towards it, which was made entirely of glass, she held her hands up in question and shouted, 'Aye, very good. What if there's a fire?'

Kristo smiled and shouted back, 'Don't light one and you'll be fine.'

He climbed into the car and reversed out of the driveway.

'Arsehole,' she shouted back, before sighing loudly and looking down at her bags. Bending down and picking them up, Molly Rose carried them down the three steps which led her into an open-plan living, kitchen and dining space. On the far wall opposite, which was almost entirely made of glass, she stared through the bifold balcony doors on to the water in front of the house. 'I suppose if I'm going to be imprisoned, it might as well be here.'

She stepped into the kitchen and opened the fridge. A bottle of Pinot Grigio stared back at her. She'd never had wine before. Only vodka, in the park that night before her best friend, Kassy, stopped that group of boys from attacking her. That had been the night they'd met for the first time. The memory of Kassy made Molly Rose stop for a moment. They hadn't been friends for long; they'd never been given that chance. One thing Molly Rose did remember was Kassy once saying that she'd always dreamed of living somewhere on the water. Staring out at the view, Molly Rose couldn't help the guilt washing over her. They'd met on the streets when Molly Rose was sleeping rough, and now she was stood inside what could only be described as a glass palace, overlooking the view Kassy had always dreamed of.

Molly Rose closed her eyes and tried not to cry. So much death. So much tragedy. She opened her eyes and pulled the wine out of the fridge before searching the cupboards for a wine glass. Upon finding one, she set them both down on the kitchen worktop, which looked almost identical to the marble floor, and poured some wine into the glass. Raising it to her lips, she glugged back a large mouthful and winced at the taste.

'*Urgh*, that tastes like vinegar,' she said, but it didn't stop her from having another mouthful. She swirled the wine around in the glass and strolled across the room towards the balcony doors. Turning the latch from the inside, she pushed the door open and stepped out onto the decking.

Feeling the cool, newly autumnal air on her skin made her shiver. A season her mum would never get to see again. Nor Kassy.

Everything was silent aside from the water lapping onto the pebbled shore just in front of her. *It's peaceful here*, she thought. Shame she was alone and not spending this time with anyone important to her.

'Maybe I'm the problem, or the curse?' Molly Rose said aloud. 'Even fucking Dean's dead.'

She sipped at the wine again, even though the taste made her scrunch up her face, as she wandered back into the house. She weaved in and out of the different rooms and wondered if Janey had chosen the décor herself, or had paid someone to do it for her.

She reached the far end of the hallway and was faced with a closed door. When she opened it, a room which looked like Janey's office presented itself to her.

Stepping inside, Molly Rose went around to the chair side of the desk and sat down on the large leather wrap-around computer chair. It was beyond comfortable and felt like a giant hug.

Placing her glass down on the desk, she ran her fingers across the Bluetooth keyboard in front of her. The office reminded her a little of her mum's office back at home. Neat, tidy. It smelled clean.

She switched on the computer and immediately a password screen came up. Tutting, Molly Rose switched it off again. Pulling open the drawer under the desk, she looked inside and saw a file marked *HR*. Information on who worked for her. Would Molly Rose's details be in there? Yes, Janey was her gran, but also an employer.

She nonchalantly skimmed through the files and quickly lost interest before closing the drawer again.

Her phone buzzed in her pocket and took her attention away from the office she was sat in. Pulling the phone from her pocket, her mum's eyes stared back at her from the screen saver she'd set after Orla died. A friend of the family's wedding a few years earlier. A memory of a happier time before Dean turned up and stole everything from her. Molly Rose didn't have the best relationship with her mum in the end, but the pain of knowing she'd never see her again was like something she'd never experienced.

A message flashed up on the screen from a withheld number. *That's odd*, she thought. *Can you withhold your number in a text?*

Opening the message, she scanned over the words and was overcome with confusion.

> There's a gift for you outside, under the
> deck. Open it. You'll like what you find.

Molly Rose gripped the phone in her hand, and the over-whelming terror clutched at her throat. Who else knew she was here? The thought of someone lurking around outside, waiting for her to go out and retrieve said gift made her feel sick. Was this one of those scam messages?

The phone buzzed again; a second message had come through.

> I spent ages thinking about what to get
> you. I'd have loved you in it. Dean x.

Her stomach lurched at reading Dean's name. Dean was *dead*.

A horrible thought entered her mind then. What if Dean *wasn't* dead? What if it had all been a trick, to make her think she was safe and then, bam! There she was, on a plane or a boat to another country with *Christ* knows what planned for her.

Molly Rose shook her head. That was ridiculous. If he wasn't truly dead, the media wouldn't have reported it. Also, if he was still alive, he'd have come after her long before now, wouldn't he?

She looked down at the message carefully. Still no number. The hairs on her arms stood on end. Whoever this was, was watching her.

*Go out and get it*, she thought to herself. *If they were here, in the house, or outside, they'd have said come out and get it, wouldn't they?*

Molly Rose stepped out of the office and moved towards the decked balcony. From inside the house, it looked so beautiful outside. But what and who was waiting for her? *Below* the deck? Did that mean that whoever was messaging her, whoever had placed this bloody gift there, could access the property from somewhere other than the driveway?

Glancing back at the front entrance to the house, Molly Rose cursed herself for not going to the hospital with Kristo to pick up Janey.

Pulling up his number, she considered calling him to come back. But then, she'd just look like a stupid little girl, who couldn't fend for herself. And that couldn't be further from the truth. This she could deal with because she'd been through much worse.

Moving towards the bifold doors, Molly Rose trembled with fear as she pushed them open and stepped out onto the deck for a second time. She stared across the water, placed her hands on the wooden railing and leaned over slightly. She shouldn't be out here, she knew that. But she was sick of being viewed as weak.

A thought occurred to her. If she was out on the balcony and the person was out there, watching her, maybe they were waiting to pounce. Why wouldn't she arm herself? Turning, she rushed back through to the kitchen and pulled the largest, sharpest knife from the block and gripped it tightly in her hand.

'Piss off, you sick *fuck*. Dean's dead. Just…' she shouted then swallowed hard. 'Just leave me alone.'

She looked around, taking in the fact that she couldn't see any other houses around her. In fact, all she could see was the water ahead and Rosneath Caravan Park beyond that. Whoever had sent the message could be looking at her right now and that thought sent chills up her spine.

# Chapter 10

'Remember, I'm doing you a favour because you've performed well with the new recruits,' he said to her. She stared at him and nodded quickly. 'And don't forget, you're being watched out here. Any funny business, any signs that you're trying to run, I'll put you in the middle of one of my parties so quickly your feet won't touch the ground. And you'd do well to keep Alina at the forefront of your mind. You fuck up, I'll make her pay for your mistakes.'

Zofia felt sick and enraged that Leo was using her sister as a threat. She didn't know where Alina was, or what she was having to go through; likely the same thing as Zofia. But she was also relieved that she was being spared from one of the parties yet again, for her co-operation in training the new people that were coming into the mix. Not that she was immune to the parties by any means, that had been made very clear to her. But so far, she'd only had to attend two since she'd arrived in Scotland. And she would do anything to help Leo if it meant never having to go through that again. Begging on the streets and being forced to mug people to get cash for Leo was a walk in the park in comparison.

'Oi, take this,' he said, handing her a small, square photograph. 'Memorise her face. You're going to help me with her.'

Zofia glanced down at it. It was a picture of a girl, around Zofia's age. She was pretty.

'What?' Zofia shrugged. 'What do I do with this?'

'I've already told you what to do with it. Memorise her face. Listen, Zofia, let me make this clear. If you help me with a job involving the girl in *that* picture, you get a bonus. Got it?'

Zofia glanced down at the picture again and sighed. They had their eye on this one too? And this one would also be taken away to a country where she barely knew the language, made to do God only knew what for absolutely nothing. These people were sick in the head.

'I'll make you a deal. You help me capture this girl, I'll make sure you're reunited with Alina. How does that sound?'

The sound of her sister's name on his lips made her shiver, but Zofia would do anything to be with Alina again.

'Yes,' she replied, unable to bear the thought of handing someone over to these monsters.

'Good. Now, get your best begging eyes on, and start collecting cash. Be careful about who you choose to rob. The ones who look harassed are the best. You know, the ones with screaming kids, or who are running for the bus. The more cash you get, the better it is for you and our deal to keep you out of the parties. Go on, get a move on, I've others to drop off and pick up.'

Leo climbed back into the minivan and, as it pulled away, Zofia looked across the car park at the Morrisons supermarket. That was her station today. Another day stood outside, begging for money that people wouldn't give because they either didn't care, or they didn't believe that Zofia was actually homeless; another day robbing people of their hard-earned cash just to stop Leo from selling her like a piece of meat like he did the rest of the girls. And boys.

Glancing back down at the photograph in her hand, Zofia sighed, swallowed down the lump in her throat and placed the picture into the pocket of her jeans before crossing the road and taking her seat on the concrete outside the supermarket. It was going to be a long day.

## Chapter 11

'Do you realise this is the longest we've ever been in a room together and not spoken?' Janey said, holding on to Ciaran's hand as he lay on the bed, linked up to all sorts of drips and machines.

*Please*, Janey thought, *just squeeze my hand*. She waited, stared down at his hand full of hope, but there was nothing. Ciaran was deep inside himself, unaware that he was even a person; unable to communicate because of what had happened to him. Being in a coma must be like being dead, Janey thought, trying to imagine what it would be like to be in Ciaran's position. The anger and the grief of her situation made her feel like she was being crushed.

'Mrs Hallahan?'

Janey took a breath and tried to keep her anger under control. She wanted to shoot her way through Glasgow if it meant finding the *bastard* who'd caused this. Finding and then losing one of her daughters was hard enough, but now she was by Ciaran's bedside, not sure that he would pull through. Even if he did, how would he be after such a bad brain injury? Would he be the same as she'd always known? They'd been together for thirty-odd years. The possibility that he wouldn't be there terrified her more than the prospect of him passing away.

'Janey?'

Janey turned around to see Kristo standing in the doorway.

'I'm sorry to interrupt,' he said softly.

'It's fine. I'm ready to go. Is Molly Rose at the house?' she replied, glad of the distraction from the horrible thoughts coursing through her mind.

'Yes, she is. I warned her not to leave, or answer the door to anyone. I do think I should have brought her with me though, if you don't mind me saying.'

Janey closed her eyes for a brief moment. 'No, I don't mind you saying. But I also know that demanding Molly Rose do what we say will result in her rebellion. I knew it would be hard enough for you to convince her to go with you to the house. You left security behind though?'

Kristo nodded. 'Yes, the team are distributed around the property. She's completely safe.'

'She doesn't know there's a team watching the house, does she? Because I think she'd kick off if she did.'

Kristo smiled. 'No, she doesn't. Unless she's tried to leave and they've stopped her, but I'd know about that by now.'

Janey sighed and turned back to Ciaran. She was still holding his hand. She didn't want to let go. Ever.

Leaning in, Janey whispered into Ciaran's ear, 'I'll be back later, sweetheart. I've just got some things to do. You rest, get strong. I need you back on this side of the plane. We all do.'

Kristo helped Janey off the seat and she looked up at him.

'Thank you.'

'Are you sure you want to discharge yourself, Janey? I mean, are you feeling well enough after the crash?'

Janey felt the niggling pains all over her body, but she knew that she was well enough to get herself out of the hospital and start her search. 'It wasn't a crash. We were run off the bloody road. And I'm fine,' she said through gritted teeth before softening her tone. 'Sorry, I know you're only trying to help.'

'It's okay. I understand your frustrations. And the doctors, they know you're leaving?'

'I discharged myself this morning. They put up a bit of a fight but I explained that Ciaran needed them more than I did. I'll be fine. The longer I'm in here, the more my family are in danger.'

Janey leaned down and kissed Ciaran on the cheek before turning and leaving his bedside. Walking away from him was like a dagger to the heart, but if she was going to keep the rest of the family and her business staff – who were almost like family – safe, then she couldn't just sit in the hospital and do nothing. And if that person – or those people – who'd run them off the road knew that Janey and Ciaran had survived, how long would it be before they tried again?

'You'll always be safe with me and the team around you,' Kristo said, allowing Janey to hang on to his arm as he led her along the corridor. 'I mean, you're our boss. If you die, who's going to pay us?'

Janey laughed loudly. 'I know. But I also want this person to know that I'm not scared of them. If they want a fight, then they can fucking have one.'

# Chapter 12

Staring down at the picture of Dean, she tried to smile. He was the only reason that Cheryl had ever stayed with her husband. Their marriage had been doomed from the start; even before that. It had always crossed her mind whether things would be different if she'd just walked away. If she'd done that, however, Dean would never have been born. And he would never have been murdered.

'Hi,' she said, picking up the phone when it rang with Leo's name on the screen.

'How's things going with Molly Rose?' he asked.

'Slow. Janey's spooked about what happened so she's taken Molly Rose away from the shop. Said she doesn't want Molly Rose out of her sight.'

Leo was quiet for a moment, and then he said, 'Okay. Well, maybe best you leave it for now?'

Cheryl frowned. '*Why?* She's one of the reasons Dean is dead.'

Not the main reason, Cheryl thought, but a major contributing factor. The idea of being in Molly Rose's company and being able to do nothing to her was tormenting. But if she didn't put all her thoughts and energy into taking her revenge, her grief would consume her.

'I know. But maybe you should just, I don't know, relax a bit.'

'*Relax?* You think I should relax? Leo, you were supposed to deal with this on your end and you messed it up. All you had to do was run them off the fucking road and kill Janey. Instead, you put Ciaran in a coma and Janey is still very much breathing. If you'd done things correctly, this would all be done by now. I'd have sorted Molly Rose out and all that would be left to do is deal with the fuckers who actually killed our son; *your* son. So, now that the original plan is scuppered, I'm dealing with the Hallahans and you can sort out Marek and the rest of them; that's if you're capable.'

How Leo was going to take down a European crime gang and their boss was, well, impossible. Cheryl knew that. But it would keep him away from her, which she was suitably pleased with. She could put all her time and energy into tormenting the Hallahans and then get justice for her son.

She heard him grunt on the other end of the phone, clearly annoyed with her bluntness. 'All I'm saying is, I'm happy to deal with all of it so you can—'

'So I can what, Leo? Curl up in a ball and die from the heartbreak of losing my son? Because that's what will happen if I stop.'

Leo was quiet again. Without Dean around, it was getting harder and harder to remember why they were together. In fact, there were no other reasons. Their marriage had fizzled out as soon as Dean was born.

'And no,' she continued. 'You *won't* deal with it all. I'll sort the Hallahans. It's my job as his mother. You sort that fucker, Marek, for ordering the hit; and while you're at it, you can find out who pulled the trigger, and who dumped his body at the scrapyard.'

She heard another sigh of annoyance. He hated that she was calling the shots here. It had never been like this; in all the years they'd been together. But now, she knew he felt guilty about what had happened to Dean. So she had the control.

Leo cleared his throat and said, 'You know I'll never get that information. No one will grass.'

'I don't give a shit, Leo. Do what you need to do. I want blood for this.'

Silence followed and Cheryl raised an eyebrow, waiting for more protest. Instead, Leo said, 'I'm working late tonight.'

'You're working late? How many washing machines and dishwashers do you think you need to plumb in?' she asked sarcastically. She knew it killed him that he had such a mundane job now. But when they'd discovered Dean was dead, Cheryl had insisted that Leo cut all ties with Marek and the gang. Surprisingly, he'd agreed.

'Sorry, but we need money, Cheryl. And I'm not earning what I used to.'

'Fine,' Cheryl replied. Because she didn't care if she never saw Leo again. If she could trade him in for seeing Dean just once, she'd hand Leo to Satan himself.

# Chapter 13

He ended the call with Cheryl and felt a low growl build inside him. He was sick of her shitty attitude and this was how she was towards him *without* knowing the full truth: that, in fact, Leo was still working for Marek and, even with the death of Dean, he had no intentions of stopping because it was a gold mine. Fuck knows how she'd react if she found out he was still very much in the thick of it. Marek might be a nasty bastard who Leo couldn't get away from through choice, but he was a good source of income and Leo wasn't about to give that up. Not for anyone. And there was no point in giving it all up for Dean because he was already dead. Yes, it hurt that he hadn't been able to stop the hit; yes, he wanted to murder Marek himself. But would he? No.

He leaned across the dash and opened the glove compartment before reaching in and pulling out a small black case. He unzipped it, opened it fully and handed it to the boy sitting in the passenger seat.

The young lad looked up at him and Leo could see the fear; it gave him such a buzz that he wondered if there was anything else on the planet that would have the same effect.

'You did well to get that cleaning job,' Leo said. 'Very well done.'

The boy regarded him, unsure of where this was going. 'Thank you,' he replied meekly.

'Now for your next task,' Leo said, licking his lips. 'Do you know what this is?'

The boy shook, his trembling hands holding on to the case. 'What am I supposed to do with it?' Antoni asked as he glanced down at the small box in his hand, his Polish accent thick yet his volume low.

'Remember when we first met?' Leo asked, not actually wishing for an answer, nor giving Antoni the time to respond. 'You told me you wanted to be a doctor, that you'd always wanted to come to the UK and go to university and eventually set up a new life here. Well, you don't have to do any of the hard work. You get to be a doctor *tonight*, and that little case contains all the equipment you'll need to carry out your work. Isn't that exciting?'

Antoni looked confused; worried. If he felt patronised, he didn't show it. 'I don't understand.'

'Oh, but you will,' Leo said, putting his arm around Antoni and pulling him in close. The boy was small, barely any meat on him at all. Leo's clients would tear him apart. But that was fine, so long as he made money out of Antoni, Leo didn't give a shit what happened to him.

Leo explained to Antoni very specific details and instructions about what he was required to do. Antoni listened, but tears glistened in his eyes.

'Oh, you've not to worry, Antoni. What you're going to do is this person's destiny. They were born for this.'

'I don't want to.'

Leo felt a sudden rage take over, like a wire had come loose. He took a breath, straightened his back and pulled

Antoni tighter to him before lowering his tone and whispering into his ear, 'I'm sorry, you don't *want* to? I don't remember giving you a choice, Antoni. You're employed by me, and you'll carry out the tasks I assign. You don't want to know what happens to people who don't do as I say. You *really* don't.'

Antoni trembled beneath his grip but remained silent.

'Are you clear on what's expected of you?' Leo asked.

Antoni nodded.

'Good. I'll pick you up after it's done. And it better be done with precision. If this fails,' Leo waved a finger and tutted, 'well, let's just hope for your sake it doesn't.'

## Chapter 14

Molly Rose sat on the sofa in the large open-plan space in Janey's house. She was yet to find the gift which the anonymous texter had claimed was under the deck. Whoever it was had been messing with her. It could have been anyone who knew what had happened to her playing some sick joke on her; trying to scare her. And it had worked. She hadn't wanted to go outside any further than the balcony. The person texting clearly knew where she was. Which meant they were watching her; they were close by. That was enough for her to take Kristo's advice and stay inside the house; happy that it had been locked before he left.

She pictured said gift in her mind. How big would it be? Was it in a box? An envelope? Was it flowers? Chocolate? A bomb? The last one made her stop. What if it was a bomb? And then she shook her head and laughed gently. 'Don't be so stupid,' she whispered to herself.

Why the hell would anyone leave a bomb under the deck and then prewarn her about it? If someone wanted to blow her up, surely they wouldn't tell her about it beforehand?

Glancing down at her phone, she noted that it was just after five o'clock. Kristo had left a few hours ago, it wouldn't be long before he and Janey were walking through the door and she was no longer alone – physically, at least. Feeling lonely had been the norm for her ever since her mum had died.

Molly Rose looked out the window and a nervous laugh crept up and escaped her lips. 'You couldn't fucking write this shit,' she said. Reaching across to the coffee table in front of her, she lifted the wine glass and reluctantly took another sip. It still tasted awful but it was better than not drinking at all. Numbing the pain of all she'd lost was better than pretending it wasn't there while sober.

The sound of a car pulling into the driveway made the faces of the dead fade and Molly Rose looked up. She set the glass down, got to her feet and made her way up to the front entrance of the house. It was Kristo, arriving with Janey in the passenger seat. Looking through the glass, Molly Rose gave a wave and stood awkwardly, waiting for them to unlock the front door and come inside. Then she noticed a man stood at the end of the driveway. He looked like some sort of security guard. Of course he was. Janey wasn't taking any chances after all that had happened. And after what she'd just read on her phone, she knew now it wasn't such a stupid decision on both Janey and Kristo's parts. But now that they were both at the house, it was time to tell Janey about the text.

Kristo helped Janey out of the car and she hobbled her way towards the door. Molly Rose couldn't help but notice the difference in Janey's appearance. When she'd first met Janey, Molly Rose had been struck by how glamorous she'd seemed. She certainly didn't look like your typical grandmother and, if anything, Molly Rose remembered thinking she hoped that she looked as good at Janey's age. But now, the dark circles under her eyes made her look like she hadn't slept in months. The lack of her usual make-up didn't help. She noticed the crow's feet at the corners of her eyes, the lines around her mouth. And as she held on to Kristo, Molly Rose realised that this woman, the head of a criminal firm who'd seemed untouchable, was just as human as the rest of the population. She looked like she was close to breaking point. The last eight weeks showed on her face. Molly Rose had lost her mum, but Janey had lost her daughter who'd only just come back into her life. On top of that, she was facing the possibility of life without her husband too. No wonder she looked so rough.

Molly Rose stood back from the door as Janey let herself in. She smiled at Molly Rose and pulled her into her arms.

'Hi,' Janey said. 'Are you okay?'

'I'm fine,' she replied, hoping that Janey wouldn't hold on to her for too long. It was weird, being hugged by a woman she hardly knew yet was a relation by blood. 'How's Ciaran?'

'He's stable, I think. Still unconscious but that's the induced coma. He'll wake up, he will,' Janey replied, pulling away and looking at Molly Rose.

'I'm sorry about what happened,' Molly Rose replied, deciding that now wasn't the best time to burden Janey with yet another problem. 'Is there any way it could have been a genuine accident and the people who caused it are just scared about what might happen to them?' she asked, hoping there wasn't someone out there trying to kill them all. Again. But that wouldn't explain the text.

Janey pursed her lips and shook her head. 'There's no way this was an accident, sweetheart. Not a chance in hell. You know our luck by now, don't you?'

*Yeah*, she thought. *I do, unfortunately.* She could also recall life before Janey had come into it. That had been a simpler time.

'Yeah.' Molly Rose smiled, pushing the thought out of her head and cursing herself for not being grateful for Janey's protection, even if it was because of her that Molly Rose needed protecting at all. 'We're cursed.'

Janey laughed a little and winced before gripping her side. Molly Rose stepped forward, took her hand and led her down slowly to the couch while Kristo brought bags in from the car and closed the door.

'Kristo,' Janey called back. 'You get home to that wife and family of yours. We'll be fine here.'

Molly Rose raised an eyebrow. Kristo didn't seem the type to have a family. When she looked at him, she saw a man who lived alone, in a flat that was plain and bland while he sat by the phone waiting for Janey to call.

'My wife and children are with family right now. They understand that I'm needed here. And if it's all the same, I'd rather not leave either of you alone.'

Molly Rose stared past him and fixed her eyes on the security guard at the end of the driveway before returning her attention to Kristo. For the first time, she saw a softer side to this man. And then she had a thought that almost crippled her with fear.

'What about my dad? What if someone is trying to get to him too?'

'He's a fair distance away, Molly Rose. He's safe,' Kristo replied. 'I've already checked.'

'And Auntie Sinead? Is she safe? I mean, this happened not far from her facility. Could that just be a coincidence?'

Janey nodded. 'Kristo and the team are making sure every one of us are safe. That's why you're staying here with me. We have a team of security surrounding the property and anytime we leave, they'll not be far from us.'

Molly Rose frowned. A *team* of security? She'd only noticed one man outside.

'I thought there was just one guy watching the house?' Molly Rose asked, just to be clear.

'No. I've enlisted an entire team,' Janey said. 'We're safe here. And Ciaran has someone with him at the hospital. And Sinead's facility is being watched too. I don't want to have to pull her out of there when she's doing so well. The stress of all of this on top of losing Orla would...' Janey cleared her throat and Molly Rose felt a lump grow in hers. 'It would set her back. She doesn't know about any of what is going on and she doesn't have to know.'

Molly Rose didn't know how she felt about that. *Should* she tell Janey about the text? About what had been left under the deck? Janey already had so much on her plate, and if there really was someone out there, watching her, then the team would get to them before they got to Molly Rose. In fact, maybe the texter hadn't planted anything beneath the house at all. Maybe they were trying to entice her out of the house, away from the safety of the place?

'Are you hungry?' Molly Rose asked, pushing the thoughts out of her head. 'I can make us some dinner?'

Janey shook her head. 'There's a lovely little Chinese takeout place along in Helensburgh and they deliver. Why don't I order us something from there?'

Molly Rose smiled as she looked at her fairly new grandmother, who didn't usually look anywhere near old enough to bear the title. She was such a strong woman, who appeared to fear nothing and no one. Molly Rose was from the same stock. She could handle whatever life threw at her because it was in her blood. 'Yeah, that sounds great.'

## Chapter 15

Packing away her paints and easel for the day, Sinead glanced up at her painting of the grounds surrounding Endrick Castle Estate and smiled. She'd made so much progress with her painting skills in such a short space of time.

'It's really stunning, Sinead. You should be proud of your achievements.' The art therapy counsellor smiled at her. Jacob had been a shoulder to lean on since Sinead had been admitted. He'd seen so much potential in her she didn't even know was there. Art had never been something she'd ever considered even before becoming an addict.

'Thanks, Jacob. I am proud of myself. Something I never thought was possible,' Sinead replied.

'You keep this up, you'll be entering into art exhibits and festivals before long,' Jacob's southern American accent purred. Sinead had never asked where he was from; she guessed Tennessee or Alabama.

'Ha, I don't know about that,' she said as she carried her paintbrushes and board to the sink. Turning on the tap, she smiled to herself.

'Are you kidding? You need to give yourself credit. This is a talent that's been hidden and suppressed for years, Sinead. Start showing it off and you're bound to get noticed. Think of the life you could have, selling your work. I'm telling you; it'll happen if you put your mind to it.'

Maybe Jacob was right. Maybe she just couldn't imagine it because she still found it difficult to see the future after everything that she'd been through in her life. All Sinead had ever been capable of was imagining how she was going to get her next bag of heroin. Conjuring up images of a good life was something she would have to train her brain to do.

She'd been clean for two months now. Having started off on her own, trying to get off the heroin without any help had been the hardest thing she'd ever had to do. But having the focus of finding Molly Rose had helped distract her a little. Then Orla was killed, and it had sent Sinead on a spiral of grief which Janey had said might cause a relapse; and Sinead had been scared she was right. Janey had paid upfront fees for the best rehab facility in Scotland, and as much as Sinead didn't like the idea that Janey contributed to the pandemic of addiction on the streets, she was grateful that she was able to get the level of help she was currently receiving at Endrick Castle Estate. At first, she'd hated it, but now Sinead was actually enjoying her time spent here. So much that she worried how she would slot back into the real world when the time came.

Washing her brushes under the warm water, Sinead was aware of someone next to her at the sink.

'Ah, Antoni, how are you getting on in your first week?' Jacob's voice floated across the room. Sinead turned to see a younger man next to her, emptying the bin.

'I'm doing fine,' the young man replied. Sinead glanced at him and smiled. He barely looked old enough to be out of school, never mind have a job.

'Settling in okay?' Jacob asked again.

'Yes, thank you,' he replied.

Sinead gave him a smile and Jacob said, 'Sinead, this is one of the new caretaker team members, Antoni. He's been with us for about a week now, is that right, Antoni?'

Antoni tied the bag up and set it to the side before pulling a new one from the roll and shaking it out. 'That's right.'

Sinead nodded, unsure of how to respond. 'Great,' she eventually said. She detected an accent even though he spoke very quietly. Eastern European. Polish, maybe? She wasn't sure. He seemed nervous.

'You don't have to look so terrified.' Jacob smiled at him and placed a hand on his shoulder. 'We're all lovely here.'

Antoni smiled, but there was a nervousness about him. Maybe he *was* just out of school. And being in a foreign country for your first job couldn't be easy. Still, Sinead thought, she'd rather be in Antoni's position than her own.

Sinead packed her art supplies into the cupboard above the sink and took a deep breath. It was time for dinner and then she planned to settle down for the night.

–

Sinead lay in bed and stared up at the ceiling. Thoughts of Orla circled around in her head. The image of the last time she saw her haunted her memory. She didn't think those horrendous stills would ever leave her. They were still so raw.

Sinead kicked herself for the amount of time she'd wasted on drink and drugs over the years, when she should have been spending those precious days with her family;

the only family she'd ever had. Instead, she'd spent all her waking moments either injecting or looking for ways to get the cash together to score more heroin.

'Such a fucking idiot,' she whispered as she turned over and lay on her side. Why had it taken her so long and for something so awful to push her to the point where she wanted to get over this? She'd never get to show Orla that she was doing better in life.

She thought about Molly Rose, her niece who'd been through far too much trauma and heartache. Only sixteen and she'd lost her mum. What kind of way was that to start adulthood?

'I hope Janey's looking after you properly,' Sinead whispered as she reached over and turned off the light.

–

Her head felt groggy, her mouth dry. Sinead tried to open her eyes but they were so heavy and gritty, it was impossible.

'Sssh,' a whisper came.

To be quiet was all she could do as her body went into some kind of paralysis. But before she went under completely, just as she felt the scratch on her arm, Sinead opened her eyes. As she stared at the face in front of her, confusion took over.

*Who are you*, she thought.

If the warmth and euphoria hadn't kicked in so quickly, Sinead would have panicked; tried to fight back. Instead, she succumbed to what she knew was being injected into her veins. She had no other choice.

# Chapter 16

Antoni ran across the grassland at the back of the building quicker than Leo thought his measly little legs could carry him. He jumped into the car and slouched down in the seat. Leo looked at him with a smile.

'Done?'

Antoni nodded and said, 'Can we leave now?'

Leo hesitated, wanted to make Antoni squirm a little more. He watched as the lad sucked air into his lungs, took a puff on his inhaler which he produced from his pocket.

Leo switched on the engine and pulled away from the building quickly. They remained silent, aside from Antoni breathing like he'd just run a marathon.

'Is she dead?' Leo asked.

'I didn't stop to check. I injected like you said and got out as fast as I could.'

Leo thought about that. He understood why Antoni hadn't hung around. But now, Leo would have to wait for word on Sinead's medical status. There was no way he was going to just sit back and allow Cheryl to take the reins on this one. Leo was the man of the family. He was a gangster who'd been made a fool of by his boss. He wasn't going to sit back and allow his wife to dictate how things would pan out. Not a chance. When she found out about this, she'd just have to accept it. As much as he would never admit it out loud, he felt powerful doing this. He felt like the man and the gangster he was supposed to be and, since Marek had ordered Dean's death, he hadn't felt very powerful. Being in control of what was happening to Sinead felt good.

'You did good,' Leo said, slapping Antoni's leg harder than necessary. His bony little leg felt like a twig under his grip. He wouldn't last five minutes in this world unless he fattened up a bit.

Leo pulled out on to the main road and hoped that the fake plates hadn't fallen off the car. Those, along with Antoni spraying the CCTV cameras on-site, would have been enough to stop anyone identifying Leo as being present when the drugging took place. But if Antoni had done his job properly, it would look like Sinead had overdosed herself, and if he'd *really* done his job properly, then she'd die and no one would be able to dispute that.

Hearing a sniff coming from Antoni, Leo looked across and saw that he was wiping away tears from his face.

'Straighten yer face,' he said. 'You don't even know the lassie. She's a shitshow; better off dead.'

Antoni didn't reply and the beat of silence gave space for the intrusive thoughts of Dean; of the conversation that Leo had had with his own boss, Marek, about Dean.

*He's better off dead, Leo. People like Dean don't last long in this game when they can't do their jobs correctly. He's lucky I was in a good mood and ordered it to be quick. He's lucky I like you.*

The words had haunted him ever since. In reality, Marek should be the one Leo was going after, like he'd said to Cheryl he would. But Marek was a force no one could go up against. His men were loyal to him. If Leo started digging around like Cheryl had told him to, to find out who actually pulled the trigger on Dean, Marek would find out about it quicker than Leo could ask the questions. Best stay on Marek's good side, for now.

Getting Leo to finish the job Dean had started was like a game to Marek and Leo had no choice but to play it, otherwise he'd end up dead, in the same scrapyard as his son.

# Chapter 17

Janey was in the shower when Molly Rose decided to step out and onto the decked balcony. The message she'd received had been swirling around in her head since it had appeared on her phone. She couldn't just ignore it and she knew that whoever sent the message would be banking on that.

Placing her hands on the wooden railing, Molly Rose leaned over the side just enough to be able to peer a little way under the deck. She couldn't see anything unusual. If said gift was there at all, then maybe it was further back. How was she supposed to get down there? Looking to her right, she noticed the wall that ran adjacent to the long driveway. At the end was a set of stairs. She used the term loosely in her head. It was a path that sloped down towards the pebbled area leading out to the water.

Glancing back inside the house, she wondered if going down there was a good idea. The idea that it could be a bomb entered her head again. A bomb? Really? Did someone want them all dead enough to plant a bomb and address it to Molly Rose via a text?

Sighing in annoyance that this was her life now, Molly Rose decided that she wasn't going to be a victim any more and went to the front door. As she passed by the bathroom, she could hear the water running. She wondered how Janey was really feeling about everything.

Ciaran being in a coma, Sinead in rehab and Orla dead. She always seemed so cool and composed. Molly Rose knew that everyone had a breaking point; but when would Janey reach hers?

Molly Rose reached the front door and, when she looked out to the front step, she froze.

'Shit,' she whispered. Now, she was looking down at a small cardboard box and panic consumed her. The person who'd left it clearly wanted it to be found and maybe they realised that Molly Rose wasn't going to climb down under the decked balcony to see if it was there; so they'd moved it so she would find it. And it was small. Really small. Too small to be a bomb?

Her initial instinct was to run to the bathroom and tell Janey to call Kristo but something held her there. No, she thought. If it was a bomb, surely it would have gone off by now?

Molly Rose looked through the glass to the end of the drive. One of Janey's men was standing with his back to the house. How had he managed to miss the box being delivered? In fact, Janey had said there was an entire team. Where were they all? On a fucking tea break?

'Shit,' Molly Rose whispered again, stepping closer to the door and turning the lock to the left. She opened the door as quietly as she possibly could and bent down to retrieve the box, all the while keeping her eye on the guard at the end of the drive and hoping that the box wouldn't explode on her.

Stepping back into the house with the box in her hands, Molly Rose headed for her bedroom, her feet padding softly across the floor before she stopped outside the bathroom. No, she wasn't going to hide this.

She needed to tell Janey about this. It wasn't a game. It could be something to do with the people who had run Janey and Ciaran off the road. The fact that the sender had signed off as Dean was a way to lure Molly Rose in. She'd been through enough trauma and met enough bad people over the last year and a half to know not to trust anyone.

'Janey, when you're done in there, I need to show you something,' Molly Rose said, knocking gently on the bathroom door.

'Won't be a minute,' Janey called back.

Molly Rose moved through to the kitchen, set the box down gently on the worktop and made a coffee for Janey.

Janey emerged from the bathroom and walked slowly into the kitchen wearing a fluffy white dressing gown and her hair in a towel.

'Ah, there you are.' Janey smiled. Then she clocked the box on the worktop and asked, 'What's that?'

'I got a text from an anonymous number to say there was a gift for me under the deck,' Molly Rose blurted out. 'Then it appeared at the front door and the person who sent it signed off the message as if it was from *Dean*.'

Janey's expression soured. '*Jesus!* How did the team miss this?' she said, clearly annoyed. 'You've not opened it yet?'

Molly Rose shook her head. 'Well, I was going to, but I keep thinking it's a bomb.'

'Yeah, I know that feeling well,' Janey said, thinking back to when she was a child living in Northern Ireland. 'I doubt it's a bomb,' she continued, staring at the box. 'If the sender has lured you in with signing it like it's from Dean, then they want you to see what's inside, not blow your head off.'

Molly Rose's eyes widened at the thought. 'Thanks for that graphic image, Janey.'

'Sorry,' Janey said, and Molly Rose noticed a smile creep across her face as she handed Janey the coffee she'd made.

'I wasn't going to bother you with it, but then I thought about it and realised that keeping it a secret was the worst thing I could do. I think it's fair to say that secrets don't lead anyone down a good path.'

Molly Rose wished Orla hadn't kept Janey a secret from the start. Maybe if she hadn't, things might have been different.

Janey took a sip from the mug and placed the coffee down on the counter. 'You thought right, Molly Rose.'

Janey moved closer to the worktop, took the box carefully in her hands and inspected it. The cardboard was new, and the box wasn't big or heavy.

'I think we can rule out a bomb, or a body part.' Janey smiled, but the idea that was even a thought in her head fuelled Molly Rose's fear even more.

'That's not funny,' she replied as Janey took a seat on the couch and placed the box on the coffee table.

'Come on, we'll open it together.'

Molly Rose sat down next to her relatively new grandmother and took a breath. 'Do you think it's from the person who ran you off the road?'

'We won't know until we open it,' Janey said as she pulled at the tape on the fold of the box. Peering inside, she frowned and put her hand inside before pulling something out.

'What is it?'

'It's a photograph. Of you,' Janey said, holding it out so Molly Rose could see it.

As she peered down at herself, sweeping the floor of Janey's newest salon, she felt sick. Cheryl was sat at the desk with the phone to her ear. Neither of them seemed to notice their photographer outside.

Molly Rose looked at the picture carefully, trying to see if there was something she was missing. She turned it over and on the back was a handwritten message.

> *I always loved to look at you. That figure, your*
> *little waist. Molly Rose, you still get me going even*
> *from the grave.*

Molly Rose felt ill. 'What a sick fuck,' she said, reading the message out to Janey.

'I'll chop the bastard's dick off when I find them,' Janey replied.

'I didn't *even* sleep with Dean,' Molly Rose said. 'So whoever has sent this clearly thinks I did.'

'There's something else in here,' Janey said. She reached in and pulled out a sultry piece of red lingerie.

'Oh my God,' Molly Rose said, throwing her hand over her mouth.

Janey blinked and handed it to Molly Rose, who read the tag out loud.

'I'd have loved you in it.'

Janey got to her feet and quickly limped out to the front door as Molly Rose dropped the skimpy outfit on the table in horror, all the while trying not to throw up.

She could hear Janey shouting and screaming at the security guard outside in the drive, about how he'd managed to let someone get past him and leave the box at the front door; demanding to know where the rest of the team were.

Molly Rose took a deep breath and tried to compose herself. She couldn't bring herself to even look at the outfit, if that's what it even was. It barely had enough material to cover one arm. But she did lift the picture and stared at it carefully, all the while wondering who had been behind the lens. It definitely wasn't Dean. He was dead. She was more certain about that than anything because the picture was so recent: of her working in Janey's salon.

Whoever sent this wanted to cause her harm. And the only way they would get to her was to harm anyone who could be seen as protecting Molly Rose.

They needed to warn Cheryl.

# Chapter 18

Zofia crouched behind the wall which led down to the private beach from Janey Hallahan's house and listened as Janey tore into the security guard about missing someone entering the property. She didn't give the man a second to answer and Zofia sighed in relief that she hadn't been seen for the second time. After having left the box under the balcony and texting Leo to say it was done, but that no one had come out, he'd instructed her to put it at the front door. That had almost been impossible, but she'd somehow managed to do it without being seen. Being small had its advantages.

She remembered the conversation she'd heard between Leo and Marek the night she was handed over by Szymon. The names had stuck in her head. Molly Rose. Dean. It couldn't be a coincidence that she'd been instructed to send those texts and write the note on the back of the photo. Addressed to and from the same people. This was the Molly Rose who Leo was going to have trafficked to Poland and Zofia was being pulled into making it happen. It made sense now as to why he'd given her the photograph of Molly Rose, although she looked quite different in real life; most people did. He was never planning to reunite Zofia with Alina if she found Molly Rose. He was using Zofia as a way to get to Molly Rose.

Her pay-as-you-go basic mobile phone buzzed in her hand.

> Will be there in a few minutes. Stay off the road and don't let yourself be seen.

For a moment, all Zofia could think about was running down to the boatyard on the main road and climbing into one before attempting her escape. But she knew it wouldn't happen. For a start, she didn't know how to work a boat, or where she would go. Just the idea of getting away from these people, by any means necessary, was all that kept her going. Maybe she could turn back and face Janey; tell her what was going on. But would she believe her? Would Zofia get back to the house before her captor arrived to take her back to base? It was worth the risk if there was a small possibility of getting away from these bastards, but also not worth it because if Zofia did get away, they'd punish Alina for it. But she had to try to save herself and in doing so, she had a better chance of saving Alina too.

Zofia stepped out from behind the wall on to the main road. She watched as Janey shouted at the security guard: the one who hadn't been paying much attention to his job as Zofia crept on to the property by climbing the fence at the opposite end of the drive. She'd kept her hood up to stop herself from being seen on any possible CCTV. She'd been warned that Janey Hallahan covered all security bases, so not to be naïve. The woman must have been so angry considering Zofia had managed to dodge all of the security guards and the cameras.

Just as Zofia was about to step off the kerb and walk towards the house, the van pulled up in front of her and the back door slid open.

'Get in,' he said.

That was it. Moment lost.

Zofia reluctantly climbed into the van and sat down before sliding the door shut.

'Done?' he asked.

She nodded.

'I didn't hear you?' he said, cupping his hand around his ear.

'Yes.'

'Yes, *Leo*.' He had a slimy smile on his face. He loved the power.

Zofia felt sick, but she knew if he thought she was being cheeky and giving him backchat, he'd cancel their little arrangement and send her right into one of his disgusting sex parties. 'Yes, Leo.'

Leo Davidson nodded happily and locked the doors from inside. 'Good. Right, back to the flat. Quick shower and then we're going to a party tonight,' he said, as though he'd heard her thoughts.

Zofia's stomach lurched. 'But, I don't do those.'

'Tonight, you do. I have a lot of important people in attendance tonight and I need more boots on the ground.'

Boots on the ground? Zofia frowned.

Leo rolled his eyes. 'More for the clients to choose from, Zofia. Come on, you're a smart girl. Work it out.'

Her stomach lurched at the way he'd rephrased the initial analogy.

'You could at least smile about it, you'll earn more from tonight than normal.'

What was there to smile about? Terror? Disgusting men? There were always so many of them. The fact that Leo thought money was what Zofia cared about baffled her.

'Oi, I *said* smile.'

Zofia forced a smile as best she could and the sound of Leo's tormenting laughter made her want to throw up. She looked at the seat belt hanging down by his side; he wasn't wearing it as he pulled out onto the road. Perhaps if she wished hard enough, they'd be in a crash and Leo would go out of the front window, head first.

Of course, that was never going to happen. She was stuck with this life, no matter what she wished for.

# Chapter 19

'I'm so sorry, Janey. If I'd known he was a lazy piece of shit, I'd never have hired him. From now on, I'll stand guard wherever you and Molly Rose are,' Kristo said.

Janey sighed loudly. 'You weren't to know, Kristo. I know your work ethic; you wouldn't have hired him if you didn't think he was capable. He clearly pulled the wool over your eyes. As for the rest of the team, they were doing perimeter checks as instructed. Whoever this was managed to slip between the gaps from one guard to the next.'

A look of frustration crossed his face, but Janey decided not to dwell on the matter, there was no time.

'I've had a thought. The box was addressed from Dean and he was murdered, wasn't he?'

'According to the newspaper, yes. I actually feel sick,' Molly Rose said. 'I mean, *physically* sick.'

Janey looked down at the contents of the box and shook her head in disgust. Whoever this was was sick in the head. And dangerous.

'I think it's likely that the person or people who did send this are the same people Dean was working for. Perhaps they see you as – I'm sorry to put it so bluntly, Molly Rose – unfinished business. It's the only thing that makes sense to me. It's highly likely to be the same people who ran me and Ciaran off the road too; there are no current feuds with other criminals. I want to speak to Cheryl, get a hold of the CCTV from the salon. She could be in danger too,' Janey said. 'I suppose anyone associated with us could be.'

She saw the look on Molly Rose's face. She'd lost all her colour, her eyes wide with fear.

'You think they're going to try to finish what Dean started?' Her voice wobbled.

'They're not going to get anywhere near you, sweetheart. Not while I've still got blood in my veins. And Kristo will be your personal guard until we sort these bastards out. Trust me, you're going to be safe.' Janey reached out and took Molly Rose's hand in hers, giving it a reassuring squeeze. She meant every word. There was nothing on the planet that would stop Janey from protecting her family. She'd already lost too much and she wasn't about to sit back and allow more loss.

Her thoughts were interrupted when her mobile phone rang. She looked down at the screen, the number for Endrick Castle Estate flashed up. Sinead's rehab facility.

'Hello?' Janey answered, her brows knitted together.

'Mrs Hallahan, this is Jacob Moffat from Endrick Castle Estate. I'm calling about your daughter, Sinead. She's on her way to hospital following a heroin overdose.'

Janey felt her heart drop into her stomach. 'Excuse me? Could you repeat that?'

Jacob spoke the words once more and Janey frowned, her eyes narrowing.

'That can't be right. Your facility assured me of strict security protocols. How did she manage to get hold of it in the first place?'

Molly Rose's eyes rested on Janey. It was clear she knew something was wrong. Like she understood that with Sinead, it really only could be one thing.

'Can you meet me at the hospital, please?' Jacob asked. 'We can go over the details there.'

Janey agreed and hung up the phone, jabbing at the screen with a perfectly manicured finger. It was the only part of her that didn't look like it had been in a car crash.

'What's happened?' Molly Rose asked.

'Sinead's overdosed on heroin,' Janey said, limping towards the front door.

'No. No way. She was clean,' Molly Rose said. 'For two months. She was doing so well.'

'Yeah,' Janey replied, lifting her handbag from the coat hook. 'Well, now it seems, she's not.'

—

Walking through the main entrance of the A & E department at the Queen Elizabeth University Hospital, Janey was met by Jacob Moffat at the door.

'Jacob?' Janey asked, recognising his face from when she'd last visited Sinead in rehab. 'Is Sinead okay?'

'Yes. She's with the doctors now. It could have been so much worse.' The worry lines at the sides of Jacob's eyes deepened.

'How has this happened, Jacob? Your facility is meant to keep her safe,' Janey said through gritted teeth.

'I can assure you, we're doing everything we can to find out how Sinead managed to do this without our knowledge. She was doing so well, she was upbeat, passionate about her painting and life again.' Jacob glanced up at Kristo who was stood next to Janey and then moved his eyes over to Molly Rose. 'Can we take a seat over there?'

Janey looked across to where Jacob had gestured and noticed an empty seating area. They moved across the A & E department and sat down.

'You need to tell us what's going on,' Molly Rose said venomously. 'How the *hell* has this happened?'

Janey placed her hand over Molly Rose's arm and shook her head. It was sweet that her granddaughter cared so much that she felt she had to put up a front, but it wasn't her place. Molly Rose frowned but fell silent.

Jacob lowered his voice and said, 'Mrs Hallahan, we believe that Sinead *may* have been drugged by someone else.'

'Excuse me?'

'We recently employed someone to fill one of the cleaning positions. He's since gone missing and we believe he may be responsible for this.'

'That's a strong claim to make,' Janey replied. 'You have evidence of this?'

Jacob nodded and a look of sadness awash with guilt crossed his face. 'We found evidence of drug paraphernalia in the maintenance room. The police are investigating as we speak and I'm expecting more to arrive soon to chat with me about what's gone on. We want to get to the bottom of this as quickly as possible, Mrs Hallahan, and of course find Antoni for questioning.'

'Can we see her?' Molly Rose asked, her tone softer now.

'I'm still waiting for one of the doctors to give us an update. I travelled in the ambulance with her but they wouldn't let me through,' Jacob replied.

Janey looked up and saw two police officers walking through the main entrance and Jacob waved to them.

Janey didn't recognise them as any on her books. She raised an eyebrow at Kristo, who stood up.

'Mr Moffat?' one of the officers asked, briefly glancing at Kristo.

'Yes, I called about my resident's heroin overdose,' Jacob replied.

Janey got to her feet and nodded. 'I'm Sinead's mum. Janey Hallahan.' She held out her hand and the look on the officer's face told her all she needed to know.

'Ah, Mrs Hallahan. Nice to meet you,' he said. 'And you must be Kristo?'

Kristo nodded and Janey felt relief that she would be able to handle this her own way.

'Molly Rose.' Janey turned to face her granddaughter. 'Why don't you go to the vending machine and get us some hot drinks?'

Molly Rose raised an eyebrow. 'On my own? After the Dean thing?'

Janey smiled and shook her head. 'No. Kristo will go with you while I chat with the police about Sinead.'

Kristo and Molly Rose left, Molly Rose somewhat reluctantly, before Janey and the officers sat down.

'Mrs Hallahan, I'm Officer Graham McCabe and this is Officer Lindsay Nelson. We're sorry to hear about what's happened to Sinead. And Ciaran for that matter.'

Janey watched him through narrowed eyes. 'Speaking of Ciaran, any intel on who is responsible for the attempted wipeout of my family, McCabe? Because I'm starting to lose my patience with this.'

McCabe lowered his chin and smiled. 'Off the record, Major Crimes are investigating a tip-off about that European trafficking gang working our streets again.'

Janey pulled her lips into a thin line. 'Again?'

'Apparently they're out to get to the top. You'll remember when that young Glasgow lad, Dean Davidson, was found murdered? He was believed to be working for them and apparently they weren't happy with his conduct so...' McCabe ran his thumb across the centre of his throat. 'Anyway, word is they're operating again.'

Janey tried to process the information as quickly as possible. 'You said Dean Davidson was involved in that operation?'

McCabe nodded. 'I would have thought with your business interests, you'd have been aware of this?'

Janey blinked. Of course she was aware of it, more than the officer realised. But she wasn't about to share that information with him. 'McCabe, who's the head of this operation? In Glasgow, I mean?'

McCabe pulled his lips into a thin line and shook his head. 'Sorry, that's all I know. We only get snippets, you know; being low down in the chain. I'd have thought DI Pearson would have filled you in?'

Janey sighed and closed her eyes. Yes, she wondered just why DI Pearson hadn't informed her. Maybe because of what she was going through with Ciaran? Perhaps he wanted to wait it out, see if there was anything to tell at all?

She'd need to do the digging herself. But judging by the fact that Dean Davidson had been involved with the previous operations in the city, it seemed more likely than ever that Ciaran and Sinead's attacks were linked and that Janey's gut instinct was right. Did the entire criminal underworld know about Janey's family? That Sinead was a recovering addict and that her other daughter was dead? Did they see it as an opportunity to swoop in and try to take over?

Whether that was true or not, someone was trying to kill them.

Pulling out her phone, she sent a text to the DI, asking him to get in touch with her as soon as possible, and that she needed information about the gang linked to Dean Davidson.

*Fuck*, she thought. *Could this get any messier?*

# Chapter 20

Zofia sat on the mattress on the floor as she waited with dread on Leo collecting her for the party. Her trembling hands rested on her lap as she jumped at every sound that could possibly be her boss walking into the building. She'd only been forced into participating in a handful of the sex parties – Leo's term, not her own; she didn't know what else to call these sordid events – and thankfully now, with Leo using her to train the new recruits, she'd not taken part in a while. Zofia had been in Scotland for four weeks now, and had been thrown in at the deep end by Leo. She'd taken part in two parties in her first week alone and had come away with physical injuries. Her wrists had been badly bruised, her groin had been in agony too. The parties were brutal, relentless and filled with some of the most disgusting people she could have ever imagined existed. The last party she'd had to take part in was when Zofia made a promise to herself it would be the last one she attended. And for a while, it had worked. She'd shown Leo loyalty, abided by his rules and done absolutely everything he'd said without question. But here she was, yet again, being forced into attending because he'd said the guest list was larger than he'd anticipated and she felt sick with the idea of how many men she would have to... She couldn't finish the thought. And what about Alina? What was she being subjected to through all of this? What part of the UK was she in? Alina could be in the flat next door for all Zofia knew. Leo was using Alina like an invisible noose around Zofia's neck. All she wanted was to find her sister and make sure she was okay. Make sure she was alive.

'Are you okay?' Antoni asked from across the room.

Zofia nodded even though she was far from it. When she looked up at him, he looked just as terrified as she felt.

'Are you going to a party tonight?' he asked.

Zofia felt the urge to vomit as she nodded again. 'Yeah, I don't even want to think about it.'

'I am too,' Antoni said. 'Apparently now that I've fulfilled my role at that rehabilitation centre, I can do other jobs. I was originally taken to another flat with different people, but it was too crowded so Leo brought me here, said I'd be useful.'

Zofia stared at him. 'Another flat?'

Antoni nodded.

'Did you see a girl who looks like me but with blonde hair? Her name is Alina? She's my sister.'

Antoni blinked and said, 'I didn't get to see anyone. Not really. Leo just told me I was going somewhere else. Now I'm here. Is your sister under Leo's control too?'

'Yes. We were taken together but split up quite quickly. I just want to know she's okay.'

'I'm sorry,' Antoni said in a sombre tone.

'It's not your fault. I just miss her so much.' Zofia blinked away the threatening tears and straightened her shoulders. 'Is this your first?' she asked, feeling awful for him that he had no idea what was coming even though she'd briefed him along with the others he'd arrived with.

'Yes. Is it as bad as I've heard?'

'It's worse. I'm sorry.' Zofia closed her eyes briefly and, when she opened them, she could have sworn a tear dropped down Antoni's cheek. 'Why do people like him exist in the world?'

Antoni shook his head. 'Because the world is actually hell, and people like Leo are the devil himself.'

He was right.

Antoni gave Zofia a look, narrowed his eyes and said, 'Don't you work for him? I mean, he always seems to have you by his side and you were the one who briefed us when we first got here.'

Zofia expelled air loudly and shook her head. 'Only because I don't have a choice like the rest of us. If I could have it another way, I would. If I could run and hope that he never catches me, I would. It's unlikely I'd ever get away safely because he's relentless. But hell is an eternal thing,' Zofia said. 'And we can only hope that people like him get their karma.'

Antoni nodded sadly and it broke Zofia's heart. 'I just don't want this to be my life forever. And what happens when we're no longer useful? Do they let us go? Or do we die?'

The words sat heavily on Zofia's chest. Antoni was right to ask the question; it wasn't something she'd thought of herself. Yes, she had managed to secure a deal with Leo in that she didn't have to attend the parties, but tonight was an exception. What if every night became an exception? What if he was just taking the piss out of her? What if he'd never intended for the agreement to last long, just long enough to lure her into a false sense of security and then she'd be the same as everyone else?

Suddenly, Zofia stood up and said, 'I don't want this to be my forever either. We need to get out of here, Antoni.'

He looked up at her through bloodshot eyes. 'What? How? We're locked in here all the time unless we're out there, doing our job. And even then, we're being watched.'

Zofia paced the small floor space she and Antoni had been forced to share. The cramped, dark room smelled of dampness. *A prison cell would be better than this*, she thought.

'That's it,' she whispered.

'What?'

'We do something that will get us arrested.'

Antoni looked up at her, confusion etched on his face. 'I don't understand.'

'We do something to get arrested and we tell the police what's been happening to us. It's the only way to guarantee our freedom from this shithole.'

'No way,' Antoni scoffed. 'It'll only make Leo angry at us when the police release us back into the community.'

'Then we do something horrific. Something terrible.'

'Like what?'

Zofia shrugged. 'I don't know.'

'Unless you're willing to kill someone, then I'd suggest you sit down and shut up, Zofia. This isn't going to work. I had to commit a crime for Leo, one that involved hurting someone so much that they could have died and all I can see is the person's face when I did it.'

'What did you have to do?'

Antoni shook his head. 'I don't want to tell you. I was warned to say nothing. What I'm trying to tell you is, doing something awful to hurt someone whether you have a choice or not, it takes so much from you. It'll never leave me, Zofia.'

'And what about what he is taking from us, Antoni?'

Antoni folded his arms and shook his head. 'Sorry, Zofia. But I'm not going to do something that could get me killed or put in prison. We'll just have to think of something else.'

Zofia was disheartened as Antoni leaned back on the wall and closed his eyes. The sound of thundering footsteps up the stairs in the hallway outside made her freeze with fear. He was here for them.

The door opened and Leo was stood in the hallway beyond their room.

'Move it,' he said. 'You two have a lot of work on tonight.'

Fear crippled Zofia as she stared at her boss. Her pimp. The man selling her to any stranger who'd pay money; not that she ever saw a penny of it.

Leo glared at both of them and anger crossed his face. 'Are you two deaf? I said move it. Now!'

Zofia and Antoni followed Leo downstairs and out of the flat that, quite frankly, wasn't even suitable for rats. They climbed into the van and Leo closed the door. Zofia looked into the eyes of two other girls and three boys. All around the same age as her and Antoni. All silent and crippled with fear.

*No*, she thought. *I'm doing this, with or without Antoni. I'm not staying in this shithole life a second longer than I need to. I'd rather go to prison for the rest of my life.*

# Chapter 21

Sitting by Sinead's bedside, Janey looked down at her only surviving daughter's face and wondered what all their futures held; and how long that future would last.

Molly Rose sat on a chair on the opposite side of the bed. She was doubled over, her head resting on the starchy hospital blanket with her eyes closed. Janey knew she wasn't asleep.

How had life come to this? Ciaran was on another floor in the same hospital, in an induced coma, and Sinead was here, in bed recovering from a forced overdose.

*It's all your fault*, she told herself. And it was true. If she'd just stayed away, left the girls to their own lives, then Orla would still be alive. It was likely that Sinead would still be on the streets, looking for her next heroin fix, but at least there would have been a possibility that she'd have been able to turn to her sister for help at some point. Now, Sinead was fighting the effects of an overdose having been two months clean and Molly Rose had another target on her back because of Janey. She had given them up to give them a better chance at life, and now they were all in a constant state of danger because she'd been selfish enough to come back into their lives.

Janey wiped furiously at the tear which had escaped her. She was going to have to get a grip if she was going to get control of this narrative. Glasgow and the rest of the major cities in the UK knew what she was all about; knew her reputation as a fierce crime boss. The only woman in her game who could negotiate the best deals for moving products in and out of Scotland. She was able to go head-to-head with some of the country's other big crime lords, and always came out on top. Janey Hallahan was as fierce and as ruthless as her old man had once been, and people knew it. It was rare that anyone tried to cross the Hallahan empire because Janey wouldn't stand for it. Putting out hits on the few men who did was enough to keep the others in line. But when it came to Janey's family, there was a weakness in her that she could do nothing about. Now that she'd finally come back into contact with her family, and had already lost Orla, she would do anything she could to protect them.

'Janey,' Molly Rose said, sitting up. 'Are you okay?'

*Don't let her see you cry. If you crumble, we all crumble.*

'I'm fine, love.'

'No, you're not,' Molly Rose replied, taking Sinead's hand in her own. 'How could you be?'

Janey regarded Molly Rose's observation. She was much older than her years because of what had happened to her. It wasn't right what she'd had to go through.

'I'm just thinking about what you've all gone through because of me,' Janey replied.

'What do you mean?'

Janey sighed and gave a gentle smile. 'Never mind. Let's just focus on making sure Sinead gets better and keeping you safe.'

Janey and Molly Rose released hands quickly and glanced down at Sinead's bed. Her eyes were closed but she was beginning to stir, slowly at first, before it quickly turned to thrashing.

'Where am I?' Sinead slurred. 'What's happening?'

'What's going on?' Molly Rose asked, looking at Janey, her expression panicked.

Sinead's eyes flew open and she started screaming.

## Chapter 22

Cheryl opened the fridge and pulled out the cheap bottle of wine. A full one. She never left wine unfinished. Not these days. All she searched for these days was a feeling of being numb, laced with the desire for revenge.

Grabbing the same glass she'd used the previous night from the draining board, Cheryl moved through the hallway and into Dean's bedroom. It was exactly how he'd left it. Bed unmade. Clothes lying on the floor. Curtains closed. She couldn't bear to change it.

Perching herself on the edge of the bed and holding the glass between her legs, Cheryl opened the wine bottle and poured until the glass was almost full. She'd never understood why people only filled their wine glasses halfway. What was the point? Surely the whole purpose of drinking wine was to get absolutely steaming drunk to the point where you became numb? That was her purpose, at least.

Placing the wine bottle on the carpet at her feet, Cheryl drank greedily from the glass and looked up at the ceiling for a moment. She thought about Janey and how she'd be hurting about Ciaran right now. *Good*, she thought. *Imagine the pain when he dies, and then the pain when I get my hands on Molly Rose. I should have killed her the first moment I was with her.* But that was another thought she was in constant battle with herself about. Cheryl was a mum, first and foremost. A killer? Even to avenge her son, she didn't know if she truly had it in her. If she did kill the Hallahans, how would she feel afterwards? If she didn't have the balls to go through with it, and asked Leo to do it for her, how would that make her feel? Disappointed? Or guilty?

Pushing the doubts from her head, Cheryl took her phone out of her pocket and pulled up a fresh WhatsApp screen under Janey's number. She typed out:

> Hi. I just wanted to let you know that everything is fine at the salon, and take as much time as you need. I hope you and Molly Rose are okay. All my best, Cheryl. X

She hit the green send icon and watched as one grey tick became two, which turned blue. Janey had read her message. And now, she was typing back.

Cheryl held her phone in her hand like it was the winning lottery ticket as she waited for the message to come through. She had to do this for Dean. Had to. She had to swallow her doubts and fears and adopt a little of Leo's attitude. Think of the Hallahans as a business detail that needed to be fixed, rather than think of them as people.

> Thank you. There is something I want to talk to you about. Can we meet?

*Fuck*, Cheryl thought. *Does she know?* But then, if Janey did know Cheryl's true identity, Janey wouldn't hang about and she certainly wouldn't warn her by asking to meet. Cheryl would be dead by now, without a doubt.

> Of course. At the salon?

> Tomorrow morning. Cancel all your appointments. Janey.

*Cancel all appointments? Fuckfuckfuck.*

She swallowed back a large mouthful of wine and breathed through her thoughts. Maybe this wasn't a bad thing. Maybe Cheryl could use this as an advantage. Gain Janey's trust. And Molly Rose's trust, which was the most important. It would be much easier to kill Molly Rose if the girl trusted her, wouldn't it?

And if that didn't work, she'd walk into that hospital and smother Ciaran Hallahan with a pillow before finishing the rest of them off herself.

# Chapter 23

Stepping out of the van, the fresh air hit her in the face like a ton of bricks. Not because it was cold, but because she knew what was coming and it terrified her more than anything she thought possible.

Zofia took in her surroundings. She'd arrived in an underground car park at the only two parties she'd attended before this one. Now, she was outside, the sky above her pink as the sun began to set. It was beautiful and still warm even though it was the beginning of autumn.

Through the gap between the apartment buildings which towered over her, she saw what looked to be an industrial site and set in the centre was a river. She narrowed her eyes, trying to read the sign at the bottom of the road but her eyes couldn't adjust. The sound of lapping water was oddly soothing, despite the depravity of what was about to happen. She glanced up and down the street, trying to take in any kind of landmark that she might be able to recall in the future if she was ever able to escape Leo's clutches. Glancing back down to the river, she eyed the industrial site for the second time. She noted some key points. Three large yellow shutters, various Portakabins stacked on top of one another.

The sound of Leo clearing his throat made her jump and the irrational fear that he knew what she'd been thinking made her turn away from the river. She glanced at him sheepishly, and realised that he was tapping on his phone. It seemed odd to her that he'd taken his attention off them for even a split second. He really must have trusted her and Antoni not to run. The trust was laced with his ability to put the fear of God into them that if they even so much as stepped an inch from him, they'd pay the price for it.

Looking up at the building, Zofia felt another part of her soul die when she remembered what was waiting for her inside. The calming effects of the water now gone, replaced with fear. The more luxurious the apartment complex, the more party attendees there would be. Therefore, Zofia would be in for a long night.

'In you go then,' Leo said quietly as he used a key fob to open the door to the main entrance of the building. They walked towards a set of lifts and stepped inside. Zofia clocked the number on the keypad Leo selected. The tenth floor. Her spoken English was good, better than she'd been letting on. But her ability to read English wasn't as good. She scanned the word closely and read it to herself slowly. *Penthouse.* Her stomach dropped as the lift began its climb to the top.

Zofia stole a glance at Antoni and she felt sad for him. The look of absolute terror on his face made her heart sink. He was holding back tears; most likely thinking about his life back home. Who was missing him? Who was out looking for him? Did his family assume he was dead? Taking in Antoni's slim build and terrified-little-boy look, she knew that what awaited him in that penthouse could kill him. It was then that something inside her clicked. She wasn't going to put up with this any more. This was *their* life. Neither she nor Antoni belonged to these people.

Zofia was going to get them out of this. Even if that meant she didn't get out of it alive.

'I don't feel well,' she said, putting her plan in motion.

Leo kept his back to her and tutted. 'Tough it out, hen. You've got a lot of people to keep happy tonight.'

Zofia gritted her teeth and Antoni kept staring straight ahead. It was obvious he didn't want to get involved in Zofia's plan. He wasn't going to change his mind. The fear of the repercussions of trying to escape outweighed the fear of what lay ahead of him in the apartment. Maybe that was because he didn't truly understand what was about to happen to him?

'Please, Leo, I think I'm going to be sick,' Zofia pleaded.

He turned, towered over her tiny frame and eyed her with suspicion. 'I don't believe you.'

*Jesus Christ, this man genuinely doesn't care about anyone,* Zofia thought.

'Will you believe me when I start vomiting on your clients? That won't look good for business, will it?' she pushed. She felt Antoni dig her in the rib with his elbow and she had to stop herself from crying out.

The bell inside the lift chimed loudly and when the doors opened, Leo stepped out and turned. 'Out. Now.'

Antoni scurried out of the lift like a terrified mouse and Zofia reluctantly followed.

'You don't look ill,' Leo said. Then he pointed a suspicious finger right at her face. 'If you're at it…'

'I'm not. I really think I'm going to be sick. If I can just go to the bathroom and get it all up, I'll be fine for the rest of the night.'

Leo raised an eyebrow and nodded at the security guard stood outside the door. The man, as tall and as built as Leo, stared at her with a glint in his eye. She recognised him. He'd been her first client and he'd been rough, made her feel sick. Her skin prickled as she felt his eyes on her.

Leo pulled another key fob out of his pocket before leading them inside the apartment, closing the door behind him. The music was loud, but not so much that it hurt her ears like the previous parties, but still loud. This place seemed a little more sophisticated. The apartment's appearance was nice; modern. It was clean. Not like the dirty, open-plan basement where the abuse that went on was on show for everyone to see. Like their dignity wasn't compromised enough. She shivered at the thought, and found herself feeling thankful that she was in a nice apartment instead of the depths of hell. Then she remembered that tonight's hell was dressed up with nice décor, and the feeling of thanks quickly disappeared.

'Right, bathroom's down the hall. You've got precisely one minute. If you're not back by then, I'm coming in to get you. You try any funny business, remember I know where Alina is. And you better make sure you clean yourself up properly. I don't want any complaints that you're stinking of spew.'

The threat of Leo using Alina as leverage should have scared Zofia enough into staying in line. But it didn't. The thought of being held captive by Leo for the rest of her life was enough to make her stick to the plan.

Antoni glared at her through terror-filled eyes before he followed Leo down the hall towards the party, where clients would be waiting for them. Zofia found the bathroom as quickly as she could and went inside and locked the door. Leaning her back against the door, she felt the beat of the music in her chest. The male voice on the vocal had a strong British accent. She didn't recognise the song, but he sang the words *Personal Jesus* and her skin crawled, because she knew that if she ever heard that song again, it would be too soon.

The bathroom was small yet luxurious with black marble tiles from floor to ceiling. The mirror on the wall was flat to the tiles, but Zofia noticed a clip on one side and moved towards it. She gently pulled at it to reveal a small cabinet.

'Bingo,' she whispered before remembering she was supposed to be in there throwing her guts up. She retched as loudly as she could, over and over as she looked through the cabinet.

Then she saw them. A pair of styling scissors and a long, sharp metal nail file. Did a woman live here? Did she know what was going on in her home?

She slipped the scissors and file out of their place and carefully up the sleeve of her short denim jacket.

Fake-retching a few more times, she flushed the toilet, ran the tap for a few seconds and splashed her face and neck with water before patting them dry. She closed the cabinet and took a breath before opening the bathroom door. Leo wasn't outside, so she'd obviously made her time frame.

*This is it*, she thought. *This is how I'm either going to get arrested, or get killed.*

# Chapter 24

Stepping into the open lounge and dining space of the luxurious apartment, Zofia was met by Leo Davidson. He stepped in front of her and glared at her through narrowed eyes.

'What?' she asked.

'You spewed?'

That word: it was relatively new to her but she knew what it meant. She'd heard it enough times since being in Glasgow.

'Unfortunately, yes. But don't worry, I've used mouthwash so all your *clients* aren't disgusted by me.'

Leo didn't seem to detect the sourness to her tone and she was glad.

Zofia looked around the room and saw so many girls and boys, all her age, some a little older maybe. Some younger too. Her stomach churned. Men were literally holding on to young girls like they were possessions of large value. Some leered as others simply chatted. All of it disgusted Zofia.

'Right,' Leo said, his voice bringing her away from the horror around her. 'You've already got three bookings. Master bedroom is back there.' He glanced behind her. 'Your first client is waiting. He's a regular. Be good to him, eh? I don't want him going elsewhere due to disappointment; he makes me a shit ton.'

Zofia wanted to pull the scissors out and slice Leo's throat in front of his fucking clients and show them what she was prepared to do for her freedom. But something stopped her. His strength and his towering height over her were just the start. They'd probably rip her to pieces while Leo Davidson bled out on the plush carpet beneath their feet. Her sister's face came to mind then. She was doing this for her own and Alina's freedom, as well as Antoni's and the others who'd been trafficked by Leo's organisation. Zofia had to go ahead with this. But what if she wasn't successful? What if she failed? She would die, that she was certain of. And they would take it out on Alina, who would never know what had happened to Zofia.

Turning, she saw Antoni standing by the doorway. His face was chalk-white. As she approached him, she glanced back and when she was sure no one was looking, she pulled him into the hallway.

'Here,' she whispered, pushing the nail file into his hand. 'Take this and do what you have to do with it to get yourself out of here.'

Antoni glared down at his hand in horror and shook his head. 'No, I can't.'

'Do you really want this to be your life, Antoni? Being sold like cattle at the fucking market? Because if you do, then I'll take that back and use it myself.'

Antoni looked deflated, like he had nothing left to give. 'I don't want to kill anyone.'

'Then don't watch them die,' Zofia replied. 'If you don't see them take their last breath, then it didn't happen. Slice the throat hard and deep and get the fuck out of here while you have a window of opportunity.' The words left her mouth so easily it was like she'd simply detached from reality. A bit like how she felt when with the men Leo called clients. It was the only way to be able to cope. And if detaching from reality made it easier to get out of here, made it easier to hurt or kill someone in order to be free, then that's what she'd do. That's what Antoni would have to do.

'I'm not a killer, Zofia. I'm just a teenager.'

Zofia looked at him and felt guilty that she was dragging him into her plan. But she had to get them out.

'I'm doing it too, Antoni. I'm about to go in there and make sure he doesn't get the chance to violate me. If you value your safety and your freedom, you'll do the same. Look, everyone in there is occupied. If you do this quickly, we can get out.'

Zofia turned her back on Antoni and headed for the bedroom where her client waited, hoping that Antoni was able to reach deep inside and some courage.

She stood outside the bedroom and took a deep breath. She didn't want to push that door open and see him lying naked on the bed, waiting for her with hunger in his eyes. But she wanted her freedom. And she knew that freedom could come in the form of death. If, however, she was as discreet as possible, then she could get out of this place and run.

Zofia placed her hand over the handle of the door and just as she was about to open it, a loud, bellowing voice stopped her in her tracks.

'What the *fuck* do we have here then?'

It was a man's voice. And it wasn't Leo's.

'Planning on doing yer fucking nails, ya wee nancy boy?'

Zofia turned and, to her horror, saw Antoni pinned up against the wall by a man three times his size.

'What the fuck is going on?' Leo's voice interrupted.

Zofia tucked herself around the corner of the hallway so she wouldn't be seen and she noticed a mirror at the end of the hallway. She could see everything that was going on in its reflection.

'This wee fucker's got a blade,' the man said.

'Put him down,' Leo said calmly. Zofia frowned. Why wasn't he angrier?

'The *fuck* I'm putting him down. He was going to fucking plug some cunt and ah'm no taking any chances.'

'If you don't put him down, the only person getting plugged is you, mate. He's *my* property. If you harm him, if you put him out of business, I'll make sure you never walk again. And I'll make sure that every cunt in this city knows you attend nonce parties. Understood?' Leo said through gritted teeth.

Zofia watched in the reflection as the man lowered Antoni to the floor. There was a moment of silence, before Leo's fist connected with Antoni's jaw and he dropped to the floor. She froze as the horror unfolded. The security guard from outside the apartment moved through the hallway and he didn't seem to notice her.

'Where'd you get this from?' Leo said, crouching down and leering over Antoni. The music still played on in the background, although it somehow seemed quieter.

If Antoni gave her up, she'd be ready. She let the scissors slip down from her sleeve and gripped them tightly in her hand, blades pointing towards the floor.

'It's mine,' Antoni said.

'So, what?' Leo asked, picking Antoni up by the shoulders of his jacket and holding him steady. 'You just fancied yourself a wee manicure while you serviced my clients? Is that it?'

Zofia blinked rapidly as the tears started to threaten. She couldn't crumble. Not now. This was her fault.

'I'm sorry,' Antoni whimpered.

'Aye, sorry you got caught.'

Just then, the bedroom door opened and the client who'd been waiting on her was stood in front of her with his huge beer belly hanging over his silk leopard-print boxer shorts. She looked up at him in disgust.

He simply stared at her and smiled. 'In you come then, little one.'

Zofia felt sick for real now. How could she just walk away from Antoni and allow him to take the fall for her?

Chaos began to unfold behind her and the man lost his concentration, lifted his gaze and stared out at what was going on. Zofia held her breath, placed her hand on the man's chest, ignoring how disgusting his hair-covered skin felt under her palm, and guided the man backwards into the bedroom. She gently closed the door with her foot. He smiled creepily at her and reached down before cupping her breasts with his disgusting fat fingers. She recoiled at his touch and he frowned, looking down at her face.

Gripping the scissors as tightly as she could, she quickly raised her arm and thrust them into his throat. His eyes widened as he let go of her. Zofia pulled the scissors out and blood spurted from the wound. She was already crying at the sight of what she'd done. She hadn't detached this time. She was very much in the room, watching him as he began to die. Her words to Antoni echoed in her memory. *If you don't see them take their last breath, then it didn't happen.*

He fell backwards onto the bed and she let out a breath before turning towards the door and opening it slightly.

Looking into the reflection of the lounge through the mirror, she could see that the fuss had moved out of the hallway. Girls were screaming, Depeche Mode blared and Zofia eyed the front door. She crept slowly along the hall towards it and prayed the entire time that the security guard hadn't locked it behind him when he came in to see what all the noise was about.

Pulling on the handle as quietly as she could, relief flooded her veins when it opened. Stepping out into the hallway, bloodied scissors still in her hand, Zofia ran for the stairs at the opposite side of the landing to where Leo had brought them from the lift.

Taking the steps two, three at a time, she made it to the bottom of the building, burst through the entrance doors onto the front street and ran as fast as she could. Cars honked as she ran out onto the road and through a tunnel under an expressway.

She wanted to go back for Antoni, but she knew it would be too late for him. He'd already be dead. And she'd be killed too. *Jesus*, she thought to herself as she ran, her heart pounding heavily in her chest as she tried to suck in as much air as her lungs would allow. Antoni's face; the panic in his eyes flashed into her mind. He was terrified. And now he was dead because of her. He'd said he wanted no part in her plan and she'd forced that nail file into his hands. She'd given him no choice, like Leo had given *her* no choice. Was she just as bad? Forcing Antoni into something he didn't want to do for her own gain? A wave of guilt began to consume her and, for a moment, she wanted to collapse on the ground and cry; sob for what she'd done and for Antoni's horrific death. But she couldn't. She had to keep going. If she stopped, it would all have been for nothing.

Reaching the end of the tunnel, Zofia's legs felt hollow and her chest and throat constricted as she tried to catch her breath. The street in front of her was deserted of people. Cars sat in their spaces all along both sides of the road and, if she had to, she'd crawl under one and stay there until she knew she was safe from the people in that flat.

The sound of thundering footsteps at the other side of the tunnel sent her into a blind panic and she started to run again. Picking up the pace, Zofia dropped to the ground and rolled under a van that was parked to the right of the street. The footsteps grew closer and closer and Zofia forced herself to breathe steadily so as not to be heard.

'She can't have gone that far,' a male voice said quietly between breaths.

'Do *you* fucking see her anywhere? Because I don't,' Leo replied between pants. 'Fuck.'

'We should split up; we'll find her that way.'

'We're not finding her. She's long gone. I would be too if I was her. Little fucking bitch has murdered one of my best clients.'

Zofia closed her eyes. She'd *actually* killed him. She didn't know where she'd found the strength but she was glad. It was one less person to worry about and it'd got her away.

'We need to get that place cleaned up,' Leo said. 'We've got two bodies to dispose of.'

Zofia swallowed hard. Two. That meant Antoni was definitely dead alongside the client she'd stabbed in the neck.

'What if she goes to the police?' the other man said. 'If she does, I'm fucked, Leo. We all are. You get that, don't you?'

Leo growled loudly. 'She won't. She's not got the guts.'

'She had the guts to murder a fucking MP, Leo. He's not just some wee jakey off the street. He's a fucking politician. This is going to be all over the news.'

Zofia's eyes flew open. A politician?

'Aye, I fucking know, mate. She'll fly low under the radar. I've dealt with girls like her before. If I didn't have my eyes off the ball with that little shit having a shitty little blade that turned out to be a fucking nail file, I'd have caught her before she left. So, we keep an eye out for her. It won't be hard to find her. She doesn't know the city let alone the country. She'll make a mistake. One of her lot will likely give her up if the price is right.'

Zofia blinked away tears. How the fuck was she going to get out of this? Who would help her?

The silence that followed Leo's words instilled a new level of fear in Zofia.

Leo was right. Zofia didn't know the city. She didn't know where she was, or where she was going. That fact was going to make it harder to stay hidden from him but, more to the point, it was going to be so much more difficult to find Alina.

Leo cleared his throat. 'Come on, let's go. We've got a mess to clean up.'

As they moved away from the van, Zofia was too terrified to move. She cried silent tears for Antoni, and for the girl she used to be.

# Chapter 25

Molly Rose looked down at her Auntie Sinead as she thrashed around the bed, screaming as though she was in pain. Janey pressed the button to call the nurse and held Sinead, shushing her like a baby.

'It's all right, love, you're safe. You're safe,' Janey said, over and over again.

Molly Rose could only watch in horror and felt utterly helpless.

A nurse ran into the room just as Sinead was beginning to calm a little, but Janey didn't let go.

'What's wrong with her?' Molly Rose asked as the nurse busied around Sinead. 'Why is she doing that?'

'It's an after-effect of the overdose,' the nurse replied.

'An after-effect?'

'There might be episodes of aggression, psychosis. At times she won't seem herself. With time, and the correct treatment, she'll get better.'

Sinead suddenly relaxed and burst into tears.

'You're safe, Sinead. Your mum and your niece are here with you.' Then she looked down at Janey. 'She was given a dose of Naloxone which reverses the effects of an opioid overdose for around twenty minutes. Enough time to get her to the hospital and get medical treatment. Her counsellor did the right thing phoning an ambulance. She might not be with us if he hadn't found her so quickly.'

Molly Rose felt sick at what could have happened had that man, Jacob, not found Sinead when he did. Shame he hadn't found the person who'd stuck that shit into her veins in the first place.

Sinead locked eyes with Molly Rose but it was as though she wasn't seeing her niece stood in front of her. In fact, it looked as though she had no idea where she was or who she was with.

'Sinead, are you okay?' Janey asked, looking down at her.

Sinead blinked and, as the tears fell, the crying turned to sobbing and the sound transported Molly Rose back to the very moment her mum died. Sinead had wailed the same way in that moment too.

Molly Rose turned her back to her gran and auntie and tried to compose herself.

All Molly Rose kept thinking about was, if this could happen to Sinead in a controlled and seemingly secure environment, then what the hell was coming for her?

# Chapter 26

She opened her eyes and looked across the bed to Leo's side. He hadn't come home last night. No call. No text. Just a no-show. It wasn't the first time it had happened in their marriage. In fact, she was used to it after all these years. She suspected what he was up to. Likely had a mistress. Cheryl didn't actually care any more. All she had room for inside her was grief for what had happened to Dean. It consumed her every waking second. But if it wasn't a mistress, then what was the reason?

Sitting up, she ran her hands through her hair and sighed before glancing at the clock. She was supposed to be meeting Janey at the salon in an hour.

Getting out of bed, Cheryl left the bedroom and crossed the hall towards the bathroom when she heard a sound from the living room.

'Leo?' she called out.

'Aye, it's me. I slept in here last night. Didn't want to wake you.'

Rolling her eyes, she stepped into the living room. 'Why were you out so late?'

'Ran into a few issues at work.'

Cheryl narrowed her eyes. 'What issues?'

'Clean-up job went tits up.'

'You were cleaning up after a washing machine install-ation into the small hours?' Cheryl asked.

'Aye. Client was a bastard. As was the kitchen, honestly, it was last installed in the Seventies. A pipe burst and we had to switch the water off, fix the pipe and then clean up. Guy wouldn't let us leave until every last drop of water was up.'

Sighing, Cheryl shook her head. 'It's still better than what you were doing before, you know the job that got our son *killed*.'

Leo raised an eyebrow and then bowed his head. 'Aye, I know, Cheryl. If you could stop throwing it in my face every second of the day, that would be great. You know if I could go back and change it, I would.'

'But you can't, which is why I'm fixing the contributing problem now. You know, the Hallahans?'

Cheryl watched Leo, waited for a reaction. Any reaction. But there was nothing. It was like he didn't care any more.

'What is it you want to do, Cheryl?'

'Well, you were supposed to take out Janey. Instead, you put her husband in a fucking coma and now, she and that little bitch Molly Rose have fucking security around them twenty-four-seven and she's no longer at the salon. So your original plan is out the fucking window,' Cheryl sneered. 'So,' she continued. 'Janey actually contacted me. Asked me to meet her at the salon today and to cancel all appointments. The last time I spoke to her, I was worried Janey had something planned for me. But she's vulnerable right now. I'm going to gain her trust and then strike from within.'

Leo scoffed. 'And you really think that's going to happen? You think Janey Hallahan is going to trust anyone? You're going about this the wrong way. Why don't you let me handle it?'

Cheryl shot an angry look at him and raised her voice. 'Because you're responsible for Marek, aren't you? Make sure you get him, and like I said before, if you can find out who actually pulled the trigger, that would be a bonus.'

'And like I said before, no one is going to grass anyone up. But I'll do my best with Marek.'

'You fucking better,' Cheryl snapped.

Leo raised his hands in defeat. 'Right, okay. Fine. I get it. Just, please don't shout. I have a pounding headache.' He rubbed at his temples and Cheryl noticed the dried blood on his knuckles.

'What happened there?' She gestured to his hand.

Leo glanced down and paused. 'I punched a wall in frustration.'

Cheryl shook her head. 'You couldn't have used that kind of energy on your boss?'

'Urgh, do you ever get sick of the sound of your own voice, Cheryl? I mean, seriously? I know it's my fault, I know Dean's dead because of my work. *Jesus*, I'm surprised the fucking neighbours don't know about it the amount you go on.'

She threw him a dirty look and wished he'd been the one run off the road and in a coma. 'Just stay the fuck out of my way, Leo, unless you want to be useful.'

She marched through to the bathroom and slammed the door shut before switching on the shower. The sooner she got this done, the better. Getting rid of all the people in her life who'd caused her grief would leave her feeling free. She hoped Leo would disappear too.

# Chapter 27

Janey Hallahan sat on the large white Chesterfield leather sofa that was against the wall across from the reception desk in the salon. It had barely been sat on, given the salon hadn't been open for that long. The place was immaculate.

Her phone beeped and, when she glanced down, a text had come through from DI James Pearson.

> Janey, I have very little info on the European gang. I'm working on it. All I know is, they went to ground for a while and now, they're rumoured to be starting up operations again. Investigations are underway. As it stands, there is no CCTV footage of the incident. Once I know more, you'll be the first person I tell. Send my love to Ciaran.

Janey had considered asking James Pearson to look into who could have injected Sinead. But that was something that she wanted to deal with on her own. She wasn't going to let that go easily. Whoever was responsible for setting Sinead back and almost killing her would pay the ultimate price. She'd already lost one daughter. She wasn't going to allow Sinead to be taken from her too, and the only way to ascertain that was to put the culprit in the ground. She'd personally chop their fucking hands off if it came to it.

'Here you go,' Molly Rose said, handing her a mug of coffee and pulling Janey from her thoughts. She slid the phone into her pocket and smiled up at Molly Rose.

'Thanks, love.'

'What are you going to say to Cheryl?'

Janey sighed and glanced out of the window. Kristo was stood outside the door of the salon like some club bouncer and it angered Janey that things had gone this far. She thought about Ciaran and the state of him lying in that hospital bed, in a coma, and wondered if he'd ever come out of it.

'I just need to be straight with her. The fact that she's in the picture that was sent to you means she could be in danger too. The people who are trying to wipe me out won't hesitate to hurt anyone close to me, no matter who they are. That's why you've got to stay by my side. I need to be able to keep you safe.'

Molly Rose gave a grim laugh. 'No offence, Janey, but wouldn't it be safer if I wasn't anywhere near you?'

'You'd think. But the second you're alone, they could come for you. It's like going for the weakest link. It has happened already, with your mum. As soon as she was on her own with...' She let the words trail off, unable to speak their depravity.

'Yeah,' Molly Rose said. 'Fair enough.'

The door to the salon opened and Janey looked up to see Cheryl walking in, with Kristo holding the door open for her. A look of confusion and concern washed over her.

'What's this about?' Cheryl asked. 'I'm not getting laid off, am I?'

Janey smiled and shook her head. 'Of course not. But there is something important that I wanted to speak to you about. It's regarding your personal safety.'

Cheryl frowned and sat down on the sofa next to Janey. 'My safety? What do you mean?'

'So, as you already know, Ciaran and I were run off the road and Ciaran is in a coma. I believe it was a deliberate act against me and my family.'

Cheryl gave a sympathetic smile and said, 'How is Ciaran?'

'He's… much the same. But I'm hopeful that he'll pull through. Cheryl,' Janey said, meeting her eye. 'This isn't going to sound very pleasant but you need to take it seriously. Molly Rose has received something quite sinister. A box came to my house. Inside that box was a picture of Molly Rose. And you were in it too.'

'Excuse me?' She frowned.

'It was taken from outside the salon. Not sure if directly or across the street and the camera had zoomed in.'

'Jesus,' Cheryl whispered. Her face paled.

'Are you okay?' Molly Rose asked, sitting down on the other side of Cheryl and placing a hand on her shoulder. 'I know, it's a lot to take in.'

'You think I'm in danger?' Cheryl asked.

'You may not be, but it's not a risk I'd like you to take. I need you to be vigilant, Cheryl. If you think there's anything strange going on at the salon, you need to tell me. I'll have security posted here every day until we figure out who sent the picture and who's behind all of this.'

Cheryl was quiet, as though she was processing it all.

'The picture had a message on the back and they'd included a really degrading piece of lingerie,' Molly Rose said.

'I'm so sorry this is happening to you. What did the message say?'

'I always loved to look at you. That figure, your little waist. Molly Rose, you still get me going even from the grave,' Molly Rose replied. 'Whoever sent it made it sound as though it was from my ex, who I already told you is dead.'

Janey saw something in Cheryl's eyes. A change. Her jaw tensed just a little and her cheeks flushed. Janey narrowed her eyes. 'Are you okay?'

'What? Sorry. I was just thinking. This is horrible. Sick, like you say. I just... I just can't get my head around it. Who would do something like that?'

'That's what we're trying to find out. And I will. Once I do, it'll all be put to a stop. But I just wanted to prewarn you about this. Anyone's involvement with my family at the moment is being closely watched. I'll weed out the bad seeds. I always do,' Janey said as she sipped at her coffee.

Cheryl nodded. 'I'm sure you will.'

'Look, take the rest of the day off. Relax, process this and come back to work tomorrow.'

Cheryl glanced at Molly Rose. 'Are you okay? I mean, getting a message like that must have been scary.'

Molly Rose raised an eyebrow and shrugged. 'I've had a lot worse happen to me in recent months. But yeah, it's like the person who sent that knew what Dean had in store for me. Which means they were probably part of that whole operation in the first place.'

Janey cleared her throat. 'That kind of package has sent us a strong message. They intend on finishing the job Dean started. I absolutely will *not* let that happen.'

Cheryl's eyes flitted from Janey to Molly Rose.

'Cheryl, you don't look too well. Are you okay?' Janey asked, her brow furrowed.

She nodded and quickly got to her feet. 'Yes, I'm fine. Thanks for letting me know. I have to get going, got stuff on today and I want to get it done while I still have the day.'

Janey got to her feet, the pain in her ankle still intense. She regarded the look on Cheryl's face. 'Look, I'm sorry if I've scared you. But you had a right to know. Here,' she said, handing the picture to Cheryl. 'This is it.'

She watched as Cheryl looked down at it briefly.

'I hope you find them,' Cheryl said. 'If there's anything I can do to help, let me know.'

Janey kept her eye on Cheryl as she walked out of the salon. She didn't even give Kristo the chance to open the door for her.

'Is it just me, or did she seem off to you?' Janey said to Molly Rose.

'Wouldn't you be if you were in her position? She won't be used to this sort of thing like you. Even I'm starting to get used to the idea that someone wants to kill me. It's like the bloody norm these days,' Molly Rose replied, sitting back on the sofa before opening the bottle of Irn-Bru. It hissed loudly as she released the lid.

'Hmm,' Janey said. 'No, she seemed off; like, too quiet.'

'She's probably shitting herself, Janey. She'll be worrying about what you just told her.'

Janey watched as Cheryl walked up the hill on the opposite side of the street to the salon. 'Yeah, she will be. I hope I haven't just lost a good manager to all this crap.'

Molly Rose shook her head and took a sip. 'Doubt it. You pay good wages. But maybe you should add in a bonus payment to your staff. You know, like danger money.'

Janey eyed her granddaughter and noticed the corners of her mouth raise a little, but they didn't form a full smile because none of what was going on was funny. And Molly Rose didn't have much to be smiling about; she'd only lost her mum eight weeks earlier. In fact, Janey couldn't remember the last time any of them had genuinely smiled.

Janey sat back down and kept her eyes on the street. She wondered if the person who'd sent that crude package to Molly Rose was out there now, taking more pictures.

She leaned over and knocked on the window. Kristo came inside.

'Can you make sure someone keeps an extra eye on Cheryl? Something about her reaction seemed off to me.'

Kristo nodded. 'I'll get one of the team on it now, Janey.'

'You think she's a threat?' Molly Rose asked, sounding shocked.

'No, not a threat. But my gut is telling me something isn't right. I just want to keep everyone that I can safe.'

Molly Rose sighed. 'All this has really fucked with your trust in people.'

'And it hasn't for you?' Janey replied.

Molly Rose didn't answer.

-

Cheryl reached the top of the hill and, when she was out of sight from the salon, she leaned her back against the wall and took a deep breath.

The mere mention that Dean's name was attached to the package that Molly Rose had received had made her feel sick. Someone had used her son's name – her *dead* son's name – to instil fear into that family. That was something that, as a mother, she could never have done. So who was using Dean's name?

It could only be Leo. But *would* he do that? Abuse Dean's memory like that? He *had* got Dean involved in the darkest part of the underworld. She supposed he was capable of anything. And, of course, she'd told Leo to stay out of it all, that Cheryl would take care of the Hallahans. Knowing Leo, he'd have ignored that instruction.

*I'll ask him*, she thought.

But if she did ask and she was spot on, he'd only lie to her.

Closing her eyes, Cheryl peered out from behind the wall and watched as Kristo guarded the door of the salon.

Getting close to Molly Rose in order to take her down, getting close to them all, was it really worth the added stress while she was still grieving for her son?

Then she remembered why she was doing it in the first place, and she felt that fire in her belly again.

Pulling out her phone, she called her husband.

'Where are you?'

'I'm still in the flat, getting ready to leave.'

'Stay there. I'm coming home. I want to talk about the Hallahans.'

As she started to make her way home, she gritted her teeth. *If he did do this, I'll fucking kill him.*

# Chapter 28

She'd managed to control the trembling for a short time. Hiding and trying to sleep under a van on a side street while making sure she stayed hidden from her captor had been exhausting and terrifying. Zofia was left feeling cold and hungry, in a foreign country, with nowhere to turn. If she went to the police, she'd be arrested for murder; the fact that a politician was one of Leo's clients and she'd killed him made it clear that Leo knew enough people at the top to make sure she was punished for going against him. She didn't have her passport to get home. And now that she'd escaped after murdering what Leo said was one of his biggest clients, the MSP, what would happen to Alina? Leo had always threatened to use her if Zofia didn't fall into line.

*What the hell have I done?*

Something came to her then. Molly Rose. Leo was determined to get her to Poland; had enlisted Zofia's help. He had such a grudge against this young girl and her grandmother.

*That's it*, she thought. *I'll go to Janey. Tell her everything that I've been forced to do. The box. The note on the back of the photograph. Being told to keep a lookout for Molly Rose on her own. If I tell her what has been going on, surely she'd help me?*

Slipping her hand into the woman's bag, she tried to remind herself that she wouldn't be doing this if she didn't have to. Zofia would never steal from anyone, especially not a young mother with a screaming baby in her arms. But then, she would kill again if it meant her safety and freedom were promised.

'Sshhh,' the woman said as she rocked the baby gently, completely unaware that Zofia had just removed her purse and was now walking the other way towards the train station.

Zofia shivered against the cold and the crimes she was now committing because of the situation she'd been forced into. Murder, theft. Who the hell was she becoming?

*A girl trying to survive*, she told herself.

Partick train station was busy, which suited her as she'd be able to blend into the crowd. Glancing up at the screen, she read when the next train to Helensburgh was due. In two minutes, apparently.

Running through the station, she reached the platform and stood with her feet on the yellow line. She wanted to be the first on that train. Getting out of this part of the city would help her get further away from Leo and however many men he had looking for her. But heading towards Helensburgh would be like walking into the lion's den as that was one of the places Leo operated from. Zofia had been one of those posted outside the supermarket to beg for spare change; she'd later discovered that Leo had made others pickpocket those who'd been kind enough to give what they had. Some of them had come back with purses and wallets, filled with cash, some empty. None of the girls ever saw any of the money. It wasn't something Zofia had ever done, until she'd been faced with getting on that train to get away. She'd always told Leo there was no opportunity for her to be able to steal without getting caught, how the public always had their wits about them. She'd been put on the street to work a few times at night too. She knew the area a little better than most like her. She was one of the oldest on what Leo called her 'team'. Antoni had been brought in just a few weeks after her.

*Antoni*, she thought. Whatever happened to him, she hoped he hadn't suffered. The thought of what he might have been subjected to because of her made her feel physically sick. But then, if the shoe had been on the other foot, she wouldn't have blamed him if he'd run and left her behind. It was what they had to do to survive.

The approaching train distracted her from her thoughts and, as it pulled up to the platform, a crowd gathered behind her. She had the biggest fear that if she turned around, Leo would be standing right there, smiling down at her with that menacing grin he had.

*Don't look behind you. Keep facing forward.*

The train doors opened and a throng of people stepped off onto the platform before Zofia climbed on and took a seat by the window. The woman's purse was in her hand, which she had tucked inside her jacket as she held on to it tightly. As the train pulled out of the station, Zofia sighed in relief and opened the purse. There was a twenty-pound note, a few coins and a driving licence. She didn't want to look at it; didn't want to know the identity of the person she'd robbed.

She was on her way to Helensburgh now. Helensburgh, the next town along from Rhu, where Janey Hallahan lived. Taking the train there was a huge risk, but it was her only option. Leo had driven her to Janey's house twice. She'd made a mental note of the route because it was so remote, she'd wanted to be able to find her way back to civilisation if she escaped. That hadn't been the case, but she'd seen a train station in Helensburgh while in Leo's van; she'd all but memorised the route from the squalid flat to Janey's house and back again. And thankfully, the road from said train station to Janey's house was pretty straight. No major turn-offs for her to remember. Of course, she didn't have her own transport, so the train was her only option; or possibly the bus, but she wanted to stick to what she knew. Not that she knew Scotland's transport system, but she was willing to take the risk if it meant she could possibly secure her safety. And it was the biggest risk of her life, heading to Helensburgh. Anyone who knew Leo, even people at her level, could contact him and she'd be right back where she started, but in a much worse situation. She had no other choice.

What was she going to say when she got there? Would she have the guts to walk up to Janey? Or Molly Rose? Would they know who she was? Would they call the police on her? If they did, being in a police cell instead of with Leo was a step up. She'd taken her chances up until now and she wasn't about to stop.

## Chapter 29

Cheryl stepped back into the flat she shared with her husband and a feeling of dread washed over her. The flat they lived in was beautiful; grand. She used to be proud of their home, but knowing how it was paid for, through dirty money made by Leo working for Marek, she couldn't bear to be there any more. Living there now made Cheryl feel ill, not just because of how it was paid for, but because of Dean's absence.

Leo stepped out of the kitchen and he looked weary.

'What's up with your face?' Cheryl asked, goading him. She couldn't help herself these days.

Ignoring her, he said, 'What did you want to talk about regarding the Hallahans?'

Cheryl walked past him and entered the living room before taking a seat on the sofa. She leaned over and started to remove her shoes, wondering how she was going to put this to him. Would he be annoyed at her accusation that he was the one who'd taken the photo and hadn't told her?

'I went to see Janey this morning, as you know. She wanted to give me a warning.'

Leo sat down on the seat opposite her and raised an eyebrow. 'A warning? About what?'

'Apparently someone has taken a photo of Molly Rose in the shop. I'm in the picture too. Janey showed it to me.'

Leo smirked. 'Shitting themselves, are they?'

Cheryl glared at him. 'No. Not at all. In fact, it's only made Janey worry about me. She thinks I could be a target.'

Leo threw back his head and laughed loudly.

'Why is that funny?'

'Because you're obviously *not* in danger.'

Cheryl looked at her husband through narrowed eyes and said, 'So it *was* you who sent the box to Janey's house?'

Leo simply nodded, an evil smile darkening his face.

'And the sick lingerie with the message signed off by Dean? Was that you too?'

Leo's smile faded a little at Cheryl's tone.

'You used our *murdered* son's name as though he was still alive? You pretended it was from Dean?'

'Calm down, Cheryl, I was only trying to scare her. He was gearing her up to become a fucking sex worker abroad. The lingerie would have been her daily attire.'

Without thinking, Cheryl raised her hand and slapped Leo so hard across the face that her hand stung.

As though stunned, Leo merely stood there in silence without making eye contact. Her heart thudded in her chest as she tried to compose herself.

'Are you still working for them?' she said accusatorily.

The lines of Leo's forehead deepened as he frowned. 'No.'

'I don't believe you.'

'Yeah, that's fucking clear.'

Cheryl stared at him, held her breath, and then she said, 'Because they won't hesitate to kill one of us again if another transaction gets messed up, Leo. In fact, I bet if you fucked up even a little bit, the most miniscule thing would give them the go ahead to put a bullet in your skull. And mine.'

Leo abruptly got to his feet and she could see the fiery rage in his eyes. 'I said I stopped working for them after Dean. If you don't believe me, that's a fucking you problem.'

She watched as he left the room and Cheryl took a long, steadying breath.

Cheryl didn't believe a word that came out of Leo's mouth. But she had no proof.

Getting to her feet, she walked out to the hallway and looked into the kitchen. Leo was sinking back a shot of whisky and it unsettled her.

'I'm sorry,' she said. 'For doubting you. And for slapping you. I just... I just don't want you to have any more dealings with those bastards, Leo. They killed our son.'

He placed the glass down on the kitchen counter and sighed. 'Yes, I *know* they did, Cheryl. You say it every fucking day.'

She sighed, a wash of sadness coming over her. How could he be sick of hearing it? It was all that kept her alive, to know that Dean did exist once. 'All I want is peace.'

Leo nodded, but he didn't look at her. His eyes stared down into the empty glass. Just like her soul. Empty. No other purpose than revenge. His cheek glowed red.

'And you think you can really achieve that, Cheryl? Peace?'

Cheryl shook her head. 'No. I don't. I don't think I'll ever know peace again. But once the Hallahans are gone, I might be able to move on.'

Leo scoffed. 'You know that's never going to be possible, don't you? Moving on after something like this. It'll live with you, for the rest of your life.'

147

'Knowing someone paid for Dean's death will be enough,' Cheryl said. But in her gut, she knew that once the Hallahans had paid for their part, she'd make sure Leo went with them. She'd do it herself if she had to. No matter how terrifying or painful it would be to look her husband in the eye just seconds before, her mind wouldn't be changed now. Leo was a dead man walking.

# Chapter 30

Stepping off the train and onto the platform at Helensburgh Central, Zofia discreetly chucked the stolen purse into a nearby bin before exiting the station on to East Princes Street. Directly across the road she eyed the Princes Street Bar. It looked dark and dingy, but it was a place to go to get herself together until she figured out what she was going to do next.

Checking the road, she crossed over and the smell of stale beer hit her as she pulled the door open.

She was right, the place was as dark and dingy on the inside as it looked on the outside. It was semi-busy, most tables occupied by one or two people; mostly men.

Zofia felt the door close behind her and she took a breath before heading to the bar. The barman looked at her and raised an eyebrow.

'You got ID, hen?' he asked suspiciously.

She smiled as sweetly as she could; it was what she'd been taught to do for men. 'Can I have a Coke, please?'

The man didn't say anything; instead, he retrieved a can from the fridge below the bar and placed it in front of her.

'Two quid,' he said.

Zofia pulled some coins out of her pocket and handed the barman a note with a five in the corner.

'Cheers,' he said, handing her three coins in return.

Zofia took the can and turned to face the tables. An unoccupied seat in the corner caught her eye and she moved quickly towards it. Sitting down with her back to the wall, she kept her head low but scanned the pub.

What the hell was she supposed to do now? Wait? For what?

'Right, ah'm away,' one of the men sitting at the table next to Zofia said to the other. 'Got an AA meeting later. Need tae freshen masel up fur it afore a go in, know?'

She could barely make out what the man had meant, but given he was putting on his jacket, she assumed he was leaving.

'Aye, how ye getting on wae that, pal?' the other man asked.

'Shite. Keep fallin aff the wagon.'

'Doesnae help ye keep comin in here, does it?'

The men gave phlegmy laughs and one of them left. They reminded her of Leo's clients; and worse. Their gruff voices, the smell of stale alcohol and cigarette smoke. Body odour. It made her want to throw up.

The second man got up from the table and headed in the direction of the door. 'Ah'l come wae ye. Need a fag.'

She watched as they both left and, when she turned back, she noticed that a mobile phone had been left on the table. And it was unlocked, the screen shining brightly up to the ceiling.

Glancing around her, Zofia discreetly slid along the bench and retrieved the phone. She quickly switched it to silent and slipped it into her pocket, before grabbing the unopened can of Coke and getting to her feet and leaving the pub.

Both men were stood outside, facing the train station, and Zofia took a sharp left before heading away from them, praying that the owner of the phone wouldn't be too quick to go back in, work out that she'd taken his phone and catch up with her.

Seeing the entrance to one of the apartment buildings above her was open, she stepped inside and leaned back against the wall.

She pulled the phone out of her pocket and breathed a sigh of relief that it was still unlocked. The Instagram icon stared at her and she wondered for a moment why a man like him would even have an Instagram account. A thought occurred to her then. Could she contact Molly Rose or Janey via that app? Tell them about Leo?

Tapping the icon, she waited for the app to load. The page filled the screen and she tapped on the profile picture, which wasn't the face of the man she'd taken the phone from, but instead, the Volkswagen car logo. *Odd*, Zofia thought.

His name was Kenny Brown.

She tapped on the search bar at the top and typed in 'Molly Rose Hunter'. A few options came up on the screen, and she recognised the face of the girl she was looking for. The girl that Leo had made Zofia deliver the package for.

She selected the profile and hit the message button and started to type out a message quickly.

> Molly Rose Hunter, you don't know me, but I have something I need to warn you about. A man.

Old, wrinkled hands snatched the phone from her grip and Zofia gasped in shock.

'What d'ye hink yer dain, ya thievin little fuck!' the man shouted in her face while grabbing at her wrist with his free hand. 'Hink ye can nick ma phone an get away wae it? Ah don't fuckin hink so, hen.'

Zofia mustered up as much strength as she could and, in true Glasgow style, struck her forehead right into the bridge of his nose. He let out a yelp like an old dog and Zofia ran as fast as she could out of the entrance to the building and along the road away from the train station.

Her feet thundered on the ground beneath her and her heart pounded in her chest. She didn't look back in fear that the man would be close behind her. Her head ached after the impact she'd made with the man's nose. Headbutting someone wasn't something she'd ever done before, but she'd had it done to her once before when she wouldn't comply with a client Leo had put her with. She'd learned it was the quickest way to debilitate someone and it was the first thing she'd thought of when that man had grabbed her arm after snatching the phone from her hand.

She ran through an open square of man-made green spaces and benches. She briefly noticed a small monument on her right, but she didn't stop. She took a left turn and found herself outside a church. St Michael's, according to the sign outside.

Zofia didn't stop for long, worried that the man would find her and do God only knew what to her. Instead, she stepped inside and tried to control her breathing. She didn't want to talk to anyone, look anyone in the eye. She just needed a moment to process and plan.

Zofia sat down on one of the benches at the back of the church and caught her breath.

*Shit*, she thought. She hadn't even got to finish that message, or send it. The whole point in sending it was to give the family prior warning and to help prepare Zofia for seeing the Hallahans face to face.

Now, she was going to have to just do what she dreaded. Turn up at Janey's door unannounced.

## Chapter 31

Kristo opened the door and helped Janey out of the car, while Molly Rose got out from the back seat.

'Thanks, Kristo,' Janey said as she steadied herself. 'The ankle feels better by the day.' It was a lie. It was still painful, but in light of what was going on, she didn't want to appear weak just because of an ankle injury. Physically, she was in pain. She felt like the world was taking her apart, piece by piece.

'Good to hear,' Kristo said. 'Right, I'll come along to the shops with you.'

Molly Rose laughed loudly and Kristo looked at her with a furrowed brow. 'Ha, aye, all right.'

'What's the problem?' Kristo asked.

Janey couldn't help but smile at Kristo's confused expression.

'No offence, but I don't want people looking at me thinking I'm up myself because I'm walking around with a bloody security guard. I'd rather go alone.'

Janey sighed. 'You know that's not an option.'

'And you know that I'm my own person and exactly like my mother. What I want, I get,' Molly Rose teased.

Janey kept her expression stern and Molly Rose rolled her eyes.

'Oh, for God's sake. I'm only going into the bloody supermarket for a few things. I'll be *surrounded* by people.

It's not like someone's going to murder me in the freezer aisle in broad daylight, is it?'

Janey glanced at Kristo, who had chosen to remain silent. Molly Rose was right, it was unlikely that anyone would attack her in the middle of the high-street supermarket. But Janey couldn't help but think that she'd been run off the road in the middle of the day, and Sinead had been injected with heroin in what was supposed to be a safe and secure facility.

'It's not impossible though,' Kristo piped up, his expression turning serious. 'It's my job to protect you.'

Molly Rose frowned and shook her head. 'I don't need protecting. Not from a bloody supermarket. I just want to be able to grab a few bits from the shop on my own.'

'I'll watch from afar then,' Kristo insisted.

Molly Rose turned to Janey and shrugged. 'I take it you're with him on this?'

Janey nodded. 'Actually, I have another idea to go alongside it. I want you to download that tracking app. Life three sixty. Have you heard of it?'

'You want to track my phone?' Molly Rose spat the words out like they were a sour taste in her mouth. 'Jesus Christ, can't I have any privacy?'

'It's not about invading your privacy, Molly Rose,' Janey said. 'It's about keeping you safe. And if you want to be able to have some freedom throughout all of this, then I think it's best you do it. Once it's on both our phones, I'll wait here and Kristo can wait outside the supermarket. Means you've only got one of us on your tail. How does that sound?'

Molly Rose sighed in annoyance and closed the car door. 'Fine,' she said sternly, pulling out her phone and tapping away furiously at the screen.

It didn't take too long before Janey could see the exact location of Molly Rose's phone. 'Perfect,' Janey said. 'That wasn't so hard, was it.'

Molly Rose gave a smirk and turned to Kristo. 'Kristo, you better find who's doing this to us and fast. I'm sick of living my life like an open prisoner.'

Molly Rose turned and walked away from both Janey and Kristo.

'Go on after her. I'll be fine waiting here. I might even take a hobble down to the water. Take in the sea air for a bit,' Janey said.

'I'd rather you didn't, Janey. It's dangerous.'

'I'll be fine,' Janey replied, echoing Molly Rose's sentiments. The difference being, Janey really could handle herself. She'd been born into this world. Molly Rose had just stumbled across it by accident.

'If you insist. Keep your wits about you,' Kristo replied. 'And take your crutch.'

'Ha,' Janey laughed. 'Yeah, if anyone suspicious approaches me, I'll take them out with it. And if you really want to, you can check my location on Molly Rose's phone.'

Kristo laughed, dropped the keys into Janey's hand and started after Molly Rose. She didn't stop to watch them disappear around the corner, but instead headed down towards the water, reluctantly lifting her crutch. The limp was bad and she still needed it, but her pride was dented for sure. The fresh air would clear her head.

Finally reaching the front, embarrassed that her walk resembled an elderly penguin, she took a seat on one of the benches and noticed the cruise ship at the port in Greenock across the water.

*It's not something we ever did, Ciaran,* Janey thought to herself. Suddenly, a lump formed in her throat at the thought of never having that option. If Ciaran died, they'd never go on a cruise. Never have a glass of wine together again. He'd no longer be there to calm her in stressful situations; something he was always so good at.

She missed the sound of his voice already. The feel of his hand in hers. He'd been by far the best person ever to have come into her life and now someone was trying to take him away from her. Her entire family, what was left of them, was in danger and she didn't know when they were going to strike next.

A cool sea breeze whipped around her, bringing her back from her thoughts. Pulling her phone from her pocket, she considered calling the hospital. There had been no further news on Ciaran or Sinead. No news was good news, she supposed. She typed out another text to DI James Pearson, this time simply stating she was following up on her previous message and she looked forward to his response. A reply came through quickly.

> I understand your frustrations, Janey. I do.
> But please, let me do my work and like I
> said before, you'll be the first to know
> anything that comes up. Trust me. You and
> Ciaran are dear to me. I won't let you
> down.

Sighing at the response and lack of update, Janey slid the phone back into her pocket and looked back at the cruise ship. The freedom of being out at sea, was it really as good as people made out?

Turning, she glanced up towards the high street and hoped that Molly Rose wasn't giving Kristo too much of a hard time.

If anyone could keep her safe, it was him.

# Chapter 32

With the basket in her hand, Molly Rose strolled leisurely through the supermarket, browsing everything and nothing. She didn't actually want or need anything, but being able to get away from Janey and Kristo (even if he was waiting outside for her and Janey could see exactly which bloody aisle she was in because of that stupid app) was bliss. She hated that she was being watched over because of the life Janey had chosen for herself. She loved her gran, as new as she was in her life and, to be fair, if it wasn't for Janey, Molly Rose would definitely be dead by now. But she couldn't remember a time when she didn't have to look over her shoulder because of her. Leaving wasn't an option. There would always be that link; the invisible chain of DNA connecting them. If someone wanted Janey dead, then Molly Rose would always be a target.

She picked up the box of fancy dark chocolate biscuits and dropped them into the basket before heading for the alcohol section. Not that she'd be able to buy any. Just being able to go from one aisle to the next was freedom enough.

Staring at the wine, she clocked the bottle her mum used to drink sometimes. Pinot Noir. And Pinot Grigio. In fact, Molly Rose recognised a lot of them and she smiled.

Feeling a presence behind her, Molly Rose turned, expecting Kristo to be at her back. But who she saw was not what she was expecting. A girl, about her own age. She was standing close; too close.

'Yes?' Molly Rose said, instinctively stepping back.

'Can I talk to you for a minute?' the girl asked, her European accent strong.

Through narrowed eyes, Molly Rose looked her up and down and instinctively thought something wasn't right.

'Sorry. I'm already running late,' she replied, trying to move around the girl.

She blocked Molly Rose's path and raised a hand. 'It won't take long. It's important.'

'Look,' Molly Rose sighed. 'I'm not interested in signing up to some charity. I don't want to set up a direct debit and, no, I'm not able to make a small donation today. Sorry.'

The girl didn't move and Molly Rose could feel herself becoming frustrated.

'If you don't move, I'll fucking do it for you,' Molly Rose said, hoping that she'd injected a little bit of Hallahan grit into her tone. And it worked. The girl stepped to the side and Molly Rose moved past.

Filling her basket with a few more items – crisps, chocolate, some lemonade – Molly Rose pulled her purse out of her crossbody bag and, just as she was about to head for the checkout, she felt a tug and the purse being ripped from her hand.

'Oi!' Molly Rose screamed, dropping the basket and eyeing the girl who'd just mugged her. The same girl from moments before. 'Come back, ya little bitch!'

Molly Rose ran after her. She glanced out of the window, saw Kristo on the phone with his back to the shop. Great, when she actually fucking needed him he was on the bloody phone.

The girl ran just a few feet in front of her. She was fast, but not as fast as Molly Rose. They were both through the door and out onto the street. Molly Rose launched herself and managed to grip her jacket.

They both went crashing to the ground, Molly Rose on top of her back.

'What the fuck do you think you're doing?' Molly Rose said, pulling the girl's shoulders and turning her.

She lay on the ground, staring up at Molly Rose.

'I said what the fuck do you think you're doing? Are you on a death wish, mugging me? Do you even know who I am?' Molly Rose pulled the purse from the girl's grip and shoved it back into her bag before getting to her feet.

'Yes, I know who you are. And I know who your grandmother is too. That's why I was trying to talk to you.'

'What are you on about, ya fucking nutter?' Molly Rose shouted. 'How the hell do you know who I am?'

'Phone your grandmother. I need to speak to her.'

The girl was crying suddenly, and Molly Rose frowned, feeling calmer than just moments before. The girl looked terrified. Not just because she'd tried and failed to mug someone; there was something else. 'Why do you need to speak to Janey? Do you know her?'

The girl covered her face with her hands and then sat up before sobbing. 'No. But please, just do it. She's the only one who can help me.'

'Molly Rose,' Kristo's voice called as he ran towards her. 'What's happened?'

'I don't know,' Molly Rose replied, a feeling of confusion washing over her. She looked down at the girl whose face was still in her hands. 'This girl said she needs to speak with Janey.'

Kristo glared down at the girl and then pulled his phone out and proceeded to make a call, Molly Rose presumed to Janey. But all Molly Rose could focus on was the state of the girl. Her hair needed a wash, her skin was dull, her clothes dirty. And it was obvious she was utterly terrified as her body trembled.

Kassy immediately popped into her head then and a sadness crept over her.

She crouched down in front of the girl and placed a hand over her wrist. 'Are you homeless?'

The girl sucked air in noisily and then she composed herself before pulling her hands away from her face. She nodded and looked at Molly Rose through glassy eyes.

'Are you hungry? Thirsty?' Molly Rose asked, remembering that she'd first met Kassy because she'd bought her a coffee in the street. She hadn't known in that moment that Kassy would become her best friend.

The girl nodded again and wiped away her tears with the back of her hand.

Turning, Molly Rose eyed Kristo and said, 'Go in and get a sandwich, a bottle of water and a bag of crisps.'

Kristo looked down at her in a wave of confusion. 'What are you on about? You said she needs to speak to Janey. Don't you think that's a bit odd considering what's going on? I'm not leaving you alone with her.'

The girl next to her sobbed and Molly Rose sighed. 'Jesus, Kristo. Look at her. She's not going to hurt me. Just do it. I'll still be here when you get back out.'

Molly Rose turned and the girl was staring right into her face, eyes wet and bloodshot.

'Let's get you up off the ground, eh?' Molly Rose said, hooking her arm under the girl and helping her up.

'Why are you being so nice to me?' the girl whimpered. 'I just tried to steal your purse.'

'I'm guessing it was a way to get my attention. I used to be like you, once. I lived on the streets for a short time. I know what it's like to be terrified and starving.'

The girl stared at her in disbelief.

Molly Rose helped her to sit down on the low wall which separated the car park from the street and took a seat beside her.

'Is that man your dad?'

Molly Rose burst out laughing. 'No way. My dad's in America. It's a long story. So, what's your name?'

The girl looked down to the ground and Molly Rose could see the hesitation.

'It's okay if you don't want to tell me. I get it. You're not from here, are you?'

Molly Rose stared at the girl and could almost see a little bit of Kassy in there. Although Kassy was a lot fiercer than this girl seemed to be. She wasn't afraid of getting caught stealing, or getting her hands dirty to get food for herself. But the vulnerability that Kassy had was present in this girl. No one saw Kassy's softer side other than Molly Rose. And Kassy had saved Molly Rose from those boys in the park that first night she'd left home. Maybe Molly Rose could do the same for this girl.

'No,' the girl replied.

163

'Going by your accent, I'd say somewhere near Poland?' Molly Rose asked, hoping she was right and hadn't just offended the girl.

'Very good,' the girl said. 'I'm from Warsaw.'

'Ah, the capital,' Molly Rose replied and was glad to see a glimmer of a smile. 'So, how'd you come to be in Glasgow?'

The girl parted her lips to speak. 'It… It's a long story.'

Molly Rose smiled. 'I like long stories. But if you're asking for my gran because you think she's the only one who can help you, then I'm sure I already know why you're here.'

'I was brought here. In the back of a lorry.'

Molly Rose closed her eyes momentarily. 'You were trafficked?'

Zofia's voice quivered. 'Yes.'

*Shit*, Molly Rose thought to herself. That sounded all too familiar.

'Do you know who brought you here?' Molly Rose asked.

The girl nodded.

'Would you be comfortable telling the police about them?'

A look of terror passed over the girl's face and she gripped Molly Rose's hand. 'No. He said that the police wouldn't believe me because he pays them to turn a blind eye to his work. That's why I need to speak to Janey. It's all connected. She needs to know what's going on.'

Molly Rose nodded. It all made sense without her even knowing the full details. 'Can I ask again, how you know me?' she asked calmly.

The girl took a deep breath, but before she could answer, she was cut short by approaching footsteps.

'Molly Rose?' Janey called, her voice full of anger and terror.

Molly Rose looked up to see Janey hobbling towards her, leaning on her crutch. 'It's okay. I'm fine,' she said, trying to calm Janey.

'Kristo said you'd been mugged.'

'Yeah. Well, no, not quite.' She smiled softly at the girl. 'Janey, this is…' She let the sentence linger, hoping it would press the girl to tell them her name.

'Zofia,' she muttered. But the girl only stared up at Janey with wide eyes and a pale face. 'Is it really you?'

Janey stared at the girl, confused and angry. She glanced at Molly Rose as if waiting for an explanation.

'I needed to get Molly Rose's attention. I have something I need to talk to you about. It's about the man who I've run away from.'

Janey's expression hardened but her tone didn't match it. She was concerned. 'Jesus Christ. Where are you from?' She paused, her expression softening as she took in Zofia's frame. Janey was likely thinking the same as Molly Rose. The girl was small; just young and scared.

Janey's voice lowered and it was like she was staring into the girl's soul. 'Did he send you to give us a message or something?'

Molly Rose's eyes darted between the two.

'Like I said, my name is Zofia. I'm sixteen and I was brought here from Poland in the back of a lorry against my will. The man I escaped from has had a lot to say about you. And you.' She turned to look at Molly Rose. 'That's why I had to get your attention.'

Molly Rose held her hand up. 'I know.'

Janey blinked and leaned in. 'Zofia, let's go somewhere safe so you can tell us what you know.'

'It's Leo. Leo Davidson. He said he's going to send Molly Rose away.'

Something in the pit of Molly Rose's stomach began to rise but she swallowed it down. That surname would haunt her for the rest of her life. And it couldn't just be a coincidence that this man had the same surname as her ex; the same person who'd tried to traffic her too.

'I'm sorry, did you say Davidson?' Molly Rose asked.

Zofia nodded.

'Oh my God,' Molly Rose said, looking at Janey with a feeling of terror creeping over her. 'I think that's a relation of Dean Davidson, my ex.'

# Chapter 33

'Christ Al-fucking-mighty,' Janey said. 'Are you sure?'

Molly Rose nodded. 'It has to be. It can't just be a coincidence. How many Davidsons would there be in that business who aren't related?'

'I think Dean was Leo's son,' Zofia interjected.

'How can you be sure about that?' Janey asked.

'I heard him talking to another man about his son, Dean – about his murder. The other man was responsible for Dean's death and Leo knew about it.'

Janey shook her head in disbelief as Zofia told her story. Once Zofia had finished telling them about her ordeal, the fact that she'd been brought to the country against her will with her sister, forced into sleeping with men to line the pockets of other men, how she'd been forced to beg and train new recruits in order to avoid participating in these parties, how she'd had no other choice but to kill that man and run away in the hope that she'd be able to stay hidden made Janey want to put her fist through the front windscreen. The poor girl had been through hell and it pained Janey just to look into her eyes and see the terror in them.

She'd known for years that trafficking was a problem in Glasgow. It had even been suggested to her that it was a side of the business she should look into because of how lucrative it could be. Think of the money she'd

167

make on top of her already huge income from drug and gun deals. But being a survivor of sexual assault herself, it wasn't something that she'd ever considered. It had been a flat-out no. She could never live with herself, being responsible for that kind of abuse of power. Janey wasn't that kind of person and no one she associated herself with was either. It was likely why the organisation had been able to go on without Janey being notified. Her team wouldn't bring anything about it to her because Kristo may have told her men not to, due to what had happened in her personal life.

Saying no to that side of business hadn't been enough though. Now that she was faced with a survivor, and the state she was in, Janey felt guilty for not trying to put a stop to it completely.

The poor girl. She had no idea where her sister was now and Leo had been using her as bait to keep Zofia in line. The bastard.

They all sat in silence in the car, Zofia in the back beside Molly Rose, Kristo in the driver's seat next to Janey. There was a deafening silence aside from the thrum of the engine as Kristo drove them all back to Janey's house.

Glancing up at the mirror in the sun visor, Janey could see the pain and anguish in Zofia's face; and Molly Rose's, for that matter. Yet again, two young girls, pulled into a world they'd never fully understand, but they'd been subjected to the horrors it could lead to.

'Are you okay?' Molly Rose whispered to Zofia, before placing a hand over hers.

The girl didn't answer; she was away in her own world, somewhere far from the events which she'd been subjected to since arriving in the UK.

'Zofia, would you be able to identify Leo Davidson if you were to see him again?' Janey asked.

Zofia shot her a look of amusement. 'Are you kidding? I could identify that bastard with my eyes shut.'

Janey watched as an attempt at humour raised the corners of Zofia's mouth. The humour almost reached Janey, but she let it go. This wasn't by any means a funny situation. So much was going on in Glasgow, in the city she had run for decades. Not one tiny detail ever got past her and now it seemed that Leo Davidson had been operating under her nose and she'd been none the wiser. What had happened to her? Since Orla had died, her mind just wasn't with it. In fact, even before that. Had she been subconsciously checking out? Ready to give it all up and slowly beginning to pack up her desk, so to speak? It would seem that even before Orla's death, Leo and his disgusting associates were trying to push Janey out, stepping on her toes, and she had been moving back without even realising it. The idea angered her to the point where her jaw clenched, knuckles whitened under the grip of her crutch.

Kristo pulled into the driveway at Janey's house and, when the engine went dead, the silence in the car rang in Janey's ears so loudly that she had to get out of the car quickly. With silence came more intrusive thoughts.

Kristo opened the doors for Molly Rose and Zofia as Janey leaned on her crutch and limped towards the front door. She shut off the alarm and let everyone into the house. Zofia walked through the entrance hall slowly and looked around her with wide eyes.

'I'm sorry,' she said, bringing her eyes to meet Janey's. 'I'm sorry for doing what he told me to do and making you feel like you were in danger.'

'We are in danger.' Janey gave a tight-lipped smile. 'But you've nothing to apologise for, Zofia. You're a child and a scared one at that. You'd do anything to keep yourself safe from him and if doing what he told you achieved that to some degree, then I understand.'

Zofia shuffled awkwardly on the spot and sighed. 'I can't believe this is my life now.'

'Was,' Molly Rose interrupted before glancing at Janey. 'She doesn't have to go back to that, does she? Not now that she's told us his plan?'

'Absolutely not. Now that we know the kind of person this Davidson character is, and that he is trying to get hold of you, Molly Rose, then Zofia will be under Hallahan protection now,' Janey replied, smiling softly, all the while thinking about watching Leo Davidson meeting his maker. 'And this Marek you told us about, he's Leo's boss?'

Zofia nodded. 'He's the one I met first, back in Poland in that warehouse. He's scarier than Leo. *Much* scarier.'

Molly Rose squeezed Zofia's hand and Janey felt her heart ache for the girls. How these monsters slept at night wasn't something she ever wanted to comprehend.

'Janey?' Kristo said, interrupting the silence. 'I've put a call out to the team, they want a description, a photo if possible?'

Zofia shook her head. 'I don't have one.'

'We'll get one, Kristo. The bastard won't be hard to find even if he doesn't have a face,' Janey said. 'He thinks he's in charge of this city now. It's about time he realises he's not and never will be.'

'Ha,' Molly Rose laughed humourlessly. 'When she's finished with him, he definitely won't have a face.'

Janey raised an eyebrow at how callous it sounded. But Molly Rose was right, and she seemed to have taken on her own hardened attitude towards these men who kept trying to hurt her and her family. Staying safe from vengeful men seemed to be the norm for them these days.

Zofia laughed awkwardly and looked down at the floor. 'Thank you for being so kind to me. You've no idea how terrified I really am. Leo, he killed my friend and if I didn't get away, I'd be dead right now too.'

'Do you know what happened to your friend?' Molly Rose asked, jolting Janey from her thoughts. Janey wondered if it was a good idea to get this young, traumatised girl to open up about something that could stir up so many more distressing memories.

Zofia shook her head. 'I don't know for sure. I just ran after killing that man myself.'

'You did what you had to do,' Molly Rose said. 'But you're safe now and no matter what happens, you'll never need to go back to that life. Janey will sort it. Won't you, Janey?'

Janey nodded and gave a reassuring smile. 'Of course.'

Something inside Janey stirred angrily. Everything was falling apart and now she was protecting a young girl from another country from some man who wanted to kill them all. These men, these monsters, taking girls from Janey's city and bringing girls from a foreign land for their own gain. No, it wasn't going to go on for much longer. Janey had had enough. Leo and Marek weren't going to get away with this any more. She needed to get rid and make sure the girls in their possession, in both Glasgow and Poland, were saved from a life of sexual abuse.

Death would come. But it wouldn't be a Hallahan who died. Not this time.

'Kristo,' Janey said, clearing her throat. 'I want extra security at the hospital. I want a camera set up at Ciaran and Sinead's bedsides and connected to our feeds. Can you do that?'

Kristo nodded. 'Of course. I can also set up so that they're connected to the police on our payroll too?'

Janey considered this. 'Yes, but if they're sent an alarm, no arrests are to be made. Just defuse the situation and contact me immediately.' She paused as a thought entered her mind. Tapping her finger on her bottom lip, she said, 'In fact, I want them moved.'

Kristo's brow furrowed. 'Moved?'

'Yes. There's a private hospital not that far from here. I'll make a call, offer cash up front.'

Kristo hesitated. 'I'm not sure that's how it works, Janey.'

Janey shot him a look of contempt. 'That's how it's going to work. Especially if the price is right. That's how private healthcare responds quickly: an injection of cash and suddenly you're treated like royalty.'

Janey lifted her phone from her pocket, looked up the number of the hospital she had in mind and made the call. If she had to inject every last penny she owned, she'd make sure Ciaran and Sinead were safe.

## Chapter 34

Staring up at the hospital building, Cheryl wondered how long it would take for Janey Hallahan to insert security outside the hospital room of her nearest and dearest. It was likely she'd already done it by now, which would make it difficult for Cheryl to get anywhere near Ciaran.

The sound of sirens approaching made her look in the rear-view mirror as an ambulance came up behind her, the sound of the siren piercing through her ears. It passed by on her right and was followed closely by a black 4x4.

Glancing down at her phone, Cheryl looked at her son's face. Leo had never cared about him, not in the way a dad should. He'd never wanted kids, he'd only lied to her about having a big family once they were married to lure her in; she knew that now. Dean's arrival had happened quickly but when she'd found out she was pregnant she'd been captivated about how life would be with a son. His childhood and all he'd achieve, his career, his future family and her grandchildren.

All Dean had done his entire life was try to make Leo want to be around him. When Dean had been old enough, Leo had sucked him into the underworld. Dean had viewed this as a breakthrough. Finally, he and his dad would bond, they'd work together and that time spent would make Leo *want* Dean around in ways other than on a work basis. Of course, Cheryl had always known that wasn't the case. Leo viewed Dean as another cog in the machine; another pay cheque. After years of being married to Leo, she'd come to realise that he wasn't the type to care about other people's feelings. He only cared about himself. That was obvious, considering how cruel he'd been to her as a wife, and Dean as a son.

Cheryl hated herself for not pulling Dean away; for not leaving all those years ago. Leo had made it impossible, using Dean as the bait to bring her back. Threatening to have him taken from her; that he had the power to do so.

Her phone rang in her hand and she saw Leo's number flash across the screen. She reluctantly answered.

'Hey,' she said.

'I have something to tell you about the Hallahans,' Leo said.

Cheryl sat forward and looked out the window towards the hospital building. The ambulance hadn't stopped off at the front like they usually did.

'The surviving daughter, Sinead; she's in the hospital. Drug overdose.'

Cheryl raised an eyebrow. 'And how do you know about it?'

'Because I organised the overdose.'

The Hallahans weren't Leo's responsibility. He was supposed to be dealing with Marek. So why had he gone over her head with this one? And why had he been so brazen to tell her? 'Another failed attempt, Leo? A failed attempt on a Hallahan yet again and you aren't even supposed to be focusing your energy on them. You're in charge of your old boss, remember?'

She heard him scoff lightly. 'It's only a failure if she pulls through,' he said, ignoring her comment. 'She *could* end up a vegetable.'

Cheryl rolled her eyes. 'I don't want vegetables, Leo. I want death. But do me a favour, stop standing on my fucking toes. Keep to your end of the deal and we'll get on a lot better. Once that's through your head, call me back.' She ended the call and chucked the phone onto the passenger seat. 'Fucking idiot,' she said in hushed tones.

Cheryl looked up at the hospital again as she was about to get out of the car; it was time Ciaran Hallahan's life support was switched off. She opened the door, stepped out of the car and placed her feet firmly on the concrete. She took a breath. This was it. The moment Ciaran would pay for all the sins of the Hallahan family. At least Sinead was in the same place as Ciaran. She could deal with them both. Maybe Leo had done her a favour, after all.

*But what if you get caught?* A voice filtered through.

Cheryl really didn't give a shit if she got caught. She'd suffered so much loss, nothing else that happened from now on could be worse.

She took her first step towards the building. Then another. And another. As she stood to the left of the main entrance, something made her freeze. A voice. That strong Northern Irish accent. It was Janey.

Cheryl slid around the side of the concrete pillar and held her breath. As much as she knew Janey could show up at any moment, the very fact that she was stood just a few feet away still caught her off guard. What would she say if Janey saw her? Would Cheryl be able to conjure up a quick yet believable lie?

And then, as if all the fear and concern had simply fallen away from her, Cheryl stepped out from behind the pillar and walked in Janey's direction. Where better to hide than in plain sight?

Janey hadn't seen her. Instead, she was focused on the door, walking into the hospital. It struck Cheryl, the look of concern on Janey's face. She was frightened for her family's safety. Usually strong, seemingly unscathed even after what she'd dealt with recently. But now, Cheryl saw fear radiating from Janey. Good, she thought. It was about time someone else felt the aches and the terror like she did.

'Cheryl?' a voice etched with surprise called. It wasn't Janey. It was Molly Rose.

Smile, she told herself. Smile and lie.

'Cheryl?' Molly Rose said as she now stood in front of her. The words made Janey look back.

Cheryl waved and gave a gentle smile. 'Hi, Janey.'

Janey frowned. 'What are you doing here?'

'Ill family member that no one else will take responsibility for,' Cheryl lied easily. Janey seemed to buy it as she nodded. Either that or her head was somewhere else. Most likely the latter. 'How're things?' Cheryl asked.

'I don't have time to stop and chat, Cheryl. I'm on a schedule here,' Janey replied, glancing down at her watch. And then, as if from nowhere, that man was by Janey's side. But he wasn't alone. Another girl, around the same age as Molly Rose, was stood next to him. No, not next to him; slightly behind him. She looked into Cheryl's eyes for a brief moment and then looked away.

'Oh, sorry,' Cheryl said. 'I won't keep you.'

Janey gave a tight-lipped smile. 'You're okay? No one odd hanging around?'

Cheryl thought about Leo and the photo and shook her head. No one odd, she thought. Just my arsehole husband. 'Not that I've noticed. But I'll keep my eyes open.'

Janey said a quick goodbye and as she hobbled into the hospital, leaning on her stick, the man, Kristo, Molly Rose and the other girl followed closely. Molly Rose gave a wave as she walked by Kristo's side. He was there, protecting them, Cheryl thought. She bet he wasn't alone either. There would be others around, watching from other areas of the hospital grounds.

Cheryl watched as the family and their minder disappeared into the hospital building and wondered who the other girl was. She hadn't uttered a word but there had been something about her that Cheryl had noticed, although she couldn't quite put her finger on what it was.

Turning, she headed back to her car.

Well then, that was today's plan scuppered. Another day in a coma for Ciaran. She'd be doing him a kindness, killing him. If she ever got to him, that was.

# Chapter 35

Zofia couldn't say for sure that she understood what was going on. One minute, she was stood inside Janey Hallahan's house, being told that she was under Janey's protection and that she would be safe, the next she was in a car, speeding through the city towards the hospital so that Janey could be with her husband and daughter while they were moved for security reasons. Her own chaos had been intertwined with this woman's and she couldn't really pinpoint the moment it had happened. This woman seemed to know how to get things done. She'd taken Zofia at face value, and she supposed that part of the reason was to do with Molly Rose and the fact that Leo was after her, ready to ship her off to Poland. She couldn't believe there was already a past connection there with Davidson and Molly Rose. Like father like son, by the sounds of it.

Just being in Janey's presence gave Zofia a sense of worth, that her word meant something, and Zofia knew she could trust the Hallahans. She hadn't felt safe ever since she'd been forced into the back of the lorry and she'd struggle to trust anyone ever again after what Szymon did to her. But now, after being able to get to Janey and tell her about Leo, she felt safe. Safer than before, at least.

'Are you okay?' Molly Rose asked as they sat outside a hospital room. Kristo was stood at the door, making sure he could see them as Janey was inside apparently signing paperwork.

Zofia shrugged. 'Honestly? I don't know.'

Molly Rose gave her a smile. 'Yeah, I know that feeling well. But you got away like I did.'

Zofia smiled back and said, 'That woman, the one outside. Who was she?'

'An employee at a beauty salon my gran owns. She's the manager.'

Zofia narrowed her eyes. Something about her had stopped her in her tracks.

'Why?' Molly Rose asked.

'There was something very familiar about her,' Zofia replied. 'But I don't know what. You know like when you get déjà vu, and you feel like you've done something before, or been to a place?'

Molly Rose frowned and said, 'Yes.'

'I got that feeling when I saw her face. I don't know, maybe I'm going crazy,' Zofia scoffed. 'It wouldn't be so shocking considering the shit I've dealt with since I got here.'

She could feel Molly Rose's eyes on her.

'I'm sorry,' Molly Rose said softly. 'I can't begin to imagine how you're feeling. But if it helps, I do know what it's like to be held against your will. I've done bad things to save myself and the people I care about...' Molly Rose's voice trailed off and Zofia detected a crack of emotion.

It seemed there was more to Molly Rose than Zofia first thought. She hadn't volunteered much about her own past other than small snippets, saying that she was able to relate to Zofia's situation a little.

'Are you okay?' Zofia asked, noticing that Molly Rose was wiping at her face with the back of her hand.

'I'm fine,' Molly Rose replied, although Zofia knew it wasn't true. By the look on her face, she could tell Molly Rose wasn't fine at all.

'Yeah, I cry when I'm fine too, sometimes,' Zofia said. Her attempt at light humour raised the corners of Molly Rose's mouth but the smile didn't last and it certainly didn't reach her eyes.

'I don't like to talk about the stuff that happened to me. I worry it will open up a black hole inside and I won't be able to close it again.'

Zofia bit the inside of her lip. 'Similar to what has happened to me?'

Molly Rose looked down at her hands, which were clasped together tightly and resting on her lap. 'Yeah, sort of. Although I think you've been through much worse. I was never actually trafficked. You were.'

'Still, it's a horrible set of circumstances.'

'Not really, Zofia. My mum stopped Dean without even realising it. I'll be forever grateful to her for that. And then she died. It wasn't the most peaceful way for her to go, either.'

'I'm sorry,' Zofia said and decided not to probe Molly Rose any more. She didn't want to upset her.

Zofia noticed as Kristo's hand fell onto Molly Rose's shoulder, and when they both looked up at him he was shaking his head in a light gesture of warning. Whatever *had* happened to Molly Rose's mum, it wasn't something that Kristo wanted her to discuss.

Molly Rose's sadness seemed to dissipate quickly then and, all of a sudden, Janey was out of the room and on the move. Molly Rose and Zofia followed her and then they were in a hospital room. A man was lying in a bed, hooked up to a machine, and Janey looked pained.

'Hi, sweetheart,' Janey whispered into his ear. 'You're being moved to a private hospital.'

Zofia frowned, and then nurses and doctors were ushering them all out of the room and things got busy and fast.

'What's going on?' Zofia asked as chaos seemed to unfold around them.

'My gran's husband is being moved. And so is my auntie,' Molly Rose replied, pulling Zofia out of the way as doctors and nurses moved around them.

'Right now?'

'Yes, right now. They're not safe here,' Kristo said without looking at her. 'Not now that we know what this Leo Davidson has planned for Molly Rose, it's likely he won't stop until the people who can protect her aren't in the picture any more.'

Kristo eyed her warily and Zofia held his gaze.

'Why are you looking at me like that?'

'I'm beginning to wonder if Leo Davidson has planted *you.*'

Zofia's eyes widened with shock and Molly Rose gasped.

'Kristo, don't be so fucking ridiculous,' Molly Rose scoffed.

'Is it ridiculous? I mean, she's here, right in the midst of things. Ciaran and Sinead are being moved. Who's to say she isn't feeding back to him?'

Molly Rose frowned, causing deep lines to appear between her eyebrows. 'And *how* would she be doing that?'

'A wire?' Janey said. They all turned to see her stood behind them.

Molly Rose stared at Zofia and Zofia hoped that, out of the three of them, she'd see the situation for what it was. As much as Zofia had put her trust in Janey, it seemed that perhaps she didn't trust Zofia as much.

'*Are* you wearing a wire?' Molly Rose's tone was sarcastic and she heard a humour to it.

'No,' Zofia said, lifting her top and spinning around slowly.

'See?' Molly Rose pointed at Zofia's torso and then opened her hands, palms facing upwards. 'Do you need to do a bloody cavity search too?'

Janey closed her eyes and Kristo's expression remained neutral but both said nothing.

'Jesus *fuck*,' Molly Rose hissed. 'The poor girl has been through Christ knows what and you're accusing her of this? And was *I* a plant for Charlie at the time? Did you consider that? Fuck sake, Kristo.'

'Molly Rose,' Janey started but Molly Rose shot her a look.

'No, don't even try to come up with an excuse. She's a *trafficked* girl the same age as me. If Dean had got to me the way Leo got to Zofia, I would be in fucking Poland right now. Or fuck knows where else they'd have moved me to. Who knows, I might even be dead by now. Wouldn't you have wanted someone like you in *my* corner, fighting for my safety and my freedom?'

Zofia fell into stunned silence. It was the first time anyone had advocated for her in this country. She was so overwhelmed with gratitude that tears pooled in her eyes.

Janey's expression hardened and then she said, 'We'll discuss this later.'

Zofia watched as disgust darkened Molly Rose's face while Janey disappeared down the corridor, with Kristo at her back.

'No, we won't,' Molly Rose called after her. 'Jesus Christ, Janey. Leo is Dean's dad. And you think Zofia's in cahoots with a Davidson? If you agree with Kristo, I'm not willing to discuss anything with you. You're supposed to be the protective adult here. In the eyes of the law, we're both still classed as children and you're fucking accusing her of that shit?'

Nurses and doctors looked at her with confusion, but continued on with their work. Zofia looked at Molly Rose as she watched Janey and Kristo disappear around the corner at the end of the corridor.

'I'm so sorry you were tarred with the same brush as the man who brought you here,' Molly Rose said. 'I don't know what he was thinking and for Janey to question it too – urgh,' she growled. 'It boils my piss.'

Zofia didn't quite understand the last phrase, but she knew Molly Rose was angry. She sighed and looked down at the floor. 'It's okay. I get it. I understand that your gran and that man, Kristo, don't trust anyone who's an outsider.'

'Technically, Kristo's an outsider too. He's not blood. He's just an employee. For all we know, he could be working against Janey,' Molly Rose replied.

Zofia raised her eyes from the floor and regarded Molly Rose curiously. 'Do you really believe that?'

Molly Rose rolled her eyes. 'No, of course I don't. But it's a good point to make. Look, it doesn't matter what they think. *I* trust you, Zofia. I believe you because I was almost in your position. I've been in some horrific situations and it's all about survival. Janey and Kristo will realise how stupid it was to suggest what they did and they'll come around. But until then, you stay by my side. I'll help you through this because we're the same.'

Zofia couldn't get her head around how lucky she'd been to find Molly Rose. Of all the people who she thought could help her, she'd never have imagined it would be a teenager and certainly not the granddaughter of a gangster. 'Why are you being so kind to me?'

'Because, when I left home and was in my darkest place, I needed a friend and was lucky to find someone who looked after me.'

Molly Rose's eyes became distant as her thoughts took her elsewhere.

'You did?'

'Yeah. Her name was Kassy. She was my best friend.'

'Where is she now?'

Molly Rose inhaled deeply. 'She was murdered by the man who kidnapped me. It's my fault, really. If she hadn't become my friend, she'd still be alive.'

'I'm sure that's not true. These men, they do what they want, when they want, with no consideration for others,' Zofia replied. They were quiet for a few moments, each reflecting on their lives and the paths which had led them to one another. Then Zofia said, 'Leo needs to die. It's the only way we'll ever be free from him.'

'And it will happen. Janey will make sure of that. But that doesn't mean we won't die in the process. We need to be ready for that, Zofia.'

The words were brutal, but she knew Molly Rose was right.

# Chapter 36

'Hello?' Janey answered the phone.

'Janey, it's James.'

It took a moment for Janey to compute who James was and then, as if her brain kicked into gear, she realised it was DI James Pearson.

'How are you?' Janey asked.

'Just checking in with you. How's Ciaran?'

'Much the same,' Janey replied, deciding to leave out the fact that she was having both Ciaran and Sinead moved to a private hospital. 'I'm hoping for the best.'

'I am too, Janey. Ciaran is a good mate of mine. I'm sorry you're going through this. I was actually calling to let you know that I've got someone following up on some CCTV footage. It might not come to much, but I just wanted to let you know.'

Janey nodded, only half focusing on what James was saying due to what was unfolding in front of her. 'Thank you.'

'We'll catch the bastards, Janey. We will. I won't stop until I find out who did this to you both.'

Feeling thankful, Janey ended the call and slid the phone back into her pocket.

She stood behind the hospital and stared into both private ambulances as her daughter and husband were loaded into them. It needed to be done quickly. Efficiently. Janey needed them away from the NHS hospital and into the private one, with little to no one knowing about it.

'Don't look so worried,' Kristo said. 'They're going to the right place. You've done the right thing.'

'I know,' Janey said as she met eyes with her daughter. 'Would you travel with Ciaran? I want to be with Sinead right now. She's awake, aware of what's happening and I want to reassure her as much as possible. Take Molly Rose and Zofia with you.'

'They won't be allowed to come in the ambulance with us. It'll be too crowded,' Kristo replied.

Shit. Now she had a decision to make. She wasn't going to leave Molly Rose behind on her own. And as much as what Kristo had said about Zofia had brought its concerns to the forefront of Janey's mind, she wasn't going to leave Zofia behind either.

'You take the girls in the car then, follow Ciaran's ambulance. I'll meet you at the private facility. Do not let them out of your sight.'

Kristo nodded and Janey turned when she heard footsteps approaching.

'Before you say anything, I'm still really angry with you both,' Molly Rose said, holding up her hand. 'But I know how much danger we're all in and I'm not about to get us killed because I let my pride get in the way.'

Janey couldn't stop the amusement raising the corners of her mouth. Molly Rose was by far the most 'Hallahan' of the entire family; other than herself, of course.

'So.' She shrugged. 'What's the plan?'

'You and Zofia will travel in the car with Kristo to the hospital. I'm going with Sinead.'

Molly Rose glanced into Ciaran's ambulance and frowned. 'You're not going with Ciaran?'

'No. He's unaware of what's going on. But Sinead is and I want to be with her.'

Molly Rose's eyes darted from Ciaran to Sinead and a look of guilt flashed across her face. 'Can I speak to her before she goes?'

Janey turned back to the ambulance and told Molly Rose to wait. She spoke quietly to the paramedic and then looked back. 'Come on.'

Molly Rose climbed into the ambulance and sat down next to Sinead. Janey decided to give them some privacy. It was a moment she thought they needed to have on their own.

Janey caught Zofia's eye then. She looked lost as she stood there awkwardly while the family she wasn't part of made arrangements. She was a small-framed girl; looked very vulnerable. Suddenly, she felt guilty for believing that Zofia would be capable of spying for the likes of Leo Davidson. Even if it had been the case, there would be no way she'd have been able to keep up the pretence for so long.

'Zofia?' Janey said. The girl looked up at her and waited for Janey to continue. 'I'm sorry about before. You didn't deserve to have the finger pointed at you. I know Molly Rose and if she trusts you, then she trusts her gut and that's all I can ask for.'

Zofia nodded slowly. 'Thank you.'

'Are you okay?'

Janey could see the desperation on Zofia's face. 'No. But Molly Rose said you'll all look after me. So I know I will be, eventually.'

Janey raised her chin slightly and glanced back at Molly Rose. That girl, she thought. Only sixteen years old with a very old head on her shoulders. No wonder, after everything she'd encountered over the last few months.

'She's right,' Janey said. And she meant it. She'd make sure they were all going to be okay.

—

'Hey you,' Sinead said as Molly Rose sat down next to her. 'How are you?'

Molly Rose stared at Sinead with tears in her eyes but Sinead detected a hint of anger.

'Was it you?' Molly Rose asked. 'Did you do this to yourself, I mean?'

Sinead shook her head. 'No.' She seemed affronted. Then she sighed, as though accepting it was a thought likely to cross the minds of those closest to her after all the years she'd been in active addiction. 'I didn't do this to myself, for once.'

'Then who did?'

Sinead sighed and then winced as the shooting pains in her stomach slowly intensified once more. 'I don't know. But someone wanted to kill me.'

Molly Rose rolled her eyes. 'It seems someone always wants to kill one of us.'

Sinead forced a smile. She wasn't sure Molly Rose understood the severity of the situation. Glancing outside, she saw Janey stood next to a girl she didn't recognise. 'Who is that?'

Molly Rose followed her gaze and said, 'Oh, that's Zofia.'

Sinead raised an eyebrow. 'And she is…?'

Molly Rose turned back and smiled. 'It's complicated. But basically, she's me, if Dean had managed to follow through on his plan to traffic me out the country.'

Sinead puffed out her cheeks. 'Why is she with Janey?'

Molly Rose hesitated. 'It's a long story.'

'Give me the short version then,' Sinead said. She wanted to know what Molly Rose was being dragged into. As much as she knew Janey would take care of her niece, she was still very much aware of Janey's background and what that might mean for Molly Rose's safety now that Orla wasn't around to protect her daughter. Sinead felt a sense of responsibility now for her niece, although she wasn't exactly in a position to preach that.

'Okay. She was on the run from the man who was selling her for sex. He told her to find me and help get me to him so he could send me to Poland like Dean, his *son*, had planned. Wants to kill the rest of the family to stop me from being protected. So she came to us to tell us about his plan and to ask for help.'

Sinead's eyes widened. 'Fuck,' she whispered.

'Yep. Fuck *indeed*.'

Silence grew between them and then, Sinead knew that she had to ask the question. 'Molly Rose, are you safe with Janey?'

Molly Rose laughed. 'Did you not hear what I just said? I don't think *anyone* is safe with Janey. Not that it's her fault. This lunatic is just out to finish what his son couldn't, so he's attacking us all. I'm sorry I got you dragged into this. I mean, it would make sense that this Leo guy is involved in what happened to you as well as Ciaran.'

Sinead shook her head. 'Look, I don't mean to bad-mouth Janey, I don't. She's my blood and even after everything that has happened, I'm still glad she came back into my life. But she's a *crime boss*, Molly Rose; a gangster. And you're smack bang in the middle of her world. I don't think your mum would be best pleased with what's going on.'

Molly Rose pulled her lips into a thin line. 'She wasn't ever happy with anything though. So no change there.' It was an attempt at light humour, but neither of them smiled.

'You know what I mean. If I was in a fit state, I'd have you with me. You know that, don't you?'

'Sinead, please don't treat me like a child. I know exactly what Janey is all about. I'm the one who's been in the thick of it. I might be young but I'm not stupid.'

Sinead reached out her hand and held Molly Rose in her grip. 'I know. But you're also vulnerable right now and—'

'Ah.' Molly Rose held up her other hand, gesturing for silence. '*Was* vulnerable. I'm not now.'

'Come on, Molly Rose. You don't fool me. I can see in your eyes that you're terrified.'

'Yes, I am terrified, Sinead. But I'm also determined. And that outweighs the fear. I am not going to let these people get me. And neither is Janey. As much as we're a target, Janey has a full team of people watching us at all times. Leo isn't going to get anywhere near me. I promise you, I'm fine.'

Sinead felt the steadiness of her hand. What had happened with her mum had hardened her to a point which wasn't healthy. Sinead had been in her fair share of dark places; the darkest. But Molly Rose had experienced more than enough in her young years. The trauma of it all was bound to hit her at some point and if it happened in amongst the shitshow she was currently in the middle of, she wouldn't be able to cope with it.

'Being with Janey is the safest place to be, weirdly. Trust me.'

Sinead regarded her niece through narrowed eyes. 'I wish I'd been like you as a teenager. If I had, maybe I wouldn't be so fucked up now.'

Molly Rose gave a gentle smile. 'I'm not like I am now because of me though. People had their parts to play. Charlie for one. But Kassy too. If it wasn't for her, I'd have died before Charlie got his hands on me. I wasn't cut out for the streets, but Kassy made it easier.'

The mere mention of Kassy's name changed Molly Rose's expression. She looked sad.

'Right, it's all getting a bit heavy,' Sinead said, deciding not to push her niece further on it all. 'Come here.'

She hugged her tightly and never wanted to let go. Now that her sister was gone, it should have fallen to Sinead to take care of Molly Rose. But given she'd been a drug addict most of her life, which resulted in her having nothing to call her own and a mother who'd only just come back into her life and paid for her rehabilitation, she didn't have a leg to stand on.

'Look out for yourself, you hear me?' Sinead said. In her head, she'd already made her plan. Once she was better, back on her feet, she was going to make sure that Molly Rose didn't end up going down the same road as Janey. Living life right in the middle of Glasgow's underbelly wasn't the right thing for any young person. And it would be something Orla would be turning in her grave for. She'd built up a legitimate business, had become a successful and independent woman; she'd never have wanted this for Molly Rose.

'Always do,' Molly Rose said, squeezing Sinead a little tighter. 'Get better. Fast. Please.'

'I'll do my best. I promise. I don't ever want to be reliant on that shit ever again.'

'Good.'

Molly Rose pulled away and smiled. Sinead looked into her eyes and the second the thought came into her head, it was leaving her mouth.

'Once I'm out of here and clean again, I want us to start a new life together.'

Molly Rose frowned. 'Really?'

'Yeah. I mean, we could go to America, see your dad.' And then Sinead frowned. America wouldn't let her in given her criminal record.

Another look of sadness flashed in Molly Rose's eyes. 'My dad isn't interested in me, why else would he have left?'

'He should have taken you with him,' Sinead said.

'I didn't want to go. He abandoned me because he couldn't handle the grief of what happened to Mum. But he thought I'd be able to handle it all on my own? Nah, I'm not interested in him. He hasn't even phoned me since he got there.'

Sinead's heart ached for her niece. 'Okay then, not America. What about Spain? Italy? New Zealand? There're a million places we can go together.'

Molly Rose raised an eyebrow. 'Yeah, maybe. Just get better first. I need you.'

The sound of someone clearing their throat made them both let go and look in the direction of the sound.

'How are you doing?' Janey said, standing with one hand on her stick and the other in her pocket. Sinead regarded her. Her birth mother. Crime boss.

'I've been better, but then again I've been much worse.'

Janey simply smiled. It was like she didn't know what to say. 'I'll look after her, you know. I won't let Orla down.'

Sinead raised an eyebrow. 'It's not Orla you'd be letting down if you didn't do right by Molly Rose.'

The unspoken words sat between them heavily and Sinead hoped that Janey would keep her word.

'I told Sinead about what's happening,' Molly Rose interrupted.

'Right,' Janey replied, keeping her eyes on Sinead. 'I may not have been able to save Orla. But I won't fail in saving the rest of you. That I can assure you of.'

Sinead blinked and then said, 'Okay.' But she knew that was an assurance no one could make.

'We need to get going,' the paramedic said.

'Okay,' Janey replied. 'Molly Rose, you go with Zofia and Kristo like planned. I'll travel to the hospital with Sinead and—'

'Erm,' Sinead interrupted. 'I'll be fine on my own.'

Janey frowned. 'You don't want me to come with you?'

A wave of guilt washed over Sinead then. Her whole life, she'd wondered about Janey. Who she was; what had happened to her. Now, she was stood right in front of her and Sinead couldn't trust her.

'No offence, but it seems that you're the catalyst in all the bad stuff that's gone on these last few months. If someone wants you dead, I'm not sure I want you near me.'

Janey's expression turned from confusion to shock. 'It's better we all stay together.'

'Yeah, that's the same idea terrorists have,' Sinead replied in a sour tone. 'Like I said, I'm fine on my own.'

The shock dissolved from Janey's face and was replaced with a sadness that Sinead tried hard not to let penetrate. She didn't want to feel sorry for Janey. She didn't much deserve pity. Not after everything she'd caused.

Sinead nodded to one of the paramedics, who ushered Janey and Molly Rose away from the doors before closing them, leaving Sinead inside.

# Chapter 37

'And you think they're being moved somewhere else?' Leo's voice slithered down the phone, making Cheryl feel uneasy. He wanted to take control of this task, she knew that. But she'd be damned if she allowed him to after all his fuck-ups.

Cheryl watched from the back of the car park which faced on to the ambulance bays. Both Sinead and Ciaran were being moved. Janey, Molly Rose, the other girl and Kristo were all there. It was likely there were more of Janey's security team watching from other parts of the hospital grounds. Janey wasn't taking any chances.

'I'm watching it all unfold now. She's spooked and she's moving them.'

'Where to?' Leo asked.

Should she tell him? Would he stand back and allow Cheryl to do what she wanted, given that he'd already gone over her head with trying to take out Sinead? 'I've no idea. But they're in private ambulances, and someone like Janey will have the money for immediate private care, so I'd assume it will be a private hospital.'

Leo was silent for a moment and, for a brief second, Cheryl thought she could hear a woman in the background.

'Where are you?' Cheryl asked suspiciously.

'Work,' Leo replied bluntly.

A chuckle almost escaped her. A woman in the background in Leo's life usually led to Cheryl believing he was up to no good. That had been his life the entire time she'd known him. 'Who's that laughing?'

Leo sighed in annoyance. 'The woman who owns the house. Jesus, Cheryl, who the hell do you think it is? A hooker?'

Cheryl raised an eyebrow. Yeah, she thought. Because he wasn't getting any from her. That side of their relationship was dead. Had been for years.

'So,' Leo continued. 'I assume you're going to follow them, find out which hospital they're going to?'

'Obviously,' Cheryl replied through gritted teeth. What did he think she was going to do?

'I'm not sure that's a good idea,' Leo replied. 'You've been seen. You spoke to Janey herself. If she finds out you followed her, she'll start to piece things together.'

She hesitated. As much as it pained her to even think it, Leo was right. 'I want to find out where she's taking them, Leo. I need to know.'

'Fine,' he replied. 'Just do it unseen. If you really want to end that family, then you need to work smart. Janey can't see you coming, although I think that ship might have sailed.'

'What do you mean?'

'Like I said, you've been seen. You spoke to Janey. If anything happens to Sinead or Ciaran now, she'll piece it all together. She's not been running the city for decades on one brain cell, Cheryl. She's a clever woman. Don't underestimate her.'

Before Cheryl could say anything else, Leo had already ended the call. She threw her phone onto the passenger seat and sighed heavily. He had no belief that she could do this. None whatsoever and it angered her. A mother grieving the death of her murdered son was more dangerous than any fucking gangster. It was time people saw what Cheryl was capable of, including Leo.

Staring back at the ambulances, she saw them pull out of the bays and head along the road.

Dean's voice crept into her mind. He was telling her what she needed to do. *Finish it. Finish* them. *They deserve to suffer. All of them.*

With Kristo driving the 4x4, the girls in the back and Janey in the first ambulance, Cheryl eased the car out of the car park and carefully followed a few car lengths behind.

# Chapter 38

Leo Davidson let the phone slip out of his hand as the girl finished him off. She was good. And free, which made it even better.

He pushed her off and spat out the words, 'Piss off, I've got shit to get on with.'

The girl didn't look at him as she shuffled out of the room. He looked around the pokey, dark and damp flat. The place was a shithole. But he wasn't going to pay over the odds for accommodation for these people. They were here to do a job, earn him cash and keep his boss on his good side, which was hard to do these days. But if he could get Molly Rose to Poland then Marek could start to trust him again and Leo could be back at the top, and hopefully one day be running Glasgow after the Hallahans were out of the picture.

Leo stood up, pulled up his jeans and left the room. He peered into the living room. One old scruffy-looking sofa sat in the centre, with a tiny TV in the corner. Three girls were on the sofa, three boys on the floor, all staring at the screen.

'Mind and be ready by ten tonight. Half of you are going to a party, the other half are working the city. Do *not* be late,' he said before leaving the flat and locking the door behind him.

It angered him that two were missing. Zofia and Antoni. Zofia, the little shit that she was, had done a runner having murdered a very important client. A fucking *MP*. As much as some of Leo's contacts were paid handsomely to keep potential issues away from the press, something like this couldn't stay hidden for long. Three days had passed. It would be all over the news soon enough. Then, the press would start digging. There was every possibility that the MP's personal devices would show up searches of his interests. Leo would put money on it. The guy had very specific needs. Young; younger than most of Leo's clients had ever expressed a need for. It wasn't always possible for Leo to provide such a thing. The client had been adamant at first, but had finally accepted that younger than fifteen wasn't going to be possible. He'd settled and that was why Leo had decided on Zofia. She was the youngest girl he had. Leo didn't give a shit if the police discovered these things, what he did care about was keeping his own interests safe. If the client hadn't been careful, covered his tracks regarding his whereabouts, it could put the operation at risk of being discovered and it had only just got started again after the Dean situation. That would make Marek a very angry man indeed. And Leo knew what anger did to Marek. Only too well.

Antoni had been taken care of. But Zofia? She could be anywhere; speaking to anyone about where she'd come from. Hopefully he'd instilled enough fear in her to keep her mouth shut.

He pulled his wallet out of his pocket and opened it before sliding the folded picture out from the little hidey-hole at the back. As he glanced down at Molly Rose Hunter's face, he couldn't help but smirk. She was going to wish it had been Dean who'd sent her away. He'd have been kinder. Leo, on the other hand, didn't have a kind bone in his body and it wasn't something he was ashamed of. It was purely in the interests of business.

If Dean had been anything like this, he'd still be alive.

# Chapter 39

'That's him settled in. You can go in and see him now,' the specialist said to Janey. She got up from the seat in the waiting room and followed the specialist through to where Ciaran was.

'How's he doing?'

'We're seeing a little progress. But I'm afraid Ciaran isn't out of the woods yet. Patience is key,' the specialist said.

Janey wanted to punch him. It wasn't like she was a child waiting for Santa to come on Christmas Eve. Her husband was in a fucking coma.

As though he'd read her mind, he quickly added, 'He's in the right place, Mrs Hallahan. You chose well to bring him here.'

'He'll recover?' she asked hopefully, her anger quickly dissipating and, in its place, anxiety about Ciaran's outcome.

'We hope so.'

Janey glanced back at the door of the private room in the hospital and saw Molly Rose standing there. She looked sad, worn out.

'I'll leave you all alone for a while. If you have any more questions, speak to the nurses and they will pass them on,' the specialist said, leaving the room.

'Are you okay?' Molly Rose asked.

Janey put on her best and bravest smile, even though in the pit of her stomach was fear and uncertainty about the outcome of it all. 'Of course.'

Molly Rose raised a suspicious eyebrow.

She was torn. Stay with Ciaran, or take the girls back to the house and wait for Kristo to come up with answers about where Leo Davidson was and finish him off?

'You don't look okay,' Molly Rose replied. 'You look exhausted.'

Janey smiled. 'That's just my age.'

Molly Rose laughed gently and shook her head. 'Here,' she said, holding out a bag. 'I've been down to the little kiosk. Got you a few things if you're going to sit in with Ciaran for a while.'

'Awe, thank you,' Janey replied, taking the bag from her granddaughter. 'If I'm honest, I don't know what to do. Sinead doesn't want me anywhere near her at the moment and Ciaran doesn't even know I'm here.'

Molly Rose bit her bottom lip. 'Sinead will come round. Once she's feeling better.'

Janey puffed out her cheeks and sat down on the chair next to Ciaran's bed. 'I don't know. She was pretty adamant that I'm not safe to be around. Maybe she's right.'

'Well, yeah, you seem to be the catalyst for all of this.' Molly Rose laughed gently. 'But I still don't want to be anywhere else. Sinead wasn't the one who was held captive by a nutter and held at knifepoint on a bridge. That was me. And you were the one who saved me.'

'Yeah, and I was also the one who got you kidnapped in the first place,' Janey replied, pulling a newspaper out of the bag. 'Where's Zofia?'

'She's just outside.'

'Bring her in here, I don't think it's a good idea to be separated, even if it's only by an open door.'

Molly Rose stuck her head out the door and told Zofia to come inside.

Janey glanced down at the newspaper and thumbed through the pages. A large report spread over two pages caught her eye. She scanned the first few lines and took in his face.

### GLASGOW MSP MISSING

MSP for Glasgow, Nigel Richardson, has been reported as missing by his family. Nigel Richardson was last seen by his wife in his private office at home. Police Scotland are working with the family and Scottish government to piece together the MSP's last known movements. It is thought that his electronic diary, which is linked to his parliamentary devices, is being searched to help aid the investigation. He has been missing for three days. The family have asked for their privacy to be respected at this time.

If anyone has any information on Nigel Richardson's whereabouts, please contact Police Scotland.

Janey shook her head and sat the paper on the seat next to her. Zofia entered the room and immediately Janey noticed that her eyes were fixed on the newspaper. Zofia's expression had changed to fear, terror, disbelief.

'What is that?' Zofia asked.

'It's the newspaper,' Janey replied, glancing at Molly Rose, wondering if she had noticed the change in Zofia.

Zofia lifted the paper and gripped it so hard the edges folded in on themselves.

'What's wrong?' Molly Rose asked, staring down at the page with Zofia.

'That's *him*,' Zofia whispered in terror.

'Who?' Janey asked, getting to her feet.

'The man I killed before I escaped from Leo,' she whispered even quieter this time. Janey watched as tears pooled in her eyes.

'What the fuck?' Molly Rose said. 'It says this guy's an MSP. Are you sure, Zofia?'

Zofia nodded, all the while her body trembling. 'I'd never forget that face. Those eyes stared into mine as I stabbed him in the neck.'

Janey eyed Molly Rose. This was big. Too big for someone like Zofia to be able to handle.

'Are you saying that this man here is one of Leo Davidson's clients?'

'Was,' Zofia corrected. 'He's dead now.'

'But the paper says he's missing,' Molly Rose replied. 'Are you absolutely sure, Zofia?'

'She looks sure enough to me.' Janey exhaled slowly and took the paper from Zofia. 'Sit down. Take a breath. Wait here.'

She left the girls in the room with Ciaran and stepped outside where Kristo was waiting. He looked at her, noticed the paper in her hand and frowned.

'What is it?'

She held the report out to Kristo and allowed him to read it. He glanced up at her, confused.

'This man isn't missing. He's dead,' she whispered.

'I don't follow.'

'Zofia said he's the one she killed before escaping Leo. He was one of Leo Davidson's clients.'

Kristo closed his eyes and when he opened them, he was staring up at the ceiling. 'Scumbags.'

'Yeah. But I'm thinking that this could be the downfall of Leo Davidson. You know what it's like, MSPs using personal devices for work and work devices for personal matters. The system is fucked. Mind that guy a couple years ago who was caught watching porn on his phone *in* parliament? I'll bet this Nigel Richardson's hard drives and histories will show up major red flags. It could be proof he's a fucking nonce.'

'Yes, but will they show a clear link to Leo Davidson?' Kristo asked. 'I'll bet no. Leo strikes me as the type not to leave any traces.'

'Maybe not. But what about this Nigel character? He might not be as careful,' Janey said.

'Yeah, it's possible,' Kristo replied with a nod.

'He's missing though. What's the likelihood that Leo's had his body disposed of because he doesn't want there to be a link to him no matter how careful either of them have been? If we can gather evidence that Nigel is a client of Leo's, that there is some kind of trace, we can get the police on our payroll to deal with him.'

Kristo frowned. 'You don't want to deal with this yourself?'

Janey sighed and shook her head. 'I mean, I could. But I'm getting tired of all this, Kristo. And I need to be here for Ciaran. Running around doing police work isn't something I have time for.'

'You think we'll find anything? I mean, with technology, everything can be wiped.'

Janey thought about this. Kristo might be right. 'But can it be wiped forever? Data doesn't always fully disappear, does it? We need to find out where Leo was holding Zofia; where the killing took place. I've had my back turned for long enough. I should have this bastard in front of me by now and I don't.'

Kristo nodded. 'Okay. What do you want me to do?'

'When we have a location, you go with a team and do some investigating of your own. Maybe stake the place out.'

'Leo's never going to do business again at the scene of a crime, Janey.'

Janey raised an eyebrow. 'Yes, I know that. But any information about the place is better than nothing. Maybe find out who owns the property, depending on if it's a residential or a business let. That way, we can deliver information to those on our payroll.'

'Okay,' Kristo said. 'If you get me an address, I'll follow it up.'

Janey nodded, took the paper back and went back into Ciaran's room. Molly Rose was comforting Zofia, who was crying into her hands.

'Zofia,' Janey said, sitting down next to her. 'I know this is difficult for you, but can you remember where you escaped from? Did you happen to get an address?'

Zofia sat up and shook her head while wiping the tears away. 'Leo never told us where we were going. I only ever got to see the place once we arrived. We travelled in the back of a van. But I do remember a river. That big one that runs through the city.'

'The Clyde,' Molly Rose said.

'Yes, that one,' Zofia agreed.

Janey smiled and took a breath. 'Okay. Have a think about that night. As scary as it was and still is, I need you to think about where you were. Distinctive buildings, road signs; anything that can help?'

Zofia went quiet and closed her eyes. 'I remember getting out of the van and looking through the gap between the apartments, seeing a big industrial site on the other side of the river. It looked like there were Portakabins all stacked on top of each other.'

'That's really helpful, Zofia,' Janey said encouragingly. 'Do you remember anything else?'

Zofia was quiet for a moment. 'It's all such a blur. And it was kind of dark. I tried to look for a street name but I couldn't see anything and I was rushed inside quickly so he could start his party.'

'It's okay,' Janey said. 'Take your time. We're going to get him for this, Zofia. But we need your help.'

A look of horror crossed Zofia's face. 'But if you do that, I'll be arrested for murder.'

Janey placed a hand over Zofia's. 'No, my lovely girl. No one will *ever* know what you did. I promise you that.'

# Chapter 40

Zofia gripped the hair on top of her head as if it would help her to think. 'I don't know the city well. I'm sorry, but I would only know it if I saw it again.'

'It's okay,' Molly Rose said. 'Just try to work your way backwards. Why don't you start from when we met.'

Zofia looked up at Molly Rose and scoffed. 'The day I tried to steal from you? I'd rather not remember that.' And that had just been three days ago. Had it? Or maybe it was less. Her days seemed to have converged into one big mess.

'You did it for a good reason,' Molly Rose said. 'You're in the best place you could be, given the circumstances.'

Zofia blinked away fresh tears. Molly Rose was right, even though there was nowhere on the planet she'd ever be safe so long as Leo Davidson was still alive.

Janey didn't pressure Zofia by asking again, but she could feel her eyes on her. She wanted, *needed*, to know where Zofia had committed murder.

She took a steadying breath and thought back to the day she'd got on the train. What was the name of the station again? She searched her memory. Port something. No, that wasn't it. Par... par...

'Partick,' Zofia said, the name finally coming to her as she envisioned the name of the station above her as she rushed away from the woman she'd pickpocketed. 'I got on a train at a station called Partick.'

'Good,' Janey said. 'I wondered if you'd say that given your description of the apartment buildings and what you saw beyond. Well done. It was only a few days ago, Zofia. Try to remember more.'

Three days, she recalled again. Not that it felt like that to Zofia. It felt like five minutes ago. She could still hear the gurgling sound coming from the man's throat as she'd dug the scissors in. It had been her only hope of getting out of a terrible situation.

'I pickpocketed someone. A woman. I took her purse. I needed money. I needed to get away from that part of the city as quickly as I could. If Leo found me, he'd have killed me. Or worse...' She didn't want to think about what worse could have been.

'Or worse?' Molly Rose asked.

'Trust me, being dead would have been the better option after what I did to his best client.'

'Hmm, I *bet* he was his best client. The ones of high-power status always are in these situations. It's a good thing that MSP is dead,' Janey said. 'If he wasn't, he'd be wishing he was when all this shit comes out about him. Because it will.'

Zofia couldn't get Nigel Richardson's face out of her head. To look at his picture in the paper, it would be hard to imagine him the way Zofia knew him. Even though she'd only known him for a matter of seconds.

'I think I was too quick to act,' Zofia said.

'Why?' Janey asked.

'Well, he hadn't actually done anything to me, had he?'

'I *dread* to think what you'd have been subjected to if you'd gone into that room without those scissors,

Zofia. You're feeling remorseful and questioning your decision because you're a good person. Do you think Nigel Richardson would have questioned his decision to sexually assault you? Or any other young person, for that matter?' Janey said.

Zofia shook her head. No, she thought. He wouldn't. If he had questioned the way he was, he wouldn't have behaved that way in the first place.

'So,' Molly Rose interrupted. 'You were at Partick train station. What happened before that?'

Zofia cleared her throat and remembered her night, and explained how she'd slept under a van on a side street somewhere near the building she'd escaped from.

'I say sleep,' Zofia explained. 'But I don't think I slept properly. Maybe just closed my eyes every now and then. But I was on high alert, waiting for Leo to grab my ankles and pull me out from underneath and drag me back to the flat I was living in. I use that word loosely. Anyway, I remember running faster than I'd ever run before. There was a pedestrian tunnel, under a motorway. I ran through that not long after escaping the apartment.'

Janey pulled her phone out of her pocket and began tapping on the screen. Zofia felt Molly Rose's hand envelop her own and she was grateful to have a friend. Someone who knew what it felt like to be terrified for your life.

'Is this it?' Janey asked. 'Is this the building?'

Zofia surveyed the images from Google Earth on the screen. She narrowed her eyes. The tallest part of the building in the image showed a large balcony which wrapped it. Then, the shape of the apartment complex sloped down to the right, with multiple smaller balconies all over the front of it.

'No.' Zofia shook her head. 'That's not it. But the river behind it? That's what I saw between the two buildings.'

Janey nodded and began swiping her finger across the screen. With each image, Zofia's heart pounded.

'That one,' Zofia said, her heart feeling like it was in her throat. She stared at the tall, blue-cladded building. 'It was that one. Top floor penthouse. It had a lift which opened up onto the apartment's own floor, but there was a stairwell to the right. I remember running down the stairs as fast as I could with the scissors still in my hand.'

Janey nodded. 'Glasgow Harbour. I suspected that when you said about the river and the industrial site on the opposite side.' Sighing as though relieved to finally be getting somewhere, Janey said, 'Good, good. We know where this happened now. We can work from there.'

Zofia frowned. 'But what will you do? Leo will have had the place cleared by now. There will be no trace of murder, no trace of the sordid things that went on there.'

'No trace, you're right. But there is one thing we need to get rid of,' Janey said.

Zofia continued to stare at her. 'What?'

'The scissors, Zofia. Where did you put the scissors? They'll have Richardson's DNA all over them. And yours. We need to find those.'

Zofia hadn't thought about that. 'I threw them away.'

'Where?'

'I... I don't know.'

'Think,' Molly Rose said. 'Can you remember the last time you had them?'

Closing her eyes again, Zofia imagined the scissors in her hand. The cold steel against her skin. The wetness of the blood causing them to slip.

'I left them behind. Under the van. I think.'

'Jesus,' Janey said, closing her eyes and massaging her temples. 'Zofia, you need to take us to where that van was parked. And we need to go now.'

'But—'

'No buts, Zofia. If the police are looking for Richardson, and somehow those scissors come into their possession, there won't be much I can do to help you. We need to get those scissors off the street. If they're still there, that is.'

*Shit*, Zofia thought. Now that she was free from Leo, she wanted to be free from all of it. Going to prison in a foreign country for murdering an MSP wasn't what she'd class as freedom. Fresh tears welled and she started to cry.

'I want to go home.'

'Zofia,' Janey said, her voice full of sympathy. 'I know you're scared, that's a very natural way to feel.'

'Can't you just send me home on a plane or something?'

Zofia watched as Janey's eyes welled up too. 'Not right away. We need to get you a new passport. But yes, we'll get you home, Zofia. I promise. However, we need to deal with this first to get you home safely.'

The only other sound in the room was that of the machines that Ciaran was hooked up to. In that moment, Zofia wished she was in a coma. Or at least somewhere that she didn't know what was happening to her.

'This is all such a nightmare,' Molly Rose said. 'But we'll get through it.'

Zofia sighed loudly and said, 'Okay. Well, we'd better go and find those scissors then.'

–

The side street where Zofia had chosen to hide under the van that night was deserted of people now. In the middle of the day, she found that strange but was glad of it.

She sat in the back of Kristo's car and watched as Kristo and a few other men she didn't know scaled the kerbs on the street. It didn't take long for one of them to notice that the scissors were sitting beside a drain where the van was still parked. Or at least, it looked like it hadn't moved. Maybe it had.

One of the men picked up the scissors with a gloved hand and wrapped them in a cloth before sliding them into a bag.

'I can't believe they've been sat there all this time and no one has noticed them,' Molly Rose said as she looked out of the window.

'It's a bit of a quiet street by the looks of it. No residential buildings; mostly garages. The road is only linked to the harbour via the pedestrian path under the expressway,' Janey said. 'There's no CCTV on this street either. It's really fortunate this is where you left them, actually.'

'What will happen to them?' Zofia asked Janey.

'They'll be cleaned, sterilised and then disposed of somewhere far from anywhere you could ever be linked to. You don't have to worry about them coming back to haunt you. Nigel Richardson's death will never be linked to you. If I can get it linked to anyone, it'll be Leo fucking Davidson.'

## Chapter 41

Leo opened the door to his flat and was startled to see Marek standing in front of him. Thankfully, Cheryl wasn't home.

'What are you doing here?' Leo gasped.

Marek pushed past him and strode into the house like he owned the place. 'Now, now. That's no way to speak to your boss. Especially not when said boss is very fucking angry.'

Leo quickly closed the door and felt a surge of dread in the pit of his stomach. An angry Marek was never good. Taking a steadying breath, Leo turned to face his boss and as calmly as possible asked, 'What's wrong?'

Marek raised an eyebrow and gave Leo a cold, hard stare. 'Oh, plenty. But let's start with Nigel *fucking* Richardson.'

Leo's stomach flipped again as each curse from Marek indicated just how angry he was. 'What about him?'

Marek's eyes darted from side to side as though looking for the answer somewhere else. He raised his arms and shouted, 'What the hell do you mean, what about him? I was informed about what happened to him. Throat cut and bled out all over the place. And of course, it wasn't you to tell me.'

'I handled it,' Leo replied, knowing that wasn't going to be enough for Marek.

Marek wagged a finger. 'No, no, Leo. You did not handle it, because if you did, he'd still be alive and we wouldn't have a situation on our hands. His wife has reported him *missing*. It's in the papers, it's on the TV. It's fucking everywhere. Apparently, the police are looking through all his personal and work devices. Contacts, diaries, appointment schedules. All of it.'

Leo closed his eyes and prayed to any God that would hear him to help pull him out of this nightmare.

Marek pulled his phone out of his jacket pocket and tapped on the screen before thrusting it into Leo's hand.

Leo stared down at the screen. The Sky News app was open with a video ready to play. Leo tapped on the play icon and watched in horror.

*'Nigel is a hard-working, loving and caring man. He wouldn't just walk away from his family or his work like this without a trace. He takes his responsibilities as an MSP, a husband and father very seriously. Something has happened to him and we just want him home.'*

The caption at the bottom of the screen named the woman speaking as Mrs Iris Richardson: Nigel Richardson's wife.

Another voice came now. A police officer, stating that they were taking the disappearance of the local politician very seriously and that his personal and work devices were being searched and monitored for any activity which could lead them to finding Nigel.

'You hear that, Leo?' Marek's loud voice made Leo jump a little. 'This investigation is going to ruin my organisation. And again, you seem to be right in the middle of it. I had to put a halt to things after the police were keeping an eye on Dean. And now this? We need Nigel

Richardson's devices in our possession as soon as possible. Have you cleaned up the crime scene?'

Leo balled his fist by his side and tried to take a breath. It wouldn't do any good to punch Marek, as much as it would make him feel better for a moment or two.

'Are you serious?' Leo asked, failing to hide the annoyance from his expression. 'I told you I'd handled it. Yes, the apartment is clean. Everyone who was there has been dealt with too. They've all been sternly warned to keep their mouths shut. I've covered all tracks.'

'Including the devices?' Marek pushed again.

*Lie*, Leo told himself. 'It's being sorted.'

'And the body? What happened with that?'

'It's at the bottom of the Clyde. Don't worry, we weighed him down. He's not resurfacing.'

'And what about the little bitch that sliced his throat?' Marek asked through gritted teeth. 'Did you deal with her?'

'She bolted before I knew what had happened.'

Marek eyed him warily. 'Are you telling me that little bitch is out there, roaming free?'

Marek's eyes darkened and, for a moment, Leo thought his time was up. If Marek thought that Leo was yet again a threat to his organisation, he could make the decision to take him out.

Leo held his hands up. 'I got her back,' he lied. 'It's sorted.'

Marek narrowed his eyes and took a step closer to Leo; so close that Leo could feel Marek's breath on his face. Then, he felt the gun pressing into his stomach and he froze.

'And you're sure she didn't tell anyone about what happened? Like the police?'

'If she was going to do that, I'd have had a visit from them by now. She thinks we run the police, Marek. She's not going to grass.' He breathed deeply, trying not to think about the pain that would come if Marek pulled the trigger and plunged a bullet into his intestines.

'Get those devices. I don't care how you have to do it. Get them and dispose of them. Make sure there is no way Nigel's interests link back to us. And do it fucking fast.'

Leo nodded. 'I will.'

'And you better pray they don't find Richardson's body. Or that young boy you had to get rid of too. That's not a link we want them to make. Now, while we're here, I want an update. Other than everything we have just discussed, how are things going? The new recruits, they're doing as told?'

'Yeah, all fine. Other than the obvious.'

'Nothing to report?'

Leo shook his head. 'No. All going as well as it should. Happy clients, money rolling in. And after what happened the other night, the rest of them will be too terrified to step out of line.'

'Good. And Molly Rose Hunter?'

'I'm on it. It won't be long before she's overseas.'

'Good. You've got forty-eight hours. I have a shipment leaving Greenock dock in two days. I want Molly Rose on that boat. If you don't pull through for me, Leo, Cheryl will take her place. And you'll be dead. Got me?'

*Two days? Two fucking days?* Leo felt the nausea intensify at the idea of Marek's threat. He would do it. Leo had no doubt.

'Understood.'

Marek pulled the gun away from Leo, slid it into his jacket, took the phone from Leo's hand and said, '*Always* good to see you, Leo. Remember, forty-eight hours.'

Marek walked out of the door and Leo closed his eyes.

He'd lied to Marek; let him down yet again. Promised he'd sort the devices, promised that he'd finish the job Dean started. But he was nowhere near achieving any of it. The police would already have the devices in their possession. And as much as Leo had claimed that the police were in his pocket, that very much wasn't the case.

'I'm fucked,' he said. '*Royally* fucked.'

# Chapter 42

The private hospital looked more like a fancy hotel than a hospital. *Must be nice to have that amount of money*, Cheryl thought as she stared up at the building.

What was she even doing there? What did she think she was going to do? It wasn't like she'd be able to get her hands on Molly Rose with Janey and Kristo so close by. And the idea that she'd be able to get anywhere near Ciaran was a joke. It was becoming apparent to Cheryl that the Hallahans were coming close to being untouchable. But no one was, not really. Even with a security ring around them. Look at JFK, John Lennon. She laughed at the thought. She wasn't a sniper or a deranged fan. She was a grieving, tortured mother, hell-bent on revenge. She straightened her shoulders and blinked away the thoughts.

And then, she saw him leave. Kristo. He'd left the hospital unattended. Left Janey and Molly Rose *unattended*. How stupid of him. And how convenient for her. But how would she explain her presence here? There would be no way to explain it. It would only alert Janey's high paranoia about who was out to get her and her family. It occurred to her then that she hadn't thought about a method. How exactly was she going to kill Molly Rose? It would have to be quick for Cheryl's sake. She'd never killed anyone in her life and she still second-guessed herself if she could actually go through with it. Molly

Rose was a young, vulnerable teenager who'd just lost her mother herself. She'd been through trauma too. But if Cheryl didn't go through with this, there would be no justice for Dean.

A short rap on the window made her jump and she turned to see Kristo staring at her. She'd been so wrapped up in her own thoughts that she hadn't seen him approach the car.

*Fuckfuckfuck!*

Painting on her best smile, Cheryl lowered the window and waited for Kristo to speak. He didn't, making things all the more difficult; awkward.

'Can I help you?' she said, drawing the words out slowly to make it seem like he was the one in the wrong place.

'I was going to ask you the same thing,' Kristo said. 'What are you doing here?'

*Think, think, think.*

The sign above the main entrance to the hospital – which read *Hotel, Spa and Medical Centre* – switched on a light in her head.

'I have an appointment at the spa. I'm early, so decided to wait here,' Cheryl said, trying to keep her voice smooth. 'You know what it's like since Covid, they never want too many people in a place at once.' She could have kicked herself for saying it. That was bullshit now. Covid, it seemed, in society no longer existed.

Kristo raised an eyebrow and glanced across at the building. He was silent for a moment and turned back with a suspicious look on his face.

'I don't believe you,' he finally said after a long silence.

She felt her eyes widen in genuine shock at his brash-ness. 'I beg your pardon?'

'I said I don't believe you. I don't believe that you're here because you have a spa appointment.'

'Look at the sign above the entrance. It clearly states there's a spa here.' Cheryl's heart began to pump harder in her chest as adrenaline coursed through her. She protested too much. 'Why *wouldn't* you believe me?'

Kristo frowned, as though he was trying to think of the words. 'I find it oddly coincidental that you are here, today of all days.'

Cheryl raised a smile and replied, 'Why? What is today?'

Kristo hesitated. Was he second-guessing himself?

'You know what today is. You know what this place is.' He leaned in, bared his teeth ever so slightly and lowered his voice. 'You were at the Queen Elizabeth hospital earlier, claiming to be visiting an ill family member. And now, you're here. It doesn't add up. I'm watching you, Cheryl. We all are.'

Cheryl let out a shaky laugh. 'What exactly are you watching? And who's *we*?'

'If you've nothing to hide, then you don't have to find out.'

He was suspicious of her. And he'd raise those concerns with Janey. Then they would start digging. Janey had resources. It wouldn't take long for Janey to work it all out.

Kristo stood up, tapped the roof of the car so loudly that it made her jump before he strode off.

Cheryl let out a long breath and put the window back up. She waited for Kristo to be completely out of sight before she pulled out of the car park and left the hospital grounds.

# Chapter 43

Leaning her head back against the wall behind the chair she was sitting on, Zofia watched as Molly Rose paced the floor, slow and steady.

'This place has a spa in it,' Molly Rose said.

'No,' Janey replied, as if she already knew what was about to come out of Molly Rose's mouth next.

'But we'd be in the same building. We could ask Sinead to join us, it would be so good for her.'

'I said no,' Janey replied a little more firmly.

Molly Rose tutted loudly. 'You know you can't stop me.'

Zofia glanced at Janey whose expression didn't change. Her eyes were firmly fixed on Ciaran, who hadn't moved since they'd all arrived in the room.

'No, I can't stop you. But I would hope you wouldn't be so stupid to go off on your own, when you're at major risk of being captured. *Again.*'

Molly Rose rolled her eyes. 'Statistically, that probably won't happen.'

'Yeah, well, *statistically*, most people's lives aren't at threat because of unhinged men like Charlie Hallahan and Leo Davidson; not to mention others Leo might be working with whom yet we don't know about. Now, I said no and I hope you'll understand why and respect it.'

Molly Rose hesitated and Zofia wondered why she was pushing to get away so much. Zofia didn't want to move away from Janey's side.

'But I have the tracker on my phone,' Molly Rose said.

'I said no. Now leave it alone,' Janey replied.

Hurried footsteps along the corridor made Janey rise and Kristo burst through the door. A look of concern darkened his eyes.

'I think we have a problem,' he said.

'Christ, another one?' Molly Rose said, rolling her eyes and falling back onto a chair next to Zofia, tutting loudly.

'What is it?' Janey asked, ignoring Molly Rose's comment.

'Your employee at the salon, Cheryl? There's something off about her.'

Zofia tried to picture the woman. She'd been outside the first hospital earlier in the day.

'What do you mean, off?'

'She's outside. In her car,' Kristo said. 'She must have followed us here from the Queen Elizabeth hospital earlier.'

Zofia looked at Janey's face; she frowned, causing a deep line to appear between her brows.

'Why would she do that?' Janey asked.

Kristo took a long, deep breath and shook his head. 'I'm not sure. But I doubt it's a coincidence. She was outside the Queen Elizabeth earlier when you went to sign the discharge papers for the transfer. And now she's here.'

'Did you talk to her?'

Kristo nodded. 'She said she had an appointment at the spa at the other end of the hospital. I told her I didn't believe her. I said I was watching her. When I walked away, she drove out of the car park. She never went into the spa. Janey, I hate to say this, but I think Cheryl might have had something to do with the crash; with Sinead's overdose.'

Janey glanced down at Ciaran and then at Molly Rose. '*Cheryl?*'

Molly Rose shrugged and said in a low, sombre tone, 'Anything's possible with this family.'

While the three were talking, Zofia searched her mind. Seeing the woman outside the hospital had sparked something in Zofia's mind. There was a familiarity about her that Zofia hadn't been able to place.

'Surely not Cheryl,' Janey said, but there was a hesitation in her voice. Uncertainty. 'Why else would she be here, if she wasn't using the spa?'

'To see where you were moving Ciaran and Sinead to? So she can finish them off?' Kristo said bluntly.

'You think she's involved with Davidson? One of his employees? I mean, having someone like her on payroll would certainly throw people off his scent. She's not who you'd expect to have working for—'

'Oh my God,' Zofia said loudly as she stood up. That was it. 'She's Leo Davidson's wife. Or girlfriend.'

Janey's frown deepened. 'How do you know that?'

Zofia recalled the day she saw the image on Leo's phone, when she'd been made to give a talk to the newer recruits about what would be expected of them at their first 'event'. A family picture. Three people. Leo, a woman and a younger man. His son, she'd presumed. The one who was dead.

'I saw a picture of her on his phone once. When she was at the hospital earlier, before Ciaran and Sinead were moved, I thought I recognised her. But I brushed it off because, well, why *would* I recognise her? I hadn't met a woman her age since I arrived here.'

'Are you sure?' Molly Rose asked.

Zofia nodded. 'Yes… It was her I saw in the picture.'

Janey placed her hands on the end of Ciaran's bed and took some breaths. Everyone was silent. Zofia felt awkward and scared.

'It makes sense now,' Janey said. 'All of it. She applied for the job at the salon to get close to us. She's been feeding Leo information. Been following us and going back to him. She's clever; she didn't use her married name in the application; she would've known it would be a red flag.'

'What are you going to do?' Molly Rose asked.

Zofia watched as Janey looked up at Kristo. 'Bring her to me.'

'Where?'

Janey was quiet for a moment while she thought and Zofia watched her, wondering what was going through her mind.

'The holiday park out at Carbeth. It's peaceful out there. Quiet. Known for having been a crime scene in a murder investigation. It'll put the frighteners on her; hopefully make her talk,' Janey replied.

'A murder investigation?' Molly Rose gasped.

Janey shook her head. 'Not because of me, sweetheart. And it's since been dealt with. Long before you came along.'

'Oh, that's all right then,' Molly Rose replied sarcastically.

Kristo folded his arms over his chest. 'When?'

'Now. I'll take the girls back to the house. There's security. You'll be safe.' She eyed them both. 'If I can get

Cheryl to talk, tell me where Leo Davidson is and what he's planning, then maybe we can end this tonight.'

'I thought you said you didn't want me out of your sight?' Molly Rose teased.

Janey closed her eyes in despair. This girl, she used sarcasm at all the wrong times. 'Yes, well, right now, it's a necessary evil. Like I said, there will be security there to protect you.' She handed a set of bulky house keys to Molly Rose, who took them with a sigh.

Zofia felt sick. There was a lot more Janey needed to know now that Leo's wife was involved.

'Janey. There's something I need to tell you about Leo.'

Their eyes met and the nausea intensified.

'About what he does; the kind of person he really is. I think it might help get Cheryl onside.'

A thought entered her mind then: what if Cheryl already knew what Leo was like? What if she was okay with it all, or turned a blind eye to it? Surely a woman wouldn't accept that her husband was a perverted, sick and twisted individual?

Zofia started to tell Janey all about Leo and what she'd witnessed or heard from the others back at the flat where Leo had kept them all. Just saying the words made the memories flood back and she felt sick to her stomach.

## Chapter 44

Janey stared at a tearful Zofia and tried to contain her anger and disgust at what she'd just heard. Not that she could say she was surprised by it all. A person like Leo had opportunistic tendencies and he had acted upon them.

'What an utter scumbag,' Janey whispered as she comforted Zofia. 'Thank you for telling me, sweetheart. I know that must have been difficult.'

'I'm one of the lucky ones,' Zofia sniffed and wiped away her tears. 'I wasn't ever forced to… you know. But he used to make me do things like massage him. That wasn't as bad as being made to hand-pick others for him. Even the boys…' Her voice trailed off. 'He's sick in the head, Janey.'

Janey nodded. 'I know. And we'll put a stop to it. There's no place for him here.'

Molly Rose scoffed and said, 'A guy like him? Even the devil would kick him out.'

'The only way to stop his kind is to put a bullet in the skull.'

Why hadn't she known about this operation, given her status in the underworld? Had Leo gone to ground? Kept his work quiet? He must have, given that Janey knew about other criminal ventures which went on in the city. There was still no more information from DI James Pearson, other than what he'd already told her on the phone about the CCTV. Maybe it had been a dead end. Was he struggling to find things out about the operation too? Was Leo Davidson cleverer than anyone gave him credit for?

Janey was beginning to question herself. After the last few months, she felt a little out of touch with everything. Perhaps it was beginning to show? Maybe her rivals were taking advantage of the fact that Janey Hallahan was going through a tough time.

'Cheryl is our lifeline here,' Janey said, pushing the thoughts out of her head. 'We need to get her onside.'

'What if she already knows about this? What if she's in on it all?' Zofia asked. 'You know, like his secretary behind the scenes or something?'

'Then we'll worry about that if it comes up. Although, don't you think you'd have recognised her quicker if she was in on it?'

Zofia bit her bottom lip. 'I don't know. Possibly.'

Janey wondered how she was going to put all this to Cheryl and how she'd react. It was just words; there was no evidence other than Zofia's account of what Leo had been doing. If Cheryl didn't want to listen, or chose not to believe, then Janey would have to go to plan B. She'd put Janey's family in danger and if she could turn her against her husband, it would all but make up for what she'd done. If not, then Janey would have to take her own form of revenge. It was something she hoped wouldn't happen.

'If Zofia is right, and Cheryl is in a relationship, albeit married or otherwise, with Leo Davidson, then that means she could be Dean's mum,' Molly Rose said. 'I mean, I'm convinced Leo is Dean's dad, so yeah, Cheryl being his mum is a strong, if not the only, possibility.'

*Christ almighty*, Janey thought, balling her fists together. She really was losing her touch. She was usually so much smarter than this. Why hadn't she done proper security checks on Cheryl? After what had happened with Orla, her head hadn't been fully focused. She'd basically left the door open for the Davidsons to wander in and plant their feet firmly under her desk.

Pulling out her phone, Janey called Cheryl, but not before holding her finger to her lips and asking the girls to keep quiet.

'Cheryl?' Janey said, but quickly continued before she could let Cheryl answer. 'Hi, I wondered if you were free for a catch-up? Just to chat about the salon.'

Cheryl faltered a little before saying yes, she was free.

'Great. I'll pick you up at your flat in, what, an hour?'

Janey ended the call and gripped the phone tightly in her hand.

'She agreed to meet you?' Kristo said, standing by the door.

Janey glanced back at Ciaran and felt a sadness creep over her. She should be by his bedside the entire way through his coma. Instead, she was fighting yet another war to protect her family.

'I didn't give her much of a choice.'

# Chapter 45

Molly Rose fell onto the sofa with a thump and Zofia sat down softly next to her. She was getting fed up with all this running around, trying to find out who their next assassin might be. She sighed loudly and glanced up at the ceiling.

'You really think that we're safe here without Janey and Kristo?' Zofia asked.

Molly Rose shrugged. 'Who the hell knows, Zofia? It seems like no matter what she's doing or where she is, there's always a fucking drama. But there are armed men standing outside the house. So if anyone tries to get in, they'll end up getting shot. Well, except you. You managed to get past to leave that box.'

Zofia's expression didn't change. 'I'm small. Can hide in small spaces if I have to stay out of sight, which was what Leo told me to do. I'm sorry I had to leave that horrible box for you to find. I'm sorry I did the things he told me to. I was terrified he'd make me go to one of those parties if I didn't. In the end, I had to anyway.'

'You don't have to say sorry, Zofia. I get it.'

Zofia rested her head back on the sofa next to Molly Rose and let out a long breath. 'I just want to go home.'

'Least you have a home to go back to,' Molly Rose replied.

'This is your home, is it not?'

Molly Rose scoffed, 'Only because I don't have anywhere else to go. My mum's dead, my dad's fucked off to America and my auntie is in hospital. I'm effectively an orphan. It was easier living on the street and in the park with Kassy.'

Molly Rose felt Zofia's eyes burn into her.

'I doubt that's true.'

'Doubt all you want. Before Charlie took Kassy away from me, I was happy. Well, happy-*ish*, if you take away the fact that my bed was a bench or a shop doorway. But I had a friend who looked after me. She never judged, never questioned me or treated me like I was a clueless teenager. She was just… Kassy. Now, I'm being dragged around the city while my gran looks for yet more psychos trying to kill us. Sometimes I wish…'

Molly Rose stopped, not sure if she should allow the words to escape her lips.

'You wish what?' Zofia asked.

Molly Rose glanced out of the window as she saw one of the security men walk past.

'I wish Charlie had done what he'd always threatened and killed me. That way, I'd be at peace.'

Zofia stared at her, her eyes curiously searching her face. 'You really wish you were dead?'

'It's the only certain thing in life, isn't it? Death, I mean. It's like, I don't want to be dead, but it would be better than waiting for some psycho trafficker to come and send me away to another country and Christ knows what would happen to me after that. With death, there isn't any anxiety about what's coming next because there is nothing. It's an eternal black abyss. To me, that sounds a lot more peaceful than what we're living right now.'

231

A sadness crossed Zofia's face. 'Do you think I'd be better off dead?'

*Shit*, Molly Rose thought. 'Oh God, sorry. I don't think you'd be better off dead at all.' She took a breath, tried to place her words properly. 'All I meant was that I want a peaceful life. And it seems I can't have that here with all this shit going on. I'm always looking over my shoulder. Always worrying what or who is coming next.'

Zofia blinked. 'You hide it well. Your face, your demeanour doesn't show that's how you're feeling. You seem so strong; so brave.'

'That's just my resting bitch face. I get it from my mum.' Molly Rose smiled. Orla's judgemental expression entered her mind then. She'd always had something to say about, well, anything. Always judging, often negative. Perhaps that was Molly Rose's fault, for getting involved with a boy who could have destroyed her life. Maybe it was Janey's fault for abandoning her babies. Not that Molly Rose saw it that way, after finding out the circumstances surrounding it. 'I used to *hate* that about her. How she'd always have that look; that one eyebrow raised. I could always tell she was thinking how much of a child I was, how I didn't know as much as I thought. Now I miss it more than anything. Sounds stupid, but I'd give anything to have one last argument with her.'

Swallowing hard, Molly Rose refused to allow the images of her mother – as she bled out in Janey's arms – to enter her mind.

She cleared her throat and glanced over at Zofia. 'What about your family? Back home in Poland? Anyone you miss, or don't miss at all?'

Zofia blinked and parted her lips. 'As I explained when we were on our way back to Janey's, I have a sister. Alina.

We were born really close together. She was born in the January and I was born in the November. We were, are, so close. I just hope she's okay.'

'If she's as hardy as you, I'll bet she's fine,' Molly Rose said, trying to inject some hope.

'She's not as brave as me. If she thought trying to escape could get her killed, she'd never even try. If she's not dead, she'll be held up somewhere, being used just like the rest of us. I can't bear to think about it.'

Molly Rose watched the despair in her eyes and couldn't help but feel sorry for Zofia. 'What about your parents?'

Zofia shook her head and fresh tears pooled. 'My mum, she's in a care home. Early-onset dementia. It came on so rapidly, she became mute. She had no idea who we were after just a few months. It was horrible to watch.'

Molly Rose closed her eyes. 'I'm so sorry, Zofia. Your family are really going through hell right now.'

Zofia shook her head, sadness in her eyes. 'To be honest, it gives me peace to know that she hasn't a clue that we're effectively missing. It would have killed her. And dying from dementia is much kinder than the pain of not knowing what happened to her two girls.'

As sad as it sounded, Molly Rose couldn't help but agree with Zofia. If blissful ignorance during her ordeal with Charlie had been an option, she'd have taken it without hesitation. 'What about your dad?'

'He left when I was born. Couldn't handle it all apparently, having two children under the age of one. I've never known him. We don't have any other family. It was just me and Alina. I suppose that's why we were so taken by Krzysztof and Szymon. They made us feel wanted; loved.

I'll bet their boss gave them a finder's fee for getting us so quickly.'

'We can help find Alina.' The words were out of Molly Rose's mouth before she could stop them. She wasn't sure that would be possible. Janey was a gang boss, but she wasn't a magician.

'No,' Zofia said. 'I don't think I'll ever see her again. Now that I've escaped Leo, he'll make sure she suffers because of my betrayal. He always threatened it. Always said that if I stepped out of line, it would be Alina who would be punished.'

Molly Rose took Zofia's hand in hers and gave a gentle squeeze. 'Alina would want you to be free. She wouldn't blame you for getting out. Would you want her to escape even if it meant you were under threat because of it?'

Zofia nodded. 'I'd do anything for my sister.'

'Yeah.' Molly Rose smiled sadly. 'It shows. Janey will help find Alina. She'll do everything she can to bring her back to you.'

The sound of the front door opening made them both look up. A security guard walked in.

'Nothing to worry about, girls,' he said softly. 'Just doing a perimeter check of the house. Carry on as if I wasn't here.'

Molly Rose stared at the gun in his hand and raised an eyebrow. This was her life now. Strange men deployed to keep her safe while Janey tried to stop yet someone else trying to kill them all.

'Any chance you've got a spare one of those?' she said, eyeing the gun. 'You know, just in case.'

The man smiled but didn't respond as he stepped out onto the balcony.

# Chapter 46

Pacing the floor of the empty flat, Cheryl had considered doing a runner. She'd tried to ring Leo so many times after her call with Janey but he wasn't picking up. Janey was on her way to pick Cheryl up to chat about the salon, but Cheryl knew it was nothing to do with that. Kristo had told her that he'd seen her outside the hospital. She was going to grill her about it and what was Cheryl going to say? She could lie. But what would be the point? Janey trusted this man with her life.

She clutched the phone in her hand so tightly it hurt as she peered out of the window and saw a car parked outside. Not the Defender, obviously. That was a write-off after Leo had run her and Ciaran off the road.

Kristo got out of the car and stood by the driver door, clasped his hands together and waited.

He smiled menacingly up at her as she stood by the window. He'd seen her. There was nowhere to run now.

In that moment, Cheryl realised that her plan to take out the Hallahans had come to an end. Janey knew what was going on. It wouldn't be hard to find out. When she thought about it, Cheryl wondered how she'd managed to go so long undetected. Still, she couldn't appear frightened or defeated. Fight or flight was kicking in, and fight was the only option for Cheryl. Dean hadn't had the chance or even the choice to fight for himself.

Cheryl wasn't going to allow the same thing to happen to her.

She grabbed her bag, locked up the flat, headed downstairs and out of the building.

'Glad you could make it,' Kristo said. His tone matched his look. *Smug bastard*, she thought.

'Where's Janey?' Cheryl asked, ignoring his sarcasm.

Just then, the driver-side window lowered and Janey leaned over from the passenger seat. 'Hi,' she said. 'Thanks for coming. I know you must be busy running the salon on your own with everything that's going on in my life right now. It's good to know I have someone I can count on to keep things running smoothly.'

Cheryl stared at her. They were both lying to each other without saying anything at all.

'Where are you taking me, Janey?' Cheryl asked. 'I know he's told you.'

Janey frowned, feigned a confused smile. 'Told me what?'

Silence fell between them and Cheryl narrowed her eyes.

Kristo opened the back door and gestured for Cheryl to get in. She hesitated. Someone could be about to die, and it was highly likely Janey wasn't going to be that someone.

She took a deep breath and got into the back of the car. Janey glanced back, smiled and turned to face the front. Cheryl placed her handbag on her knee and looked down at it. She'd placed a kitchen knife inside before Kristo and Janey had arrived. She had to have some form of protection if things were going to come out.

'That he doesn't trust me,' Cheryl finally replied.

Janey scoffed. 'I don't trust anyone, Cheryl. If you knew what I'd been through in my life you'd understand that.'

Kristo pulled out of the building complex and headed towards Great Western Road. Cheryl took in the grand buildings as the car travelled towards Anniesland. She might never return home.

'Where are we going?' Cheryl asked again, realising that Janey hadn't answered the question.

'Out to one of my business locations. It's beautiful. Really quiet. It'll give us time and peace to talk things over,' Janey replied without turning to look at Cheryl.

'Talk things over?' Cheryl repeated and then Janey's fake smile fell and was replaced by darkness.

'Okay, time to stop pretending on both our parts. I know who you are.'

Cheryl's stomach flipped. Licking her tongue across her teeth, she inhaled deeply and quietly. 'And who am I?'

'You're Leo Davidson's wife. The man whose son tried to arrange for my granddaughter to be trafficked out of the country. The man who, I assume, made an attempt on mine and my husband's life. The man who has left my husband in a coma and the man who somehow managed to almost overdose my daughter on heroin while she was at a rehab facility.' Janey turned then, stared right through Cheryl. 'Does that all sound about right?'

Cheryl knew that Janey had no concrete proof that Leo had anything to do with her and Ciaran being run off the road. She could just be saying all this in an attempt to get Cheryl to admit it all. But then, perhaps she did know for sure. Cheryl couldn't tell.

Kristo pulled up to a red light just outside the Gartnavel hospital and the car came to a standstill. Cheryl tried the handle. It was locked, of course.

'You're not going anywhere until we've had it out, Cheryl. I don't want violence, but I don't want resistance either. You comply, you get to walk away from this. If you don't...'

The words weighed heavily and Cheryl glanced down at her bag. Pull out the knife, slit Kristo's throat, threaten Janey and she could get out. But was she actually capable of such brutality? It had taken her so long to get this close to the Hallahans and she hadn't yet executed her plan to kill Molly Rose. Given the chance, would she ever have done it?

She gripped the zip of the bag, but Janey saw what she was doing.

'Nah-ah,' she said. Cheryl looked up and watched as Janey pointed a gun at her torso. 'Hand it over.'

*Fuck.* There was no way out of this.

'Now,' Janey said softly. 'Like I said, I don't want any violence. But I won't hesitate if you kick off.'

Cheryl picked up the bag and handed it over to Janey, who put it at her feet without looking inside.

'Right. Now we can enjoy the drive out here. And when we get there, I've got something to tell you. Something you *really* need to know.'

Cheryl's brow furrowed and she said, 'Can't you just tell me now, if it's so important?'

Janey shook her head and glanced across at Kristo. 'It's not something someone should hear while sitting in the back of a car.'

The rest of the journey was made in silence, aside from the low hum of music from the radio. Cheryl couldn't make out what was playing because all she could hear was the voice inside her head. It kept telling her to get out now. To run. But she couldn't. Cheryl had no choice but to go along with Janey's plan; whatever that was.

–

Kristo opened the door and Cheryl reluctantly stepped out of the car onto grass. She glanced around, took in her surroundings.

'What is this place?' she asked.

'It's Carbeth Holiday Park,' Janey said, looking up at the towering trees which surrounded them.

Cheryl frowned. 'I didn't have you pegged as the type to own a holiday park.'

Janey smiled. 'That's apparent. You obviously don't know much about me, otherwise you wouldn't be here right now.'

Kristo placed a hand on Cheryl's back and gently guided her towards a small chalet-style building. Once inside, Janey opened a hatch and headed down a set of stairs. Cheryl stopped and glanced back at Kristo.

'Go on,' he said.

'No way, I'm not going down there until you tell me why I'm here.'

Kristo rolled his eyes. 'You already know why you're here, Cheryl. You've been lying to Janey. And she has information that you can't afford not to hear.'

Cheryl peered down the hatch and saw Janey standing at the bottom. She had already taken off her coat.

'Don't just stand up there staring at me. Get down here. The sooner you hear what I'm about to tell you, the better for all of us.'

239

There was something about Janey's expression that sat heavy with Cheryl. It was like she was angry, but it was mixed with something. Empathy.

Staring down the staircase, Cheryl paused. She could be walking to her death before having avenged Dean. Of course, she'd always known the risks of taking on the Hallahan family. But she really didn't want things to end this way. Not yet and not like this.

Taking a breath, Cheryl placed her right foot on the first step and headed down the stairs carefully, taking them slower than necessary. Once at the bottom, they walked along a steel corridor and entered what looked to be a container. Cheryl saw a long table placed in the centre of the clinical-looking room. The space was unbearably bright, lit by industrial-style long bulbs above them.

'Take a seat,' Janey said as she herself sat down, but not at the top of the table like Cheryl had expected.

Cheryl took a seat opposite Janey, and Kristo stood at the door, as though he was guarding it.

'Leo Davidson is your husband, correct?' Janey asked, her hands clasped and resting on the surface of the table.

'You already know he is.'

'Which makes Dean Davidson your son,' Janey replied, and the sound of her son's name on Janey's lips made her want to be sick.

She took a long, deep breath and nodded. 'Yes.'

'I'm sorry about what happened to him.'

She glared at Janey through narrowed eyes and shook her head. 'I doubt that very much.'

'No young person deserves an execution like that.'

Cheryl frowned. She was apologising for what happened to Dean, even though Janey knew that he was involved in the attempted trafficking of her grand-daughter. Was she being nice as a way to lure Cheryl in? To soften her up so that she would think Janey didn't have something dangerous planned for her?

'How long have you been married?' Janey asked, pulling Cheryl back out of her thoughts.

'Too long,' she replied, thinking back to the day she married Leo; and beyond. The memories made her feel so many different emotions. Happy wasn't one of them.

'Too long?' Janey echoed.

'Let's just say that Leo is a shit husband to me, and he was an even shittier dad to Dean.'

'And it's *because* of Dean that you want us all dead?' Janey asked rhetorically.

Cheryl bit the inside of her cheek and closed her eyes briefly. Grief had left her with a bitterness inside her that craved revenge.

'I want justice for my son's murder,' she replied.

Janey narrowed her eyes and sat back on her chair. Staring at Cheryl, she said, 'I get that. I wanted immediate justice for my own daughter.'

'And did you get it?'

Janey looked down at her lap and gave a wry smile. 'Not in the way I'd have liked, but yes, I did.'

'And did it help your grief? How you felt inside?' Cheryl asked. It was a genuine question. She wanted to know if the feelings she had deep inside would ever leave her.

Janey looked up at her and sighed. 'No. It didn't.'

Cheryl's heart was heavy, like someone was holding her down and pushing into her chest. Her breath caught in her throat at the very idea that she would feel the suffocating void of her loss for the rest of her existence.

'Can I ask,' Janey continued, 'why you felt that it was down to me and my family that your son was murdered? It wasn't me, or any of my family, who executed him and dumped his body in a scrapyard. Messy work, I'd say. In my line of work, if you're going to execute someone, you don't leave the evidence behind.'

The blasé manner in which Janey spoke about Dean's death made Cheryl frown in disgust. 'Are you serious?'

Janey nodded.

'If it wasn't for *your* granddaughter,' Cheryl raised her voice and it echoed off the steel walls of the underground room, 'my Dean would still be alive!'

Janey raised an eyebrow. 'Explain that to me.'

The words were on the tip of her tongue, ready to burst out of her. And then, she considered the request. *Explain that to me.*

'What is there to explain?' Cheryl said, lowering her tone.

'Explain *how* it was Molly Rose's fault that Dean died. Was it my granddaughter who executed him? Was it Molly Rose who ordered his death?'

Cheryl gritted her teeth so hard that she heard them crunch in her mouth. 'That's not the point.'

'That's exactly the point. I need to understand *your* way of thinking, Cheryl. I need to know why my husband is lying in hospital in a coma; why my daughter is back at square one with her recovery from drugs. And I want to know why I'm having to set up a shit ton of security for my granddaughter just to feel safe in her own home. So, please, tell me how you think Dean is dead because of Molly Rose, if it wasn't her who pulled the trigger?'

Cheryl frowned; sat forward. She glared at Janey, felt fury like she had when she first set eyes on Molly Rose.

'Because…'

Because what?

Janey stood up, leaned her hands on the table and stared down at Cheryl. Janey seemed taller than before; seemed more intimidating even with the limp and the fact that her walking crutch leaned against the table next to her.

'I'll tell you what I think. I think you're blaming the easy target. I think that you know you can't get the revenge on the people who killed your son because they're more powerful than you could ever imagine, so you went for someone lower down the food chain. A teenage girl who wouldn't be able to defend herself against you.'

Words failed her. She opened her mouth to speak, but there was nothing remotely feasible ready to come out.

'I'm right, aren't I? Leo's boss killed Dean because he couldn't deliver on a promise. *My* granddaughter. Dean was murdered because he failed in his task to get Molly Rose out of the UK and into another country to earn money for his sex-trafficking boss but you can't get to him, so you thought you'd go for Molly Rose instead. But that wasn't enough to scratch the surface, so you decided to go for all of us? I'm piping hot, aren't I, Cheryl?'

Cheryl closed her eyes and when she opened them, tears fell onto her cheeks. How did she know all this? She had all the details. Every single one.

'Sounds utterly ridiculous when you say it out loud, doesn't it?' Janey said.

Janey sat back down across from Cheryl and clasped her hands on the desk again and Cheryl tried to stop herself from falling apart.

'I get it, you know. As mothers we'd do anything for our kids; our grandkids. But you targeted the wrong ones, Cheryl.'

Janey's tone surprised her. It was empathetic, peppered with a sadness she hadn't expected.

'Get on with it then,' Cheryl said. 'Put me out my misery and kill me, eh? I'm done with all the bullshit life has dealt me recently. Blissful death would end all of it.'

Janey was quiet for a moment and then said, 'I'm not going to kill you, Cheryl. But what I'm about to tell you might.'

Cheryl wiped her hand over her cheeks to get rid of the tears and frowned. 'What do you mean?'

'Did you ever look closer to home for who might have been responsible for Dean's death?'

'If by closer to home you mean Leo, then no. He'd never hurt our son. Not in that way, anyway.'

Janey nodded. 'Perhaps he didn't pull the trigger, but it's likely he'd have known about the hit before it happened.'

Cheryl glared at Janey. 'Are you asking me, or telling me?'

'I'm asking,' Janey replied softly.

'No way. As soon as it happened – well, as soon as Dean went missing, Leo quit.'

Janey's expression fell. 'He quit?'

'Yeah, he walked away from all that shit as soon as it happened. I told him to. Said that he couldn't work with the people who killed our son.'

'So, you were okay for Leo to work for a trafficking gang, along with your son, but as soon as he died, that's when you decided enough was enough?' Janey's eyes widened.

'I didn't know that's what they were doing. I thought it was just drug dealing at first. If I'd known, I'd have made them both walk away a lot sooner.'

'Cheryl, sweetheart, that's not the kind of job you can just quit your way out of. Not the ones at the top of the chain or the bottom. Leo *didn't* walk away. He's still very much working for those people. Marek is still very much Leo's boss in every sense of the word. Leo's *still* in the trafficking business, in more ways than you can imagine.'

'No, he's not,' Cheryl said. 'I think I would know, I'm his wife, for fuck sake.'

'Oh, I can assure you he is, Cheryl. I have an eyewitness.'

Cheryl's eyes darted around the room as she tried to think. She knew Leo was capable of some horrible things, but *this*?

'An eyewitness?' she asked curiously, hoping to God that Janey had got it wrong; that Leo hadn't been lying to her for all this time.

'A young girl who managed to, *thankfully*, escape Leo's clutches. I don't know how she managed it, being so young and vulnerable, but she did.'

Cheryl rubbed at her eyes as though doing so would make her see things more clearly. Of course, it didn't. 'Okay then, who is she? What does she think she knows?'

'She's from Poland. And she's now under my care until we can get her home safely. When she got here, she was forced into some horrific situations which I won't go into detail about. What I will tell you though is what she said about Leo. That he…' Janey hesitated, blinked and adjusted herself on the seat. She was staring at Cheryl, deep into her eyes, like she was trying to work out what Cheryl was thinking.

Raising her hands in question, Cheryl said, 'That Leo what?'

'That he doesn't *just* bring the young people in; and when I say young, I mean younger than you would ever expect. Less than sixteen, Cheryl. I'm sorry to have to be the one to tell you this, but Leo makes *use* of them; her words, not mine,' Janey replied.

Staring at Janey through narrowed eyes, Cheryl glanced at Kristo and then back to Janey. 'Makes use of them? What the hell is that supposed to mean?'

'Oh, come on, Cheryl,' Kristo said, his voice a little louder than she'd expected, causing her to jump in her seat. 'You've been married to this man for years; had a son with him. You know what he had Dean involved in. Use your brain. Think about it.'

She did think about it, but not for long. The word *use*; to make *use* of them… She pushed the idea out of her head. 'No. No way. Leo might be a bit of a prick, but he's not like *that*. He's not a fucking paedo.'

'Can you be sure of that? I mean, it's bad enough that he brings these people here under false pretences. What makes him any different to the people who pay for these young people to engage in… God, I can't even bring myself to say it,' Janey said.

Cheryl stood up suddenly and heard the chair fall to the floor behind her. 'No,' she said loudly as she shook her head. 'Leo wouldn't… He *wouldn't*.'

And that's when it hit her. *Oh no. Oh fuck. What the hell am I married to?*

'It's a lot to take in, Cheryl. But you need to know that the person you're married to isn't who you think he is. He's not a husband or a dad. He's a human trafficker; recruiter and consumer, for want of a better fucking expression.'

Cheryl heard the chair being placed back in position behind her just in time to catch her fall. She felt Janey and Kristo's eyes burn into her as she remembered the day she met Leo. The day she turned fifteen years old. Then the wedding and how none of her family had been there. She'd thought it had all been her own choice. But had it? Truly?

'Are you okay? Do you need water?' Janey asked.

Cheryl couldn't answer. She was too busy going over her life with Leo, from the day she married him in Gretna Green just after her sixteenth birthday. On that day, she'd been certain that she'd made the right decision. Other than losing her parents over it, Cheryl had been happy. For the first few years anyway. After Dean was born, things started to change between Cheryl and Leo. Not because there was a new baby. But because Leo himself changed. He'd become distant, sometimes verbally and emotionally abusive. The distance had led her to think all sorts and there had been suspicions that he was cheating. With who, Cheryl had never known.

'Cheryl?' Janey pressed. 'Are you all right? Are you taking all this in?'

She couldn't speak. All she kept thinking about was her life for the past twenty-five years. Had it *all* been a lie? Had Leo been doing this the entire time and she'd only found out about it later in life, when she was in too deep and had no way of escape?

'Cheryl?' Janey said, firmer this time.

'Yeah,' she said, nodding. But she couldn't bring herself to look at Janey. Of all the people in the world to open Cheryl's eyes to what her life had been, she'd never have imagined it would be Janey Hallahan.

'Tell me what you're thinking,' Janey said.

'I married him when I was sixteen; as soon as I turned sixteen,' Cheryl blurted out. 'I started sleeping with him when I was fifteen.'

Janey's eyes glanced up at Kristo.

'Was I his first? Was I a guinea pig to see how easy it would be?'

'Did he...' Janey cleared her throat. 'Did he ever make you do things with other men for money?'

'No. Nothing like that. But... Oh my God, I was fifteen. I married him almost as soon as I turned sixteen. I lost my family. All I've ever had was Leo and Dean. Did he groom me? Was I *fucking* groomed?'

Janey's eyes softened. 'It looks like it. You *were* underage, and he knew.'

'I was the one who suggested getting married. Once he proposed, I pushed for us to do it before telling my parents we were together. Fucking hell. What was I thinking?'

Janey leaned across the table and stretched out her hand. 'You were thinking exactly what he wanted you to think, Cheryl. He planted the seed and allowed you to grow it. This is what he does. Promises a good life. And now look at you. Miserable, trying to kill people because Leo made you think a certain way. This is all him, Cheryl. What I've told you about him, it's all true. And it seems it stems back a lot longer than I could have imagined. You're a victim too, Cheryl, possibly his first. I'm sorry.'

Cheryl leaned forward, pressing her forehead into the table. She couldn't breathe; heart thundering in her chest.

'He dragged our boy into this. He made my son a monster. Dean was a good boy. He was...' The tears began to pour and she couldn't stop them as she banged her fist on the table. 'Janey... Janey, I'm sorry.'

Cheryl looked up at Janey Hallahan through pleading eyes.

'I know. I see it. He manipulated you into thinking it was all you wanted, Cheryl. He took everything from you so he would have someone on his side. Someone who would see the best in him so that if the time came, he could use you as a fucking character reference.'

'I need to get out of here,' Cheryl said, gulping back bile as she stood up, chair falling to the floor behind her again.

Janey got to her feet, as did Kristo. 'No, you need to stay here. We're not done yet.'

'Look, you might as well kill me. I've got nothing left anyway. He's ruined everything. Me, my son,' Cheryl sobbed before doubling over.

'I'm not going to kill you,' Janey said. 'I need you. I need you to help me deal with this bastard. You started a reign of terror on my family, Cheryl. I feel for you, I really do, but you're not going to walk away from this without helping me to finish it.'

Cheryl tried to compose herself. 'How?'

'I need you to tell me everything you know about Leo. Who his bosses are, where they are, what they do, how they operate. All of it.'

Shaking her head and wiping tears away with trembling hands, Cheryl said, 'I don't know any of it. Not really. I've never met his bosses. I've never seen him in action when it comes to his job. Fuck,' she tutted. 'His job, like that's what it is. He's a fucking animal.'

'Yes, he is. And we need to put a stop to this. So if you don't know anything like you claim, then we need to think of something else. I'll need you to set up a meeting with him. Arrange something that will put me in a room with him.'

Eyes wide, Cheryl said, 'I don't think that's a good idea.'

'Cheryl, my husband is lying in a hospital in a coma. My daughter is recovering from being injected with heroin and I'm trying to protect my granddaughter from this scumbag. As much as I feel for you, you *will* do what I tell you.'

'No, I can't do that.'

'Okay. I didn't want to tell you this myself, I thought it should come from Zofia; she'd be able to give you the full picture from her own eyes. But since you're not listening to me, then I'll tell you. It's about Dean.'

Cheryl's thundering heart almost came to a complete standstill.

'Zofia was in a room with Leo and Marek, his boss, along with some other people who would be able to corroborate her story if we get given the chance to save them. They were talking about Dean's death and how if Marek thought it would stop Leo questioning him so much, he'd kill Dean *again* and make Leo watch the second time. You see, Cheryl? Leo did know about the hit all along and he didn't do anything to stop it.'

No longer able to swallow the bile rising from her stomach, Cheryl retched until there was nothing left.

'I need to speak to her,' Cheryl said, wiping the back of her hand over her mouth.

'No.'

'I'm not going to hurt her. I need to hear it from her.'

'You'll scare her,' Janey said. 'I don't want that for her. She's been through enough.'

Cheryl closed her eyes and took a breath, the stench of bile still in her nostrils. 'If you want my help, you'll let me talk to her. I only want answers, Janey. It's all I've ever wanted.'

'Actually, you wanted revenge. But yes, fine.' Janey was quiet for a moment, then nodded. 'I'll call her. You can speak to her over the phone.'

# Chapter 47

Sinead's body ached as she dressed herself. Even the thought of moving made her wince. But she wasn't staying here in this private hospital to get clean again. She'd been drugged against her will; she'd still *be* clean if that hadn't happened. She had the strength to do it, she knew she could; not even just for herself but for Molly Rose too.

With Orla dead and Oliver in the US, Sinead felt it was her responsibility to be a good role model for Molly Rose. If the only adult in her niece's life was Janey, then it was inevitable she'd go down the wrong path and that wasn't something she wanted for Molly Rose.

Glancing up at the ceiling, Sinead fought off the urge to scream. She was so angry with Janey, yet grateful at the same time. They were all in a dangerous situation yet again because of her birth mother. It was because of Janey that Sinead had been used as a way to hurt her. But at the same time, if it wasn't for Janey's money, Sinead might still be on the streets, injecting shit into her veins and expecting that with every score, she could die. Either way, Sinead could end up dead.

'Sinead, you've only just arrived. I really don't think it's a good idea for you to be doing this. You're not fit enough yet. The side effects will still be present; and that's not to mention the withdrawal symptoms I'm expecting to creep back in,' the nurse said. 'I really think it would be best to stay here and recover fully.'

Sinead rolled her eyes. 'Did Janey pay you to say that?'

The nurse frowned, but there were no signs of confusion. The nurse knew exactly who Janey was. Not only Sinead's mother, but the woman who'd paid a substantial amount to have her cared for.

'Look, I don't need to be here. What I need is to get out and get to my family; or at least what's left of them. I'm fine. I was clean for long enough. I can do it again.'

'Two months? That's not a very long time in comparison to how long you struggled for,' the nurse said, a little too accusatorily for Sinead's liking.

'Look, love, I get that you're a nurse and you probably think you know better than I do about recovery, and I'm sure you mean well, but two months is a big deal to people like me considering I was on the junk for most of my adult life without a day off it. And I mean that literally. So, if you'll excuse me, I want to get out of here.'

The nurse stood in the doorway of Sinead's private room and it made her think of a prison guard outside a cell.

'Are you going to move yourself, or am I going to have to force my way past?' Sinead said, not asking for permission.

Reluctantly, the nurse stepped aside with a wash of disappointment crossing her face. Or was it guilt for speaking her mind a little too much?

Sinead gave a nod, picked up her bag and walked out of the room and down the corridor towards the exit. It did cross her mind that she should check in on Ciaran but, then again, the only person on her mind right now was Molly Rose. After Orla, it was difficult to believe that Molly Rose was as fine as she said. And given what was going on now, that yet someone else was out to get them all, the last thing she was going to do was sit in a hospital bed and wait for the news that her niece had been murdered, or worse.

She reached the exit door and pushed it open, feeling the fresh air on her face and in her lungs.

'I can do this,' she whispered to herself. 'I can stay clean on my own. No matter how hard it is; no matter how brutally awful the withdrawal gets. I can do it.' It was all about making the right choices. She just had to choose to say no when the withdrawal was at its most challenging. That's what she'd been doing in the rehab facility before some fucker ruined it for her.

Taking a deep breath, Sinead pushed back her shoulders, walked out of the grounds of the hospital and headed for the nearest bus stop.

—

The bus pulled out of the last stop in Helensburgh and made its way along towards the small village of Rhu, where Janey's house sat on the waterfront. Sinead had never been there; only had an address. But she knew Molly Rose was living there and, as much as Sinead had been happy for Janey to come back into her life, with her she brought carnage and destruction for Sinead's family. Her twin was dead, Sinead had almost been killed and Molly Rose had been through far too much trauma for a girl her age. It had all come to them because of Janey. That was something that Sinead couldn't forget. That, coupled with the fact that Janey was a crime boss whose fortunes were made through drugs, had caused Sinead to realise that she wasn't the type of person to be in charge of the care of Molly Rose. Orla would be mortified at the idea. It was up to Sinead now to take Molly Rose away from it all.

'That's you now, hen,' the driver called out to her. 'That's the house just up there on the left. Ye cannae really see it fae the road but it's definitely there. I watched it getting built maself. Been on this run for years. When ye dae ma job, it's hard tae miss new stuff on yer route, ye know whit I mean?'

Sinead smiled as she reached the driver's cab. His life sounded so simple. Normal. She couldn't wait for normal.

'Thank you,' she said, giving him a smile as he pulled into the bus stop.

'Nae bother, hen, catch ye later.'

Sinead stepped off the bus and, just a few yards ahead, she saw the entrance to the driveway, which curved around before you could see the front door of the house itself.

*Right*, she told herself. *Stay calm, tell Janey what you think should happen with Molly Rose and what Orla would have wanted, and don't get personal. Stick to facts.*

'Well, well, well,' a deep voice came from behind her, one she didn't recognise. 'Nice to see you on your feet again.'

Turning, Sinead saw a man standing closer than necessary. He was tall, his eyes dark and his smile menacing. She didn't recognise him; he could be anyone. An old dealer, an old druggie acquaintance. No, she thought, as much as she was off her face over the years, she'd never forget a dealer. And if this guy was a former fellow junkie, she was sure he wouldn't look as healthy and strong as he did.

'Who the hell are you?' Sinead said.

'Someone who is so utterly elated to find that Janey doesn't put as much security at the house as she should,' he said, and all too quickly he flew at her, punching her so hard in the face she felt her nose explode. Blood dripped down into the back of her throat as she tried to scramble to her feet. He was too quick for her as he gripped the hair at the back of her head and pulled her up to her feet. 'Ssh,' he whispered, as though she was making a noise. But she wasn't; she was too stunned to do anything and, with the blood almost choking her, she couldn't do anything other than concentrate on breathing.

'What the fuck?' Another male voice came from the direction of the house. Before Sinead could process what was happening, a loud pop made her flinch violently in the man's grip and she watched as the man coming towards her dropped to the ground.

He wasn't the only one. There were two more and the man holding her shot them too. All three lay on the white gravel drive, blood pouring from their heads.

'Let me go,' Sinead demanded, almost forgetting that, in an instant, he could kill her too. But all she could think about was Molly Rose.

'Oh no, Sinead,' he replied sinisterly. 'You were supposed to die in that fucking rehab place and the person I tasked with the job fucked it up. No, you're not going anywhere.'

She struggled in his grip, tried to pull away from him. But instead, she felt a sharp pain in the side of her head this time. The blow wasn't enough to knock her out completely but it did render her unable to move much. Was that the shock of the blow itself, or had he paralysed her?

He laid her down on the gravel and stared down at her. He wasn't smiling, nor did he look angry. But there was something about his expression that Sinead couldn't place. Determination? Fear? Perhaps both.

'I'm sorry, Sinead. But I'm not going to let anyone get in my way this time. Molly Rose is mine.'

Sinead tried to speak, tried to move but she couldn't, her limbs heavy like setting concrete. He bound her hands together, then her ankles.

*No, no this isn't happening. I need to get to Molly Rose. She can't go through this again*, she thought to herself, although the words were cloudy in her head.

He lifted her over his shoulder and carried her a short distance towards a van. She hadn't heard it approach from behind her. He must have come in just after she'd got off the bus.

He opened the boot and threw her in as though he was chucking in an old gym bag. Her head thumped and she closed her eyes against the pain. She felt her hands being tied, a gag was shoved into her mouth and a piece of material was tied roughly around her head before being pulled over her eyes. She froze with fear. If she resisted, he could kill her.

Where the fuck was Janey? And Molly Rose? Had this lunatic already got to them?

Before she could think of anything else, she heard the tailgate slam shut on her and the distant sound of crunching gravel underfoot.

## Chapter 48

Alina's face had been in Zofia's mind ever since she'd told Molly Rose about her. The thought that she had no idea where her sister was killed her. She could be somewhere in the UK, or further afield in Europe. She *could* be dead. Or, worse, locked up somewhere, being abused every single day. Did she have someone looking out for her like Zofia did with the Hallahan family? It was unlikely. Alina wasn't as strong as Zofia. She was much more of a people-pleaser; whereas Zofia, well, she was smart enough to know that people-pleasing got you nowhere. Of course, that wasn't the case when working for Leo. That was exactly the kind of trait he had been looking for in his employees. The word made her sick. They weren't employees. They were slaves.

The shrill ring of Molly Rose's mobile phone made Zofia jump; she'd been so deep in dark thoughts she'd completely detached from the present.

'Janey?' Molly Rose said as she answered it.

Zofia looked out the window and saw the security guard standing at the front door. She thought his presence would make her feel better, but it didn't. If anything it made her feel worse. The fact that he was there at all meant there was still a high threat level that Leo was coming for them.

'Yeah, okay. Hang on,' Molly Rose said before sitting closer to Zofia. 'Janey wants me to switch to loudspeaker. She wants to talk to you.' Zofia frowned as Molly Rose tapped the screen and said, 'That's you on.'

'Zofia?' Janey started. 'Can you hear me?'

'Yes, I can,' Zofia replied with a frown. 'What's wrong?'

'Molly Rose, I want you to hold Zofia's hand through this. Okay?' Janey said.

The girls stared at each other and Zofia could see the fear in Molly Rose's eyes, the same fear that Zofia felt in her chest. Was it news about Alina? Had they found her?

'Why?' Zofia asked, the word coming out in a long drawl.

'Zofia, I have someone here that I need you to explain something to. Remember when you told me about Leo; the conversation he had with his boss from Poland?'

Zofia swallowed hard. 'Yes. What about it?'

'Well, I have Cheryl Davidson here, Leo's wife. She needs to know about that conversation. Can you reiterate it to her, please? As clear and precise as when you told me.'

Zofia gripped Molly Rose's hand a little tighter. Zofia felt like she wanted to be sick.

'Go on,' Molly Rose said reassuringly. 'Just tell her what you told us.'

Zofia puffed out her cheeks and closed her eyes. 'Okay,' she started. 'Cheryl?'

'What did you hear between them?' Cheryl asked bluntly.

Zofia pushed through the fear of telling Cheryl the truth and continued. 'The other man, Leo's boss, basically said something along the lines of that Leo would know what would happen if things didn't go as planned.'

259

Cheryl cleared her throat and said, 'That doesn't prove anything.'

Zofia bit her lip in annoyance. 'I'm not finished yet.' She took a breath and continued. 'Then he went on to say that he would have him killed again if he could, and make Leo watch second time round if it would shut Leo up; or something to that effect.'

Silence fell on the other side of the call. Zofia glanced at Molly Rose who was smiling sympathetically at her. 'You did well,' she mouthed, but Zofia still felt sick. Had Cheryl believed her? Or would she take the side of her husband even after the truth? Surely not, after she'd heard that.

'Thank you, Zofia,' Janey said. 'I'll see you girls soon.'

The call ended and Zofia threw herself back onto the sofa and sighed loudly. 'I hate this.'

'Yeah, it's not pleasant. But it'll be over soon. I'm sure of it.'

Zofia went to speak, to say that she hoped Molly Rose was right, but before she could, a loud bang rang in her ears. Then another. And a third.

'What the *fuck* was that?' Molly Rose said, cautiously getting to her feet. As she rose, Zofia's eyes darted towards the balcony. There was nobody there. There was a short period of silence which seemed to last forever.

'What's going on?' Zofia asked. 'Where are the security guys? Did they shoot?'

Silence, other than the rushing of blood in Zofia's ears, and then the soft crunch of gravel out in the driveway. Slow, steady footsteps, edging closer and closer.

'Yeah, but I don't think it was our guards' guns.' Molly Rose's voice trembled.

The glass panel in the front door smashed and Molly Rose gasped as Leo Davidson rushed into the living room, a gun in his hand. Zofia moved to behind the sofa and crouched down as low as she could.

She couldn't see what was going on, but there was the sound of a struggle; Molly Rose was fighting back.

'Don't even *think* about it, you little bitch,' Leo hissed. 'Or you'll end up like your fucking mother.'

'Get the *fuck* out of here,' Molly Rose screamed. 'Let me fucking go!'

A deep thump followed by silence made Zofia freeze as she lay on the floor behind the sofa. She held her breath, desperate not to be heard; not to be found.

Footsteps approached. One. Two. Three. A shadow appeared over her.

'Well, well, well. Isn't this a fucking surprise? It's like waiting for a bus and two come along all at once. I feel like I've hit the fucking jackpot.'

Looking up and into the eyes of Leo Davidson, Zofia felt like something inside her died. He pointed the gun at her face with an evil glint in his eye and a smile on his face.

'Please.' Her voice broke into a whisper. 'I just want to go home.'

Leo pulled his lips into a thin line. 'Yeah, that's probably what Nigel thought before you fucking killed him, ya fiery little bastard. I'd love to help you out, Zofia, but you've made my life very fucking hard these last three days and I'm on a schedule. Up,' he said, gesturing for her to rise.

She remained where she was on the floor, trembling with fear.

261

He leaned down, gun still pointed in her face, and grabbed her by the neck. 'I said get up.'

His eyes were wild, a mixture of anger and sheer delight that he'd found her.

Zofia wanted to plead, beg with him to let her go free. But then she saw Molly Rose lying on the floor next to the edge of the sofa with blood on the side of her face. She wasn't moving.

'What did you do to her?' Zofia cried.

'I silenced her; for now. I'm sorry, wee girl, but you're going to have to be silenced too. I can't have you ruining this for me. You already fucked me over with Richardson. And because of that, you've fucked it for your sister too.'

White-hot pain shot through her head, blinding her. She was vaguely aware of movement. Was she walking, or being carried?

Then, as though someone switched off the light, the darkness quickly descended.

# Chapter 49

Janey placed the phone down on the table and waited for Cheryl to compose herself.

'This can't be happening,' Cheryl said as she rested her head in her hands.

'I wish I could say it wasn't,' Janey replied. 'But it's better that you know what you're married to.'

Cheryl took a long, deep breath. 'My Dean, he was brainwashed.'

'That, I think we can agree on.'

'Leo as good as killed him with his own bare hands. I can't just let that go.'

Janey nodded, happy that Cheryl was coming round to the idea that the revenge plot from their side had been utterly ridiculous. 'You've been brainwashed too, Cheryl. Leo made you believe that we were the bad ones in all of this, when in truth, he's been the one causing all the chaos; all the terror.'

Cheryl closed her eyes as tears fell. She cried in silence.

'We need to know where he is, right now,' Kristo said, his voice low as though he was trying to be sympathetic. But Janey knew him, he'd be raring to go right now, desperate to bring Leo in and put a stop to all this.

Cheryl glanced up at Kristo and frowned. 'You probably know more than me. He rarely tells me the truth, it would seem. Fuck, he's told me he's been working as a fucking handyman since Dean was killed; doing odd jobs with a few other guys. What kind of a man would still work with the people who killed his son?'

Janey sighed. 'The kind who's probably been told that if he walks away, he and the rest of his family are at risk of being next. By the sounds of this Marek guy, he doesn't fuck about.'

'And in your line of work, you've never heard of this Marek? Never come across him?'

Janey raised an eyebrow. 'I deal in many things, Cheryl, but not people. I don't associate myself with that shit. Its inhumane.' In hindsight, Janey knew she should have made herself more aware of the situation. She should have known more about what was going on in her city. She might have been able to stop all of this from happening if she had.

'Each criminal transaction funds the next, though? Am I right? The money does the rounds, surely? The money that buys the drugs, buys the guns, buys the people?'

The thought made Janey sick. Cheryl was right. It was all one big pot, shared among the crime bosses of the country, filtered down to the street players and the drug addicts. Her work had contributed to it all.

'So,' Janey said, swallowing hard and pushing the very true statement out of her head. She switched the subject back. 'You can't tell us where he is?'

'No. But Leo isn't one to let things go. If that girl, Zofia, has got away from him, and Molly Rose is still on his radar, then there's a strong possibility that he's hanging around somewhere, watching for his chance to move.'

Janey blinked. 'We have security.'

'And Leo is one determined man. You might want to go and check on the girls. I'll go home, see what I can find out.'

Janey laughed a little louder than she intended to. 'You'll *go* home? Ha, Cheryl, I love how you think you can just walk away from this of your own free will. You're not going anywhere without me now. I feel sorry for you but I wouldn't trust you to look after a jar of fresh air. I'm not letting you out of my sight. Where you go, I go.'

'Janey,' Cheryl replied. 'No offence, but how am I to know you and this girl haven't concocted a load of shit to corner me? Sorry, but I don't trust you as much as you don't trust me.'

'You think I care that you don't trust me?' Janey frowned.

'No. But I can't just take your word for it, or this girl's, for that matter.'

Janey pulled her lips into a thin line and nodded slowly. 'So, you're saying you don't believe a young sixteen-year-old Polish girl that she was brought over here and abused by people your husband set on her? You don't believe what she said about him knowing that your son was going to be murdered? But you can take his word on it all?'

'That's not what I'm saying.'

'That's exactly what you're saying.' Janey took a long, deep breath. 'I mean, I sort of get it. You were one of his first victims. You're probably still, in some shape or form, brainwashed by him; the younger version of yourself which is still buried deep inside you hopes that it's all a misunderstanding and that the man you fell for is still in there. I can imagine you would believe a lot of what he says. But let me suggest something: men like him, they're not very good at covering their tracks. Perhaps you'll get your proof, if you look in the right places. I'd imagine he'll have a second phone, possibly multiple phones. Maybe a second laptop or tablet you might not know about. It could have a list of contacts, client details.'

Cheryl's brow crinkled as if she was trying to think. 'Yeah,' she said. 'Possibly.'

Janey lowered her tone, realising just how vulnerable Cheryl was right now. 'What is it he said he does for work now?'

'Plumber and all-round handyman. Works with a few other guys but mostly for himself, *apparently*.'

Janey sneered. 'Definitely working for himself; I'll give him that.' She looked at Cheryl in sympathy; as much as she could at a woman who'd conspired to have her family killed. That was the thing with men like Leo Davidson, he'd use women as weapons against each other to protect himself, no matter the cost.

'This isn't happening,' Cheryl said, sounding as though she was struggling for breath.

'It is. And if we're going to put a stop to him hurting anyone else, including you, Cheryl, then we need to move fast. I can help you find the evidence you want. It wouldn't harm to have something against him in black and white.'

Cheryl stared at her through glassy eyes and nodded. 'Yeah, fine. Okay.'

Kristo led them back up to the ground floor and out to the car. Cheryl very well could be bluffing, Janey thought. If she was, it would be easy enough to deal with. But by the look on her face, Janey wasn't sure that Cheryl had the strength to lie. She'd just been told her husband knew his own son was going to be murdered and had done nothing to stop it. What kind of father did that, regardless of anything else he was?

Janey watched as Cheryl climbed into the back of the car, Kristo into the driver seat, and stared out at the grounds around her. The last time she'd been in the holiday park had been when Danny McInroy had tried to cross her. She closed her eyes at the memory of his destructive behaviours, his need for power. He'd been an angel in comparison to Leo Davidson. Still, the devil had once been an angel, hadn't he?

She got into the car and they all sat in silence as Kristo drove them back to the West End of the city. Janey pulled her phone out of her pocket and typed out and sent a WhatsApp to Molly Rose that she was on her way back but might still be a while given what she was about to do with Cheryl.

Happy that the message had been delivered successfully when two blue ticks appeared, Janey slipped the phone back into her pocket and hoped that they would find something incriminating in Leo and Cheryl's flat; something that would snap Cheryl out of her brainwashed state. She was close to coming out of it, Janey could see that in her eyes. Surely no one could hear that about the man they were married to and not have doubts about the truth that lay behind it.

'Janey?' Cheryl said, her voice piercing through her thoughts.

Janey turned and looked at Cheryl.

'I know Leo isn't a good person. I do. I don't want this life any more. I'll make sure we find something.'

Pursing her lips, Janey felt a sadness wash over her at the look on Cheryl's face. Her entire life had been a lie because Leo had made it that way.

# Chapter 50

She struggled against the plastic ties which bound her wrists and ankles together, all the while trying to breathe steadily and not panic at the idea that, this time, she wasn't going to get out of this alive.

Pain seared in the back of her head as she tried to remember what happened. They'd been sitting there, talking about what had been going on when a gunshot made them freeze. Had there been more than one? Maybe two? She couldn't remember. All she could think of was the pain.

'Zofia?' Molly Rose whispered, hoping that she was still with her.

'Shh,' came the sound of Zofia's hushed, panicked tone. 'Don't speak. If he hears us, he'll...' Her voice trailed off. Something was off, aside from the blatantly obvious.

And then she heard it. A voice she had not expected.

'Molly Rose?'

The sound was croaky, like the person had smoked a twenty pack just that day.

'*Sinead?*'

Molly Rose blinked against the darkness, trying to see better. But it was no use. They were in complete darkness.

'Are you okay, Sinead?'

'I'm fine. Head's fucking thumping; the bastard smashed me with something. Are you okay?' Sinead asked, sounding a little clearer this time.

'What the hell are you doing here?' Molly Rose whispered.

Sinead tried to clear her throat quietly and said, 'I was coming to check on you.'

'Why aren't you in the hospital?'

'I don't think now is the time to discuss it, do you? I think we should be talking about getting us the hell out of the boot of this nutjob's car,' Sinead said.

Molly Rose rolled her eyes in the darkness. No chance of that happening. She knew how this went. It only seemed like yesterday that she'd been running through Kelvingrove Park to get away from Charlie before he'd snatched her and put her in the boot next to Kassy. At least this time, no one was dead. For now.

'We're going to die,' Zofia said from the other side of Sinead.

'No, we're not,' Molly Rose replied with a determination she hadn't even felt the first time she'd been taken.

She couldn't think over the sound of the engine and the music. A song Molly Rose actually liked, one that had trended on TikTok back in 2021 before her life had gone to shit. Måneskin, 'I Wanna Be Your Slave'. It was ironic given that, yes, she and Zofia were going to be slaves to Leo, but no, he wasn't searching for redemption. It didn't strike her as the type of song that Leo Davidson would like. She pushed the unnecessary thoughts out of her head and took a breath.

'We are… we're going to die. He's not going to let us live after this,' Zofia replied in a panic. 'Especially me.'

269

'Oi, get a grip. Think about it, he *needs* us alive so his boss doesn't kill him. You said it yourself, Zofia: his boss threatened him with the same fate as his son. He's not going to want that to happen. All we have to do is survive.'

'No offence, Molly Rose, but you've not seen survival in this life. It means being a sex slave to the most horrific people you can imagine. I don't know what I'd prefer, death or that life.'

Those words rendered Molly Rose silent and caused her heart to skip a beat.

'We have to get away,' Sinead said.

'I know,' Molly Rose said. 'But how? I mean, I can't imagine I'm the only one of us tied up and blindfolded in here?'

Quiet sobs from Zofia answered her question.

'Right then. So we have no choice but to wait, do we?'

Silence, as much as silence could be over the roar of the engine, fell between them.

'We wait,' Molly Rose finally said. 'And when we get the chance...' She stopped. *If we get the chance*, her inner voice rung pessimistically in her ears. 'We *fucking* run.'

# Chapter 51

Cheryl tried to control her jittery hand as she entered the home she shared with a man she now realised she truly knew nothing about. It made her feel sick to think about how she'd been taken in by his lies and charm back when she'd first met him. And he'd done it so easily. She'd been so bloody stupid. So easily manipulated into leaving her entire life behind for Leo. For Christ's sake, she was only fifteen when they'd met; sixteen when they'd married. A choice she'd thought had come from her own mind; but he'd coerced her into it without having to do anything other than fucking love-bombing her. Why had that realisation only come to her now, years and years later when it was all too late?

'Jesus,' she whispered as she tried to turn the key. It wouldn't budge. *Wrong one*, she thought as she pulled it out of the lock and tried to select the correct one.

'Problem?' Janey asked from behind her.

'No, just put the wrong key in, that's all.'

That's all? That's *all*? If only that was all she had to worry about.

Turning the key, this time the door opened. But a new sense of dread washed over her now. What the hell was she going to find that would have been under her nose the entire time she'd been living with him? How many years' worth of clients had he racked up, people who would pay a pretty penny, or as little as possible, to abuse young women? Cheryl wanted to believe that it wasn't true, that there had been some kind of mistake, a mix-up. Leo wasn't the person Janey thought. In reality, it was Cheryl who'd been wrong about him for all of the twenty-four years she'd been tied to him by the law of marriage.

As they stepped into the flat, Cheryl couldn't help but notice the look on Janey's face.

'What is it?' Cheryl asked, curious to know what she was thinking.

Pursing her lips, Janey replied, 'By the looks of it, Leo hasn't been paid well for his involvement in the organisation.'

Cheryl frowned. The thought that her home and life as a wife and mum had been funded by Leo's activities made her feel sick with guilt.

'Seriously,' Janey continued. 'No offence, Cheryl, but this is a basic flat. I'd have expected Leo to have been compensated well for his involvement.'

'Are you actually serious?' Cheryl said, her face crinkling with disgust. 'You say it like he works in a fucking office or something.'

'All I'm saying is, I was expecting a little more grandeur than this. Either Leo's been hiding his money from you, or he's on basic pay.'

Cheryl closed her eyes and counted to ten, breathing through the anger that followed the situation she was in.

Even if Leo had been making more than he was letting on and hiding it from Cheryl, she didn't care. Not about the money. All she cared about was how stupid she'd been to let this happen to her and her son. Why hadn't she been more observant? Why had she allowed Dean to go on to work with Leo even though all she thought they were doing was dealing drugs? That in itself was bad enough. She hadn't wanted that for Dean, but seeing him happy that he was getting close to Leo was enough to allow her to take a step back and let them get on with it. If she'd intervened…

'I'd rather not think about him getting paid to traffic young people, thanks. If we can just get on with it,' she said, pushing away the images of what Leo had been getting up to, what he'd been forcing Dean to do.

'Okay,' Janey said, holding her hands up in defeat. 'Where do you think he'd keep a second laptop? Or tablet? Under the bed? Under the sink in the kitchen? Taped to the back of the TV?'

Cheryl glanced back at Janey and raised an eyebrow. 'Well, considering I had *no* idea who my husband actually *was* until very recently, I can't say that I'd have any idea where to start looking.' She glanced around the entrance hall of the flat and felt the weight of the world press down on her chest. All Cheryl wanted to do was run away, disappear from it all and start over, but even then, she didn't know if she had the mental strength to be able to do something like that without Dean by her side.

*Fuck*, she thought. She should have done that long ago, got her son away while she had the chance. Now he was dead and it was likely that Molly Rose and that other girl would be next if they didn't figure something out.

'Think, Cheryl. Where's the last place you'd look for anything like that? Where would Leo put something like a laptop or tablet; Christ, even a fucking diary that he wouldn't want you to know about, that you'd never think to find there?' Janey pressed.

Cheryl noticed how Kristo was distracted. He was looking up at the ceiling, his arms stretched up and feeling his fingers along the top of the wall, where it met the ceiling.

'What are you doing?' she asked, genuinely baffled.

'I'm feeling for a weak spot,' Kristo replied. 'I'll check all the walls. Every inch of them. You never know, there could be a spot where he's installed a safe; even a cupboard that you don't know about.'

Cheryl looked at Kristo, dumbfounded. 'Seriously? You think I wouldn't notice something like that in my own house?'

Kristo lowered his arms and his lips formed a thin, cynical smile. 'Well, to be fair, Cheryl, you didn't notice that your husband and son were sex traffickers.'

Cheryl bit her tongue. Cheeky fucking bastard. He was right though. She'd missed everything. *Everything.*

'Okay,' Janey said, leaning her crutch against the wall. 'What about the living room? Should we start there?'

A thought sprung to Cheryl's mind then. A thought that made her stomach roll. But it would make perfect sense. The last place she'd ever think to look, as Janey put it.

'No, actually, I think we start in Dean's bedroom.'

Janey and Kristo gave each other a fleeting glance, then turned back to her. Janey frowned. 'You think if Leo was keeping things hidden that could incriminate him, he'd hide them in his *son's* bedroom?' she asked.

'Yeah,' Cheryl said, sighing in annoyance. 'Like you said, it's the last place I'd think of to look because I rarely go in there now; it's too painful. He had a shitty attitude towards Dean. This would be something I'd imagine he'd do. Another one of his sick ideas, probably.'

Janey nodded slowly and a flicker of sadness crossed her face before she said, 'Okay. Lead the way.'

Cheryl moved towards Dean's bedroom and she stopped for a moment outside it, wishing that she could hear those old sounds coming from behind it. *FIFA* or *Call of Duty* coming from the PlayStation, or laughter as he scrolled on TikTok. He was just a normal lad, really. Just a normal lad who felt like he had something to prove to his old man and allowed himself to be sucked into the most horrific of circumstances.

The sound of Janey clearing her throat jarred her from her thoughts and Cheryl pushed the door open. The room smelled the same as it had when Dean was still alive, although it was fainter; something that triggered Cheryl's grief even more. It was why she hadn't touched it since he'd last been in there.

'Where to start?' Janey said, her voice softer than probably necessary.

'Anywhere you like,' Cheryl replied, sitting down on the crumpled bed.

Janey and Kristo began searching through wardrobes and drawers, under the bed, behind furniture. It was as though they were trying to be respectful as much as possible while trying to pin anything they could on Leo. But they were disturbing Dean's room as he'd left it when he'd died. Not that it was tidy. It was an absolute mess. A typical young lad's bedroom.

'Was this Dean's?' Janey said, stretching her arm under the set of drawers and pulling out a small laptop bag. She glanced up at Cheryl.

She shook her head. 'Not that I know of. He was more a PlayStation kind of lad.'

Janey slowly unzipped the bag and inside lay a tablet and charger. Cheryl frowned. It was too easy for him to hide it there. Either too easy, or Leo was just that stupid. Then again, it was Cheryl who'd been stupid.

Switching it on, Janey waited for the screen to light up.

'I mean, it could be nothing,' Cheryl said. 'It could *just* be a tablet.'

Janey didn't answer. Instead, she sighed when the tablet prompted her for a password. She glanced up at Cheryl. 'Any idea?'

She shrugged. 'Not a clue. Maybe try Dean's date of birth? First of October two thousand and two.'

'Jackpot,' Janey said as the screen opened up.

Cheryl's eyes widened. She glanced down at the tablet and, to her horror, the screen saver was a picture of Leo and Dean together. Leo was grinning out from the screen, looking high as a kite; while Dean, he wasn't smiling. Not even a hint of a smile. His expression was neutral. The background was alien to Cheryl. A dark space, people in the background she couldn't make out. Next to Dean in the image was a table with playing cards, a bottle of whisky and countless empty beer bottles and cans. She could even make out several lines of cocaine which had obviously just been laid out before the picture had been taken.

'Leo looks like he's just won the lottery in that picture,' Cheryl said, feeling her heart fill with venom for him.

'Yeah, well, hopefully we're about to strip him of his winnings,' Janey said, swiping her finger across the screen.

'I'll stand by the door, keep an eye in case he comes back,' Kristo said before leaving the room. Although Cheryl wondered what Kristo would actually do if Leo did appear. Shoot him? The prospect of seeing him lying on the ground with his own blood pooling beneath him was a sight she'd gladly see right now. She'd be willing to pull the trigger herself.

Janey pulled herself up onto the bed next to Cheryl and said, 'There only seems to be one extra app other than the ones a tablet usually comes with. It's a cryptocurrency app. It's next to a contact app and a photo gallery; like they've all been put together.'

Cheryl glanced down at them as Janey pointed them out. 'Well, the crypto app is something I wouldn't be able to help you with. I'm shite with technology.'

'That's fine. I can deal with getting into that. It would be good to look through the contacts. If Leo is as thick as I hope he is, then I'd imagine that all of his sick clients' details would be in here.'

Cheryl shook her head. 'Yeah, possibly.' But she couldn't keep her eye off the photo gallery.

Janey opened the contacts app and started to look through them. There were hundreds, Cheryl noticed. All male names.

'Well, I think it's safe to say that he really is as thick as shit,' Janey said, her finger hovering over one name in particular.

'Isn't that the guy who's been on the news? The MSP?' Cheryl asked, staring down at the very memorable and recognisable name.

'It sure is,' Janey replied. 'That's our missing MSP. Good old *clean-cut* Nigel Richardson. Pillar of the fucking community.'

'Jesus,' Cheryl gasped. 'He was a client of Leo's?'

'Yep. Don't worry. He got his karma,' Janey said through gritted teeth.

Cheryl chose not to ask what that meant, she could work it out for herself. And the less she knew, the better.

'And what about the other names?' Cheryl asked, scrolling her finger down the screen.

'I recognise a few,' Janey replied. 'In fact…' Her voice trailed off and then she shouted on Kristo, who came back into Dean's bedroom. Janey took the tablet from Cheryl and held it out to Kristo, whose eyes widened.

'What the fuck is he doing on there?' he asked, sounding more shocked than Cheryl ever thought possible.

'Seems this just opened up to be much bigger than any of us could have guessed,' Janey replied.

'Who is it?' Cheryl asked, glancing between them.

'He's a very high-ranking police detective,' Janey hissed. 'One of ours. Jesus fuck.'

Cheryl frowned. How many more men of power were in this digital contact book? How many of them were abusing their position?

'Can I see that?' Cheryl asked, holding her hand out for the tablet.

'I don't think that's such a good idea, Cheryl,' Janey replied.

She swallowed hard. 'I know. But I have to see for myself the kind of animal he is. And I need to know that Dean isn't involved in,' she hesitated, took a breath, 'in *that* side of things.'

Janey sighed and handed the tablet to Cheryl. She went into the gallery app and closed her eyes briefly before she began to scroll. What she saw made her feel sick to her stomach. Scrolling some more through the images, she averted her eyes from the abuse and concentrated on the faces in the background as she looked for her son. If he was involved in the direct abuse, she didn't know what she'd do. Praying with everything she had that she wouldn't see Dean as she slid her finger across the screen, her heart rate slowed a little as she came to the end of the gallery. There weren't that many of them, but he wasn't there. *Definitely* not.

'I think we need to pay this *bastard* a visit,' Janey said to Kristo, her voice forcing Cheryl's thoughts back to the present.

'He's not in any of them,' Cheryl said distantly, having closed the tablet down.

'Who?' Janey asked.

'Dean, he's not in any of the pictures.'

Kristo gave her a cynical look. 'Doesn't mean he wasn't there, Cheryl. Ask yourself who might have taken the pictures?'

Jesus, she hadn't considered that. Setting the tablet down on the bed, Cheryl got to her feet and looked around the room. Dean's Superdry hoody was hanging over the back of the bedroom door and she lifted it, raised it to her nose and sniffed. His scent was almost gone and she felt like a knife sliced through her heart at the thought nothing in the house would smell like him ever again. As time went on, the scent would fade.

Hugging the hoody tight to her, a rustling sound came from the front pocket. Holding it out from her body, she slid her hand inside and pulled out an envelope. It was simply addressed to *Mum*.

'Oh my God,' she whispered, staring down at what was very clearly Dean's handwriting. A surge of panic consumed her and a lump formed in her throat.

'What's that?' Janey asked.

'A letter from Dean. I've just found it.'

'Are you going to open it?'

'I don't know if I can,' Cheryl choked.

'Cheryl, if Dean has left you a letter, there must be something in it he wanted you to know,' Janey said. 'Open it.'

Cheryl sat down on Dean's bed, took a deep breath and tore open the envelope.

Mum,

If you're reading this, I'm probably dead. I just wanted to tell you that I'm sorry. I didn't want any of it. Not really. But you know what he's like, always pushing me to be better, to be like him. I didn't know what I was getting into at first. I thought it was just a bit of dealing. But before I knew it, I was producing fake passports and recruiting girls.

I fucked up a job and because of that, I fucked up another and I know it's only a matter of time before Marek will kill me. He isn't going to let what I did go. I wouldn't be surprised if he has Dad do it himself. He's that kind of guy.

Just know, I'm not like him. I'm not a pervert. I'm not some kind of sicko who likes to abuse people. I didn't want to take the pictures on the tablet. But I had to. I had to copy everything so that you could know the truth. He liked having them to look back on, to admire his own fucked-up sense of power. I saw it as an opportunity to take him down. If you're reading this, I'm one step closer to achieving that.

You need to get away from him, Mum. He's a monster and he turned me into one too. Had me thinking I had something to prove to him but in all honesty, I'd have been better off walking away *from him. He's a scumbag, Mum. Get away from him.*

*I love you and I don't want you to think of me in the same light as him, especially when you see everything on this tablet.*

*Stay safe. Get free.*

*Dean.*

Cheryl swiped angrily at the tears running down her face and folded the letter back up and slid it back into the envelope before handing it to Janey, who read it quickly. Her face darkened.

'Even his own son, the one who tried to traffic my granddaughter out of the country, knew he was a scumbag. Another brainwashed product of Leo *fucking* Davidson,' Janey said through gritted teeth as she handed the letter to Kristo, who sneered upon taking in the words but said nothing. She looked down at Cheryl and nodded. 'I'm sorry your life is in such chaos, Cheryl. You've been so helpful in pinning Leo down.' Janey glanced at Kristo and nodded. 'We have to go.'

Cheryl didn't want to stand by and wait for Leo to come home. She didn't want to be near him.

'Can't I come with you?' Cheryl got to her feet.

Janey frowned. 'You want to come with me? I would have thought you'd want away from us the second you got the chance.'

'No,' Cheryl replied, shaking her head. 'I just can't stay here. I can't just wait for him. If I see him, I don't know what I'll do.'

Sighing, Janey frowned. 'I'm sorry, Cheryl. But I have some business to attend to regarding the list on that tablet. I'd rather you weren't around while I deal with it. You can keep in touch. Let me know when, *if*, he comes back. Tell me what state of mind he's in. You need to be able to feed me information. You're on our side now. Do you understand me?'

Nodding, she watched Janey and Kristo leave the flat and glanced down at the floor. Her shoes were muddy. All their shoes had been muddy from being at Carbeth. They'd dragged mud through to the carpet in Dean's bedroom.

She bent down and removed her shoes with shaking hands, before going into the kitchen and filling a basin with hot soapy water. Lifting a scrubbing brush from under the sink, Cheryl walked through to Dean's room and placed the basin on the floor in the middle of the room. Glancing at the bed, she frowned at the mess of the duvet. It wasn't the mess Dean had left it in. It was now tainted with the presence of others.

She got down onto her hands and knees and scrubbed furiously at the carpet, wishing that she could scrub away the last twenty-five years of her life. Scrub out all the cruelty, all the lies that Leo had brought to her life and all the turmoil he'd caused their son. She wished she'd never met him, although it pained her to think such a thing, as that would have meant never having Dean. What kind of life had he had anyway because of his scumbag dad? None at all. He'd have ended up in prison if he hadn't been murdered. She didn't know how she felt about the letter. Did it make things worse? Or was it a good thing? Dean was trying to do the right thing in the end, wasn't he? Or was he trying something that would mean, if he did get caught, he'd get off on lighter charges for showing remorse and pinning down those at the top of the organisation?

The sound of the bristles on the carpet weren't enough to drown out her crippling thoughts and the words from Dean's letter. She got up and switched on the PlayStation. Once it had loaded up, Cheryl opened up Dean's Spotify playlist, which she still paid for every month, and hit play. Kasabian, 'Shoot the Runner', blared out of the speaker from the TV and Cheryl closed her eyes briefly, remembering Dean's voice belting out the words of the song while getting ready to go out at night with his dad. He'd hidden his feelings about Leo well, so much so that the letter told her more than she could have ever imagined. Cheryl opened her eyes and turned back to face the room before she continued to scrub the mud off the carpet. She scrubbed until her fingers bled.

## Chapter 52

'I have them,' he said as he drove back to Glasgow, using the back road from Helensburgh.

'You have *them*?' Marek asked. 'Forgive me, who are you talking about?'

Leo gritted his teeth as he saw the build-up of traffic in the usual spot of the A82 just outside the turn-off for Cameron House hotel and the Duck Bay marina. No matter the time of year, it was always so busy at that junction.

'Molly Rose Hunter and Zofia,' he replied. 'Along with an additional extra. And I'm not letting them go this time.'

'You have Zofia *back*? I thought you said that she didn't get away after Nigel?'

*Fuck*, Leo thought. He had told Marek so many lies that he'd lost track. 'I meant I have them all together now.'

Marek was silent, as though he knew Leo was lying. He was expecting Marek to lose his temper but instead, he said, 'The extra?'

'It's Sinead. Janey Hallahan's daughter. Molly Rose's auntie. She was at the house when I went to get Molly Rose. She got in my way.'

'Is she dead?' Marek queried.

Leo bit the inside of his lip. 'No.'

'Is she sedated? Restrained?'

'Aye, the blow to the face knocked her out. She's in the back of the van with the other two.'

Marek sighed loudly on the other end of the call and then, surprisingly, he laughed. 'I'll make space for her. I'll consider her a bonus for all your fuck-ups in the past.'

Leo slowly raised an eyebrow as the traffic began moving again. 'You want her on the cargo ship with the others?'

'Why wouldn't I?'

'But… but she's not young. Well, not as young.'

'Everyone has a type, Leo. I'll make use of her. Does she have any flaws?'

'She's a recovering junkie. In fact, I had one of my lads inject her with heroin just a few days ago.'

'Why?'

'She was a link to Molly Rose. Someone who would want to see her safe. I had to snuff her out. Only, it didn't go as planned.'

Marek sneered. 'Nothing you ever do goes to plan, Leo. You're a royal fuck-up.'

As the traffic began to pick up speed again, Leo imagined Marek in the boot of his car. Imagined strangling him with a plastic zip tie. Releasing his grip a little, giving him hope that he might live and then pulling tightly again, so tightly that Marek's eyes would pop out.

'I won't let you down,' Leo said.

'Doubtful, Leo. Very doubtful. The cargo ship leaves tomorrow. If those girls, including Sinead, are not on it when it leaves the dock, I'll cement your ankles into breeze blocks and throw you in the fucking Clyde myself. Understood?'

Leo closed his eyes briefly, let out a long breath. *Don't retaliate. Don't react.* 'Yes, boss. Understood.'

The line went dead and Leo kept his eyes on the road. The girls were in his possession. The cargo ship was leaving the dock in less than twenty-four hours. The question Leo had to ask himself was where the fuck he was going to keep them until then. Then it came to him. The one person he knew who could help him with a place; someone who had helped him to sort out locations for the gatherings and the parties. Not all of them, but some. His venues had been discreet. He pulled up the number in his phone and hit call.

'Hello?' the voice on the other end of the call said.

'All right, Inspector Gadget. How you doing?' Leo said with a smile.

The line was silent for a moment, and Leo had to glance back at the dash screen to check they hadn't been disconnected.

'Jimmy boy? You there?'

'I'm here, Leo. What do you want?'

Leo frowned. 'What's up with you? You're usually excited when I contact you. Usually *right* up for a party.'

'Aye, well…' There was a long pause. 'All that's behind me now.'

Leo's smile fell and he raised an eyebrow. 'Is that right?'

'Aye. I should never have got involved with you in the first place. It was wrong. I'm a fucking detective. I abused my position.'

Leo spat out a laugh. 'Since when the fuck did you develop a guilty conscience, *DI Pearson*?'

James Pearson fell silent and Leo decided to fill the gap.

'Look, the reason I'm phoning is, well, I have a bit of an issue.'

'What's that?'

'I need temporary accommodation. Just for the night. I've got some… cargo that needs storing until the ship leaves the dock tomorrow.'

He let the information sink in with James.

'Cargo?'

'Aye. You know, the kind you like to make use of when you're not on duty.'

'No chance. I'm having nothing to do with it,' James replied sharply.

'Oh really? Then you won't mind the bigwigs at the top knowing what you've been up to then? That you like… well, let's just say you have a particular taste in women. You wouldn't mind all that coming out, would you? Just the click of a button, Jimmy boy, and all your secrets would be laid bare to your bosses, all your colleagues. Your family? What would they say, eh? To know that good old daddy, good old husband and good old Inspector James Pearson is a fucking nonce.'

'If I go down, I'll take you with me, Leo. I'll take all of you,' James replied with a quiver in his voice.

A wide, sinister smile spread across Leo's face and laugher erupted. 'No, you fucking won't. You'd die before you ever saw the inside of a jail cell. Marek wouldn't have it. You know what he's like, James. He had my son killed. My *son*. If he can do that to me, think about what he'd do to you if you broke your silence. You know what he's like; he has no mercy. Brutal killings, long, drawn-out suffering.' The thought of what Dean would have went through almost caught in his throat. He swallowed down the hard lump and continued. 'So, like I said, I need emergency accommodation. I would take them back to one of the flats but this is a special order that has to be handled delicately. I need them isolated.'

There was a long, hard sigh and then, 'I assume the dock you're talking about is Greenock?'

'Yes. Leaves tomorrow at four in the morning.'

Another long pause. Leo allowed James the time to think.

'Okay. Meet me at the bottom of Station Road just off the A82. I know a place.'

'Good man,' Leo replied. 'I'm on my way.'

# Chapter 53

As Kristo drove them to Detective Inspector James Pearson's house, Janey was furious. Furious that she'd had the wool pulled over her eyes by him. The bastard had actually checked in on her, told her that there was CCTV he was investigating for when Janey and Ciaran were run off the road. He must have known that was Leo, especially if James was using Leo's services. The fucker must have been on the payroll with Marek too.

The fact his name was on that list was bad enough, but the pictures on that tablet made her feel sick. James abused his position of power and had been captured by Dean Davidson behind the lens of that camera along with many, many others. She and Kristo had gone through the gallery after Cheryl had, or at least gone through it until they couldn't stomach it any more. She couldn't fathom them, how anyone could be so sick in the head. Young people, practically kids, being... and by Leo Davidson himself, as well as Nigel Richardson, among others. But Detective Inspector James Pearson: the man Janey and Ciaran had on their payroll to keep their name out of things, to turn a blind eye to drug and gun running from their end. To be in the pockets of gangsters like them was one thing, but to participate in that kind of shit? *Jesus*, she thought.

'We're here,' Kristo said as he pulled the car into a space outside the house.

'Look,' Janey said as she saw James coming out of the car on his driveway, his face white as chalk. 'Ooft, he looks rough.'

Kristo nodded. '*Dog* rough.'

Narrowing her eyes, Janey got out of the car, deciding to leave the crutch inside. She didn't want to look weak. Just looking at him made her skin crawl, knowing what he was capable of; what he'd done.

'James?' she called just as he unlocked his car, the sound of his name on her lips making her feel sick.

Turning sharply, his eyes flickered with something as he caught her gaze. Surprise? Fear?

'Janey? What are you doing here?'

His voice triggered suspicion in her. Did he know that she knew? No, he'd have disappeared by now if he thought his name was linked to a trafficking organisation.

'I was coming to see if you had any news on who may or may not have run Ciaran and I off the road? Last time we spoke you told me there was possible CCTV footage you were having investigated. Any word on who may have injected Sinead with heroin?' Her voice went up a little on that last word. It was a test, to see if he would crumble and tell her everything that she already knew about him. Of course, she knew he wouldn't. Who in their right mind would freely admit *that* was who they were? 'You've not really been responding to my messages when I've asked about the European gang either.'

'Nothing, I'm afraid. CCTV didn't show anything suspicious,' he said, and she knew fine well he was lying. There'd never been any footage. It had all been a ploy to keep her onside because he was involved with Davidson. 'And no one from the public have come forward either. There was nothing on any of the road cameras in the surrounding area. No witnesses. As for Sinead, we've got nothing. I'm sorry, Janey. But it looks like we've hit a dead end,' James replied. 'And the gang; well, I'm working on it.'

Janey nodded slowly and heard Kristo's door open. James's eyes flickered towards him but only briefly.

'That's frustrating,' Janey replied.

'Sorry,' James said. 'I thought so too. But like I said, I'm working on it.'

Then he glanced down at the laptop bag she carried in her hand.

'I'm actually on my way into the office,' James said unconvincingly.

'Okay,' Janey said. 'Can I just ask, you don't happen to know anything about the missing MP Nigel Richardson, do you?'

His expression remained the same but she knew it had affected him. A man on Leo's list was missing – although she already knew he was dead – and he didn't even blink? She wasn't buying it.

'What do you mean?'

'Well, what happened to him? You've no leads on that?'

James opened the door to his car and said, 'It's a mystery to us at the station, Janey. But why are you asking?'

'I wondered if it might have something to do with the man who ran us off the road.'

Raising an eyebrow, James replied, 'You think *Nigel Richardson* was the one who ran you off the road? But, why would he do that?'

'At this stage, anything is possible,' Janey said. 'This time last year, I had no family other than Ciaran. Now, one of my twin daughters is dead, one was spiked, my husband is lying in an induced coma, and that's *after* my granddaughter was kidnapped and almost killed. Forgive me, James, but I'm struggling to see the good in anyone right now.'

Silence fell between them and then James gave a soft smile. 'I can't begin to imagine how you're feeling, Janey. That's a lot of trauma to process in such a short space of time. There are bad people out there, Janey. Between us, we do our bit to stop them.'

She was about to open her mouth, to tell him what she'd found, when Kristo's phone rang. She turned as he answered it. As soon as he did, the look on his face told her something was very, *very* wrong.

'Shit, shit, shit,' Kristo said, hanging up the phone.

'What's wrong?' Janey asked, watching him rushing around the car towards her.

'We have to go, *right* now. There's been an incident at the house.'

Her stomach flipped. 'What do you mean, an incident?'

'Three of my men are dead. Only Brendan survived. The girls, they're gone.'

Janey felt her mouth drop open. 'What the fuck do you mean, they're gone? Gone where?'

'I don't know. He didn't say. All he said was a shooter came to the house and put a bullet in all of them. Seemed the guy thought he'd killed Brendan too but it skimmed the side of his face. He played dead. But the guy took the girls. And Sinead.'

Janey grabbed on to the door handle of the car to steady herself. 'She's meant to be in the fucking hospital.'

'Yeah, well, she's not. She's gone. We need to find them.'

Janey felt like her head was swimming. She glanced at James, who was simply staring at them.

'Okay, time to cut the shit, James. I know about your involvement with Leo Davidson.'

His face darkened.

'You need to tell me everything you know about him, James.'

He shook his head. 'I don't know anything about a Leo Davidson.'

Kristo spun on his heel and pointed a gun at DI James Pearson's face. 'Your name is on his *fucking* client list. We have fucking images of you with girls young enough to be your fucking daughter; girls he's trafficked into the UK. You know everything there is to know and you're going to start talking right now.'

James's eyes darted to Janey. 'Could you please keep your voice down? I don't want my neighbours hearing this. And I have *no* idea what you're talking about.'

'I think we should go somewhere more private, don't you, *Detective* Inspector Pearson? That is, of course, unless you *want* to have this conversation out in the open? You know, the one where we expose you for being a fucking paedophile?'

His expression fell then, along with his jaw. 'I'm *not* a paedophile.'

'Then what are you?' Kristo asked, the gun still pointed in James's direction.

'Best go inside,' James said, closing the car door.

–

Janey stood by Kristo's side, the gun still very much in line with James Pearson's head.

293

'Nice house you've got here. Gorgeous place to bring up a family,' Janey said, pointedly. 'Tell me, how are the missus and the kids? I'm assuming they don't have a clue that you're a fucking nonce?'

James shook his head. 'We didn't come up here to talk about my private life, did we?'

Janey laughed loudly. 'That's exactly what we came up here to talk about, you fucking idiot. You don't think I've seen them? The pictures?'

James frowned, a deep line forming between his brows. He looked genuinely confused. 'What pictures?'

'The sick parties you attended, with Leo, with Nigel fucking Richardson? It's all there on Leo's tablet. Your face is there. A detective in amongst the vilest humans.'

His eyes widened. 'I… I didn't know.'

'You didn't know what?' Janey pressed. 'That they were kids, or that you were being photographed?'

He bowed his head in what looked like shame, but most likely despair that he'd been caught.

'Where is he?' Janey asked, glaring at him.

'I don't know.'

'I don't believe you. Where were you going when we pulled up outside?'

James didn't answer.

'Give me your phone,' Janey said, holding out her hand.

'No.'

'I don't think you're in a position to argue, detective,' Kristo said, taking a step closer. 'Phone, now.'

James hesitated and then pulled the phone from his pocket and handed it to Kristo, who passed it to Janey.

'It's locked,' she said. 'Passcode?'

'Six seven eight six seven five.'

She tapped in the numbers and stared at the screen. She went to the phone icon and last calls. There it was. Leo Davidson's number.

'Wow,' she said sarcastically. 'You've actually saved his number under his own name. You really did think you would never be caught, didn't you? I don't believe how easy you've made this for me. Tell me, why did he call you around ten minutes before you were setting off to work, as you said outside? What did he want?'

James closed his eyes and raised his chin towards the ceiling before opening them again. 'He said he wanted my help with something?'

'And what would that be?'

James fell back on the sofa, his face sheet-white. 'I can't do this,' he muttered.

'Oh, you fucking can, and you fucking will. I can't kill you, James, because you have information I need, but I can make this process as painful as possible if you'd prefer? Your decision. Easy way or the hard way?'

'You think any of this is easy for me?' James queried.

'Was it easy for those kids you were abusing in those pictures I saw?'

He winced at the words. 'They were of age.'

'Aye, just because they were of age doesn't make it right, does it? Tell me, what's the going rate these days? What does Leo charge?' Janey spat. 'You probably want Kristo here to put a bullet in your skull right now just so you don't have to answer my questions. Rest assured, that's not going to happen. Now, tell me, *where* is he?'

James sat back up straight and shook his head. 'Fuck sake,' he hissed. 'Right, he asked me to help him out with some accommodation.'

'For who?'

'He said he had cargo to store until four tomorrow morning.'

Raising an eyebrow, she briefly glanced at Kristo. 'Cargo? As in people?'

'Yeah. He wasn't specific, but that's usually how he refers to them. That or product.'

'What a fucker,' Janey said through gritted teeth, then she turned to Kristo. 'It's Molly Rose and Zofia. He has them.' Then she turned back to James. 'Did he say how many?'

'Like I said, he said cargo, not people.'

'And you were on your way to meet him just as we showed up?'

He nodded slightly, like a scorned schoolboy.

'We go with him?' Janey asked Kristo.

His brow furrowed as he pulled his lips into a thin line. 'I'm not sure that's such a good idea. He'll take one look at us and could panic that he's going to lose out with his boss again. It could put the girls in real danger.'

'True,' Janey replied. She glanced down at James and raised an eyebrow. 'Looks like you're going to have to lead the way, James. We'll be following. One foot out of line, and I'll do worse than kill you. I'll send all of the evidence I have right to your bosses; your family. So, you'll do exactly what I say. Got it?'

The DI was quiet for a moment, as if he was thinking. Then he looked Janey in the eye and said, 'And what if I don't?'

Janey frowned. 'Are you fucking deaf? I just told you what would happen.'

He shook his head.

'You don't have a choice, James,' Janey replied.

'Everyone has a choice, Janey. I've helped you out enough times over the years to cover up bad choices to come from your firm.'

Janey felt a burning rage rise up through her body. 'Are you threatening me, James?'

'I'm trying to level with you, Janey.'

'I don't level with paedophiles,' Janey tutted as she turned to Kristo, nodded and turned her back.

'No, wait. I was…' James started but the sound of bone crunching under the handle of Kristo's gun stopped him. Janey turned back round, her eyes to the floor. She took a steadying, calming breath.

'I'm utterly fucking sick of men trying to threaten and intimidate me and my family. In fact, sick of it doesn't even come close. Now, if I need to bleed you fucking dry, James, I will.'

She watched as his nose streamed with blood. His eyes were already beginning to swell.

'I'll say it one more time, James. You will do *exactly* as I say. You will not threaten me or my family. You will not expose any of our connections, past or current, because you will only implicate yourself.' Janey leaned down so her face was close enough to smell the blood and said slowly, 'Do I make myself clear?'

DI James Pearson closed his eyes and sighed loudly as blood dripped off his chin. 'Aye, I've fucking got it.'

## Chapter 54

Pulling into the side of the road where James had suggested they meet, Leo kept the engine running and listened carefully for any movement in the back. The girls were silent, which he was surprised at given women were usually noisy, talkative pains in the arse. He glanced down at the lock icon on the dash for the millionth time and was secure knowing that they weren't going anywhere.

The place was deserted and Leo was happy with that. The fewer people around, the less he had to worry about.

His phone rang through the speakers and seeing his wife's name flash up on the screen immediately annoyed him. This was not the time for Cheryl's shit.

'I'm kind of busy. What's up?' Leo said upon answering.

'Is it true?' Cheryl asked, sounding tearful; anxious.

Screwing up his face at the odd random question, he asked, 'What are you talking about? Is what true?'

'You know, even when I saw the pictures, I still hoped that there was a chance I was seeing wrong. Does that make sense?'

Leo raised an eyebrow. *She's officially lost it*, he thought. 'Cheryl, I don't know what's going on, but you need to cut the cryptic crap and just spit it out. *Is. What. True?*'

A small bout of silence, and then a sound he'd only ever heard from her once. When she found out Dean was dead. Not just missing. But *dead*. The guttural, painful sound that came from the very depths of her soul pierced through the speakers in the van and he instantly reached for the volume control, turning it down quickly.

'You *utter* fucking scumbag bastard!'

Something inside him chilled. 'What the hell are you on about?'

'You… you knew,' she cried. 'You knew he was going to be killed and you stood back and allowed it to happen. Your boss called the hit and you just stood there like a scared little boy. You could have stopped it. You could have *protected* our boy but you didn't. Even Dean knew he was going to die and he tried to warn me, but I found his letter too late.'

Leo stared out of the windscreen, stunned by the words coming from Cheryl.

'And to make it all a million times worse, if it could ever actually get worse, is that you're still working for that person. You're *still* bringing young people into the country illegally and subjecting them to…' The sound of a hard swallow filled the car and then a deep, gagging breath. 'You put them in rooms with people who do the most disgusting things to them. But you… you do it too, Leo. I found your tablet, Leo. With everything on it. The client list. The photographs. Did you make Dean take them?'

Leo sat forward and turned the volume down even more. He felt sick to his stomach. How had she found the tablet? And when? Because he had it in his possession all of the time. Had Dean made a copy? Those pictures were leverage against clients who might threaten the organisation. Yes, Dean had been the one to take them. Had he taken pictures of Leo too? Had he planned on grassing on his dad the entire time?

'Cheryl, I don't know what or who has got into your head, but you need to stop talking right now. You're being deluded.' His words had no edge to them now. What she'd seen, it was enough to send her into this spiral.

'I've got the fucking evidence to prove it!' she screamed. 'You, I saw you.'

Leo closed his eyes. Jesus.

*The wee bastard*, he thought.

He parted his lips to speak, to try to say anything to calm her down. But she got in there first.

'You're never going to get away with this.'

Leo couldn't stop the laugh that escaped his lips. 'Aye, right, Cheryl.'

'You think I'm kidding? I'm deadly serious. I won't stop until you pay for our son's death. He's dead because of you. I'll make sure you suffer, you selfish, self-centred fucking prick.'

'I'll fucking bury you, Cheryl. What makes you think you'd be able to overpower me?'

'I won't have to. You won't see me coming.'

Leo shook his head and a little smile raised the corner of his mouth. 'You knew what I was when you married me, Cheryl. Let's not pretend for a moment that you didn't. You weren't bothered back then, were you? Dating a twenty-year-old suited you. I had a car, the looks. You were spoiled rotten and you loved it.'

A quiet gasp came. 'Are you *actually* kidding? You're telling me it's my fault?'

'No, all I'm saying is, well, you were fifteen when we met. You should have known better.'

'Wow. And is it the fault of those young people you smuggled into the country that you are what you are? You know what, Leo, I can't wait to watch you die. I hope it's fucking brutal and painful and I hope that the second you're about to take your last breath that you regret every decision you've ever made to make people's lives a misery.'

Leo jabbed at the end call icon on the screen and dug his body back on the seat behind him. *Shit shit shit.*

Turning the car around, Leo pulled off Station Road and on to Mount Pleasant Drive. He needed a minute to get his thoughts straight. He needed Marek to know that he could be relied on.

'Think,' he said out loud. Glancing up at the Erskine Bridge, he remembered seeing a sign that it was closed to all traffic. Something to do with maintenance. He could just drive to the dock and wait until Marek got there. But he had three live humans in the back of his van. If the police stopped him, he was fucked. If he didn't make it to the dock, Marek would kill him.

Pulling up maps on his phone, he looked at the surrounding area and, on it, an abandoned house featured at the end of the road. The most up-to-date image was just a few months ago. What were the chances it was still unoccupied? Likely, he thought.

Taking a breath, he turned the van around and drove slowly to the end of the road. Sure enough, the house he'd seen on the maps was there, looking just as abandoned as it did online.

'Perfect,' he said quietly.

# Chapter 55

The engine died. She instinctively tried to glance around in the dark space of the van but she could see nothing behind the blindfold. Could only feel her own fear, and that of Sinead and Zofia.

Where were they? Where had he taken them? But most importantly, what was he going to do with them next? She knew the answer to that, but not the detail. Molly Rose wasn't going to allow Leo Davidson to send her off to some foreign land without a fight.

Molly Rose listened carefully as she heard Leo get out of the van. Footsteps. One, two, three. He stopped. She couldn't judge where he was in relation to the car. But he was still close by. She could hear Sinead and Zofia breathing. Slow, steady breaths. Yeah, she thought. That's it. Stay calm. The calmer we are, the calmer he'll be and the closer we are to getting the hell away from him.

A gentle tap came then, on the back doors. Then his leering, disgusting voice.

'We're going to be staying somewhere for the night until it's time to ship you off,' Leo said. 'I'll be back in a moment, just going to check the place is good for us to stay and then I'll help you all in, one at a time.'

Help them in, like he was some kind of fucking butler. Molly Rose shuddered at the sound of his voice but relief flooded her at the sound of his footsteps getting further and further away.

'Now,' Sinead's muffled voice came from behind her gag.

'How? We're still tied up,' Molly Rose replied as clearly as she could. And he wouldn't have left the car unlocked. 'No, we need to wait until we're inside wherever it is he's going to be keeping us.'

A crunching of gravel underfoot getting closer and closer made Molly Rose freeze. He was coming back, quicker than when he'd walked away at first. The lock clicked, the doors opened, and a little light filtered through her blindfold, but not enough to be able to make anything out around her.

'Okay, Molly Rose, you first,' he grunted as he pulled her up and then, suddenly, she was up on his shoulder, her head dangling upside down behind him, her hands tied at her back and her feet bumping off the front of his body. They must be somewhere remote for him to be carelessly carrying her out of the back of the van and over his shoulder in such an open space.

She felt the air around her change, from outdoor to indoor. And the place stunk to high heaven of musty old wood and a faint scent of old urine. The same scents contained in the building where Charlie had kept her just months earlier. Suddenly, panic began to rise and Molly Rose realised that she wasn't as tough as Janey: a hardened gangster who'd experienced enough trauma in her life that she knew how to cope with it. Molly Rose was not an experienced gangster. She was a sixteen-year-old girl who'd been through far too much in her short life.

*I don't want to die. I want my mum.*

'Right,' he said, throwing her down onto a some-what softer surface than she was expecting, knocking the thoughts out of her head. 'Next one.'

He was gone, out of wherever he'd left her, back to the van for the others. The place was silent and she remembered trying to work out where she was when Charlie had taken her. It had been impossible, there had been no starting point, not really. All she'd felt back then was fear; much the same as she felt now. But she had to swallow it down. Being scared wasn't going to save her or the others now.

He returned, threw someone down but not right next to her, not even in the same room. Shit, she thought, he was keeping them separate. She could hear his breath, and felt him move around her, slowly, like he was trying to suss her out. What was there to suss? She was tied up, completely at his mercy, containing a shiver at the memory of what Zofia had told her about him: that he wasn't just the guy who had brought her here, but he was also *that* guy. The kind who would... She couldn't even think it. And she was alone, in a room with him. *Fuck.*

–

Out of nowhere, her blindfold was removed with a harsh tug. Narrowing her eyes, she blinked up at him as he removed her gag.

'Right,' he said in a low voice. 'I want to know everything there is to know about your gran.'

Molly Rose's brow crinkled. 'Eh?'

'You heard.'

She pursed her lips. 'Aye,' she replied, licking her tongue around the inside of her mouth, trying desperately to stem the thirst. 'I heard you, I just don't get it.'

'What's not to get? I want to know the ins and outs of Janey's businesses, who she deals with, the lot.'

'What would make you think I know the ins and outs of her business dealings? I'm sixteen.'

'Don't give me that shit,' Leo said as he paced the room slowly.

'It's not shit.'

He stopped, stared at her. 'You really expect me to believe that you don't know anything?'

Molly Rose took a breath. She was going to be shipped off to some other country, where Christ knew what would happen to her. She'd rather die than that. There wasn't much to live for right now anyway, was there? The constant battle of trying to get away from people who wanted her dead *because* of Janey was tiring.

'Even if I did, I wouldn't tell you, would I?'

'Ha.' He laughed so loudly it made Molly Rose jump. 'You're fucking ballsy. Just like her, I suppose.' Leo leaned in, his nose almost touching hers. She stared into his eyes. She could see Dean in there. Shame he had such a dickhead for a dad, otherwise he might have turned out differently and he wouldn't be dead. 'What about the salon? She's laundering through that, right?' Leo said, and Molly Rose shrugged.

'Why don't you ask your wife? She works there, after all.'

Leo glared at her through narrowed eyes. 'Fucking hell, give me something, you stupid little bitch.'

A backhanded slap threw her back onto the sofa she'd been dumped on. It stung so much it started to go numb.

'Dean hated you, did you know that?' she said, her entire body trembling.

Leo glared down at her. He was quiet for a moment, as though thinking about what she'd just said. 'What did you just say to me? Are you on a death wish?'

'It's better than what you've got planned for us, isn't it?' Molly Rose pulled herself back up and, before she could stop herself, she spat a mouthful of saliva at him, spraying his jeans at the knee.

He looked down as if unfazed and then met her eye.

'My son didn't hate me, Molly Rose. Far from it.' He sat down on an old wooden coffee table in front of her.

'He used those exact words to me,' Molly Rose replied. 'You're lying.'

Molly Rose kept her eye on him. She wanted to hurt him, if that was possible. The man didn't seem to possess the ability to feel anything for anyone other than himself.

'My son was just like me, only a few years behind.'

Molly Rose didn't believe that to be the case. If Dean was anything like Leo, then why was she still a virgin? Surely if Dean was the same as his dad, then he'd have raped her? Or at least talked her into having sex before she was ready. Not that she was going to say that to Leo, it could trigger him into doing something that couldn't be undone; something that Molly Rose might never get over.

'Only difference was he had more of a conscience; too much so for the work we were carrying out. Even if he did complete his task of getting you out of the country, he'd have probably been eaten up by guilt eventually. I tried to toughen him up, but he was more like his mum than me. I tried to bond with him. But it was hard when he didn't share the same interests as me. But never for one moment did I ever think he would…' He let the words trail off into the darkness of the room and Molly Rose frowned.

'Think he would what?'

Leo didn't answer. He seemed distant. Had something happened between them before Dean was murdered that made him question Dean's loyalty to the job?

'Is that why you let your boss kill him?' Molly Rose asked flatly, knowing fine well it could result in another slap, or worse.

Leo shot her a look. 'That's not what happened.'

'So what *did* happen then? Because going by what I've been told, that's exactly how it went down. You *knew* he was going to be murdered and you allowed it to go ahead. Some hardman you are if you can't even protect your own son,' Molly Rose said with as much venom as possible, although inside she was trembling.

'It's none of your fucking business,' Leo spat before getting up and pacing the room.

'It is my business though. He was trying to traffic me out of the country. If my mum hadn't intervened, I'd be in some other country being used as some kind of fucking sex slave and Dean would still be alive. That's what caused it, wasn't it? I was too hot to touch given that she got involved so he backed off and then he was killed for failing to complete the job.'

Leo lurched forward and grabbed Molly Rose's face, digging his fingernails into her cheeks. Her stomach lurched with fear but she needed to keep going. She needed to try to break him down. 'You think you're a smart little bitch, don't you? Think you know it all. You know *fuck* all.'

'I know a lot more than you think. Dean told me things. About you. About Cheryl.'

He let go of her, pushed her back on the sofa. 'It was all a way to pull you in, Molly Rose. It was his job. He was *doing* the job he was being paid for. And if you believed it all, then I suppose he did something right.'

'Yeah, maybe he did. I suppose that's one thing you can be proud of him for,' Molly Rose said, raising an eyebrow.

Leo glared at her, but there was a hint of curiosity about his expression.

'Don't you want to know what he had to say about you?' Molly Rose pressed, knowing that her luck would run out soon.

Leo didn't say anything as Molly Rose studied his face. Was he feeling guilty about his son? Did this man feel any emotions?

'You're cocky for a young girl who's about to become a slave,' Leo replied, although Molly Rose knew it was an attempt at deflection.

'He really did hate you, you know? I'm not lying.'

Leo frowned, regarded her through narrowed eyes.

'Like, *really* hated you. I mean, obviously I didn't know who you were but he said you were a… now, let me try to remember his exact words. Oh yeah, he called you a big bullying bastard. Yeah, that's right. Said you were always shouting at him as a kid. Never showed any pride in his achievements when he was growing up. If he was good at football, he got no reaction from you. Good at maths, nothing. But then this one time, he got into a fight at school and suddenly you were so happy. He said that you told him you were "proud as fuck" that he'd showed this other boy what he was made of. Proper Davidson stuff, according to him.'

She could see it, a vulnerability about him as he stared down at the floor. He parted his lips and said very quietly, 'Shut up.'

'I felt sorry for him,' Molly Rose continued. 'I mean, I spent so much time with him before he was killed. I actually got to see a side that now, when I look back, I'm still sure was real. I mean, I didn't believe it when it all came out about him. I remember reading about it in the paper and I just couldn't believe it. I don't even know how the police never linked you to his crimes. Like, how did you get off but he was on the police radar?'

'I said, shut up,' he said more firmly this time.

'But then, when I thought about it all, as much as Dean was successful in grooming me – I mean, I fell for him, that was his plan – I still felt sorry for him. Now, the person I feel most sorry for is Cheryl.'

Leo was visibly chewing on the inside of his cheek; Molly Rose could tell she was getting a rise out of him.

'Dean actually told me how he knew you regularly cheated on his mum. Dean hated lying to her; hated pretending that he knew nothing of what was going on. But what's worse is now I know it wasn't just cheating, was it, Leo? It was you *abusing* young fucking kids. People like me and younger. People like Zofia.'

She watched as he raised his hand and Molly Rose braced herself for impact. He brought his hand down on her face, slapping her so hard it would have hurt him. She felt her face explode then, and a warm, wet sensation of blood trickling down her cheek made her wince.

'Just because my boss wants you on that ship doesn't mean I won't fucking kill you,' Leo said through gritted teeth.

Molly Rose looked up at him. She couldn't show weakness. That was how she'd managed to get through her ordeal with Charlie, by being strong, by feigning bravery. She wasn't about to crumble now.

'But you won't, because if your boss doesn't get what he wants this time, the only person getting killed is you. Same boss, two Davidsons within, what, a year of each other? That's brutal, if you ask me.'

'If you really want to know the meaning of the word brutal, Molly Rose, then keep running that cheeky little fucking mouth of yours; see where you end up,' Leo snarled at her.

She knew she was pressing her luck; if this had been Charlie she'd have lost a few teeth by now.

'What is it with men? I mean first there was Dean, although that failed *spectacularly*. Then Charlie: he was a fucking disaster too, left me free on a bridge because he shat it from my gran. Now you. I wonder how you'll get caught?'

Leo laughed. 'You think you're getting out of this?'

'They say things happen in threes, don't they?'

'You truly believe that you're not getting put on that boat and shipped off to serve *my* punters?'

Molly Rose shook her head. 'They're not your punters though. They're your bosses. You're nothing but a middleman, a dogsbody. You're nothing more than Dean was, Leo. At least Dean had some kind of humanity left about him; I mean, he actually gave a shit about people, about his mum. You? You couldn't give two fucks about anyone other than yourself.'

That's what did it. He delivered a third blow, this time to the jaw. He hit so hard the pain shot through her teeth right into the back of her head.

'I should have left that gag on, saved you from your fucking self,' he said, replacing the blindfold and gag before throwing her over his shoulder and carrying her out of the room. He threw her down and placed his lips against her ear. 'Not another fucking peep out of you, Molly Rose, or I'll terrorise one of your wee mates here and make you watch. Under*fucking*stood?'

Molly Rose nodded and remained silent. Good, she thought, as much as her face and jaw hurt like hell, she'd got him thinking about Dean. That would make him vulnerable, even if he'd never admit it to himself. He'd be thinking about his son, what he'd done to get him killed. While he was doing that, she could try to work out how to get them out of there before it was too late.

## Chapter 56

*Little fucking bitch*, he thought as he paced the room back and forth. He should have killed her there and then. All that bullshit about Dean. He'd never have spoken to her about his family. Never. Then again, the things that Molly Rose had said were true. Leo *had* been unfaithful to Cheryl. And Dean himself had told Leo that he hated him on numerous occasions, although not in recent years. Then there was the letter Cheryl claimed she'd found, alongside the tablet. *Fuck*. Maybe Molly Rose knew more than Leo was giving her credit for.

His phone buzzed in his pocket and, when he pulled it out, that same feeling of loathing and dread he always felt when he saw Marek's name flash up on the screen washed over him.

'Marek?' Leo answered, hoping that his boss was in a good mood.

'You've got them secured?'

'I do. They're tied up and I have them in a safe house just off the junction for the bridge so I can get them down to the dock in plenty of time.'

'You know the bridge is closed?' Marek asked, sounding annoyed.

'Only for maintenance on the underside. The road itself is still useable,' Leo replied, feeling frustrated that

Marek still didn't trust him to get the job done after all this time.

'I'd do it myself,' Marek replied, 'but I have other business to tend to beforehand. You won't fuck this up, Leo.' It wasn't a question, more of a demand.

'Far from it.'

'And using the bridge when it's closed, it's not something that's going to get you pulled over, is it?'

Leo smiled. 'I've already done a check. Last night, actually. There are only cones at the entry slip, easily moved. And the bridge itself is fine, like I said. The workers are on the underside at the south side of the bridge. So by the time I cross it, they won't have had a chance to see me.'

'And cameras?' Marek asked.

'I've got fake plates and my face will be covered. I've got it all under control, Marek, it's not a problem. The girls will be there in plenty time. You'll get your Molly Rose plus two bonus girls. You're good.'

A short spell of silence made Leo feel nervous. Molly Rose had been right, he hated to admit. But if Leo did anything to mess this up like Dean had, if Marek didn't get this girl in particular, Leo was dead.

'Right, I suppose I'll have to trust you then,' Marek said.

Marek ended the call and Leo fell back onto the old sofa. Then he remembered the six-pack of beers in the front seat of the car. One or two wouldn't do him any harm. He wouldn't be driving down to Greenock for a good few hours anyway.

Pushing himself up from the sofa, Leo headed outside to get the beer. He peeked into the other room where the girls were held up. They were sitting there in silence; Molly Rose subdued due to the beating he'd given her for her cheek. Good, he thought. If they continued to behave like that for the rest of the time they were here, he'd have no trouble at all.

# Chapter 57

'Molly Rose?' A muffled voice came from behind a gag.

'Uh ah,' she replied, her mind foggy from the beating she'd taken. She didn't want to use up any more of her energy trying to speak. She needed to try to think clearly about their next move. 'Ssh.'

She couldn't even tell who was next to her.

'Right then,' Leo said, his sudden presence jolting Molly Rose like an electric shock. 'I need a beer. I'll be checking on you three. So don't go doing anything stupid. Not that you can,' he laughed. 'I've made sure of that. Boss man's expecting you. How's the face, Molly Rose? Still sore from all that cheek you gave me?'

*The boss man.* The words echoed in Molly Rose's mind.

Molly Rose winced from the pain in her jaw as it shot up her head.

And then, as if without a care in the world, Leo left the room. A door closed just a short distance away. Footsteps fell further. The skoosh of a can opening, and his voice, echoing somewhere in another room. He was on the phone but his words were inaudible.

Molly Rose lay down on her side and rubbed the side of her face Leo hadn't battered on what felt like the arm of a sofa, pulling at the material around her face. It loosened so much that she was able to push it up above her eyes.

She squinted, adjusted her eyes, ignoring the pain in her jaw and face.

They were definitely in a house; the room she was in now was similar to the one she'd been in with Leo just moments earlier. To her right, a window, or at least where a window used to be. Now, it was just a wooden board. A flimsy-looking one at that. She glanced back at Zofia and Sinead who were lying on their sides, their arms behind them and looking like they'd given up.

She needed to get the gag out of her mouth; needed to untie her hands. She looked around the room, her eyes almost fully adjusted to the dark.

*How the hell am I here again*, she thought to herself, trying to sit up properly.

There wasn't much in the room from what she could see. No furniture, no sharp objects to rub the plastic ties against. *Shit.*

And then she remembered. Keys. She had keys to Janey's house in her pocket. On those keys was one of those multitool key rings. She'd barely looked at it when Janey had handed her the keys. But they usually had a bottle opener, a mini screwdriver. Maybe there was something sharp she could use to cut the ties. But how?

Glancing back at Sinead and Zofia, she knew she needed to get their blindfolds off and gags out. She needed to get her own gag out.

'Sinead,' she muffled, shuffling towards her.

Sinead seemed to be paying attention; it was hard to tell without being able to see her eyes or hear her voice.

'Sinead, pull my gag out,' Molly Rose whispered so quietly she barely heard the words herself. As if she knew what to do, instantly Sinead sat up, turned her back to Molly Rose and wiggled her fingers. Molly Rose lowered herself towards Sinead's hands and placed the gag against her. Sinead hooked a finger in and, to her surprise, Molly Rose was able to wiggle the gag out of her mouth and down onto her chin. It was uncomfortable as it was still tight, but more bearable. She licked her tongue around the inside of her mouth, trying to wet it, and tasted more blood. 'Turn around, I'll try to remove your blindfold.'

Sinead did what Molly Rose said and then Molly Rose tried to stand as best she could with her ankles bound together. The sound of Leo's distant voice still speaking down the phone was reassuring that they still had a window of time.

Molly Rose's fingers fumbled around the blindfold, but she managed to hook a finger under the material and lift it up and over the top of Sinead's head. Molly Rose then moved her fingers down and did the same with the gag. It was still in place, but out of Sinead's mouth now.

'Jesus,' Sinead whispered, licking her lips. 'Where are we? What did he do to you?' she asked, glaring at Molly Rose's face.

Molly Rose shook her head and silently shushed Sinead. Then, trying her best to ignore the pain as she moved her lips, she slowly mouthed, 'I have a tool in my pocket on Janey's keys. I need you to get it out and try to cut me out of the ties.'

Sinead watched her lips closely, trying to read every word. Then she nodded and, awkwardly, they manoeuvred themselves into a position where Molly Rose had her front pocket pressed up against Sinead's hand, which was still tied behind her back.

Glancing down, Molly Rose could see how difficult this was going to be, if possible at all. But she wasn't going to give up. Not now that they were this close. She'd managed to get away from Charlie when he had a knife pressed into her spine on that bridge. She *could* do this.

'A bit higher,' she whispered. 'Wait, I'll lower myself. Yeah, now slip your fingers in. Even if you can hook a finger in and just slide it out. Just try not to drop it, otherwise he'll hear us.'

Molly Rose focused so hard her vision blurred a little. But it was slowly coming up from the bottom of her pocket, inching closer and closer. And then, it was falling from the pocket towards the hard floor. It hit the floor with a metallic jangle and Molly Rose held her breath. *Shit.* If he heard it, he'd come in. And if that happened, he'd see that two out of the three were minus a blindfold and a gag and he'd lose his shit.

As if by a miracle, Leo was still chatting loudly on the phone in another room. He hadn't heard a thing. She and Sinead let out a breath of relief at the same time and Molly Rose glanced down at the keys on the floor. How the fuck were they going to be able to pick them up?

'Use your mouth,' Sinead whispered.

Molly Rose nodded, and attempted to get down on to the floor, making as little noise as possible. She sat down and shimmied off the old, disgusting-smelling sofa onto the floor. Leaning on her side, pressing the left side of her face to the dusty wooden floor, Molly Rose opened her mouth and gently picked up the keys with her teeth, feeling a sharp pain surge through her gums. He'd really done a number on her. She raised herself slowly, waiting for the inevitable jangle once more. It came, softer this time. She kept the keys firmly clamped in her jaw, pinkish saliva pooling at the side of her mouth. Then Sinead's hands appeared at her mouth, and she took the keys from Molly Rose. Sinead was going to have to try to manoeuvre her fingers to release the correct tool for cutting the plastic tie at Molly Rose's back.

'Okay, I think I see it. Your fingers are actually on it,' she whispered as quietly as she could. 'You need to hook your thumb through the ring and then use both index fingers to slide the small blade out from its safety cover.'

Molly Rose watched in disbelief as Sinead actually managed it. She gripped it in her bound hands and Molly Rose smiled.

Molly Rose took a steadying breath and mouthed slowly, 'Right, I'm going to take it in my mouth and try to cut you free. I'll try my best not to hurt you. I'm sorry if I do.'

Sinead nodded in agreement.

Molly Rose glanced back at Zofia, who had been silent the entire time. She was waiting on her turn to be set free.

Clamping the chunky end of the tool in her teeth, Molly Rose moved towards the plastic ties around Sinead's wrists and prayed to anyone who would hear her that she wouldn't slit her auntie's wrists.

And then she started, slow, steady cuts, back and forward. She didn't want to take the blade off the plastic and not meet the same point. In a way she was sawing her out of the ties. Again, saliva pooled and dripped from her mouth, making it difficult to keep the key ring in one place.

'It feels looser,' Sinead whispered. And then, finally, after what felt like forever, the zip tie broke and Sinead's hands were free.

She turned, took the key ring from Molly Rose's mouth and cut the tie on her ankles. Then the ties on Molly Rose's wrists too.

They both breathed a sigh of relief again, and Sinead freed Zofia, who stood up and all three of them hugged for a moment, in utter silence. No one cried. In fact, Molly Rose couldn't be sure any of them even breathed in that moment.

'Now we just need to work out how to get out without him hearing or seeing us,' Zofia whispered.

Molly Rose glanced at the door, and then down at the key ring in Sinead's hand.

'That doesn't look very sturdy,' Sinead said, glancing at the board covering the window.

'It would still make a lot of noise,' Molly Rose replied. 'I know this sounds mad, but I say we wait.'

They both looked at her, dumbfounded.

'Wait?'

'What else? We don't even know our way out of here. Look, he said he needed a beer. I heard him open a can. If he drinks enough, he might fall asleep.'

Sinead glared at Molly Rose in the dark, studying the marks left by Leo's hands. She gave Sinead a reassuring smile that she was okay, even though she was in agony. But she had to keep focused on getting away from him.

'Are you okay?' Zofia asked so quietly Molly Rose barely heard her.

'I will be. We all will. I'm getting us out of here.'

## Chapter 58

Janey couldn't help but revel in the look on DI James Pearson's face when he watched her team of men filter through his front door and into his living room. He'd had no choice in the matter when Janey had suggested they all meet at his house before going to take down Leo Davidson.

'Thank you all for coming,' Janey started. 'I know how difficult it must be for you all to come together for a job today considering you lost two out of three of your men at the hands of Leo Davidson at my house today. I'm so sorry for your loss, I know you're all very close. I want to thank you for coming together in my family's name. You've no idea how much that means to me, given the fact that Ciaran is still in hospital and Sinead checked herself out without telling me. Thankfully, Brendan survived the shooting today and was able to identify Sinead being there. He'll be rewarded handsomely for his dedication to the Hallahan empire. As will you all.'

The men were silent, their eyes on her. It seemed like only yesterday she'd called them all together to help her family. Now, here she was again, fighting for her family once more.

'Mrs Hallahan, could we have an update on Mr Hallahan? How's he doing?' one of her security team asked.

'He's still in an induced coma. From what I understand, it will only be for a few days and then they'll attempt to bring him around. Keep everything crossed for him that he pulls through without any lasting effects.'

Kristo was stood by her side and cleared his throat. 'Now, Detective Inspector James Pearson here has had some, let's just say, *disgusting* involvement with Leo Davidson. He had a call, just an hour or so ago, from Davidson himself, requesting the DI's help in getting some *cargo* to a safe location until he can get it to the shipping dock in Greenock by four in the morning.'

Janey took a breath. How anyone could compare people to cargo was beyond her. This Davidson was the worst kind of criminal she'd ever come across.

'We believe that *cargo* is our Molly Rose, along with Zofia and Sinead. He is planning to ship them off in the early hours. We *cannot* let this happen. So, James here is going to tell us where he was planning to meet Davidson. I want you boys to go there, take him out the second you have the chance and get those girls back to me. Sounds a lot simpler than it will be, but I trust you all. You've been with me since day one.'

They all nodded, but there was a fiery anger to their expressions as they all glanced down at James Pearson, sitting down on the sofa.

'Go on,' Janey said. 'Tell them what you told me.'

James took a breath, blinked and said, 'I arranged to meet him on Station Road. I was going to show him an unoccupied house where he could keep the… cargo.'

Janey shook her head. 'Get in your car. Two of my men will travel with you in the back. You so much as blink the wrong way and they'll take your head off. Any signs that you've warned him about us, they'll take your balls off first. Understood?'

James nodded frantically. *Snivelling little git*, she thought.

'Right, up,' Kristo said, stepping forward and hooking an arm under James's, pulling him up roughly from the sofa. He glanced at two of the men and said, 'You two are in charge of this paedo rat. You heard Janey, any shit from him and he suffers.'

'Aye,' they both said as they followed Kristo out to the car. Janey watched them go and turned back to the rest of the team.

'The rest of you, I want some of you behind them, some of you behind me. When we get there, do what you think is best. I just want the girls back safe and sound.'

They all nodded. 'And what about this Davidson's boss, Janey? What would you like done with him?'

Janey glanced up at the ceiling. 'Well, from what I can gather, he's still here in Scotland. As brazen as it is, I think he's planning on travelling on that ship. He has this obsession about getting Molly Rose overseas. It's like a cockfight between him and Davidson. If I can end him too, it means Molly Rose is finally safe from all these lunatic bastards. I'm thinking we could surprise him at the dock? I could pull a few strings to get us in there, what with my connections at Belfast and Stranraer. I'm sure it wouldn't be a problem. He won't know we're coming.'

'Got it,' one replied before they all headed out of the house.

Janey glanced out of the window and down at the car park. She watched as James climbed into the driver seat and two of her men climbed into the back. He looked utterly terrified.

*Good*, she thought. These men needed putting in the ground, a lot further down than six feet. *Below devil level*, she thought as she walked out of James Pearson's flat and down the stairs to the car park.

'Good to go, Janey,' Kristo said as the last of the team climbed into their cars.

Nodding, Janey looked up at the windows of the surrounding houses. Were curtains twitching? People around here would know who James was. A DI who'd been escorted from his home by men dressed in black trousers and bomber jackets. Nosy neighbours might call the police about it. They might contact the press or post it on social media.

It wouldn't be a bad thing. Maybe it was time these people were called out online.

But when she really looked, there were no faces at windows; no phones recording what was happening. Because the truth of it was no one cared what went on outside of their own lives. And that suited Janey down to the ground.

She got into Kristo's car and closed the door, glancing around at the interior.

'You're missing the Defender, aren't you?' he asked as he pulled his belt on.

'I'm just missing being able to drive. I'm missing being able to live a normal life without constant threat. The Defender is just metal. It can be replaced.'

Kristo looked at her with a worrying stare. 'It's going to be okay, you know. We're going to get them back and put an end to all this.'

'Hmm,' Janey said, looking out the window as the cars started to pull out of the private car park. 'I'm beginning to wonder if I'm a contributing factor to *all this*.'

'What do you mean?'

Kristo started the engine and pulled out behind one of the team cars.

'This world that we live in, the drugs, the guns, the crime, even down to the trafficking, I'm part of it all. It's all connected, isn't it?'

Kristo pulled a face. 'Your empire has nothing to do with Leo Davidson and his organisation, Janey.'

'Doesn't it?'

Kristo fell silent.

'I mean, think about it. People get hooked on drugs, they become vulnerable, homeless. They've lost everything. And then people like Leo Davidson come along and offer these people a new life. Then, bam, before they know it, they're in a fucking brothel somewhere in Eastern Europe, still addicted to the drugs I put out on the streets, but to make matters worse, they're being sold to serve the most disgusting people known to humanity.'

She glanced out of the window and fell silent again.

'So, what do you want to do about it? Give it all up?' Kristo asked as they headed along Great Western Road. Grand sandstone buildings and detached houses flashed by as Kristo kept up with the rest of the team cars.

'Honestly? I don't know. Maybe I'm too old for all this now. Maybe I should never have taken over from my dad at all. If I hadn't, Orla would still be alive, that's for sure. And my other daughter and granddaughter's lives wouldn't be at risk either.'

'You can't blame yourself for the decisions of people like Charlie and Leo Davidson, Janey.'

'Can't I? Like I said, it's because of me this is all happening.'

Maybe it *was* time to give it all up. To try to live some kind of normal life away from organised crime.

But what if Ciaran didn't survive?

What if they *didn't* get to the girls in time?

What would she do then?

# Chapter 59

The itch had crept over her entire body now, the cold sweats had taken over and all she wanted was one, just one hit of heroin to get her through. If Sinead hadn't been spiked, she wouldn't be feeling this way right now.

*Fuckfuckfuck*, she thought as she took a deep breath. She'd been good. She'd been clean. Now this fucker in the next room was responsible for her being spiked and she was back at square one. Would it be better if she didn't survive this? If she died, she wouldn't have to suffer the withdrawal any more; the constant gnawing in the back of her mind that screamed out for heroin. The withdrawal was accompanied by guilt and grief. Guilt that her sixteen-year-old niece seemed to be the one with a plan to get them out, guilt that Sinead's brain couldn't function to even come up with one suggestion. The grief constricted in her chest. Orla. Her twin. She shouldn't have been the one to die in the way that she did. It should have been Sinead. Orla had everything going for her, a husband, a successful business, a beautiful home. What did Sinead have? Nothing. Not even a fucking toothbrush.

*Jesus*, she thought as the itching intensified. She tried desperately not to scratch. It was bad enough being locked up in an abandoned house. Throwing withdrawal into the mix wasn't something she wanted to pile onto Molly Rose's already full plate right now.

Glancing up at Molly Rose as she stood at the door of the room, her heart was in her throat.

Tiptoeing across the floor, Sinead stood next to her and shrugged, her expression questioning what she was doing.

Molly Rose raised her finger to her mouth and silently shushed her. The swelling on her cheek was getting bigger and her jaw was already starting to bruise. It didn't seem to faze her. How was this girl *only* sixteen? She'd been through more in the last couple of years than most people went through in a lifetime and she always seemed to face things head on, with a strength Sinead could only dream of. Just like her mum. Orla had always been able to face things head on too.

'I think he's fallen asleep,' Molly Rose mouthed slowly.

Sinead raised an eyebrow. 'Really?' she mouthed back.

Molly Rose nodded and Sinead peered around the door. She was right. Leo Davidson was sat on a sofa, his head resting on the back of it so his face was raised to the ceiling. A gentle snore came from him and Sinead let out a slow breath. This could be it, their chance to run. But how?

Molly Rose shifted her position and pulled the key tool out of her pocket, the one they'd used to free themselves. Sinead glanced down at it and then back up, meeting her niece's eye.

'No,' she mouthed clearly as she shook her head.

Of course, Molly Rose ignored her and flicked open the small blade that was only meant to be used as a box opener, or a letter opener.

Sinead gripped Molly Rose's elbow and mouthed, 'No.'

'It's him or us, Sinead. I know what I'd rather,' Molly Rose whispered, pulling her arm from Sinead's grip. 'Go check the door.'

'It will be locked. He's a criminal, an organised crime boss, he's not going to kidnap us and forget to lock the door.'

'Just do it.'

Sinead puffed out her cheeks quietly and felt a presence next to her. Zofia had joined them.

'What's going on?' she mouthed.

'Ask this lunatic,' Sinead replied, tiptoeing her way to the door at the end of the hall. Taking a breath, fully expecting that the door would be locked, Sinead glanced down to see that the door wasn't even closed properly. 'What the hell?' she said quietly, before pulling on it. It opened inwardly and a second door presented itself. Of course it did. It was a newer door to the interior one. A long glass panel set in the centre.

Stepping forward, she pulled on the second handle. It was, of course, locked. They could smash their way out. But that would wake Leo. Turning back to look at Molly Rose, she shook her head.

Smiling a little, Molly Rose crept across the floor and came to stand next to Sinead. Zofia was still by the door of the room they were in.

'Something isn't right,' Sinead said, her hands trembling with fear and withdrawal. 'Why would he randomly just go to sleep knowing that we're in here and that we would be attempting to free ourselves?'

'Because he's a fucking idiot,' Molly Rose said. 'And doesn't realise that we're clever enough to attempt to get free. Right, you know how to pick locks, don't you?'

'It's not the skill I'm most proud of, but yeah. I'll do it as quickly as I can,' Sinead stated.

'Yeah. But when it opens we have to take him out before we run. If we don't, he'll only come after us. This won't end unless he's dead, Sinead. You have to understand that.'

Sinead did understand that. But killing him?

'Can't you just wound him?'

Molly Rose shook her head. 'He can't come after us if he's dead.'

'You can't do it, Molly Rose.'

Looking at Sinead through narrowed eyes, Molly Rose raised an eyebrow. 'It's him or us, Sinead. I'm not willing to lose my life in a brutal manner for this piece of scum.'

Sinead went to speak but Molly Rose shoved the multitool key ring into her hand. Glancing down at it, she sighed and turned to face the door before getting to work. As she studied the tool, Sinead realised there was nothing thin enough to be able to wiggle into the keyhole.

*Shit.*

As if hearing her thoughts, Molly Rose glanced down at her. 'What's wrong?'

'I can't do it.'

'Do what?' Leo's voice filtered down the hallway.

They all turned sharply towards him. He stood there, filling the space in the doorway. Sinead froze, Zofia rushed backwards into the room and Sinead heard a thump, like she'd thrown herself to the floor. But Molly Rose just stood there, calm as ever, staring back at him. She opened her hand and wiggled her fingers a little. Sinead placed the tool into her hand, the blade still facing outward.

'Did you really think I was asleep?' Leo asked with humour to his tone. 'I was just testing you, to see if you would try. Seems like I was right. I knew you'd try to escape.'

'That was a big risk. How did you know we wouldn't just kill you?'

'But you didn't,' Leo replied.

'You're not taking us, Leo. It's as simple as that,' Molly Rose said.

'Funny. You're *dead* funny, Molly Rose,' Leo replied.

Sinead noticed how he seemed a little nervous. What was he thinking? Was he considering how he was going to tie them all back up? How would he manage that when there were three of them and one of him?

'Right, back in. On you go,' he said, like he was talking to a dog he'd let out in the garden for a late-night pee.

'No,' Molly Rose replied sternly. 'I'm not doing anything you tell me.'

Leo stepped forward and glanced into the room. Then he frowned. Something was wrong.

'What the fuck?' he said, turning his body towards the room. Just then, his eyes widened and a wooden table came flying towards him from inside the room. The small one that looked like it had seen better days. It hit him in the face and, as it did, he stumbled back and fell over a box on the floor. Zofia rushed out of the room with something large in her grip. A wooden chair. She brought it crashing down over Leo's head and let out a scream at the same time. Leo groaned underneath the smashed wood and Sinead stared wide-eyed at Zofia.

Before she could pull her back, Molly Rose rushed at Leo and plunged the small blade into his side, one, two, three times. Then a fourth and, suddenly, Sinead lost count of how many times Molly Rose had stabbed him. He tried to fight from underneath the pile of wood but before he could do anything, Zofia came rushing back out of the room with another piece of battered old furniture, a small table that could have come from a set of three, and raised her arms again.

'Fuck!' Sinead shouted. 'We need to get out of here, come on.'

She grabbed out at Molly Rose's arm and pulled her back, taking the tool from her hand. It almost slipped from her grip from the blood dripping from it but it didn't deter her. Pulling out the emergency car window tool, she jabbed it at the glass a couple of times before it shattered in the centre. Raising her foot, Sinead kicked out the remainder of the glass and turned to Molly Rose and Zofia.

'Go,' Molly Rose said, almost knocking Sinead from her feet as she pulled Zofia behind her. 'Go, go, go!'

They were out of the house and Molly Rose was leading them towards the van. Sinead heard a click and the van lit up.

'You're driving?' Sinead said as Molly Rose and Zofia climbed in.

'I grabbed the keys out his pocket; it's the only way for us to get away from here.'

Sinead glanced back at the house at the sound of falling wood and Leo's voice shouting after them. She got into the back seat and shut the door. 'Then you'd better hurry the fuck up because he's coming.'

Molly Rose's blood-streaked, trembling hands fumbled with the key. 'There's no ignition,' she said in a panic.

'Press the button on the left-hand side and put it into drive,' Sinead shouted from the back seat. She turned to see Leo stumbling down through the overgrown front garden.

The engine roared to life and, just as Molly Rose started to pull away from the horror house, Sinead's door opened and Leo threw himself inside. Zofia and Sinead started to scream and Sinead kicked out at him, but he was already inside the van, scrambling to get to Molly Rose.

'We're going to die,' Zofia shouted as Molly Rose threw the van round the corner and down onto the main road. Sinead noticed that they were travelling along a one-way slip road in the wrong direction.

'Molly Rose, turn us around,' Sinead screamed, trying desperately to fight Leo off as he lunged on top of her, his fingers snaking around her neck.

The van bumped and juddered and Sinead couldn't figure out where they were going.

'Where's the fucking blade?' Molly Rose shouted as she tried to keep her eyes on the road.

Sinead fought as hard as she could against Leo, who was bleeding all over her in the back seat.

'Shit!' Molly Rose shouted, her voice loud and hoarse. 'The road, it's shut!'

Sinead turned her head to the right and sunk her teeth into Leo's hand as hard as she could. He let out a guttural cry and then his fist came down on her face. He punched, again and again.

'Stop!' Zofia cried as the van swerved from side to side. 'You're going to kill her.'

'That's the fucking idea,' Leo slurred on top of her.

Sinead felt herself drifting. She couldn't hold on as blows rained down on her.

'Molly Rose, watch out!'

# Chapter 60

'My phone,' Molly Rose said, almost as if she'd forgotten she had one in the first place. 'Where's my phone?'

'Concentrate on the fucking road,' Zofia said, glancing back at the chaos and violence unfolding in the back seat.

Molly Rose glanced back quickly. Zofia was right, he was going to kill her if he kept punching her that way.

She reached over, opened the glove compartment and slipped her hand inside while trying to keep her eyes on the road, all the while hoping that Sinead wasn't going to die. Her fingers gripped on to something and she pulled it out. It was her phone.

'Turn that on,' she said to Zofia, handing it to her. 'Phone Janey. Now.'

Zofia took the phone from her and then she screamed, 'Molly Rose, watch out!'

The car crashed through a no-entry barrier. They were on the Erskine Bridge. How the fuck had they ended up there?

'Jesus!' Molly Rose said as she tried to control the car. 'Leo, stop!'

He had stopped. He'd passed out on top of Sinead. They were both unconscious.

'Oh shit, they're dead, Molly Rose. They're both dead.'

Molly Rose turned and looked, before turning her eyes back to the road. 'Brace yourself,' she said as she tried to slam on the brakes. It was too late, they'd careered through another barrier and the car flipped once, landing on its roof.

Molly Rose's head pounded along with her jaw. Sinead and Leo were silent and covered in blood in the back. Zofia was sobbing next to them.

'The phone,' Molly Rose muttered as she raised a hand to her head. 'Where's the phone?'

Then she closed her eyes.

## Chapter 61

Pulling into the side of the road, Janey glanced around. It wasn't a surprise that Leo was nowhere to be seen. Had James played them?

'Where is he?' Janey said.

Kristo got out of the car, as did DI James Pearson with the other security men. Janey opened the door and leaned out.

'So, where is he?' she shouted.

'I don't know. He should have been here by now,' the DI replied. 'I should have been here before now. I'm surprised he's not tried to contact me.'

'Then you'd better fucking call him and find out what the hold-up is.'

The sound of an approaching car made everyone's ears prick up. As it drove down the street towards them, Janey rolled her eyes. 'What the hell is she doing here?'

Cheryl pulled her car up in front of Kristo's and got out.

'You shouldn't be here,' Kristo said, taking a step towards her.

'My husband, soon to be ex, has Janey's granddaughter, I've just found out that he knew our son was going to be murdered and didn't stop it and he's also a fucking paedophile. I have every right to be here as the rest of you.'

336

Janey sighed in annoyance. 'How did you even find us?'

'I followed you, obviously. I'm not going to sit in the flat and wait for news. I want to see his face when he dies.'

Janey looked at Cheryl in disbelief that she thought she'd get the chance to do that. 'Just, I don't know, just be quiet, eh? Keep your mouth shut unless you've got something helpful to say.'

Cheryl raised an eyebrow and drew her eyes away from Janey.

Janey glanced back at James Pearson, who had his phone at his ear. 'He's not picking up,' he said.

'Could he have known we were coming?' Kristo asked.

'I didn't tell him a thing, only that I knew what he was and that I found the tablet and the letter,' Cheryl said.

Janey glanced down at her phone to check the time and, when she did, it pinged. She took in the information on the screen. Molly Rose had turned her mobile phone on.

'Kristo, the car, now. We need to go.'

Cheryl frowned. 'What is that?'

'It's the tracker I put on Molly Rose's phone. She's turned it on,' Janey said, waiting for the signal to come through. When she saw the location flash up on the screen, she frowned. 'Why the *hell* have they stopped on the Erskine Bridge?' she said out loud.

Cheryl climbed into the back seat.

Janey turned and looked at her in horror. 'What are you doing?'

'I'm coming with you.'

Kristo turned to the team and said, 'Right, I want two cars up there with us, two cars tracking the perimeter on either side of the bridge. The villages beneath it, the entryways to the forest just down there and any other places you think necessary.' Then he looked at DI James Pearson. 'You, back in the car. You're coming with us all.'

The team deployed to their specified locations and Kristo climbed in beside Janey.

'Get there, Kristo. I can't let another family member die because of me.'

## Chapter 62

Silence and darkness enveloped them and Molly Rose held her breath. The engine was dead. No sound coming from the radio. Outside it was dark, the only lights came from the lamp posts on the side of the road. *On the bridge*, she thought.

Zofia unclipped her belt and fell onto the ceiling. Leo didn't move; didn't make a sound. Neither did Sinead.

'Are you okay?' Zofia said, moving slow but steady towards Molly Rose. Surprisingly, there was no pain. No injuries from what she could tell.

'I think so,' Molly Rose replied as she fumbled with the seat-belt fastener before tumbling onto the ceiling.

The window on Zofia's side had caved in during the crash. 'Come on,' Zofia said. 'This way.'

Molly Rose hesitated. Why hadn't Leo tied them up? Put them in the back of the van? She couldn't remember. It was all such a blur. And where were they going? Where was he taking them? And then it came to her. They'd escaped from the house. Molly Rose and Zofia had attacked him. But it hadn't worked. He'd come after them.

'My phone,' Molly Rose said again.

Then she spotted it. Her mobile was in Zofia's hand and she sighed with relief.

Zofia looked around as Molly Rose got to her feet. 'We're on a bridge,' she said.

Molly Rose turned on her mobile and hoped that the tracking signal would reach Janey quickly.

'Can you walk?' Zofia asked.

Molly Rose nodded. 'We need to get Sinead out of there.'

'I think she's dead, Molly Rose,' Zofia said. Her tone was gentle, but rushed. 'But Leo might not be. We need to get as far away from this car as possible.'

Molly Rose looked at the wrecked van and suddenly she was cold. Tilting her head up to the night sky, she only just realised that it was dark. She took the phone from Zofia's hand and pulled up Janey's number, but as she hit call, the car rocked a little.

'Sinead?' Molly Rose spoke into the air.

Glancing up, she watched as Leo moved slightly inside the car, making it rock gently on its roof.

Turning to Zofia, she simply said, 'Run.'

The sound of their feet hammering on the ground as they ran across the bridge was coupled with the gushing of blood in her ears.

'Here,' Molly Rose said, seeing a large scaffolding platform come into view. 'Climb up there.'

'Are you fucking crazy?' Zofia replied, sounding breathless. 'We'll die.'

'And if we don't hide, Leo will kill us anyway,' Molly Rose replied, stopping at the part of the bridge which had a ladder leading onto the scaffolding. She read the sign.

BRIDGE MAINTENANCE
ENGINEERS ONLY. DO NOT
MOUNT WITHOUT SAFETY
HARNESS.

Peering over, Molly Rose noticed a platform below. It disappeared beneath them, and she wondered if they might stand a chance if they were able to get down there.

Molly Rose looked at Zofia. 'It's up to you, but I'm chancing it. I'd rather fall to my death than allow Leo to get me. Even though he's probably going to bleed out and die soon, he'll make sure we suffer before he does.'

Zofia didn't hesitate as she moved towards Molly Rose, who already had her left foot up on one of the poles and was hauling herself up. As she did, she turned to her left. Leo was still in the van. He'd stopped moving. Maybe he was dead? Molly Rose wasn't stopping to check. Once down on that platform, she'd contact Janey.

Taking a breath as she reached the top platform, all the while her wrist still in terrible pain, she gently lowered herself onto it and eyed the ladder to her right. It led down onto the platform below which stretched under the bridge.

*Don't look down*, she thought, but she'd already cast her eye on to the car park beneath. Concrete, she thought. If she fell, it would be quick. Hopefully she'd die before impact. The thought made her heart lurch in her chest.

'Are you okay?' Molly Rose looked up to see Zofia lowering herself onto the platform above.

'No, I'm not. I'm dangling about a hundred and fifty feet above ground,' Zofia said, sounding panicked.

'Take a breath,' Molly Rose said. 'You're doing great.'

'Why are there no cars?' Zofia asked. 'I mean, this is a main road bridge to connect two sides of a city? Why are no others here?'

Molly Rose remembered. 'Because the road is shut. Now come on, get down here.'

Molly Rose lowered herself down onto the platform beneath her and held on tightly to the pole to her left as she waited on Zofia coming down.

'I hate heights,' Zofia puffed as her feet landed on the metal floor.

'Ssh.' Molly Rose held her finger up to her mouth and gestured for Zofia to follow her.

Molly Rose fell to her hands and knees and slowly crawled as far back under the bridge as she could. It was deathly quiet up there, and cold. The water beneath them was black like the sky.

Zofia followed her and they both stood up, breathing as quietly as possible.

Molly Rose listened for movement on the scaffolding. There was nothing. Leo must still be in the car.

She pulled out her phone and pulled up Janey's number. It barely rang once and Janey picked up.

'Are you all right?' Janey asked.

'No. You need to find us now, Janey. We crashed on a bridge and me and Zofia managed to climb out.' The words caught in her throat and she let out a sob.

'It's okay. I know where you are. You're on the Erskine Bridge? It's closed to all traffic for maintenance but we're coming.'

Molly Rose glanced at Zofia and said down the phone, 'That'll be why there's no other cars here then.'

'Where's Leo?' Janey asked.

'He was still in the car. Sinead is too. Janey, I think she might be dead.' She let out another sob and Janey was quiet for a moment. That would mean another dead daughter for her. Two in the space of a short few months.

Janey cleared her throat. 'Where are you now? Your location is still reading on the bridge. Is that right?'

Molly Rose took a deep breath and decided now was not the time to question why there was a tracker on her phone. She looked out at the view of the city from where she and Zofia were hiding. It was a sight to behold in better circumstances. The blackest of nights illuminated by the city lights.

'We're *under* the bridge on the maintenance scaffolding.'

'Jesus Christ,' Janey said. 'Okay, stay there. We're on our way. Won't be more than a few minutes. Stay on the phone but don't speak. You need to keep quiet. If he didn't see you go down there, then he might think you've gone down to the village in Old Kilpatrick or even over to the Erskine side.'

'Why can't he just die?' she whispered into the phone, tears pouring down her face.

Zofia sat down on the metal floor and began shivering. Molly Rose stared down at her and wondered if she was going into shock or if she was just cold.

'I'm going to go quiet, Molly Rose,' Janey said down the phone. 'But I'll still be here. Keep the phone on you. I can track your exact location that way.'

Molly Rose nodded, but didn't speak, like her gran had instructed. She stood there, holding the phone in her hand, all the while looking up at the underside of the bridge. Leo had been planning to take them somewhere they'd never be able to return from. Using the closed bridge was a risk for him. Now they were all stuck and she had no idea if Leo was dead or alive above them.

'I'm so cold.' Zofia shivered.

Molly Rose bent down in front of her and raised a finger to her mouth and shook her head.

She stood back up and felt a gentle sway from the metal floor under her feet. It suddenly dawned on her how high up they were. How close to death.

The sound of scuffling above them made Molly Rose look up. The bridge was shut. It was obvious the entrances and exits of the bridge weren't being watched otherwise people would be there to help.

'Where the *fuck* did you go?' he grunted, probably from the pain of the amount of stab wounds Molly Rose had inflicted with the tool on the key ring.

Leo's voice echoed out above them and Molly Rose closed her eyes. *Don't breathe. Don't move.*

The sound of feet on metal made her toes curl. He was coming down. And there was nowhere for them to go.

Molly Rose's eyes met Zofia's.

'Boo!'

Leo jumped down onto the platform, causing it to sway. He stumbled a little, clutched his side with a blood-soaked hand. Molly Rose tried to catch her balance, reaching out to hold on to the pole for support. The phone fell from her hand and disappeared into the darkness below. Zofia screamed. Molly Rose froze.

This was it. This was the end.

# Chapter 63

'Molly Rose?' Janey said into the phone as Kristo's car sped down the A82 towards the exit slip road for the Erskine Bridge. 'Can you hear me?'

She glanced down at the screen and noticed that she was still able to track the signal. It no longer stated the bridge as the location. It now read The Saltings.

'Kristo. Take the Old Kilpatrick exit.'

'Why?'

'I don't want to think about why. Just do it.'

Kristo glanced at her. 'The location has changed?'

Janey nodded. 'Fuck. Either they've fallen from the bridge or they've dropped the phone.'

Cheryl sat in the back of the car in silence and all Janey could think about was what they were going to find when they got to that car park.

'Share the location with the team, Janey,' Kristo said.

Janey did that as Kristo passed by the exit to the bridge. Janey peered through the window, trying her best to see if she could see the car. She saw nothing as Kristo took the Old Kilpatrick slip road and made his way down into the village as quickly as possible. The roads were quiet as he weaved in and out of parked cars on the road, before taking a left at the bottom of the street. The bridge came into full view above them, just a few feet along the road. From down here, all looked calm and normal. She could see the scaffolding platform Molly Rose and Zofia had climbed onto, but she couldn't see if they were still up there.

'Leo won't have pushed them off,' Cheryl piped up. 'They're too valuable to him, moneywise and...' She trailed off. 'His boss would kill him like they killed Dean, if he lost them. They'll still be alive.'

Janey turned in her seat and looked Cheryl square in the eye. 'I hope to God, for all our sakes, that you're right.'

Janey was angry with Cheryl. In some ways, this was her fault. If she'd just been honest from the start, they could have dealt with Leo immediately.

The car passed under the bridge and turned right into The Saltings car park. They all got out of the car and Janey continued to stare down at the phone. It still registered the car park as where Molly Rose's phone was situated.

She looked up at the scaffolding platform. She couldn't see a thing. It was too dark and the street lights below were skewing her vision.

'Molly Rose!' Janey called, her voice echoing around them. Another car pulled up with a team of Janey's men getting out.

'They're still up there,' Cheryl said.

'How do you know?' Kristo asked.

Cheryl outstretched her arms and rotated left to right. 'Do you see any bodies?'

Janey glared at Cheryl and then turned her attention to the team who'd just arrived. 'Get up onto that bridge. Do what you have to. Just bring the girls back safely.'

They jumped back into the car and sped off out of the car park.

Ahead of the car park was a woodland, with the bridge above. To the right, a pub. If anyone was going to fall, it wasn't going to be discreet.

Janey headed into the woodland, keeping her eye on the bridge. 'He could have got them back in the car, Cheryl. They could be long gone by now.'

Cheryl shook her head as she walked alongside her. 'I hope he's dead.'

Kristo walked behind them silently. Janey continued to look up.

# Chapter 64

Molly Rose gripped at the pole and held out the other hand. 'Don't come anywhere near me,' she shouted.

Leo laughed. 'My boss knows I was on my way to the dock with you both. You think he's going to just sit there, twiddling his thumbs if I'm late?'

Molly Rose glared at him. 'No wonder Dean was so fucked up. He didn't have a chance with a dad like you.'

'You shut your mouth. My son's name never crosses your lips again,' Leo snarled.

'Or what? You'll throw me off? Good. Means I won't have to endure the shit you're planning on putting me through. Go on then!'

Leo frowned at Molly Rose's sudden outburst and then he laughed.

'Molly Rose,' Zofia said. 'Shut up.'

She didn't take her eyes off Leo as Zofia spoke words of desperation. She wasn't going to die without a fight. This man, or so he thought of himself, was nothing but a predator. Saw people like Molly Rose and Zofia as income. She wasn't going to let him do this. She'd rather die than end up a sex slave.

'No. He should know that Janey's team are all around, waiting for him.'

'Bullshit,' he hissed. 'If that was the case, I'd be dead by now.'

'Give it time.'

Leo glared at her through darkened eyes. Molly Rose knew this was the end of the road for all of them. Not one of them on that scaffolding platform was going to survive.

Leo took a step forward and stopped, still clutching his blood-soaked side. 'Come on, back up on to the bridge.'

Molly Rose shook her head and glanced down at the wound. 'Probably won't be long until you bleed out.'

'I'm not fucking around here, Molly Rose. If you think I'm bad, you really don't want to know how my boss will deal with you if he has to come all the way up from Greenock to find us in this predicament.'

'I don't give a fuck about you or your boss.'

'Right then,' Leo said, trying to straighten up. 'How's this? You don't come voluntarily; I'll throw Zofia off the edge.'

Zofia sobbed beside Molly Rose.

'No, you won't.'

'Won't I?'

'She's worth too much to you. And you already fucked up the last job because of Dean. You're on a final warning with your boss. He wants us both alive,' Molly Rose said, recalling the phone call she'd overheard when she was locked in the room he'd put them in after capturing them.

'You don't know what you're talking about,' Leo said. 'Up onto the bridge. Now!'

His bellowing voice made Molly Rose move back, and that's when she felt it. The loose pole. If she'd moved any quicker, bore any more weight onto it, she might have gone over.

'And I said, no! I'm not fucking scared of dying. But you? You're scared that your boss will do to you what he did to Dean; and you don't really know what that was, do you? Although I don't think you have that much time on your hands by the looks of how much blood you're losing.'

'I'm fucking warning you, you little bitch. You don't do what I say and I'll—'

'You'll what? Throw yourself off? Because that would be the best option for all of us, wouldn't it? You'd rather die by your own doing than your boss's, wouldn't you?'

He was like a caged animal in the way he stared at her.

'You were a vulnerable mess of a girl when Dean got a hold of you. What changed?' Leo asked, as though he was genuinely interested, but his breathing became raspy. He was slowly dying.

Molly Rose shrugged. 'When you're almost trafficked for sex slavery on more than one occasion, and have had to stab someone with the smallest tool to hand, you tend to harden up a bit.'

She leaned down and hooked her hand under Zofia's arm before pulling her up. Zofia stood next to her, shivering and sobbing.

'Shame it's not enough to save you,' Leo said.

'The universe has been trying to kill me for a couple years now. I knew it was going to catch up with me eventually. But I'll tell you this, if I go, you're coming with me.'

Leo gave a throaty laugh and blood gurgled in his mouth. He was almost out. He reached out his hands and ran at her. Just as his bloodied hands were about to grab on to her, she ducked to the side and pushed Zofia down onto the metal floor, before scrambling to get back up and turn just in time to see Leo grab on to the loose pole and crash over the edge.

He didn't make a sound as he went over. No scream, no call out for help. He simply fell into the darkness. The platform rocked slightly and the only other sound she heard was Zofia's sobs, before the imminent slap of flesh and bone connecting with the concrete beneath.

Molly Rose lay down next to Zofia and held her face as sobs began to escape her own throat. 'He's gone, Zofia. Leo's dead.'

# Chapter 65

She let out a scream she didn't know she had in her. A sound she hadn't even made when she found out Dean was dead. It wasn't through overwhelming grief, but absolute terror. The sound of Leo's body hitting the ground like that; crunching bones and organs exploding was a thing of nightmares. He was nothing now but a mass of blood and guts on the woodland path. Tree debris lay around him; on top of him. *Jesus.*

Janey turned her away from what was left of Leo and pulled Cheryl towards the car.

'Ssh,' Janey said. 'You have to stop making so much noise. You'll alert people that something is wrong.'

Cheryl tried to breathe, but she couldn't get air into her lungs. Janey opened the car door before helping her inside.

'Breathe,' Janey said, cupping Cheryl's face in her hands. They were cold, that much Cheryl noticed. 'In and out. Slowly.'

Cheryl did what Janey said and slowly her breathing evened out.

'I need to know if Molly Rose and Zofia are okay.'

'The boys are at the bridge,' Kristo said, phone in his hand. 'The girls, they're safe. The team are bringing them down now. Sinead's in the van. She's in a bad way but she's alive.'

Janey let out a steady breath and glanced back at Cheryl, who now had an overwhelming urge to throw up. She quickly climbed out of the car and emptied the contents of her stomach on the gravel path.

'I'm sorry,' Cheryl said, wiping the back of her hand across her mouth. 'I'm sorry for everything. I just wanted justice for my Dean. If I'd known then what I know now, I'd never...' She cleared her throat. 'I'd have taken it out on Leo.'

Janey stared at her with, what was that, sympathy?

'You were his victim too, Cheryl. Both you and Dean. And everyone else he's manipulated.'

'I'm sorry,' she said again.

'What's done is done. But your husband's boss will want answers, Cheryl. We're now left to deal with that, you know that, don't you?'

Cheryl nodded. 'Marek, he's... a horrible, horrible man. Capable of the most horrific things.'

'Yeah, we know. Trafficked children, Cheryl. That's what Molly Rose and Zofia are. Children. Molly Rose likes to think she's an adult but she's not.'

'I'm sorry,' Cheryl muttered again. 'If I could change things, I would. I don't want Marek to come after anyone because Leo promised to fulfil Dean's unfinished business. Dean was just a kid himself. If Leo had been any sort of a man, never mind a dad, he wouldn't have dragged him into this shit. People like Marek, they get away with everything because of how powerful they are.'

Janey frowned and then shook her head in disbelief. 'Up until now, maybe. But no more. His sick operation will be stopped. Now.'

With Janey's words echoing in Cheryl's ears, a car pulled into the car park and came to a halt in front of them. The back doors opened and Molly Rose climbed out before falling into Janey's arms. The other girl, Zofia, ran around and Janey held her hand out to her.

Janey's arms were full. The majority of her family were still alive and she'd done whatever it took to keep them all safe.

As Cheryl glanced back at Leo, or what was left of him, she slowly came to realise that she was just as bad as he was. She'd planned to put an end to all of the Hallahans when, in reality, the only person who needed to be stopped was Leo. And Marek.

'Are you girls okay? What happened?' Janey asked.

Zofia sobbed; couldn't speak. But Molly Rose... she seemed unusually calm. Like she was numb to it all, after what she'd been through.

'I think we've been better.' Molly Rose smiled. 'But that's another evil bastard dead. Nothing bad about that.'

'Yeah,' Janey sighed. 'I suppose you're right.'

Molly Rose glanced across at Cheryl with a sadness in her eyes. 'We never did get to meet when I was with Dean.'

Cheryl's stomach rolled. 'No, we didn't.'

'You look like him,' Molly Rose said.

Guilt and terrible sadness washed over her like a tidal wave and her legs buckled as she fell to the ground. She let out a sob as arms enveloped her.

'It's not your fault,' Molly Rose said into her ear.

'Yes, it is. I should have left when Dean was still little. If I had, none of this would have happened,' Cheryl cried.

Molly Rose cradled Cheryl like a child. 'Yes, it would. It just may not have happened to me. Leo was a monster. Dean was his son, just looking to be accepted by his dad. He'd have done anything to gain that.'

Cheryl looked up at Molly Rose, saw sympathy in her eyes. 'How are you only sixteen? You're so strong; mature for your age.'

Molly Rose shrugged. 'When you've had numerous attempts on your life, you're bound to grow up quickly.'

Janey was by their side then, crouched down next to them. 'We need to go. A team have been called in to clear the scene. We can't be here.'

Molly Rose nodded and helped Cheryl to her feet. 'Are you going to be okay?'

Cheryl glanced up at the sky for a moment and then back at Leo's final resting place.

'Yeah,' she replied. 'I'll be fine. You all go.'

Janey shook her head. 'I'm not leaving you here. We'll drop you off.'

'You don't have to worry about me, Janey. I'm not going to do anything that will jeopardise you or the girls' freedom or safety. But I will ask one thing of you.'

Janey raised an eyebrow. 'What is it?'

'I want to be there when you find Marek.'

Letting out a long breath, Janey's shoulders dropped. 'Are you sure? He's dangerous, much more so than Leo ever was.'

Cheryl wiped the tears from her cheeks, straightened her back and swallowed hard.

'Dead sure.'

# Chapter 66

'I can't believe Leo's phone survived the fall,' Janey said as she glanced down at it in Kristo's hand.

'Seems burner phones are made of tougher stuff than any human,' Kristo replied.

The image of Leo Davidson was burnt on to Janey's brain. She'd never forget the sound, the image of what had become of him.

'It would seem that Leo didn't use this to send messages. He'd have used the tablet for that. But we do have a few numbers stored in this,' Kristo continued as he tapped the phone in his hand, bringing Janey out from her own thoughts.

'I suppose they're not stored under the names of those belonging to the numbers?' Janey asked, picking up her coffee mug and taking a sip. She glanced through the window at Molly Rose and Zofia who were sitting on the chairs in Sinead's room at the hospital. Molly Rose seemed fine, but Zofia had gone quiet.

'Surprisingly...' Kristo let the words hang in the air.

'No way,' Janey said, her eyes wide.

'Marek has called a few times, texts too.' He held the phone up and she read the message to herself. 'It seems the tablet was only for Leo's use. Client details, his own personal camera. I don't know why he thought it was a good idea to keep images like the ones he did. Surely, he knew it would incriminate him if he ever got caught.'

'People like Leo believe they'll never be caught. He was a narcissist,' Janey replied, taking the phone from Kristo and looking down at the text on the screen.

> What the fuck is going on Leo? If you have fucked up this transaction like your boy did, I will kill you and that fucking wife of yours as slowly and as painfully as possible.
> ANSWER YOUR FUCKING PHONE

'He's angry,' Janey said. 'So, what's your plan?'

Kristo slipped the phone into his pocket. 'I'm going to message him back, apologise for messing up. Offer to meet to discuss a plan going forward.'

Janey frowned. 'He doesn't know Leo is dead?' she whispered.

Kristo shook his head. 'No. And he won't be around for much longer.'

'I want men stationed here; the hospital staff are on high alert for any intruders. I'm coming with you.'

Kristo hesitated and then said, 'You want to leave the girls? After what happened last time?'

'No, I don't want to leave them. But I do want to make sure this Marek character is dead and in the ground. I can't risk him coming after us now that Leo's dead. My family have been through enough.'

'We'll be fine,' Molly Rose's voice came from the door. 'Someone needs to stay with Sinead. Just leave as many security personnel outside as you can. But to be honest, the man who really wanted to fuck us up no longer even resembles a human, so I think we'll be fine.'

Janey glanced at Kristo. She was worried about Molly Rose. She should be more worried, scared even. But she seemed fine. Too fine.

'Go back in and sit with Zofia. She looks like she needs a friend right now,' Janey said. She watched Molly Rose go back inside and Janey pulled the door closed.

'I'm worried about her. She doesn't seem to be processing the horrors of what's gone on these last few months,' Janey said.

Kristo sighed. 'It's a lot to take for anyone but for someone of her age, and the fact that she was thrown into all this because of what happened to Orla, I'd say it's all going to come out at some point.'

'Yeah, I hope so. It's not healthy how…' Janey tried to think of the word. 'Blasé she is about it all.'

'She'll be trying to stay strong. I mean, you're not exactly having an easy time yourself, are you? Ciaran's still in a coma, and Sinead's been through hell. Your grand-daughter's life was targeted again. She'll be acting this way to support you.'

Janey wanted to cry. 'But that's *not* her job.'

'I know. I don't have much else to say that will help. But I can get rid of this Marek and hope that, with his death, it'll be the end of all this shit and you can get on with life.'

Janey smiled gently. 'What would we do without you, Kristo?' Then she pulled him in and held him tight. 'You're like family. Ciaran will be so thankful of you when he wakes up.'

*If he wakes up*, a voice inside her brain said.

'Let me get the security organised and then we can get this shit sorted,' Kristo said. 'Oh, what do you want done with Pearson?'

'Exposure,' Janey said. 'I'm going to send the files we found on that tablet to his bosses, his family. I'm going to send the entire tablet in to the police. He needs a taste of his own justice system because, well, you know what they do to police in prison, don't you?'

'So, I just let him go for now?' Kristo asked.

Janey nodded. 'Yeah, just tell him he's done his bit. Let him think he's free. Although I'm sure he probably knows deep down this isn't how things end for him. But, yeah, let him walk.'

'Got it,' Kristo said. 'I'll keep in touch, let you know when everything is in place. It won't take long. Marek's going to want Leo's head on a plate right now. So he'll go wherever Leo leads him to.'

As she stood there on her own, watching Kristo head down the corridor, the enormity of what had happened in her life in the last few months hit her. Orla's death. Sinead's spiking and attack. The several attempts on Molly Rose's life. It was all her fault. If she wasn't in the line of work she was, none of it would have happened.

She stepped into Sinead's room and glanced down at her only surviving daughter. She was awake.

'How are you?' Janey asked, staring down at her, wondering how she could have let any of this happen.

'I've been better. Desperate for a hit. I've been battered so badly I can't see out of my left eye. My sister is dead. My mum's a...' She let the remainder of her words hang.

Janey closed her eyes briefly. Sinead was so right. Silence followed before Molly Rose broke it with an attempt at humour.

'So, who's going to take out this other guy then, so we can all get on with boring old life?'

Janey rolled her eyes. 'It's not funny, Molly Rose.'

'You're telling me,' she remarked. 'Having someone constantly trying to kill you definitely isn't what I'd define as fun.'

Molly Rose eyed Zofia, who'd been silent since they'd got in the car after Leo fell from the bridge.

'You don't need to know any details about what is going to happen next. All you need to know is that you're both safe and no one else is coming for you; for any of us.'

Molly Rose's face contorted. 'I don't think I'll ever believe that, if I'm honest.'

If Janey was being true to herself, she wasn't sure she believed it either.

# Chapter 67

Cheryl stood at the window of her flat and watched as the car pulled up outside. She moved through the flat to the front door and waited until she heard the footsteps approaching before unlocking the door and quickly moving into Dean's bedroom.

Closing the bedroom door behind her, she listened carefully as the men moved through the flat and into the living room. No words were spoken but their presence was heavy. She didn't know how many of them were there. She guessed two or three?

Sitting down on Dean's bed, she placed her hands on the duvet and inhaled deeply. His scent was gone. Nothing smelled like him now. His short existence in this world had disappeared.

What if he didn't turn up, she thought. What if Marek knew he was about to be ambushed and decided not to come to the flat? But why would he think that? It had been his suggestion.

There it was, the sound of the front door opening. The way he walked made her skin prickle. The fact that he was sharing the same air as her made her feel sick.

'Are you ready for this?' Janey mouthed from the corner of the room. She'd arrived just before her team of men had, and Cheryl had asked her to wait in Dean's room. That in itself must have been hard for Janey, given what Dean had planned to do with Molly Rose; rather, what he'd been *forced* to do by Leo and Marek. Although, Cheryl knew that Dean had been an adult. And there had been no way of forcing him to do anything, unless it meant gaining his dad's acceptance. Molly Rose had been right about that.

Cheryl nodded as Janey handed her the gun. Kristo had instructed her to wait for the signal before leaving the bedroom and entering the lounge.

As she waited, her heart thumped inside her chest. She was about to do something that she'd wanted ever since Dean had died, and now she wasn't sure she'd be able to go through with it when the time came.

Janey was by her side now, gently gripping her arm. 'And you're sure, given the fact that the police will be all over this place and you'll get arrested?'

'I'd do eternity a million times over,' Cheryl replied. 'It'll be worth it.'

Janey nodded. She would get it. She was also the mother of a murdered child.

Cheryl reached into her pocket and pulled out a piece of paper. She handed it to Janey and whispered, 'Don't read it yet. Wait until all this is over.'

Janey stared at Cheryl and nodded.

'I'm sorry,' she whispered. 'For everything.'

Janey closed her eyes briefly. She'd be thinking about Ciaran, lying in the hospital in his coma. No one knew if he'd ever come out of it. That had been because of Cheryl.

'I know.'

Someone tapped gently on the outside of the bedroom door. The signal Kristo had told Cheryl to wait for. She took a deep breath, steadied the gun in her hand and pulled the door open before walking through to the living room. She felt Janey at her back.

Kristo was stood in the centre of the room, pointing his own gun at Marek, who was sat on the sofa. But not on just any spot. On the spot Dean used to sit, every single day. While he ate his breakfast. Scrolled on his phone.

'Ah, Mrs Davidson. What a lovely surprise,' Marek said, sounding chirpy for a man who had a gun pointed at his head. Marek looked down and eyed the gun in her hand.

'We've never met,' Cheryl said.

'No, we haven't,' Marek said warily. 'I was expecting Leo. But I've been met by these men.' The word 'men' sounded venomous.

'Leo's dead,' Cheryl replied.

'So I heard. I was tricked into coming here by *him*.' Marek stared at Kristo, who was still firmly pointing the gun at Marek.

'If you knew Leo was dead before now, I wouldn't be standing in front of you,' Cheryl said. 'In front of the man who killed my son.'

Marek raised an eyebrow and a darkness crossed his face. 'Dean,' he said. 'We all have to pay for our mistakes.'

Cheryl nodded. 'True.'

Silence fell between them and Janey stepped forward. 'You were using children to traffic children. Were you abused yourself as a child?'

Marek eyed Janey and the dark shadow across his face grew darker. 'Ah, the crime boss with a heart. I've heard a lot about you. Seems as though the Davidsons can't follow through on much. Dean couldn't finish the job he started for me, Leo couldn't finish the job for me and… well,

363

Cheryl, I thought you wanted Janey Hallahan dead too? Now you're working *alongside* her?'

'I discovered she isn't the enemy. Janey wasn't the one who killed my son. That was you.'

'I *ordered* the kill. Bit of a difference there,' Marek replied.

Cheryl glared at Marek. She didn't want to just shoot him once in the head. She wanted to pump his brain full of bullets. She wanted to burn his body and watch as it turned to ash. But there wasn't time for that. And she wasn't that kind of person. Although grief did many strange things to your way of thinking.

'You as good as killed him yourself. That's enough for me,' Cheryl replied, raising the gun.

Marek let out a laugh. 'I bet you don't even know how to—'

Cheryl pulled the trigger, the silencer on the gun muting the sound of the shot as the bullet left the barrel, hitting Marek in the eye. His head shot back against the leather sofa, blood spattering everywhere. She flinched as her shoulder almost popped out of the socket from the force of the gun going off.

'I know how to use it all right,' Cheryl muttered, rubbing at her shoulder. 'Fucking prick.'

She turned to Janey, who had a look of empathy on her face. 'Agreed.'

'I'll third that,' Kristo said.

Cheryl glanced down at the bloodied mess that used to be Marek's face and closed her eyes. 'Thank you for allowing me the privilege to kill him, Janey.'

'That's your prerogative,' Janey said. 'I'd have done the same for Orla, given the chance.'

Cheryl turned back, gave Janey a smile and said, 'I hope you and Molly Rose can live in peace after all this. I need to be with my son now.'

'Cheryl, no!' Janey shouted.

She reached out as Cheryl raised the gun to her head.

# Chapter 68

*Dear Janey,*

*I wanted to write this letter to you for a number of reasons. The main one is to say, again, how truly sorry I am for allowing Leo to fill my head with his reasoning that you and your family were to blame for Dean's death. The only person at fault for what happened to Dean was Leo. His own father.*

*I want you and Molly Rose to know that I understand now. I was also one of Leo's victims. But I also enabled him. I will never forgive myself for that.*

*I hope Ciaran pulls through. And Sinead. I'm sorry for what Leo did to her. I should never have allowed any of it.*

*I don't expect your forgiveness. I understand if you can't bring yourself to reach that level. I also don't expect you to not feel so much anger towards me that you want to kill me. I'd be the same. In fact, I am the same. I want the person responsible for Dean's death to be dead too. So if you're reading this, I'm probably dead already. That was my plan all along, to finally let go once I ended the person who took my baby from me.*

*You don't owe me anything, but if you could find it in yourself to do this one thing for me, I'd be more grateful than you'll ever know.*

*I'd like to be buried in with my son. Could you arrange that for me please? I've left details for my funeral in an envelope in the safe in my bedroom. The key is lying next to it. All the paperwork is in there, you only have to hand it in to the funeral director.*

*I don't expect anyone to be at my funeral given what I've done and what I've allowed to happen. And if I'm honest, I don't mind. All I want is to be with my boy, no matter where that might be. If it's in blissful darkness, or burning hell, I'll take it either way.*

*Janey, you're more of a mother than I ever was. I just wish I hadn't allowed Leo to control me for so many years. I could have got Dean away. We could have had a different life.*

*Sincerely,*
*Cheryl Davidson*

# Chapter 69

## THREE DAYS LATER

She sat in the corner of the dark, damp room within the flat. No one had come for them in a week. They'd been left, locked in the flat with little to no food and only the water from the tap to survive on. The flat was crowded. Usually, half of them were out at work, while the other half were there to catch up on rest before they were carted off to the next party, or private client appointment. Each time she'd been told it was her turn, she'd thrown up. The fear never diminished.

Alina thought about Zofia. Wondered where she was. Was she alive? Safe?

'Did you hear that?' one of the girls from the other side of the flat whispered, interrupting her thoughts.

She had heard it. The closing of car doors. The *quiet* closing of doors.

Footsteps on the communal stairway outside the door.

Then the door was rammed open and she closed her eyes, not wishing to know what or who was coming for them.

'It's okay, you're all safe,' a woman said in a strong accent.

She looked up to see the place swarmed with armed police and a few females. Were they officers too?

'My name is Georgia Munro, I'm a detective with Greater Manchester Police. You don't have to worry any more. No one else is coming for you. You're all safe.'

The flashing of torches blinded Alina momentarily. Was it all a dream?

'Hey.' The woman bent down in front of her, the light of the torch making her look like an aura surrounded her. 'Are you okay?'

Alina shook her head. 'No. But I will be. Are you real?'

The woman nodded her head and Alina glanced around. The others were being spoken to, cared for. They had blankets wrapped around them; cups handed to them with steam swirling out of the top.

'What is your name?' the woman asked.

'Alina,' she replied with a shaky voice.

The woman bowed her head a little and then stared back. 'Hi, Alina. Let's get you out of here.'

Alina felt her entire centre shift, and if she hadn't been sitting down already on a cold, hard floor, she'd have fallen. She was finally free.

## Chapter 70

### ONE MONTH LATER

Janey closed the boot and sighed. This wasn't going to be easy, but it was something she had expected. After everything that Molly Rose had been through in her short adult life, it was expected that she'd make this kind of decision.

'Are you sure about this?' Janey asked, smiling at her while carrying her hand luggage bag over her left shoulder.

'Well, I could stay here and anticipate the next attempt on my life?' Molly Rose replied with the most sarcastic expression Janey had ever seen on another person's face. 'But that's boring, isn't it?'

Janey rolled her eyes and laughed. 'I've never known anyone to be so…'

'So what?' Molly Rose opened the passenger door and slung her bag into the footwell.

'So put together after what you've dealt with. You really don't take anything too seriously. I don't know how you do it.'

'It must be in the blood. You never seem fazed by all the death that surrounds you. That's not a dig, by the way. It's just, well, in your job, it's kind of inevitable, isn't it?'

That hit Janey like a freight train. It was true. Death had been all around her for years, whether it was in or out of her control. And it had taken a teenager to get that message through to her. That, and the fact that her own family, who she'd not long found, had been dragged into it all. One dead, one leaving and one... well, Sinead wasn't going anywhere, but she certainly had made it clear how she felt about Janey's world.

'I suppose it is. That's why I'm giving it all up,' Janey said.

Molly Rose raised an eyebrow. 'Really?'

Nodding, Janey breathed out and felt a little weight of everything she was responsible for leave her. 'I'm handing it all over to Kristo. I'm done.'

'This isn't a last-minute ploy to get me to stay, is it?'

'No. As much as I want you to stay – for selfish reasons, of course – I wouldn't lie to get you to do it. I'd been toying with the idea of retirement a while ago. Not long before I met you, actually. Maybe if I'd done it sooner, none of this would have happened.'

'Hmm.' Molly Rose pulled her lips into a thin line and narrowed her eyes. 'Nah, I doubt that. But hey, I'm glad we found each other. I just wish it had been under better circumstances.'

A short bout of silence fell between them but it was broken by the sound of Sinead closing the door to the house behind her. Janey glanced up and watched as Sinead approached the car with a bag of her own.

'Ready?' she asked solemnly.

Molly Rose turned and pulled Sinead into her arms. 'Never ready to leave you. Are you sure you can't come with me?'

'Molly Rose, I have a criminal record. I'd be laughed at for attempting to even get off the plane at JFK.'

'I'm flying into Bangor Airport, actually.' Molly Rose pulled away.

'Very funny,' Sinead said. 'And I'd love to come with you. But honestly, I want to get my life together. I need to start off small here, where I can get my shit together.'

'No more drugs?' Molly Rose asked.

'Not even paracetamol if I can help it,' Sinead said with a smile.

Janey glanced down at her watch and back at the girls. 'I don't mean to break this up, but if we don't get going now, Molly Rose might miss her flight.'

They all climbed into the car and Janey started the engine. She looked back at the house before pulling out of the drive and sighed. When she returned, Molly Rose would be on a plane, and Sinead would be settling into her own place.

'Right.' Molly Rose tapped the dash. 'Get me the hell out of this shithole.'

Sinead laughed loudly in the back seat and Janey couldn't help but smile as she glanced over at her granddaughter. The bruising on her face had almost completely gone; it was only visible now if you were looking for it.

But Janey would never forgive herself for the part she had played in everything that had happened to her family. That was why now was the time to stop. No more drugs. No more illegal businesses. No more fighting for survival.

'Right then,' she said, pulling herself away from her thoughts. 'Glasgow Airport and then, Sinead, where are you meeting your social worker again?'

'George Square in the town. Then she's taking me to the bus station,' Sinead replied, with a little excitement in her voice. 'Wales, here I come.'

'You don't know anyone in Wales,' Janey said.

Sinead nodded with the biggest grin on her face. 'Exactly.'

Janey nodded and pulled out of the driveway.

## Chapter 71

Tucking her passport back into her hand luggage, she placed her hand over the strap and made her way through the security lounge towards the shops and various restaurants. Molly Rose wasn't hungry; she was too nervous about the flight. Not so much the flight itself, but the fact that she was flying halfway across the world on her own to start a new life in America. There was nothing left for her in Scotland. Not really. Staying behind for the sake of Janey wasn't something she'd even considered, although she had thought about staying for Sinead. But when she'd discussed it with Sinead, it became clear that it wasn't what either of them wanted.

'I need to be able to do this on my own. I can't rely on my teenage niece to keep me clean and sober, can I?' Sinead had said.

With the thought swirling around her head, Molly Rose found herself standing outside a WHSmith, looking inside at the bookshelves. Reading wasn't something she'd really done in her life. Why not start now?

Stepping into the shop, she stood in front of the selection of books and immediately the horror section took her interest. As she browsed, it was apparent that this Stephen King writer was highly popular. She picked up a copy of *It* and read the description on the back.

'Yeah.' She drew the word out. 'I don't fancy reading a horror set in the place I'm moving to. No, thanks.' She placed the book back on the shelf and noticed the woman who was standing beside her smile.

'It's very good,' she said. 'But yeah, I wouldn't want to read that and then be walking down the street wondering if I was going to be pulled into one of those drains.'

Molly Rose smiled back and thought about how being pulled into a drain was nowhere near as terrifying as what she'd been through herself.

Molly Rose grabbed some snacks for the plane, picked up a magazine and paid at the till before heading for the gate.

Finally, it was all over. Her life as she'd known it. No more being scared of who was going to try to kill her next. No more looking over her shoulder for Leo Davidson, or Marek. She'd go through life as normally as she could now.

From now on, the only person she was going to allow to fill her memories was her mum. Orla. But not in her last moments. She didn't want to remember Orla that way.

*Maybe one day, I'll write a book about all this*, she thought.

Then she opened the magazine and began to read.

## Chapter 72

The sun beat down on her skin as she sat on the bench in front of the fountain in Krasiński Park in Warsaw. The splashing sound soothed her as the fountain sprayed water up into the air.

'I never thought I'd ever feel this relaxed again,' Zofia said, leaning her head back on the bench and feeling the sun on her face.

Her sister Alina's hand slipped into hers and she felt an overwhelming sense of sadness at what they'd been through. Alina more so; she'd suffered so much more than Zofia had. So much that Alina hadn't spoken a word since she'd been rescued by the police in Manchester.

'I know you're not ready to talk about what happened yet. Maybe you won't ever be ready to speak the words out loud. But just know that I'm here for you, no matter what. We won't ever be apart again, Alina.'

Alina didn't speak. She didn't smile. But they were together, and to Zofia, that was all that mattered.

Szymon and Krzysztof had been arrested at the warehouse just a few days ago and were awaiting trial. Both Zofia and Alina had been assured that they'd go away for a very long time and the girls wouldn't need to go to court to face them; their evidence would be delivered via video link for their protection.

Zofia gripped her sister's hand tightly and pulled out her mobile with her free hand. There was a message from Molly Rose.

> Hey, how are you? I miss you. Hope you're doing okay. America is wild. So different to Scotland. I'm really enjoying it. I hope you and Alina are doing well. Is she talking yet? Do you know much about where she was or what happened to her? Maybe you two could come to visit me? My dad has a good job here, and I've just started working as a waitress but hoping that once my citizenship comes through I'll be able to go to uni. Not got a clue what to study right enough. But hey, life is full of endless opportunities when you're free, right? Speak soon. MR x

A smile raised the corner of Zofia's mouth. Molly Rose had been incredible for Zofia. She'd come along at the right time, took her under her wing and, if it hadn't been for the Hallahans, Zofia would be dead. The same way Antoni was dead and, likely, Alina would have died too, eventually. Marek and Leo would have grown their trafficking empire and more people would have suffered.

Zofia tucked the phone back into her pocket and turned to Alina. 'Fancy some lunch? I'm starving.'

Alina took a deep breath. 'I'm hungry too.'

Zofia raised an eyebrow and her eyes filled with tears. 'What do you want to eat?'

Alina shrugged. 'I don't mind. You choose.'

Zofia wiped the tears away and got to her feet, still holding Alina's hand.

# Chapter 73

Janey sat the steaming mug of coffee on the table in the garden and sat down on the seat.

'Thanks,' Ciaran said. 'As soon as I'm out of this bloody thing, I'll make you more than just a cuppa.'

Janey sighed inwardly. There was a strong possibility that Ciaran would never walk again, and if he did, he'd likely always need the wheelchair as a backup. Another thing that was her fault.

'I'll hold you to that,' Janey replied, lighting her cigarette and staring out over the North Channel. This was where she had been sitting when Kristo called her to tell her that the club back in Glasgow had been the target of an arson attack, later learning that Charlie had been responsible. It had been the last place she'd sat when she'd decided she wasn't ready to give up the Hallahan legacy. So much had changed since then.

'Good morning.' Kristo's voice came from behind them. Janey turned to see him emerge from the house, all suited and booted, ready for the day.

'Jesus, man, you don't hang about, do you?' Ciaran laughed.

'Got a lot to do today. Flying back to Glasgow to take on my first day as a new businessman,' Kristo replied.

'And a fine one you'll be at that. Your family deserve all the fortunes it will bring too,' Janey replied. 'And I admire you for going legit too, Kristo. I think we've both learned a valuable lesson over the last year or so.'

Kristo nodded as he looked across the water to Copeland Island. 'I saw what your family went through. I don't want that for me. I'm glad you respected my decision. My wife is happy with the path we've chosen to go down.'

Janey smiled. Never in a million years had she planned out her life as a crime boss. It had been hard graft with a lot of unnecessary loss and bloodshed. Her entire life had been dedicated to making sure the Hallahan empire and legacy ran smoothly. Had it been worth it? She wasn't sure.

'I'm glad to hear it,' she said.

'So Janey, what do you plan to do in your retirement?' Kristo asked.

Janey puffed on her cigarette and smirked. 'I plan to take up knitting, crocheting, that sort of thing.'

She felt Kristo and Ciaran's eyes on her and she couldn't keep a straight face before she burst out laughing.

'Fuck retirement,' she replied. 'That's for old people. I'm not sinking into a sofa for the rest of my life. I plan on Ciaran and I doing something worthwhile. Maybe travelling. Maybe just running a small, *legit* business. I also plan to do something good with my free time now.'

'Besides wheeling me around in this bloody thing?' Ciaran suggested sarcastically.

'I think it would be a good idea to get involved with a charity who help support victims of trafficking.'

Again, she felt their eyes on her.

'Like how?' Ciaran asked.

'I don't know. But I feel like I want to give something back. I want to do something good with my time, Ciaran.

I spent too many years building an empire that caused harm. I was part of the problem.'

Ciaran sighed. 'Janey…' But then he stopped. 'Can we just rest first? You know, take some time to process all the fuckery that you've had to deal with.'

Janey closed her eyes, felt the sea breeze on her face. 'Yeah, maybe,' she said.

'You lost your daughter, almost lost your grand-daughter *again*. I almost died; Sinead too. Can't you just relax, take it all in. Take time to heal, Janey. You don't have to pour yourself into something else; not yet.'

She opened her eyes and took another draw on the cigarette. 'I don't want to process it. I want to remember it like it was yesterday. It keeps me checked into reality; reminds me of the person I don't want to be ever again.'

She felt Ciaran's hand slip into hers and, in that moment, she was so grateful that Leo had failed in all of his plans to take out her family. Would he have left her to suffer on her own without them?

'You're a good person, Janey. You are.'

*I'm not*, she thought, but didn't say out loud. *But I'm going to try to be.*

What would life be like as *just* Janey, and not Janey Hallahan? She stared out at the water ahead. Life from now on was going to be very, very different.

# A letter from Alex

Hello. I hope you're all doing well. I want to thank you for reading *A Mother's Revenge*, which is my eleventh novel and my third book featuring Janey Hallahan (my absolute favourite character of all my books). Also, whenever I see a Defender, I call it the Janey mobile. And yes, now I want one. We can but dream.

This one has been a hard task, due to lots of varying reasons, but I have thoroughly enjoyed writing this book. I especially loved featuring real places which are local to me. The Erskine Bridge, which is a big landmark in West Dunbartonshire and Renfrewshire, played a big part in this book. I often found myself down at Erskine beach, staring up at the bridge and visualising *that* scene. If you know, you know.

As ever, a huge thank you goes to you, for coming back, or for picking my books up for the first time. In equal measures, I really am so appreciative that people read and enjoy my work. So, from the bottom of my heart, thank you.

As always, you can find me on all the socials if you want to contact me, including TikTok.

Alternatively, you can email me directly at alexkaneauthor@gmail.com.

# Acknowledgements

To all at Hera Books. Keshini, Dan and Jennie. Without you, my books wouldn't have a home. You're all fabulous to work with and make the entire process so easy. Thank you, Keshini, for being so flexible and understanding over the last few months.

Thank you to my copy editor, Ross, who was very thorough and kept leaving little comments in the margins about how much he was enjoying the book.

Thank you to my proof reader, Vicki Vrint, for keeping an eye on all those little details in the final stage.

The fantastic and hardest-working woman I know, my agent, Jo Bell. Thank you for all the hard, behind-the-scenes work you do for me. Forever grateful.

My husband, for always encouraging and supporting, even when I feel like I'm failing, you always give me that boost that is mostly needed.

My daughter, for being the inspiration for me to keep writing so that I can be with her as often as possible.

My family and friends who support and continually champion what I do. You're all amazing.